More Praise for *Catching Genius*

"With precise and evocative prose, Kristy Kiernan weaves a story of family and history that is as nuanced and finely wrought as it is compelling. *Catching Genius* draws you in with its genuine characters, and it holds you there with its truthful exploration of the enduring bonds of love and family... This affecting novel shines a new light on the concept of genius—what it is and what it isn't. And speaking of genius, Kristy Kiernan looks like a debut novelist who will be around for a long time to come." —Elizabeth Letts, author of
Family Planning and *Quality of Care*

"Kristy Kiernan bursts from the gate with this skillful rendering of a family's reckoning with its painful past. Kiernan peels away the layers in a lilting and luminous voice, exposing strata after strata of family secrets made murkier by the passage of time. Kiernan proves she's a writer to watch—find a comfortable spot, turn off the phone, and lose yourself in this gorgeous debut."
  —Sara Gruen, *New York Times* bestselling author of
Water for Elephants, Riding Lessons, and *Flying Changes*

"A warm, moving novel about the power of familial bonds."
  —*Booklist*

"Kristy Kiernan's fluent storytelling and fully-drawn, credible characters make for an affecting novel. With effortless grace, her lyrical prose drops the reader into scenes rich with details and powerful emotions." —Tasha Alexander, author of *And Only to Deceive*
and *A Poisoned Season*

"*Catching Genius* is the real thing: a rich, compelling, and deeply nuanced story delivered in language that's as luminous as it is authoritative. To judge by this affecting first novel, I'd say Kiernan's the real thing, too." —Jon Clinch, author of *Finn*

continued...

"*Catching Genius* is the total package; a beautiful story beautifully told. Kristy Kiernan pulls you into a deep and fully realized world; exactly the place a reader wants to be taken."

—Lorna Landvik, *New York Times* bestselling author of
Angry Housewives Eating Bon Bons and *Oh My Stars*

"In her beautifully written debut novel, *Catching Genius*, Kristy Kiernan portrays the complexity of familial relationships with a depth, candor, and insight that can only be called exceptional."

—Sandra Kring, author of
The Book of Bright Ideas and *Carry Me Home*

"Kristy Kiernan deftly captures the complicated relationship between sisters and succeeds in showing the ways families can make us crazy and angry and lost, but ultimately, how families can and do save us. With her fine eye for detail and obvious love of the beach, math, and music, Kiernan draws the reader into a family and lets us revel in a summer that reconciles the pain of their past and provides a glimpse of their hopeful future." —Judy Merrill Larsen, author of *All the Numbers*

"What is there not to like about this novel? A beach setting. Love and heartbreak. Regret and redemption. And a plot with surprising twists and turns that will leave your hankie damp and your heart feeling good." —Ad Hudler, author of *Househusband* and *All This Belongs to Me*

"*Catching Genius* is simply mesmerizing, not only because it expertly captures the unbreakable bond between sisters. The novel also explores the many facets of very real characters, breathing life into the seamlessly plotted story line. This author's first novel is a must-read for women's fiction fans of all ages." —*BookPage*

"Kiernan is a compellingly talented writer and one to watch...hauntingly beautiful." —*Florida Today*

"Kiernan writes about family, forgiveness, and the allure of the Gulf Coast with authority and assurance, producing a smoothly plotted story peppered with revelations that lead to a rousing, heartfelt finish." —*Mostly Fiction*

Matters of Faith

KRISTY KIERNAN

BERKLEY BOOKS, NEW YORK

THE BERKLEY PUBLISHING GROUP
Published by the Penguin Group
Penguin Group (USA) Inc.
375 Hudson Street, New York, New York 10014, USA
Penguin Group (Canada), 90 Eglinton Avenue East, Suite 700, Toronto, Ontario M4P 2Y3, Canada
(a division of Pearson Penguin Canada Inc.)
Penguin Books Ltd., 80 Strand, London WC2R 0RL, England
Penguin Group Ireland, 25 St. Stephen's Green, Dublin 2, Ireland (a division of Penguin Books Ltd.)
Penguin Group (Australia), 250 Camberwell Road, Camberwell, Victoria 3124, Australia
(a division of Pearson Australia Group Pty. Ltd.)
Penguin Books India Pvt. Ltd., 11 Community Centre, Panchsheel Park, New Delhi—110 017, India
Penguin Group (NZ), 67 Apollo Drive, Rosedale, North Shore 0632, New Zealand
(a division of Pearson New Zealand Ltd.)
Penguin Books (South Africa) (Pty.) Ltd., 24 Sturdee Avenue, Rosebank, Johannesburg 2196,
South Africa

Penguin Books Ltd., Registered Offices: 80 Strand, London WC2R 0RL, England

This book is an original publication of The Berkley Publishing Group.

PRINTING HISTORY
Berkley trade paperback edition / August 2008

Library of Congress Cataloging-in-Publication Data

Kiernan, Kristy.
    Matters of faith / Kristy Kiernan.—Berkley trade paperback ed.
        p. cm.
    ISBN 978-0-425-22179-2
    1. Faith—Fiction.   2. Spiritual healing—Fiction.   3. Domestic fiction.   I. Title.
    PS3611.I4455M38 2008
    813'.6—dc22

                                                                2007050600

PRINTED IN THE UNITED STATES OF AMERICA

10   9   8   7   6   5   4   3   2   1

For my husband, Richard W. Kiernan,
who lets me chase my dreams and rejoices when I catch one

Acknowledgments

My deepest gratitude to the following professionals, who are so efficient and talented, and who allow me to do my job without daily psychiatric intervention:

Anne Hawkins, my agent

Jackie Cantor, my editor

Tom Robinson and Michele Langley, my publicists

Tasha Tyska, my sanity wrangler

Thank you to the Naples Divas, who teach me something new every month, and who don't throw things at me when I haven't read the book: Sue Bankosky, Stephanie Coburn, Karyn Conrath, Betty Keigler, Terry Knight, Pat Kumicich, Tanya Oosterhous, Ellen Schmidt, Sharon Smaldone, Barbara Taefi, and Joyce Thornton.

As always, thank you to my family and friends for all of their support, especially to my husband, Richard, for his unflagging belief, and our own personal troll, Niko, for her companionship.

A person will worship something, have no doubt about that.

—Ralph Waldo Emerson

One

THE turning points in my life have always arrived disguised as daily life. I never get the opportunity or have the sixth sense to stop and examine them, to time-stamp them on my soul, whisper to myself that *this*, this thing, this simple boat ride in the Everglades, this phone ringing, this drive home twenty minutes late, was the thing that might do me in.

They never appear important enough to stop the things I'm already doing—like sparring with my husband over the developing nothingness of our marriage, like mixing the right amount of black into the red of a fire sky painting, like sitting down at my computer and reading an e-mail from my son.

"He's coming home for spring break," I called down to Cal through the open window, scanning Marshall's message for more information. "And he's bringing someone with him."

"I can't hear you," Cal yelled back, the hollow, river rush of water beating against the house for a moment. I read the rest of the e-mail, committing the pertinent facts to memory as a flutter in my stomach began to make itself known, before I headed downstairs and out the kitchen door. The edge of the screen caught the back of my heel before I could get out of its way.

Cal, shirtless and browned, his shorts riding low enough to expose a strip of white skin, squinted at me as he hosed off two bright blue coolers. "What's up?"

"Marshall's coming home for spring break," I repeated, surveying the sparkle of fish scales caught in the crisp grass at the sides of the driveway like diamonds in straw. "And he's bringing company."

"The Dalai Lama?" Cal asked, flipping a cooler over and sending a rush of tepid water over my bare feet.

"A girl," I said, and was rewarded for my timing with a squirt of water up my calves. Cal turned to me in surprise, a smile flashing quick and white across his face. I grinned back, raising my eyebrows, a joke, half-formed, about to spill out, before I remembered that we weren't joking much these days.

"Really? A girl?"

"Ada," I said, the unfamiliar name hard on my tongue, a good complement wrapped in the downy softness of *Marshall*. "She's pre-law."

"What else is she?" Cal asked, turning back to his coolers.

"He didn't say."

"That's new. And you didn't ask?"

I didn't answer the criticism, not nearly as subtle as his words suggested. The method our son took to find himself was a never-ending fracture, but it was a method I was open-minded enough to indulge, and one Cal barely abided. The possibilities of Ada's religious affiliation skated through my mind as I watched him move on to the next cooler, sluicing the remains of his second fishing tour of the day across the drive.

"What should I do about sleeping arrangements?" I asked.

"Put her in your office and let them sneak around."

"Nice. I'll ask Marshall. Good trip today?"

He shrugged and flipped the second cooler over before turning the hose on himself, talking behind the water cascading down through his hair and across his face. "Couple of idiots from Minnesota. Talked about ice fishing the whole time. They want to go out tomorrow, but they wouldn't put on any sunscreen, so I'm pretty sure I've got the day off."

His words dimmed out, as Cal's stories about paper-white Yankees were destined to after twenty years of marriage. I imagine he barely heard my talk about warping Upson board or paint loss on a Highwayman painting these days.

I envisioned a girl named Ada. She would be sturdy, blonde, and no taller than I. Trying to fit Marshall beside this Ada in my imagination was harder work. He'd never brought a girl home before.

Boys, there'd always been boys. Interesting boys he sought out when he was tired of being Jewish, or Buddhist, or Methodist. Earnest-looking boys who wore various amulets and indicators of their faith, who Marshall engaged in fascinating theological discussions over dinner. Fascinating to me anyway. Cal, his fire-and-brimstone minister father never far from his mind, would leave the table, taking his plate to the living room, where he'd turn up the television loud enough that those of us left in the dining room would fall silent, intent on our food.

I was proud of Marshall. He was curious, about this world and the possibility of the next. Curiosity was an admirable trait, one my own parents cultivated in me. Meghan, our daughter, was as curious as Marshall and I were about the world. And she was due home any second.

"Did you pick up the EpiPens?" I asked.

"On the counter."

And we were done. Marshall, check. Fishing trip, check. Meghan's EpiPens, check. I turned to go back inside, the screen door catching my heel again. I'd asked Cal a hundred times to slow it down. If I didn't have to endure the pained sighs and protests that he had been *just about to do it*—the implication that I was an ever-impatient, never-satisfied wife—I would look up how to do it myself. It was just a screen door. How hard could it be? Maybe he would do it before Marshall came home.

But right now the screen door didn't bother me. Marshall was coming home, and he was bringing a girlfriend. It would be good to have someone new in the house.

For all of us.

SWITCHING out Meghan's EpiPens that night, I told her about Marshall and Ada. She grinned as she handed me the old injector from her backpack and fit her new one in.

"I know," she said, with a coy look up through her lashes, something that had been happening a lot lately. Meghan had begun to flirt like a silent screen siren. With everyone. Me, her father, the UPS man. I was hoping it was a phase that would pass, though I'd hoped that with her fixation on Winona Ryder too.

"How do you know?" I asked.

She shrugged. "She e-mailed me."

I sat back on my heels in surprise. "She e-mailed you? You mean Ada?"

"Uh-huh. She's a vegetarian."

"Wait a minute. When did she e-mail you?" Meghan was twelve. I vetted all of her e-mail from anyone other than Marshall.

"A little while ago. She used Marshall's account."

"Oh. Well, what else did she say?" I asked, a little disgruntled at Marshall for allowing Meghan the first, albeit electronic, glimpse of his girlfriend.

Meghan shook her head and pulled brightly colored folders out of her backpack, arranging them carefully on her desk, preparing to start her homework. With Marshall I'd had to stay on top of homework or I'd find him studying some religious text or another; with Meghan I rarely even needed to remind her.

"Nothing. She sounds really nice. She said she'd stay in my room if you said she could. Can she?"

"I have the pull-out sofa in my office for guests, Meghan," I said, looking at her bunk beds doubtfully, finding it hard to imagine a college girl wanting to play sleepover with a twelve-year-old. Besides, what if Cal were right and she ventured out to visit Marshall? "I think we'll wait and talk to Marshall about this, okay?"

Meghan chewed her bottom lip and stared up at her *Edward Scissorhands* poster, but said nothing. I sighed. She was such a good child. And she followed directions. Always. Following directions might save her life one day. That had been drilled into them, her. And they'd had to drill it into everyone around them. They'd spent years educating themselves and Meghan's schools.

They now had a peanut-free zone for lunch in Meghan's middle school. Thanks to new laws, Meghan was able to carry an Epi-Pen, that ever-present, life-saving cylinder, with her everywhere in school, with a backup in the nurse's office.

Unfortunately, with education came a certain amount of isolation in our small town, and so far Meghan was the only child to come through the local school system with a life-threatening food allergy. The lunch area was in a small room separate from the regular lunchroom, and she ate alone. It all set her apart, and not in a way that made her the most popular girl in school.

It was no wonder she was looking forward to Ada's visit. I looked up at the *Edward Scissorhands* poster above Meghan's desk, with Winona partially obscured by the blades at the ends of Depp's delicate wrists, and wondered if she saw herself in Ryder's character, held safely behind sharp objects. I nudged her shoulder.

"You think she'd like the peony sheets or the Little Mermaid?"

"Mom!" she gasped. "Not the Little Mermaid—" She broke off when she saw the grin on my face. She threw her thin arms around me, and I'd have gladly attached blades to my own hands at that moment to keep her safe.

I e-mailed Marshall repeatedly over the next three weeks. Asking questions about Ada under the guise of making sure we were prepared for her visit. I asked about the food she liked (*she's a vegetarian mom, very whole foods, i've stopped eating red meat and feel so much better, you should really think about restricting meghan's exposure to additives and stuff...*), and her sleeping habits, (*i don't know mom*), and skirted around the issue of her religion with vague questions about her family (*they're really close...some interesting ideas...their church sent her to school on a full scholarship*).

I researched vegetarianism and whole foods and stocked up on tofu and grains, and in the week leading up to their arrival I stopped work altogether, closing the door to my studio with three paintings in various stages of restoration, and worked on cleaning the house.

Meghan's allergies had turned me into a late-in-life clean freak, and our home was spotless most of the time. After the first horrifying anaphylactic episode when she was two—a friend's daughter babysat and made Meghan homemade Play-Doh out of peanut butter—we'd gotten her tested for other allergies, and the results changed our lives. A whole host of airborne irritants threatened

Meghan's airways: dust mites, an endless variety of flower pollens, dander, mold. And food allergies, peanuts and shellfish, threatened her systemically. Thank God she was fine with fish, or our entire livelihood would have been threatened.

Now our home was tiled throughout with only a few scattered throw rugs, no more drapes, no more overstuffed sofas. Marshall's two cats had been pressed upon neighbors, and I learned how to steam clean everything.

But this was different. This wasn't cleaning for my daughter's health; this was cleaning to impress. We didn't have many house-guests, and I was a bit surprised to find that there was a difference. Meghan and I got haircuts, and she talked me into buying her two new tops, several pairs of shorts, and flip-flops with rhinestones on them, all of them a clear maturity level above what she had been wearing.

Two days before their arrival, I put fresh sheets on Marshall's bed, smoothing his pillows, running my hands down the spread, tugging at wrinkles that weren't there. I missed him. His fresh-man year at college he'd come home as often as he could, called every other day, made me feel needed and missed. But this year I was lucky to get an e-mail once a week, and questions about his friends and classes that he used to answer readily had been met with silence.

All natural, of course. All the way it was supposed to be. And, in fact, Marshall's pulling away had probably come later than might have been considered normal. But then Marshall had never been a typical kid.

I dusted his dresser, picked up the large wood cross he'd hung all his necklaces on, and wiped under that as the pendants swung and clinked against each other—crosses, crucifixes, ankhs, and spirals and stars—mixing happily, without rancor, the way their representative religions seemed unable to manage in the real world. I fingered the gold Star of David that Ira's parents had given him after their son's funeral.

Poor Ira. At least his end had come rather quickly. There's not much time for suffering when you are, literally, hit by a train. It was Ira's parents who suffered, and Marshall, of course. Cal would say that was where all of Marshall's issues started, but Marshall and I had been having theological discussions for years before that.

True, it had escalated, more rapidly than I'd been aware of at the time. But he'd also been on the cusp of puberty, a natural time to start exploring the larger questions in life.

Marshall's first cross, small and silver, on a thin leather cord, hung between Ira's star and a red, knotted kabbalah string. I clicked it with my fingernail and looked around Marshall's room one last time, wondering what Ada would think of the lack of decoration—no posters, no sports equipment in the corners. Aside from the necklaces on the dresser and the religion books on the shelf above his bed, it was practically monklike.

I gave the room one last glance as I backed out the door. The sun winked off a crystal pendant, throwing prisms across the otherwise bare walls, dagger-shaped rainbows as beautiful as any painting.

CAL had watched our preparations throughout the week with a bemused smile, but the day before they were due he came home with a fresh haircut and offered to make whole grain bread, something he hadn't done in years. The three of us worked in the kitchen together, music floating in from the living room, the windows open and the smell of the Gulf of Mexico and the bay filling the house, as soft as hope.

A rush of affection for Cal, something I hadn't felt in a long time, hit me when I saw him bent over the counter, kneading dough. He and Meghan were talking about fishing, and I studied him, seeing the young man I'd met when I was younger than Marshall was now.

He'd come out of the backwoods of middle Florida, land weary and religion exhausted, running from his mother, the reputation of his brother, the memory of his father. We'd met when my boyfriend, a fellow art major, took me on an airboat tour of the Everglades. Cal had been our boat captain, silent while our guide yelled over the engine, staring at me while everyone else stared at ospreys on their massive nests and alligators slipping into the grassy water.

I'd felt his eyes on me the whole time, and when I finally got off the boat, my knees weak, ears ringing, shaking wind-flattened bugs out of my clothes and hair, I was flush with more than sunburn. He handed me a phone number along with a warm can of Coke, and I'd slipped it into my pocket with a breathless glance at my boyfriend.

I called him that night and he picked me up at my dorm. We'd only spent a handful of nights apart since. He got me through college, he got me through the disappearance of my parents—on sabbatical in the Galápagos the year after we married when their boat went down—and he got me through the births of Marshall and Meghan.

And then somewhere along the line, he—the determined man who wouldn't take his eyes off me—had slowly disappeared, into work, into his workshop to tinker with engines and fishing gear, into the Gulf and the Everglades. Or perhaps I'd simply lost sight of him. Who knows how a marriage disintegrates, by what degrees, what its half-life is?

Now, as he shaped the dough into a ball and gently slipped it into an oiled bowl, I thought I saw him again. He looked up, and I didn't look away but smiled at him, feeling a laugh bubble up in my throat when he did a double take. He grinned and winked at me while our daughter's sweet voice splashed through the kitchen in bright, happy colors. And for a moment we were back, and I couldn't wait for Marshall and his first girlfriend to walk through that door and remind us of ourselves.

MARSHALL

He was letting Ada drive the last half. He was exhausted with the telling of Ira's story. He'd never told anyone at college about it before; he'd never wanted to take the chance that he would break down, maybe cry in front of people who had not known Ira, could not understand how close they had been.

But Ada was different. She was so very different. And she had been rapt as he'd told the story, gasping when he told her about the train, how massive it had seemed, how close, how fast. She placed her hand on his leg, rubbing his thigh sympathetically. To his surprise, he hadn't cried. Just her presence, just her listening to the most pivotal moment of his life, was enough to comfort him, and when they'd stopped to gas up the car and change places, she'd held him and kissed him right there in front of truckers and everyone.

And he'd let her drive, not just because he was tired, but because she'd asked so—there was no other word for it—she'd asked so damn *cutely*, he could not resist, and because now he could look at her rather than the road. Every time he looked at her he found something new, something more delicate, something more astonishing than the last thing he'd noticed.

Like right then, she downshifted into fourth gear, and when she flexed her foot on the gas pedal he noticed the line of muscle running down her thigh. His mouth suddenly got dry, and he wanted more than anything to lean over the console and run his tongue over that line of muscle.

He swallowed and looked out the window. *Jesus.* He swallowed again, reforming the unconscious epithet into a short prayer. She made him think in ways he'd never thought before, never knew he could think before.

They'd been weak. He'd tasted the skin over that muscle before, the night she'd teased him into inviting her home for spring break. He'd professed as much regret as she had. But it was all he could think about.

She shifted up to fifth and tossed her head, trying to get a lock of dark hair blown by the wind out of the side of her mouth. He reached for it at the same time as she did, but she got there first, hooking her index finger over it and drawing it out, and had she drawn her shirt over her head it couldn't have left him more breathless. He shifted in his seat and nearly groaned aloud.

His hands curled of their own accord, his fingers grasping the air beside his thighs the way they wanted to grab hold of her hair.

"So what else did your mom say?" she asked. "What should I call her?"

He shrugged, irritated to have the image of his mother sliding over Ada's, but relieved too. "Chloe, I guess," he said. His mother had always told his friends to call her Chloe. He didn't figure it would be any different for Ada.

"Chloe," Ada repeated, drawing it out, glancing at him sideways. "Chloe and Calvin. Cute. Chloe and Cal and Meghan. And joining them for the weekend, Marshall and Ada the vegetarian," she sang, squeezing his knee playfully.

He laughed, his irritation and bordering-on-violent desire fading, pride at the thought of walking into his house with this beautiful girl lifting his spirits and filling his lungs with something lighter than air. He went with it, praising God for the sheer miracle going ninety miles an hour in the driver's seat beside him.

Two

"THEY'RE here," Meghan cried, "they're here!"

She flew past me, pounding down the steps before the screen door had a chance to maim her. My hands stilled under the faucet, the strawberries falling from my fingers to thump into the colander as I peered out the window. I could hear Marshall's car now, moving too fast up the drive, sending a flock of ibis winging for the safety of the sky.

"Cal!" I called, drying my hands and trying to slow my heart. The car came into view, shell dust and sand obscuring its lower half as though it were being deposited beside the house by a cloud. I took a quick glance around the kitchen, satisfied with the dish of hummus, the white corn chips, and the beautiful green edamame in my mother's blue ceramic bowl.

I stood on the porch while Meghan danced around the car, the dust settling enough to see that Marshall wasn't driving. I felt a twitch of disapproval, but it quickly disappeared when the passenger door opened and Marshall unfolded himself.

Meghan threw herself at him and he caught her with a grunt, swinging her sideways and holding her captive while she squealed to be released. He swung her back upright and she hit him on the shoulder, brushing her hair back into place with her other hand while he ducked her fist. I laughed and heard Cal moving in the kitchen just as the driver's side door slowly opened. I watched as Ada exited the car, smiling shyly, nothing at all like my vision of her as an athletic blonde. You could nearly hear Meghan's awed inhale, and I wondered if Marshall had somehow, subconsciously, picked this girl just for his little sister.

This waif, this pixie, was a near dead ringer for Winona Ryder in Meghan's favorite years—the funky leggings, spiky bangs, lots of buckles years. She grinned at Meghan and held her arms out. I almost cringed in embarrassment for her, trying too hard, too soon. But I underestimated something, either my daughter or Ada, and Meghan circled the car and hugged the girl, briefly, but hard. I moved down the steps quickly, and Marshall met me at the front of the car, lifting me off my feet for a moment.

"What's up, Mom?" he asked, letting me inspect his face. He hadn't shaved, not that anyone more than three feet away from him would notice. He flushed and ran his hand across his jaw. "Come on." He took my arm and turned me toward Ada. She flashed me the same grin she'd given Meghan. Thankfully—for both of us—she didn't open her arms for a hug, but held her hand out. I shook with her, instinctively clasping my other hand over hers when I felt how cold her slender fingers were.

"It's so nice to meet you, Mrs.—"

"No, call me Chloe."

"Thank you, and thank you for having me to your home," she said, pulling her hand from my grasp and looking up at the house, its three stories towering before her. She slid her dark sunglasses up into her hair as she tilted her head back, and I saw with a little shock that she had a thin, silver hoop through her left eyebrow. It winked in the sun, sparking cold and white like a star. She turned on that brilliant smile again, and I heard the screen door squeal open at the same time.

"Cal," I said, turning around and motioning him down the steps. He hadn't needed my encouragement and was nearly upon us. "This is Ada, Marshall's friend."

"Great to meet you, Ada," Cal said, taking her tiny white hand in his. It disappeared up to the wrist in his big brown hand, like a bait fish, caught and calm with inevitability. "We've been looking forward to meeting you."

"Dad," Marshall said, appearing at Ada's side and placing a proprietary arm across her shoulders. "How's it going?"

Oh, I thought with a start at his tone. Oh, this was new, this attitude, this was completely new. I didn't even know what it was, some male thing, some claiming of manhood on Marshall's part, some test. The very air was charged, with more than humidity, more than happiness at our son being home. Cal released Ada's hand and clasped Marshall's shoulder, giving him a shake. Marshall stood his ground, though I could tell it took effort.

"It's good, kid," Cal said, and I nearly flinched when I saw Marshall's bravado collapse in the face of his father's condescension. Cal had won for a moment.

"Come on, come on," Meghan said, tugging on Ada's elbow. Ada ducked out from under Marshall's arm and allowed herself to be pulled into the house, scattering the tension like so many flies. I reached out for Marshall and we walked into the house behind them, with Cal trailing after us. I heard the screen door catch his heel and felt a nasty little measure of satisfaction for that small, well-deserved punishment.

* * *

As Marshall finished unloading the car, he and Cal maneuvering around each other, I followed Ada. She trailed Meghan up the stairs slowly, glancing at the family photos that ran up the wall in their mismatched frames. Meghan was clutching an old-fashioned, battered train case in one hand, and with the other she steadied herself on the railing as she twisted back and forth to catch glimpses of Ada.

I hung back when we reached Meghan's room, leaning against the doorframe while Meghan gave her the grand tour.

"Do you want the top?" Meghan asked, gesturing toward the bunk beds, freshly made with the bright red splashes of the peony sheets. "Or the bottom, because I don't mind either one, and when I have sleepovers sometimes my friends want the top. So that's okay."

Meghan had never had a sleepover, something that had somehow escaped me before and that broke my heart now.

"I'd love the top," Ada said with a smile at me, making her eyes crinkle and the silver loop in her eyebrow glitter. The corners of my own mouth tugged up of their own volition. It was hard to resist her smile or the fact that she was making my child happy.

Meghan deposited the train case on the top bunk, and I noticed that her usual zoo of stuffed animals was nowhere to be seen, likely hidden in her closet to avoid any whiff of immaturity.

"Hey, I love Winona Ryder," Ada said, looking admiringly up at a *Beetlejuice* poster. Meghan nearly swooned.

"I have almost all her movies," she said and ran to the little TV with the built-in DVD player we got her for Christmas. She opened her dresser drawer and pulled out a stack of movies to prove her devotion. "We can watch any of them you want. I mean, we can stay up, you know?"

"I'd love that," Ada said. "If your mom thinks it's okay."

They both looked to me and I nodded. "Sure, of course. It's not a school night."

"Yes," Meghan whooped. She ran to the bottom bunk and laid the movies out in a neat row. As Ada bent over to inspect them, her shirt rode up, and above her low-slung cargo pants peeked a black, tribal tattoo. I nearly gasped aloud. I am not necessarily against tattoos, but seeing it, so stark against the perfect white skin of this young girl, this young girl who was my son's new girlfriend, and who, according to Marshall, was deeply religious, was shocking.

"So, Ada," I started, unsure of what I would say next. "Marshall tells us you're from Nebraska."

She turned around and flopped back on the bed, making the DVDs bounce out of their orderly row. Meghan frowned slightly, but then she, too, turned and flopped onto the bed, trying to mimic Ada's loose-limbed grace.

"That's right. Have you ever been there?" Without waiting for an answer, she reached over and with her black-painted fingernails tickled Meghan's belly. "It's *freezing* there right now. I'm so glad we're here instead. Have you ever seen snow, Meghan? Meggie? Does anyone call you Meggie? That's cute."

Meghan giggled, at the tickling, at the nickname, at the fact that this incredibly cool girl with a wire through her eyebrow was here in her room. I hoped she wouldn't notice the tattoo.

"Meghan's never seen snow," I said. "We're planning a trip for her thirteenth birthday, though, aren't we?"

Meghan inhaled sharply, flashing me a grateful look for the entry. "We're going to go to New York City. Just me and Mom, when they have the Christmas decorations up. As soon as it snows she said we'd go, I don't have to wait for my actual birthday. Have you been to New York?"

"No," Ada said, somewhat wistfully. "You're so lucky to have a mom who's so cool."

Meghan grinned at me. I appreciated the sentiment, but I wasn't the cool mom. I was the mom who had to watch everything, every morsel Meghan placed in her mouth, every bit of dust in the house, every well-meaning adult who tried to tell me about a homespun remedy for Meghan's allergies. That hadn't left much time for cool.

"What do your parents do?" I asked, as Meghan gathered up the DVDs and Ada rose to inspect Meghan's desk.

"My mom runs the commissary and my dad is a foreman for the orchards."

"The orchards?"

"Apples. Mostly Jonathans, Winesaps, Red and Golden Delicious," she answered, picking up one of Meghan's EpiPens and turning it over in her hands, her voice turning vague and painfully bored. "All-natural, no pesticides, natural fertilizers. We grow everything in the community. Whole foods, no preservatives."

"Is everyone a vegetarian?" I asked. Meghan slid the drawer shut on her DVDs and turned to listen to Ada.

"No," she said with a shrug. "Hey, what's this about?" She held the EpiPen out to Meghan, who cast a quick, doubtful glance in my direction.

"That's Meghan's EpiPen. It's a shot of epinephrine, in case she has an allergic reaction," I answered.

"Marshall told me about that," Ada said, placing it back on Meghan's desk. "You know, all these allergies now, they're really just the result of preservatives and altered foods. Have you ever tried a whole foods diet? Cutting out all preservatives, additives, anything not totally organic?"

I laughed. Not just at the question: What hadn't we tried? But at the audacity of this child to even ask the question. "Meghan's allergies are tied to her immune system, not to preservatives."

Ada looked skeptically at Meghan. "So, you've tried a whole foods approach?"

Meghan shook her head. "No. But eating animals is gross," she said, and I looked at her in surprise. She'd never mentioned being interested in vegetarianism. Meghan glanced quickly between us. "I mean, I like a hamburger sometimes, but, I don't know, maybe we could try the whole foods thing? Maybe I wouldn't need the EpiPen?"

"Sweetie," I said, "there's a difference between being a vegetarian and what Ada's talking about—"

"You know there's a lot about exposure therapy online," Ada said. "Have you looked into that at all? Marshall and I were reading about it—"

"Meghan's first exposure was plenty enough," I said firmly. "Thank you, Ada, but we have a good system now and everything is fine."

"But, Mom," Meghan protested, "you're not even—"

"Your mom's right," Ada quickly interrupted. "Of course. I shouldn't have even said anything. I'm sorry."

Meghan shrugged and looked uncomfortable. "It's no big deal, Mom," she muttered.

The silence was full and seemed somehow specific, weighted, as if it were pushing softly at me. They clearly wanted to be alone. I felt, for the first time with Meghan, that it was time for me to back off; she didn't need a chaperone.

"Well. You girls get to know each other and come down when

you're ready for a snack," I said, and they looked at each other with small, satisfied, and very adult smiles. I heard Meghan's door close quietly, and I stopped for a moment, listening to the low laughter that filtered out of my daughter's room.

Marshall rounded the corner with two suitcases and seemed surprised to see me at the top of the stairs. I motioned for him to come up.

"Hey, you. Need some help?" I asked, holding my hand out for a suitcase.

He shook his head. "No, I got it." He pounded up the stairs, skipping every other step, and covered their length in seconds, landing beside me without even losing a breath. "Ada in with Meghan?" he asked as he passed Meghan's closed door. I followed him to his room, where he swung his suitcase up on the bed and dropped the other one, Ada's I presumed, by the door.

"Yeah, they seem to have hit it off," I said, now leaning against my son's doorframe, keeping that Mom distance, feeling more natural about it now that I was with Marshall. "She's very pretty."

He fumbled with the clasp on his suitcase, his face in quarter profile to me, enough to see a smile tease his lips. But he didn't answer me, just flipped the lid of his suitcase up, allowing it to fall back on the bed with a muffled thump. I moved into the room and sat lightly on the edge of the bed.

"Your father and I are trusting that there's not going to be any nighttime activity while you're here, Marshall."

"Mom," he began to protest.

"No, just listen to me. I'm allowing Ada to stay with your sister because it seemed to have been worked out beforehand, and I didn't want to disappoint her. And you're the one who let them e-mail, so you have only yourself to blame for that. I don't want to have to talk to Meghan about why Ada slipped out of her room in the middle of the night. Is that clear?"

Marshall took a deep breath, as though about to explain something obvious to a rather dull child. I called upon my own patience, remembering the times I had thought my own dear parents astonishingly stupid and how they tolerated me with such good humor. But I was mistaken about the object of his forbearance.

"We don't—we don't do that," he said, nearly strangling on the words. "She's very committed to her faith, and I support her, I—she makes a lot of sense."

"What is her faith, Marshall?"

"Well, it's sort of a mixture of fundamental Christianity, evangelical, maybe even a little separatist, but it's cool. They share everything with the community, but there's a lot more to it than that. Their guiding principle is really all about hard work, responsibility for each other, and to God. It might seem a bit rigid, but that's good. Faith requires something of you, right?"

"She said her mother works in the commissary and her father works in the orchards. Are those church businesses?"

He nodded. "Yeah, it's all pretty self-sufficient." He gave up on unpacking and picked up his suitcase, still splayed open, and dropped it on the floor next to his dresser. He shrugged when he turned back to me. "I'll just be repacking it next week anyway. I was thinking about taking Ada out fishing tomorrow. Is Dad booked?"

I shook my head. "I'm not sure. Ask him at dinner. If she's a vegetarian, I doubt she wants to fish, Marshall."

"We probably won't fish. I'd just like to take her for a ride, maybe see some dolphins, have some lunch. She's never been out on the Gulf or in the 'Glades."

"What about your father?"

"What about him?" He leaned against his dresser, sending his necklaces and charms gently swaying and clinking against each other.

"Are you going to ask him to go along?"

"I wasn't planning on it. I've taken the boat plenty of times by myself."

"I know, and don't think your father won't remember the last time you did. I'd be prepared for that little conversation again if I were you. I was just thinking you might want to spend some time with him, let him get to know Ada."

He smiled a wry, sideways smile, something new, something lopsided and slightly cruel. A man's smile. And, like a man, or at least like the man his father was, he didn't answer me. Instead he asked about dinner, and asked about my work, and when I left him, he was knocking on Meghan's door to reclaim his girlfriend.

MARSHALL

It was startling enough having his mother sit on his bed and address sex so directly, but now the very embodiment of it was standing there, in his bedroom, her hip jutting at him like a challenge. Technically, Ada had been in his room before, his dorm room, when his roommate was gone, studying, wherever the hell he went, but this was his *bedroom*.

His every boyhood fantasy had played out in this room. He'd splayed more Playmates across that worn blue spread in his mind. More than Playmates. The most bizarre choices had been flung in all manner of disarray across every inch of this room. Classmates, teachers, movie stars, the woman who delivered the mail. Even, occasionally, friend's mothers.

Actually, Ira's mother had appeared frequently. She still did sometimes. He'd never noticed her in more than an *Ira's mother who makes us brownies from scratch after school* way, until after Ira died. She'd held him so often after that, rocking with him, whispering in his ear. Taking as much consolation as she gave.

But he was no longer fourteen, and Ada was nobody's mother, and she was here, in *his* room. His skin felt tight, not just the insistent pressure against his zipper, but everywhere. His wrists felt thick, strong, the back of his neck, his calves, the muscles he was rarely conscious of full and ready to move in some new way he had never even considered.

Ada, still hipshot against the dresser's top edge, reached out and flicked the row of necklaces with her index finger, sending them tinkling against each other, flashing silver and gold.

"So what's all this?" she asked. Her voice was light, but he saw the tension in the set of her jaw, the crease between her eyebrows, the way her eyes roamed over the books on the shelf. He stood and moved in behind her, inhaling the scent of her hair, before he reached past her and stilled the necklaces in his fist. They felt fragile, like childhood, and he picked up the cross, opened the top drawer, and dropped it in with a clatter.

The necklaces tangled there in the bottom of the drawer, messy, unimportant, and he slid the drawer closed while she kept him at a distance with that hip and a turned head.

"Nothing," he murmured.

She twisted away from him and shut the door, startling him with her assumption of what was allowed and appropriate in his parents' house, his house. He resisted the urge to open the door again, to call down the stairs that it was all right, they weren't *doing* anything.

"So it's easy like that?" she asked, leaning her back against the door. "How many of those are there? Did you really believe in all that, all those?"

"Hey, what did I do? You know, I've told you—you know I've been searching for the right thing, the right path."

She narrowed her eyes at him and it didn't matter, it did not slant her face toward ugly, no matter the emotion under it. She was simply, differently, perfectly perfect.

"Yeah. You told me," she said.

He moved toward her and she allowed him to come. She uncrossed her arms and let them drop to her sides, placing her palms flat against the door, turning her head so her throat was vulnerable to him. He placed his hands on her hips, pressed her into the door, and leaned down to kiss her neck just above her collarbone. She didn't move anything but her head, turning it slightly toward him again and then spoke softly, her breath lightly ruffling against his ear, the promise of her lips nearly unbearable.

"How do I know you won't just leave me like you left them?"

"No," he whispered, moving his lips up her neck to her ear. "No, I won't leave you."

She swiveled her head back and forth slowly, her hair brushing against his face, and then pushed him away from her, picking up her suitcase, turning, and opening the door all in the same liquid motion. He was left in the doorway, watching her walk down the hall away from him in his own house with a suitcase in her hand, as though they had already been married for forty years and she was leaving him.

Just before she turned into Meghan's room she threw a final comment over her shoulder.

"Faith in our Lord requires sacrifice, Marshall. Not jewelry."

Three

I PEEKED at the vegetarian tomato alfredo sauce while keeping one ear tuned to the footsteps and doors opening and closing above me. We'd never had a noisy house, not even when the kids were younger. Even Meghan's piano lessons and practice had been muted, muffled somehow by the three stories of the house, the humidity of the Gulf of Mexico, and her hesitancy on the keys.

But tonight there were three of them up there and it sounded like twelve to me. I knew mothers who loved a raucous house full of children, but I'd never gotten the hang of relaxing into the din, never been the placid earth mother with multiple, wide-eyed children gathered beneath her skirts.

We did not tiptoe around; there was no ban on noise. Our family had just always had a certain amount of reserve, a reluctance to startle. But at the sound of Meghan's bright peal of laughter, slipping down the stairway and into the kitchen like a jazz riff, I smiled, and when Cal entered the kitchen I turned it on him.

"Hey," he said, jerking his head up, indicating the noise from upstairs. "Guess they're getting along. She seems nice. Marshall got some of his old man's genes after all. We know how to pick 'em."

I laughed. It had been a long time since we'd flirted. "Did you ever consider that maybe you weren't the one doing the picking?" I asked, coy but out of practice. He grabbed me around the waist and bent me over backward, going after my neck. I played along and protested for a minute, allowing him the barest graze of a kiss before I pushed him away.

"So, really," I said, lifting the lid again, stirring where there was no need, looking to add something there was no absence of. "What do you think?"

Cal sniffed at the sauce, wrinkling his nose. "I think making sauce out of tofu is really weird, and I don't care how much V8 you put in it, I'll still know it started out looking like a slimy brick of candle wax."

"Come on," I said. "What do you think of her, of Ada?"

He shrugged. "I'm glad the kid has a girlfriend."

"She has a tattoo." That got a raised eyebrow.

"Where?" he asked.

I pointed to the top of the back of my jeans.

"Really? What's it of?"

"Some black tribal thing. And what about the eyebrow piercing?"

"I thought she was religious? A tribal tattoo seems a little at odds with that, doesn't it?"

"I don't know," I said, knocking the edge of the spoon against the rim of the pot and turning to face him. "I don't know of any religions specifically against tattoos. Judaism says something about defacing your body, scraping your skin or something. But she's definitely not Jewish. It sounds like a commune, one of those big, happy family things. It's certainly not something I'm against;

I just don't know what their beliefs are. What if they're polyga-mists or something?"

"You've been watching too much cable. And since when did that matter to you, anyway?" he asked, and we were back to our usual poking at each other.

"I guess since I considered the fact that he's old enough to get married," I said. "And even if he doesn't marry her, and even if it isn't anytime soon, he will probably marry someone, someday."

"This is just occurring to you?"

"Yes," I said, angry at the defensiveness I felt well up within me. "I mean, no, of course I've thought about him getting married before, I just never gave much thought to *who* he'd marry."

"Or how many wives he might have?" he pressed.

"Look, I just—I think it changes when they get older." I turned back to the sauce, but I could feel him staring at my back. I let the silence hold until I couldn't stand it any longer. Without turning around, I said, "What, Cal?"

"I think it's very strange that you've fought with me for years over this, like he's had some perfectly acceptable hobby, and suddenly, because he brings a girl home, it's a potential problem? Jesus, Chloe, this is the first normal thing that kid's done since he was ten."

"That's ridiculous. And don't say Jesus in front of her," I said, dismissing him. I heard the screen door slam before I could replace the lid on the sauce.

DESPITE Cal's reservations, the tofu tomato alfredo was fantastic, silky and full on the tongue. Ada seemed impressed, and Marshall turned grateful, leading the conversation with topics designed to maintain peace at the dinner table. He asked about Meghan's schoolwork and she practically glowed when he asked her something in French and she could respond fluently.

"What did you take?" Meghan asked Ada.

"I didn't take any foreign languages," she said. "I was home-schooled. I'm pretty good at sign language though."

"Really? Show me my name," Meghan demanded. Ada taught us Meghan's name, and then did everyone's, patiently repeating the configurations over and over until we each knew at least our own names, even if we dissolved into hopeless laughter if we tried anyone else's.

She signed something at Marshall, quickly, with more intricate gestures than the simple finger spellings she'd taught us, and he nodded but did not include us in the conversation, such as it was. Neither Meghan nor Cal noticed, caught up in testing their names out on each other. Marshall saw me looking at them and smiled, not the sly grin he'd given me upstairs, but his old, open, boy smile.

"So, Dad, are you booked tomorrow or can we go out on the boat?" Marshall asked.

Cal seemed surprised, but smiled at him, and I realized he thought he'd be going. "Where do you want to go?" he asked. "We can take you to Meghan's favorite spot, lots of redfish there. What do you say, Meg?"

Meghan bounced in her seat. "Yeah, we could—"

"No, Dad, I meant maybe I could take Ada out. No fishing," he interrupted Meghan, as though she hadn't spoken. She fell silent. "She won't even eat fish, you think she's gonna put a hook in one?"

It was the exact wrong tone to take with Cal, and I sighed at the inevitability of it all, neither of them giving an inch. I'd warned him, and we were not to be disappointed. Cal did a dramatic choke on his pasta and turned red before making a great show of swallowing and wiping his mouth with his napkin before responding. His real talents were lost on the fish of Florida; the man should have been an actor. Ada watched with her mouth slightly open, a forkful of pasta hovering in midair, as if debating whether she should flee or keep eating.

"Why, exactly, do you think I should let you take my boat out by yourself? Didn't the last time teach you anything? Taught me something, something I'm not ready to forget, Marshall. The answer is no. You can take your girlfriend out on the water by yourself when you get your own boat."

Two years ago, right after graduation, Marshall had not come home for dinner. Calls to his cell phone went directly to his voice mail. We didn't start to worry until after dark, and by midnight we were frantic. Meghan had finally come to us, interrupting me on the phone with Corbin, Marshall's friend, who professed to have not heard from Marshall.

"Mom," she'd whispered, sidling against me and avoiding Cal. "I think I might know where he is." I filtered this astonishing announcement through Corbin's vague suppositions about Marshall's whereabouts and hung up on him without explanation.

"What?" I cried, leaning down into her face, my hands tight upon her small shoulders. "Where? Why have you waited so long? Where is he, Meghan?"

She cast a doubtful glance at her father and then said, in an even smaller voice, "I think maybe he took Daddy's boat."

"What?" I asked, even as Cal bolted for the back door where a row of keys hung on pegs. I heard him shout, "Dammit!" and knew his second set of keys, on their ubiquitous red-and-white buoy key ring, weren't there.

I left Meghan, nearly shaking with the unknown outcome of her revelation, and met up with Cal in the outbuilding where he stored all of his charter equipment and kept his records in a small office. He'd already raised Marshall on the radio, and I hung back as I listened to him yell at him, reminding myself that my son deserved every bit of it. After pinpointing Marshall's location, Cal arranged for Sea Tow to haul him and the boat, simply out of gas, back to the marina.

When Marshall arrived home, things only got worse, and we all suffered with it. Marshall had been allowed to take the smaller boat, *McKale's Ferry*, by himself since he was fourteen, but it had always been arranged beforehand, and never had he been allowed to take it after dark. I was just glad he'd left the large boat, *Trillium's Edge*, designed for overnight trips out in deep water, at the marina and was now safe at home.

But Cal took it as a personal affront, a slap in the face of his trust in Marshall, in his assurance that his son knew the dangers of the water and boating in the 'Glades, how quickly things could go wrong. He hadn't been allowed to take the boat on his own since, and hadn't asked.

Ada gaped at Cal while Meghan slipped lower in her seat. Marshall simply nodded. "Maybe we can talk about it later," he said, calm and reasonable, to my surprise, deflating the tension like a pinprick to a balloon. Cal flicked his gaze my way and I raised my eyebrows at him. He seemed nearly ready to laugh.

"Yeah, later," he finally said. "Like when you're forty." And at that Marshall was the one to laugh, causing Ada and Meghan to glance between them in confusion. I was a little confused myself. Ada recovered first.

"What sort of art do you restore?" she asked me, and I silently thanked her for the change of topic.

"I mainly work on oils, but I can do just about anything," I replied. "I've wound up specializing in Highwaymen for the past few years. Word gets around with collectors."

"Highwaymen?" she repeated.

"They were a group of artists who specialized in Florida landscapes back in the sixties," I said. "Their work wasn't very expensive at the time, and it wasn't always treated very well. I clean them up, fix some paint loss, kill some mold."

"Is that what you went to school for?" she asked. I shook my head.

"Not really. I sort of fell into it by default; I was an art history major. What about you? Marshall says you're pre-law?"

She nodded, keeping her eyes on her plate. "Well, there's not actually a pre-law major or anything. There's just classes they suggest you take. I'm a political science major, so law schools can tell that I'm serious about being a lawyer. I'd rather do something like what you do though."

"Why don't you?" Meghan asked.

Ada shrugged, color splotching her cheeks unevenly. "I don't know. I used to want to be a writer, or an artist. It's more important that I become a lawyer though."

"Why is that?" I asked. "The world needs writers and artists more than it needs another lawyer."

"Not where I live," Ada said. "Anyway, my scholarship is for political science, so that's sort of a lot to concentrate on."

"You lose your scholarship if you're not going to law school?" Cal asked. "That doesn't seem very supportive."

"No, everyone is really supportive," she replied quickly, her color heightening again. "I do want to be a lawyer. Just sometimes I think it would be nice to do something creative, too, that's all. What did you go to school for?"

"I didn't," Cal said, without a trace of self-consciousness. It had never bothered him that he hadn't gone to college. It bothered me considerably that I hadn't earned my degree. After my parents disappeared, it was just too hard to go back, and then I was pregnant with Marshall. It felt right at the time, but I'd never gotten comfortable admitting that I'd gone to school but never graduated. People tend to ask where you went to college, not whether you graduated or not, and so my answer was always honest, but perhaps not always complete.

"Really?" Ada said.

"Never wanted to. My parents couldn't afford it, and I wasn't good enough in high school to get a scholarship, but it didn't matter. I knew what I wanted to do, and I knew how to do it. College isn't for everyone."

"You told me I had to go," Marshall said.

"You didn't have any idea of what you wanted to do," Cal pointed out. "Still don't, as far as I can tell."

"Of course you had to go," I said, shooting a cautionary glance at Cal. "And Meghan will go too."

Meghan nodded. "I want to go," she said.

"Will you study music?" Ada asked. "Marshall says you're a great pianist."

Meghan shook her head. "No, I'm no good."

"She is," I protested. "She just doesn't have the confidence."

"No," Meghan said again, firmly, and I sighed.

"Do you want to do what your mom does?" Ada asked. Meghan looked at me briefly, almost scientifically.

"No," she said. "I think...I don't know. Maybe I'll be a lawyer."

I made some sound; I don't know exactly what it was. A laugh, a choke, down in my throat, and she added quickly, "Or maybe a teacher."

"I bet you'd make a great teacher," Ada said.

"Sure she would," Marshall said. His hand stole under the table, and I could tell he'd grasped Ada's. "And you'll make a great lawyer."

"And what will you make?" Cal asked.

"I was thinking about moving to poli-sci," Marshall said. "You're right. I haven't been able to focus on what I want to do. But Ada's really helping with that. I think there's a plan for me."

"And do those plans include dessert?" I asked, standing too quickly and making the legs of the chair scrape against the floor. "Cal, want to help me?" I turned away with my plate before I could register his response.

"What was that all about?" he asked as I dumped the remains of my pasta down the sink.

"I just—What's all this about becoming lawyers?"

"So what? They're just reacting to Ada. Meghan will change her mind twenty times before she even reaches high school. And I'd be happy if Marshall would decide on anything. What do you have against lawyers, anyway? That's a pretty unoriginal bias for you."

"It's not that I have anything against them. I just thought our kids would do something less...corporate."

He sighed. "I don't know, Chloe. Could you just try to have a good time this week? Stop criticizing their future before they even get there."

"Oh," I said, turning around with my hand to my throat. "Forgive me. Was I being critical? I thought that was your job."

"Stop," he whispered fiercely. "Just stop, Chloe. Damn, what's wrong with you? Is it the tattoo? What? Let the kid grow up, would you?"

"Like you have?"

"At least I'm trying."

"That's why you won't let him take the boat? In broad day-light? After asking nicely?"

"Is that what this is about? You're trying to get me to let him take the boat?"

I shrugged. It was a non-answer for me. In fact, I couldn't decide what was keeping me on edge. Nothing I touched upon—tattoo? her still unspecified religion? Marshall growing up?—settled in me as concrete. But apparently my shrug was answer enough for Cal.

"All right. I'll bite. I let him take the boat, you'll relax?"

"Do what you want," I said. We stared at each other, silent now, daring the other to up the ante or fold. We did this in our marriage. This was our shorthand. This was our passive-aggressive, avoid-a-fight way. It worked. Passive-aggressive is hugely underrated when it comes to marriage.

"Mom?"

Meghan startled us out of our cold war. She'd poked her head around the swinging door and was looking at us with a mixture of irritation and concern.

"You want me to help with dessert?"

"Sure, honey," I said with a bright smile at Cal. If he rolled his eyes, he did it after he turned away.

When the three of us carried in the bowls of strawberries and tofu flan, Ada and Marshall were leaning in to each other, their temples touching as Marshall said something in Ada's ear. She was laughing softly. The intimacy of it nearly took my breath away. They did not jump and pull apart the way I would have when I was their age. The way I would have expected. The way I was still standing there waiting for.

It was only when I placed Ada's bowl in front of her that they drew back. Both smiled up at me without guile, and warmth filled my belly. I thought it might be nausea for a moment, but it seemed that whatever reservations I'd had simply burned up, like a scrap of paper afire, a brief blaze and then gone off the tips of the fingers, into the wind. I couldn't help but take a deep breath and something seemed to expand and ease inside me as I sat down and let it out, nearly expecting to see a wisp of smoke. Just a rough start, I thought.

It was new. That was all. When had new stopped being a good thing? When Meghan was diagnosed? That was new. That was a whole world of new to learn. Who wants new after that? What you want after that is *safe*.

And we'd been safe. Amazingly enough, after all the tests and adjustments and frightening trials of new food, we'd been safe. And nothing new had happened in a very long time. Until now. Or maybe we'd been ignoring the new things that had been presented to us over the years. Maybe we had stagnated in our pool of safe. Maybe this was why Cal and I swallowed jokes untold, restrained hands meant to touch.

"Your father has something to tell you," I said.

"Oh, yeah. You can take *McKale* tomorrow," Cal said. "But I want the radio on at all times."

Marshall glanced at me and broke into a wide grin. "Great! Great, Dad, thanks."

Meghan clattered her spoon into her bowl and looked panic-stricken. "Can I go? I want to go. Can I?" she asked, turning, not to Cal or me, but to Marshall and Ada.

"Sweetie," I said gently, "I think Marshall and Ada would like to have a little time alone."

"Meghan, come on," Marshall said. "We'll do something when we get home, okay?"

"Why can't she come?" Ada asked. A short silence changed

everything again, as if we'd all inhaled at the same time, pulling the oxygen from the room faster than it could filter in.

"Can I, Mom?" Meghan asked, her eyes wide.

"Ask your brother," I said, keeping my tone light.

"Marsh, can I? I won't get in the way or anything," she pleaded.

Marshall didn't look at Ada. He shrugged and said, "Yeah, all right, I guess."

Cal looked at me and nodded, as if to say, *See?* I would have pretended to not see that look last week. I lifted a shoulder, tilted my head, and in that off-balance motion of acquiescence I saw Cal for the first time in years.

New.

MARSHALL

Dinner. He could scream with the cheesy conversation. His dad, practically preening in front of Ada. It was disgusting. And his mom. He'd had no idea she could be so...prissy. She kept putting her hand on her throat like she was trying to close a collar up.

Meghan was a huge pain in the ass. He'd wanted to blast over the Gulf, listen to Ada scream with excitement, then slow it down and wend through the back canals and tributaries on the edge of the Everglades, drift through the mangroves alone with her. He'd already pictured it, could feel the thick air, feel the vibration of the quiet motor as it pushed them through, the muffled flap of wood stork wings and the quickening of the water as an alligator slid beneath the surface.

Unless something was fighting against becoming dinner, it was a languid world. He wanted to see Ada languid, wanted to see her body slow down as the humidity infused it, wanted to see if her hair softened out of its spikes and if her angles, beloved though they were, turned to curves.

None of that would happen with Meghan there. Instead the day would turn bright and happy, filled with the giggling laughter of his sister looking for a mentor of femininity. Meghan could never understand, much less learn, the solemnity of the river that ran through Ada, the serenity of faith only present in someone who *knew*.

This was what had been missing for him. There were gulfs between belief, faith, and certain knowledge. He'd stood on the banks of faith and belief, but never *knew*. Ada was on the other side. She so assuredly *knew* that she could afford to be nearly frivolous with her faith, careless with her belief, like trust-fund babies could toss cash around, as if they didn't care about it. But, in fact, it was the very fabric of their cells, their souls. Without it they would be dismantled, they would disintegrate, dissolve.

He wanted to feel that. He wanted to eat that knowledge whole and feel it spread out from his center to nourish his soul. That was what God was. That wholeness. He couldn't wait to meet Ada's family, the community. Couldn't wait to see them all, as one being, working toward the same goal of sustained enlightenment.

He could meet them soon, she'd said. But she wanted to meet his family first, and now they were proving themselves as surface and prosaic as he'd feared they would. They didn't understand how much he'd evolved over the past year, and now there was so damn little common ground. But then perhaps that's what Ada was trying to do with Meghan. He closed his eyes and let their conversation flow around him, praying the way she'd taught him, allowing himself to become still and allow the chaos around him to resolve itself without feeling the need to manipulate it.

It took so little time. In a matter of moments he felt able to re-enter the discussion, now centering around the one modern art class Ada had taken last semester. He listened to Ada and his mother circle around each other, his mother patiently explaining why Ada was wrong about something, some artist.

"I think you probably mean Graham," his mother said.

"No, but that's a common misconception," Ada replied. He nearly choked on a slice of strawberry.

"Really?" His mother's voice was low and pleasant, but Marshall heard the patient condescension in it. Ada didn't know, didn't realize.

"Smith's influence was really Xceron, but because they were both named John and both had been employed by Hilla, Hilla..." Ada faded off for a minute, searching for whatever name eluded her. Marshall thought his mother would rush to fill in the blank, to prove that she was the more knowledgeable after all, but when he looked at her he could tell that she didn't know the name either. He, Meghan, and their father watched the two women in silence, mouths not exactly hanging open, but close enough, amazed, not only at the fact that Ada dared to contradict his mother on an art point, but also that his mother couldn't seem to come up with an answer.

"Rebay!" Ada cried. "Hilla Rebay. Anyway, because they'd both been employed by her and had the same name, a lot of the American critics thought Smith was saying he was influenced by Graham, but really, he meant Xceron."

"Wow. That's quite a conclusion," his mother said, obviously unconvinced. Marshall felt his anger getting the best of him again. She always acted like she was so open to everything, but she was never open to the fact that perhaps she might be wrong about something.

"Let's look," he said, rising from his seat. Four pairs of startled eyes turned toward him. "Should be easy enough to find. I need to check my e-mail anyway. Come on, Ada."

Ada looked uncertainly at his parents, but then she rose, with Meghan leaping to follow, and they tramped upstairs to the computer in the attic office. It was an old, crappy desktop and they were still on dial-up at the house, but he hadn't bothered taking his laptop out of the trunk yet.

But he found what they were looking for in less than ten minutes, printed off the pertinent information, and the three of them entered the kitchen, triumphant.

His mother wasn't always right, and they had the evidence in hand.

Four

I COULD have been angry when they showed up in the kitchen with their dossier detailing the intricacies of David Smith's Surrealist influences. And, indeed, from the evidence they presented it appeared that he meant John Xceron rather than John Graham. I'm sure I hid my irritation well.

And it wasn't the fact that I was proven wrong. It was the fact that not only did Marshall obviously feel such a compelling need to prove me wrong, but that the three of them, even Meghan, seemed to take such glee in it. I tried to recall my earlier expansive feelings, my willing embrace of *new*.

Ada smiled at me tentatively as Marshall and Meghan jostled each other around the kitchen. "Can I help you clean up?" she asked softly.

"No, of course not," I said. "You're our guest."

But she pushed through the swinging door and came back in with the empty hummus plate and the still half-full bowl of edamame in her hands, giving Marshall a pointed glance.

"Come on," he said to Meghan, and they returned to the dining room to help clear the table. I gave Ada a little thank you wink as she placed the dishes on the counter.

"That's a beautiful bowl," she said, running her fingers around the pierced edge of the blue ceramic bowl my mother had given me when Cal and I married.

"Thank you," I said. "It was my mother's. She always had it on her kitchen table, and now I always have it on mine." I shook the edamame out of the bowl and into a plastic bag as she watched.

"I thought it was probably a family thing," she said. "We had one exactly like it, my mom had it, I mean. She said it was her mother's."

"Really? How funny," I said, appraising the bowl, wondering how many women my mother's age had the bowl, if it had been one of those giveaways they used to do at grocery stores. I had never asked where my mother had gotten it, and I now envisioned thousands of them tucked away in a second and third generation's kitchen cupboards around the country.

"Does she keep it on her kitchen table?" I asked, making light conversation as Meghan and Marshall filed in with plates and silverware.

"Oh," she said, flushing. "No, it disappeared a long time ago. We sort of moved around a lot, so I guess it got lost. She did, though, when we had it. I really liked it."

She sounded so bereft for a moment that I actually considered handing her the bowl right then and there. But Marshall appeared behind her, his hands on her shoulders, and smiled at me over her head.

"I want to show Ada around," he said. "Can we be excused from slave duty?"

"Marshall—" Ada began to protest.

"No, that's fine," I said, waving them off. "Meghan and I can finish up here."

"Mom," Meghan started to whine, but quieted when I gave her a warning look.

I held on to Meghan in the kitchen, her back against me, my right arm slung around her chest, just above the soft beginnings of her breasts as Marshall and Ada headed out on their walk. We watched through the screen door as Cal accompanied the couple out to the road, veering away toward his outbuilding and leaving them to make their way, slowly, their arms wrapped around each other's waists, down the pine needle–littered street.

He led her away from the path that led to the beach and the romantic sunset over the Gulf of Mexico that was every Southwest Floridian's pride. Instead he veered toward the path to the bay, where the sunset would be muted, filling the sky with a light that made everything green glow, everything red a torch. It was less showy than the brilliant fireball sinking into the Gulf, but there was a softening beauty in it, and it was, for me and evidently for my son, even more romantic than the beach.

There were other advantages to ushering in the stars on the bay. I knew that he would show her the right way to leap from rock to rock to make it over to the tiny island without soaking her boots, would identify the wading birds that came out to feed, and might even be able to point out an alligator. And, of course, the real draw was that the bay was almost always empty of people, locals and tourists alike, at this time of day.

I watched them go and had a nostalgic longing for Cal to come gather my hand in his and lead me through the palms and pines, to find me an orchid in a tree, to guide me over a root or make sure I avoided a snake. I envied them their romance.

Meghan held no such notions yet and strained lightly against me. I felt myself tightening my arm before I let her go. She opened the dishwasher and began sliding our dessert bowls into their slots in the top rack, the way I preferred it done.

"So, you like Ada, don't you?" I asked, moving beside her at the sink to rinse and hand her the dishes. She reached up and turned the radio over the sink on, fiddling with the knob until she found the station she liked, moody, alternative. She bobbed her head as she answered.

"Yeah, she's cool. Don't you think so? And she knows a lot about a lot of different things. She said she'd teach me more sign language. And she said she'd help me research stuff, like my allergies. And she said maybe I could visit. Sometime."

"Really? Well, I think you're a little young to go visit a college…"

"No, I mean when her and Marshall go to meet *her* family."

"She and Marshall," I responded without thinking. "When is this supposed to happen?" I asked, trying to sound casual.

"This summer. Can I go?"

"Oh, sweetie, let's cross that bridge when we get to it, okay? I've never met her family, I don't even know…" I trailed off. Ada had communicated with Meghan. Perhaps all my less-than-subtle questioning had been directed at the wrong people all along. "Meggie," I said, guilt flashing through me at my conscious use of Ada's nickname for her. Ah, see? New. I was getting the hang of things. "What has Ada said about her family?"

She slid the dishwasher rack in and manually lifted the door into place, yet another broken hinge in our home. "Just the same stuff she told you. They're really into, like, no chemicals and stuff."

"Right," I said. "I mean, what about their beliefs?"

"You mean their religion."

"Yes. I suppose." Meghan had grown up with Marshall's interest in religion, and she turned to me when she had questions. I always enjoyed our conversations. They gave me an opportunity to remember my parents and their interest in the world, their absolute willingness to discuss every theory as a possibility, and Meghan was learning to be inquisitive about life, which, I admit, I adored.

I loved having these two interesting children here, growing up on the backwater edge of the Everglades. Surrounded by people who'd lived here for generations, who made their livings from fishing or manual labor, it thrilled me to be raising children who could move easily in both worlds. It was vanity, of course, arrogance even, but I could not help but enjoy the thought that I was somehow diluting Cal's hard genes with my more genteel ones, making a lovely cocktail of children who knew how to think in abstract and didn't wince at getting their hands dirty or toughened by honest work.

I loved it when Meghan looked at me as she was looking at me now, thoughtful and curious, her brown eyes, flecked with the gold of her father's, pensive. "I think they're sort of like Kyle. I don't really know what the name of their church is, but it's, you know, their way of life?"

I nodded. Kyle, a friend Marshall had met his senior year in high school, had been a member of The Church of Jesus Christ of Latter-day Saints and an interesting young man, but the friendship, for whatever reason, had been short-lived. I wasn't completely clear on all their beliefs, but at least I had some direction to go in. "Interesting. What makes you think she's like Kyle?"

"Well, he talked about healing and laying on of hands and stuff, and that's why she knows sign language, because she learned it before their church healed her sister."

"What was wrong with her?" I asked, fascinated now.

"She couldn't talk, or hear, and she was sort of learning challenged, or something. But they healed her, I mean, the people in the church did."

"She can talk, and hear now?" I asked.

"She didn't say, she just said they healed her. Do you think that really works?"

And here was where Cal and I differed. Cal would have simply said "no." I didn't believe in absolutes. Who was I to say? I couldn't say that I believed it, but how could I say that it never happened? Because I'd never seen it? Because it wasn't widely accepted?

"I don't know," I answered. "Wouldn't that be wonderful though?" I wanted her to see possibilities, to accept the right of others to believe what they wanted to, even if it wasn't what she, or her parents, believed.

She nodded, and then looked out the window, searching the driveway. "Ada said she'd watch *Heathers* with me if you let us," she said.

Ah. This? Definitely *not* new. "Sorry, honey. We've discussed this."

She sighed, a huge, precursor-to-teen-angst sigh. And that was when I knew that yes, this new was good. Because I did not feel dread well in me at the thought of Meghan turning into a teenager. Instead, I could not keep my mouth from curling into a delighted smile. I was looking forward to every bit of it, to seeing her change, and test her boundaries, and blossom—yes, I actually thought the word *blossom*—into a young woman I was going to be so proud of.

After Marshall and Ada returned we set up the Scrabble board in the living room, and when Cal returned from working in his outbuilding, he joined Meghan as a team. None of us were any match for Marshall though, who seemed lit from within, and this, too, I reveled in.

Cal and I left the children in the living room sometime after eleven, when Ada finally cajoled Meghan into playing the piano for her, and as we climbed the stairs he reached back and took my hand to the strains of Bach. We shared space amicably in the bathroom, and, as couples who have been married for a certain amount of time often do, there were enough allowances between us, an extra carefulness in passing the toothpaste, a courteous holding out of a face towel, that the path was being gently cleared for sex. This was the romance in our marriage, and, I believed, in most long-term marriages.

We laughed softly, talked softly, fell together softly, and then softly drew apart, aware of and pleased that this was one of the good times and our distance had been successfully breached once again. It was an aftermath with a subtly hopeful sheen, a small, quiet bit of promise.

CAL fell asleep quickly, but I was still awake when I heard the kitchen door open and close. I pulled one of Cal's buttery soft T-shirts over my head and padded to the window. Marshall, Ada, and Meghan moved in the moonlight like reeds, any difference in their build or sex smoothed out from this height. I could have opened the window, called down to them to find out what they were doing, but I felt too satisfied with my children, magnanimous in my newfound acceptance of them as young adults.

It startled me to see Marshall walk up the bumper of his car and onto the hood, oddly reminiscent of the way it had startled me to watch him climb the steps to his first day of elementary school. He got his balance on the shape of the hood, then turned around and held out a hand to Ada. She turned her face up to him and raised her arm. I could see that she was laughing, her mouth open in joy as he helped her up on the bumper and then the hood. She clambered onto the roof while Marshall helped Meghan onto the hood.

They joined Ada on the roof and the three of them lay across it, Marshall in the middle, and gazed up at the stars. My children beneath me, safe in the moonlight, my husband sleeping behind me in our sweetly scented bed, I was all rare, feminine contentment.

Had I known what the next twenty-four hours would bring, I would have flung open the window and launched myself out of it, arcing toward my children in an attempt to cover their fragile bodies with my own, to keep them safe from all that was new.

MARSHALL

If she wasn't talking, Marshall could imagine that Meghan wasn't there, and he and Ada were alone, looking at the stars. Of course, the times she wasn't talking were remarkably few and far between. But eventually her small voice faded away as she succumbed to the late hour, and Ada took his hand as they stared up at the sky.

He rolled toward her, raising up on one elbow so he could look down on her face, the skin across her high cheekbones stretched taut and nearly translucent in the moonlight. The soft rush of the surf on the beach filtered through the trees in the quiet, and a barred owl hooted in the distance.

He pushed her collar out of the way with one finger, trailed his fingertips across the base of her neck. She breathed evenly under him, gazing past him at the sky, as if she weren't aware of his presence.

If he stared hard enough, he thought he could see right through her skin, could see the fine arch of her collarbone, the badge of her sternum. Ada remained still as he pressed his lips to hers and tasted the softness of the inside of her top lip.

He ran his fingertips against the side of her breast and nearly moaned when she arched slightly under him and drew a quick breath, the air flowing in past his lips between them. He pulled his head back so he could see her eyes as he pressed more firmly against her breast, and as he did he heard the train coming.

The sound was faint. Ada was likely confusing it with the sound of the surf, and from years of hearing it he knew it wouldn't get much louder before fading away again, but before it did...and there it was. Her eyes widened as the whistle sounded and her mouth opened slightly.

"Is that it?" she whispered.

He nodded, but remained silent, waiting. There were always two at night. Unless the engineer saw that something was on the tracks. But usually it was just two. And there the second one was.

As the sound filtered through the pines and palms, Ada closed her eyes and pulled him down toward her, letting him melt into her, responsive rather than passive now, staying quiet so as not to disturb Meghan. When she moved her hand down and pressed hard through his jeans, he nearly expired with sheer happiness.

The whistle died away without him noticing, and as the sound of the engine faded she pushed him away. Clouds moved across the moon, and when he looked at her now, her eyes were dark and shadowed, her lips a deep, swollen stain.

"Come on," she said. They woke Meghan and got her into bed without waking his parents, and then, after enough time had passed for Meghan to enter a deep sleep, Ada came to him in his childhood room.

When she left him, before dawn, he knew that there was nothing else he would ever want. Everything he had been looking for had been found.

He found his life.

He found salvation.

And, oh yes, he found God.

Five

THE kids were gone by the time I rose that morning, and the sun had already evaporated any traces of the cool night. Cal had been up for hours, as was his custom, and a half-pot of coffee was waiting for me. I poured a cup and padded across the yard to the outbuilding, pausing for a moment to check on the sunflowers, happy that the rabbits hadn't yet found the tender shoots. Heavy white and green buds were nearly ready to pop on the gardenia. I could already smell them and knew that by this evening at least a few of them would be open, their lush petals as soft as velvet.

I made plans to snip them off their bases and float them in a glass bowl in Meghan's room, as a treat for Ada. I doubted she'd seen, or smelled, many gardenias in Nebraska, and it was a flower that Meghan tolerated beautifully. Brown thrashers, like tiny hawks with their spotted breasts and sharp yellow eyes, flitted away under the ficus hedge as I reached the door to Cal's workroom, and I smiled at the sound of him singing along with the Eagles.

"Hey," I said, stepping over the raised metal threshold. He

smiled over a boat engine, his forehead lightly slicked with sweat. "You should have woken me."

"Ah, I figured I'd worn you out last night. It was only fair of me to let you sleep."

"The kids get off okay? Did they take something to eat?"

"I gave them a few bananas and fifty bucks. They said they were going to stop at the store."

"That was generous of you."

He shrugged. "Don't want him to run out of gas again."

"Oh, Cal, you didn't say that to him, did you?"

"No," he said, drawing it out as he wiped his oily hands on a pink rag and came around the engine to plant a kiss on my cheek. "I'm keeping our deal in mind. How about you?"

"Well," I said. "I watched the three of them leave the house last night long after midnight—"

"What?" he interrupted me, his hands still wrapped up in the rag. "You let Meghan go out in the middle of the night?"

"Not finished," I teased him. He looked at me expectantly. "Of course not. They just hung out in the yard. Climbed up on the car, actually, but never got in it."

"So spying on them out the window counts as letting them grow up? Hell, if I'd known that I'd have joined you with my binoculars."

"I wasn't spying," I protested. "I heard the door and looked to make sure they didn't drive off. I saw them lie down on the car and then I got back in bed. I fell asleep before I even heard them come back in."

He appraised me thoughtfully and finally nodded his head. "Well, all right, Mom. Aren't we mature?"

"Aren't we though?" I grinned at him. "No, it—it feels good actually. I think. We've made the next step in parenting. This is what we're supposed to do, right?"

He sighed. "So I hear," he said. "Never thought it would be this hard though. How you doing on Ada?"

I shrugged. "Meghan told me a little more about her last night. I don't know. They're young. Chances are Marshall is going to move on to someone else soon anyway. I suppose I'm getting worked up for nothing. What do you think? Do you think this is love? Temporary?"

"Who knows. You've always been closer to him than I have. I've tried talking to him about girls a few times before, but it always devolved into our same old thing."

"Arguing religion."

"Yeah. I don't know. Maybe it is love. Or maybe he just thinks it is."

"Is there a difference?"

Cal looked at me in surprise. "Well, yes, there's a difference. Damn, Chloe. That's pretty cynical."

I turned away from him, tears suddenly pricking my eyes. The tears didn't feel cynical. Had I turned cynical? And if I had, why was it a surprise to my husband? The same reason that Ada's appearance in our lives was a surprise to me, I supposed. I was too sure I knew Marshall.

I had touched every inch of his skin, wiped and cleaned and inspected places I had never, would never, touch on Cal. I thought I knew Marshall so well that it shocked and nearly confused me to consider hair anywhere on his body but his head. It was the great conceit of motherhood perhaps, that my having birthed, fed, and bathed him gave me never-ending access to his psyche.

Meghan had not pulled away from me yet. Had she? How long had it been since I had seen my daughter naked? Unselfconscious without clothing? And why did allowing them to grow up seem exhilarating until anything sexual came into the picture?

The surprises of motherhood seemed dubious gifts, at best. And the stages—I could no longer call them surprises—of marriage not only seemed dubious but...dangerous. A slick, long-grassed slope of dulled emotion, and yes, perhaps even cynicism.

And I cannot deny that the fact that it was a surprise to my husband was both depressing and yet oddly satisfying. I knew he wasn't paying attention. And didn't that just prove it?

I wandered over to Cal's workbench and picked up a wrench. It must have been twenty years old, its shank no longer shiny but lustrous. I tapped it against the side of the bench and then turned back to Cal with it in my hand, enjoying the slightly unbalanced weight of it.

"Think you could fix that screen door today?" I asked.

"I'll try to get to it," he replied, gazing at me steadily.

I nodded and, tossing the wrench onto the bench with a clatter, left for my workroom.

Where I got little to nothing done. After the energy and noise of the previous night, the house now seemed too quiet, too still to support creativity. I mixed a green to replace some paint loss on a palm tree, but couldn't get the right shade. My black wasn't even, not usually a problem in the frequently less technically correct Highwaymen paintings, but this was a Harold Newton, and the man had known what he was doing with color.

I finally turned to the other Highwayman I was working on, a "fire sky," filled with brilliant reds and yellows, almost absurdly lurid to anyone unused to southwest Florida's sunsets. I'd seen plenty of sunsets to rival the fire sky painting, and this time I got my colors right and was finally able to lose myself in my work. By the time I was ready for lunch, I'd worked my shoulders into satisfying knots and managed to replace my irritation with Cal with more pleasant remembrances of the previous night.

This, too, was one of those stages of marriage that nobody tells you about. Like the pain of childbirth fades, allowing us to do it again and again, eventually the time spent on petty resentments shortens, and we move from angry to settled in hours rather than days. Cal and I did anyway. My parents were gone too young for me to ask them about the intricacies of marriage, the secrets, if they had them, and the pitfalls.

And Calvin's parents were no example to turn to. According to him anyway. I'd never met his father, dead of a massive heart attack on their sofa when Cal was only sixteen, but his stories about him were both frightening and exhilarating, tales of impassioned sermons on the lure of the devil and the pain of the fiery pits of hell. Cal's brother, Randy, had been the quintessential preacher's kid, and was, the last time anyone had heard from him, evading warrants in Florida, Georgia, and Alabama.

Cal had removed himself entirely from the family the day he graduated from high school. We received occasional letters from his mother, her looping hand childlike, filled with misspellings, guilt-laden entreaties to visit her, and unselfconscious Bible references along with portents of doom and random news of obscure relatives.

Cal read these letters quickly, silently, occasionally allowed me to read them, and then threw them away. We did not discuss it, but I knew that he feared Marshall would read one and get intrigued, would possibly want to visit his grandmother, and would disappear into the bug-infested wilds of undeveloped Florida and spend his life convincing others that Satan was just a step behind them, waiting for the chance to claim their souls.

We'd taken him to visit once, when he was a toddler, at my insistence. Our first days there had been good, strained but polite. But once the initial busyness of food preparation and catching up on third cousins thrice removed was over, Cal and his mother seemed to deflate, as though all of their social niceties had simply leaked out, like so much air, and all that was left was the sour, stale remnant of a relationship long over. Their conversations, already terse, decreased in word count but increased exponentially in hidden meaning.

I watched, as one might watch snakes behind glass, certain of my safety but fascinated by the proximity to danger anyway. I did not miss a word, or a glance. I held Marshall while they jabbed at each other and vowed that I would never speak in riddles to my son.

She quoted Bible passages that seemed to be written specifically for her perceived lot in life, that of wronged mother, grievously harmed by the insensitivity and ungratefulness of her family. Cal countered with bits of Bible I'd never known he knew, all of it streaming from his mouth in a rounded, thickened accent I'd never heard.

My son and I were visiting with strangers.

Two days before we were to leave, we sat on the porch after dinner, eating homemade peach ice cream and listening to crickets, and it all ended. Marshall finished his ice cream and began to cry for more. He was up too late, and his cries rose fast and high in the air. Cal's mother stared hard at Marshall, his lips soft and red and still smeared with ice cream, and I saw her eyes narrow as she turned to Cal.

Ignoring me completely, she pointed her spoon at Marshall and said: " '*Withhold not correction from the child: for if thou beatest him with the rod, he shall not die. Thou shalt beat him with the rod, and shalt deliver his soul from hell.*' "

Before I could even begin to make sense of this, Cal stood, his bowl clattering at his feet, and said, "That's it, we're done." He strode past her and grasped me by the arm, pulling me from my chair as he scooped Marshall up in his other arm. Marshall's crying escalated to screaming, and though I pulled my arm from Cal's hand, I moved.

I never protested, I simply followed him quickly to the room he and his brother had shared as children, threw our belongings into our bags, and we were gone. I didn't dare speak, to her or to him, as we left. It was almost two hours later, after Marshall had cried himself out in the backseat and we were hurtling toward the west coast, that Cal finally spoke.

"We're not going back," he said. "Don't ask."

"Okay," I said quietly. And we did not. I wrote her Christmas cards, and I occasionally sent her photos of the children. But I never responded to her letters, and could never get the chill out of my heart when I recalled her words.

It was no wonder that Cal worried about Marshall and his interest in religion. It was hard for him to separate Marshall's more scholarly approach to religion from his own upbringing. I wondered if Cal had heard anything from the kids on his radio, and made him a sandwich for lunch so I had an excuse to visit the workshop, give my peace offering, and ask him.

He gave me a tentative smile as I entered, a tuna salad sandwich and chips on a plate held in front of me, and it was as though the nasty words had never been uttered. He washed his hands and sat on a stool to eat.

"Anything from the kids?" I asked.

He nodded, his mouth full, and swallowed, wiping the back of his hand across his mouth before he spoke. "Marshall said he figures they'll be back around six."

"Okay. I'm going to run out and grab some things for dinner. Need anything?"

"Nope. Maybe get a movie?"

"Sure. See you in while." I leaned over to peck him on the

cheek. Just a small kiss, nothing memorable about it until much, much later.

I spent the afternoon doing errands in town. I picked up some summer clothes for Marshall and Meghan, taking care to pass over the childish items Meghan would balk at. After waffling for too long in the underwear department, I also picked her up a bra. I stopped at the produce stand, thinking that the kids would be happy to know I was buying organic and supporting a small, local business. Sandy, the owner, dressed in a long, purple skirt and red tank top, her white hair in long braids, greeted me.

"Well, am I going to see the whole Tobias clan today?"

I grinned at her. She had to have been approaching seventy, and I aspired to develop her easy style, her assurance that she was always exactly where she should be. She radiated calm and wit, and I always swore that as soon as my hair was more than fifty percent white I was going to strip the rest of its color and emulate her.

"Hey, Sandy. Were the kids in?" I asked, smelling the end of a cantaloupe. Sandy pulled it from my grasp, hefted another one, and then handed it to me.

"Yep. Marshall's gal is a little spitfire, hmmm?"

"Seems like it. What did you think?"

She cocked her head to study me for a moment. This was a small town. She'd been here for years before me, and she knew our family's history, as did almost everyone else in town. She belonged to the small nondenominational church just down the road from us. The church itself was ancient, but they kept it up beautifully, painting it bright white every year when the rainy season ended. Marshall had attended services for a brief period, but their laid-back style of worship hadn't seemed to keep him interested, and he'd moved on quickly.

"Well, she's not a shy young lady, that's for certain. Told me I needed to stock yak milk and then called the integrity of my flax-seed into question."

I laughed and tucked some tomatoes into my basket. "I can't imagine anyone calling the integrity of anything you touch into question. If it makes you feel any better, she showed me up last night at dinner."

Sandy nodded. "It's good to question, but I seem to have less patience for it in children these days. Perhaps I'm getting old and crotchety."

"Or perhaps they're just young and brash," I offered, taking my basket to the counter.

"Perhaps. Made fresh cookies," she said, nodding toward the basket of homemade cookies next to the register. I looked long-ingly at them and inhaled. The aroma managed to seep out of the plastic wrap that covered them. There were more chocolate chunks than dough, and the peanut butter cookies had little hash marks made by a fork, just like my mother had made when I was a child. But I shook my head and paid her for the produce, promising to pass a kiss along to Cal.

I stashed the bags behind my seat and headed to the video store, my final stop. Nothing too grown-up, nothing too childish. Choosing for this new dynamic was more trying than I would have thought. Did other parents go through this? I never noticed moth-ers agonizing over tiny bras, or picking up and putting down an R-rated movie seven times. Had I truly become so protective that my own decision-making skills had been warped beyond repair?

Finally I chose a comedy, and then, as I approached the coun-ter, my eye was caught by Winona Ryder in a blue skirt, held from behind by a leering Christian Slater. I grabbed the box before I could go into another fugue of mothering and plopped *Heathers* on the counter along with the other movie.

I drove home with the windows down, the spring already steamy with a humidity that I loved feeling on my skin, and the radio loud I had a couple of hours before the kids got home, and even thought that perhaps I could convince Cal to bake some more bread and maybe join me in the shower. The night before had been tense, enjoyable, frightening, and exhilarating all at once. I was ready to plan for a more relaxing time tonight, all the jitters gone, the jagged edges smoothed.

I was singing along with the radio, some Justin Timberlake thing that I would never in a million years have admitted to Cal that I liked, when I turned onto our drive. I hadn't even slowed down when I saw the workshop door fling open and Cal come running out, his mouth open, tearing at the passenger door handle before I could come to a stop to hear what he was screaming.

Everyone talks about their heart pounding, jumping out of their chest, but when I heard that he was screaming our daughter's name over and over I never felt my heart at all. There was nothing but a great sucking hole in my chest, with nothing to fill it but the echo of *Meghan*.

Six

WHEN we reached the marina, all the emergency vehicles were already there, their lights going but their sirens off. I didn't know what that meant and stuttered, "What's happening?" at Cal, but Cal was already out of the car while it was still rolling, stumbling when his feet hit the pavement before righting himself and tearing for the dock.

I slammed into park and took a different route, toward the ambulance, grasping at the handle of the cab, startling a young woman in a paramedic's uniform. I was talking before she could get a foot on the ground, spewing forth Meghan's medical history, the list of things that could go wrong, and what needed to happen now, right now, and where was she, where was my daughter and what exactly had happened, and why was everyone just standing around and why weren't the sirens on?

"They're almost here," she said, placing her hands on my upper arms, trying to hold me together. "We can't do anything yet. Coast

Guard is still a mile off. It was faster for them to come in than for us to go out. Everything is going to be fine, they're almost here."

I spun out of her grasp and headed for the dock, where I could see Cal, gesturing toward the marina where the big boat was, and as I got closer I could hear him shouting.

"God dammit, where are they? I can get her, I can get her!"

"Sir, listen, listen!"

As I arrived by Cal's side, we all fell silent and sure enough, we could hear a boat, going flat-out, balls-to-the-wall as Cal would say with a disapproving shake of his head whenever he saw some idiot speeding through a no-wake zone. The engine whined, and we all watched the mouth of the canal, waiting—helpless and fairly vibrating with adrenaline—for the boat to round the peninsula.

Within seconds it roared into view, swinging a wide rooster tail as Marshall overcompensated for the speed and then straightening, flying at us, his face, hidden behind the windshield, just a smudge of white with hollows of dark sunglasses for eyes, like a skull with a shock of dark hair.

We all moved at once: the paramedics poised themselves on the edge of the dock, gloves already on, the driver ran back to the ambulance, Cal readied himself with ropes, and I started my mouth again, talking about anaphylactic shock and the need, above everything else, for speed, for instant action, all the while aware that nothing had been instant because Meghan hadn't been with me, and nobody else could possibly understand.

But Marshall did, of course, Marshall understood. Meghan was his little sister; he'd been there for all of it. We'd shielded him, of course, to an extent, until we'd know what was wrong, how it could be prevented. But he knew everything now, he knew what to do, and he'd never have allowed anything to happen to her.

And then the boat hit the dock, literally, hit it with the side of the bow, sending one paramedic nearly off the edge while the rest of us reeled and got our first glimpse of the horror show in the cockpit. Blood, everywhere, Ada keening gibberish, her eyes rolled back in her head, more blood on the seats, on Marshall and Ada, and on Meghan, dear God, Meghan.

I started to scream then. Because there was no way that was my child, there was no way that my child, my girl, could have become that poor thing on that boat. I launched myself into the cockpit, pushing myself past Ada, who wouldn't shut up, and past the paramedics, who had already shot Meghan full of epinephrine, and they fought with me, shouting to keep me back while trying to intubate her.

Cal, done wrestling with ropes, pulled Ada unceremoniously off the boat, dragging her useless, bloody legs, and tossed her on the dock like a rag doll so he could get to me, and then he hauled me away, my hands reaching for the only recognizable part of my daughter, her hair, her long, dark hair, streaming across the dirty white mesh of the cushions.

Cal held me from behind, and I sagged over his forearms while the men struggled with my unrecognizable daughter. Ada had crabbed her way off the dock and was huddled over her knees on the curb by the ambulance, with the driver patting her, as if she were the one who needed comfort. Ada was pushing her away, shaking her head.

I straightened up quickly, startling Cal and smacking the back of my head into his chin when I realized that I hadn't seen Marshall since laying eyes on Meghan. There he was, still in the cockpit, his back pressed against the dash as far as he could get, watching the paramedics work with his mouth agape.

"Marshall!" I cried, pulling away from Cal, who held on for a moment while I struggled, but finally released me. I made my way on board at the bow and crawled over to the windshield to bang on it. He jumped and finally turned toward me.

"What happened, Marshall, what happened?"

He didn't say anything, just shook his head at me, his mouth still slightly open, his eyes hidden by his sunglasses. The paramedics suddenly shifted and the boat rocked, making us both clutch for balance and breaking whatever tenuous contact we'd made. Cal, seeing that they were attempting to lift Meghan, jumped in the cockpit, and the three of them managed to get her out of the boat and on the stretcher. I scrambled my way off the boat and rushed with them to the ambulance, Cal right beside me, both of us talking to the unresponsive lump that used to be Meghan, telling her it was going to be okay.

The driver left her ministrations of Ada as another EMT from the fire truck took over, and as they slid the stretcher in Cal handed me up into the back, saying, "I'll meet you there," before the doors closed and the ambulance raced off, sirens, finally, blessedly, going now.

There was less room in the ambulance than I would have thought, and I made myself as small as I could while they continued to work on Meghan and talked to the hospital on their radio. I gingerly snaked my hand onto her ankle, the only place I could reach, the only area of her bloated body they didn't seem to be working on.

"Is she breathing?" I finally asked, my voice breaking on the words.

"We have a pulse," the paramedic nearest me said. "Right now we have to be thankful for that. They're ready for us, we're almost there."

As we pulled into the emergency room drive there was a sea of people in green and blue scrubs waiting, and they swarmed over her and ran her in through the automatic doors with the paramedics while a nurse guided me behind them and asked me about Meghan's medical conditions.

I lost sight of her and answered rapid-fire questions as Cal finally arrived, Marshall padding silently behind him, Ada limping ten paces behind him, blood running down her leg. A nurse rushed over to her and she was led away while Cal joined me. Marshall hung back, silent, his sunglasses still on.

"What's happening?" Cal asked, his voice hoarse. "Where is she?"

"They're doing everything they can for her right now," the nurse answered soothingly. Cal was in no mood to be soothed, and he grasped me by the upper arm and started down the hall, the nurse hurrying to keep up.

"Where is she?" he asked when the hallway split.

"Mr. Tobias, please, let me see what's happening and I'll be right out to tell you," the nurse said. "There's a private room right here. Please, have a seat, I'll be right back, I promise."

Cal looked in the open door of the room, then looked at the nurse. "If you're not back in five minutes to tell me what's going on with my daughter, I'm turning this hospital upside down."

"Cal," I cautioned him. "They're doing everything they can." And was immediately ashamed. *I* should have been turning the hospital upside down. But I needed to follow the rules, be courteous. If I did, if I did everything right, everything would be okay. Let the doctors work, let the nurses work, let the drugs work. Stay calm, cooperate, stay calm.

"Go!" he said, and the nurse went, flying on her soft-soled shoes. Cal finally let go of my arm and stepped into the waiting room, falling heavily into one of the low, burgundy chairs. A muted TV flashed news across the screen in the corner. I beckoned to Marshall, still watching us silently from the corridor, and he slowly joined me, following me into the room and sitting in the chair next to mine.

"Where's Ada?" I asked, suddenly remembering her bloody legs. He shook his head. "What happened, honey? Did Meghan get stung?" He shook his head again, and Cal and I exchanged glances.

"What happened, Marshall?" Cal asked.

Marshall looked at his father and started to shake his head again, but Cal stood and, covering the space between them in a split second, ripped the sunglasses from Marshall's face. I flinched and nearly cautioned Cal again, but this time I was more afraid of Cal than of not being courteous, and my hand landed on Marshall's arm instead, keeping him from shrinking away as his father loomed over him. "What the hell happened, Marshall?" Cal said.

"I—I don't know," he said. "I don't know. It was okay, I mean, we, Ada, I mean—"

"Slow down," I said. "It's okay. Just take it easy. Now, everything was fine, until when?"

"The cookie."

"What cookie?" I asked.

"We got— Ada got cookies at the produce stand."

"What kind of cookies, Marshall?" Cal asked, his face beginning to turn red, his voice lowering. My stomach bottomed out, but I fought the growing certainty, recalling the cookies with the little hash marks in them, the exquisite smell of the peanut butter coming right through the plastic wrap, the extraordinary kindness of Sandy, whom I would never again be able to look at the same way. Meghan wouldn't eat a cookie with peanuts, and Marshall wouldn't let one near her. There was no question. There had been some horrible mistake, a bit of peanut had worked its way into a chocolate chip cookie, peanut oil on the wrapper, something.

"Chocolate chip," Marshall said, his voice dropping to a whisper. We waited. "And a peanut butter."

Cal exploded. He dragged Marshall up from his seat and thrust him back so his shoulders were pressed against the wall while he fought to keep his feet in front of his chair. I was on my feet just as quickly, pulling on Cal's arms, as terrified of what he might do as I was of what Marshall was saying.

"What did you do?" Cal yelled. "What the hell did you do?"

Marshall broke, his face crumpled, and he sagged against the wall as Cal struggled to hold him upright. "I didn't think—"

"You didn't think? You didn't think what? You didn't think your little sister would die? What the hell? I don't even know what you're saying here. You let your girlfriend buy a peanut butter cookie and then sat there while she fed it to her? While she tried to kill your sister?"

"No, no, I—she said it was organic, and that it was such a small bit—" He broke off again, obviously too horrified to continue. Cal abruptly let go, and Marshall dropped into the chair and folded in upon himself, sobs shaking his body. "I tried the EpiPen, I did, and it worked at first, but then she stopped breathing again, and I couldn't find another one."

This time he looked at us accusingly, hurt and bewildered. "I looked," he cried. "I looked, and there wasn't one there, and then Ada said, she said we could..."

I leaned over him, my hands rubbing his back. "That you could what, honey? What?" I asked. I had to hear this. What horrible experiment were they performing with Meghan's life? Marshall whispered something and both Cal and I leaned closer to hear. "What?"

He lifted his face to us, agony etched across it, and said, "She said we could pray."

There was more, but I didn't hear much of it after that.

*   *   *

LATE that night, while Cal slept fitfully in a chair beside Meg-han's hospital bed, and I spoke softly to her, holding her hand, a police officer arrived and waited outside the door while a nurse whispered in my ear. I'd already told the story over and over again, to doctors, nurses, to everyone who asked how she'd gotten some-thing with peanuts in it, and it did not strike me as strange to be telling the story one more time in the hallway while a uniformed officer took notes.

How they, the children, Ada and Marshall, had broken a tiny piece of the peanut butter cookie off and mashed it into the top of a chocolate chip cookie and given it to Meghan. How Ada had explained to Marshall that it would be okay, that it was organic, that the exposure to such a tiny bit would help her build her immu-nity. And how Meghan had seemed fine, until she started pushing on her lips with her fingertips, until she started to panic and gasp for breath.

And how they'd prayed. How they'd watched Meghan struggle for air and clutched each other and raised their voices in prayer. Until Marshall finally broke, broke and scrambled for the EpiPen and jammed it into her thigh, and their joy when she came back, and they prayed over her again, and how she'd tentatively joined them.

He said Meghan was okay, that she was talking, that she held their hands . . . until she started gasping again. And that was when she started to vomit, and when Ada clutched him and told him to stay steady, that God was working through Meghan, was testing his faith, his commitment to him, to her. And he'd tried, he'd tried, but his faith wasn't strong enough, and when Meghan lost con-sciousness, he'd struggled out of Ada's grasp, finally throwing her to the side, and started the boat and gunned it, sending Ada flying across the cockpit to split her knees open on the floor, one knee bad enough to need stitches.

"Where are Marshall and Ada now, ma'am?" the officer asked softly. I shook my head.

"I told him to take her back to our house and to call her parents to come get her," I said. "I assume they're there."

He nodded his head and closed his notebook before looking at me solemnly. "I hope your daughter comes out of it, ma'am. Here's my card. Please call me if you think of anything else."

I nodded, tucked the card in my pocket, and went back into the hospital room where Meghan lay.

She'd never regained consciousness. She was alive, but the doctor told us she hadn't been for a few moments, that she'd been starved for oxygen, and that they didn't know when, or if, she would wake again.

MARSHALL

They'd gone home near dinnertime. His father, unable to even look at him, had left the waiting room to go in search of the nurse, and his mother, crying quietly, told him to go home, to find Ada and go home, and to have her parents arrange to get her. The directive was clear.

Get her out of their house.

He didn't want to see her at all. He wanted his mother to take care of it. He only wanted to curl up in a ball and allow his mind to blank, to find the spiritual clarity he'd been so high on just that morning. Faith was supposed to sustain people in times of crisis, but it had fled his soul at the first sign of trouble. And this was such trouble, such horrible, nightmarish trouble.

He'd found Ada sitting in a chair in the corner of the emergency room waiting area, crutches leaning on the table beside her, her legs bandaged. When she saw him, he could do little more than shake his head at her before saying gruffly, his voice foreign to himself: "Let's go."

He'd allowed her to make her way alone across the parking lot on her crutches and started the car, watching her hobble toward him in the rearview mirror, wishing he had the guts to put it in reverse and extinguish her from his view.

She worked her crutches into the backseat and got in the car, groaning as she bent her legs, and finally slammed the door shut with a sigh. She was clutching a sheaf of papers in her left hand and as they brushed the hairs of his arm he recoiled as if singed.

She didn't speak until they had pulled out of the parking lot. "Is she—is everything okay?"

He rolled to a stop at a red light and looked at her, really looked at her. Her tiny face was pinched in pain, her mouth drawn into a tight line—a mouth he'd placed his own lips on. The lines of her delicate shoulders he'd run his hands across, small, perfect breasts he'd caressed, the first he'd held, kissed, her slender hips tucked back into the seat cupping her perfect bottom that fit right in his hands as if sculpted just for them.

He hated her.

And he hated himself for wanting her so desperately at the same time, for feeling his cock stir while his sister lay dying. If he had the guts to cut it off right then, he would have.

She glanced at him and then down at her lap. When the light turned green and he moved forward, she reached over and placed her hand on his leg. He shifted gears and then gingerly, not trusting himself to touch any more of her skin than he had to, picked her hand up and dropped it back on her lap.

"Do you want to pray with me?" she asked.

He could not seem to bring his mouth to move, could not push words up out of his throat. He'd always had a vague notion of words coming from his brain, falling down into the back of his throat and rolling out through his lips, effortless, gravity allowing them to drop into the world. But he had been wrong. Words were grave and serious work for the body, formed in the chest, too heavy to move unless forced out on explosive bursts of air from the lungs.

Simply breathing seemed like such an effort. The air leaked in and out; it was impossible to think of it being able to sustain something so heavy as a single word, much less several of them strung in a row. He had no idea how he'd ever had entire conversations.

Ada snuffled beside him, huddled against the passenger door, her left knee wrapped in an outlandishly bulky bandage, her right bandaged less dramatically. He had a nearly overwhelming urge to reach over and squeeze her knee, to make her scream in fright and pain, to just keep the pressure on, let her scream all the way home.

"Are you going to talk to me?" she asked in a tiny voice, and he hated her for that, for being able to sustain voice, even the weak, pathetic one that it was. He didn't look at her, just clicked the directional to turn on the road toward home, not bothering with the route he'd taken her just the day before, along the water, empty road spooling out ahead of them like their future, the smell of the Gulf and the bay mingling like lovers.

She began to chant. It didn't matter what. They were words he once recognized, but no longer did or wanted to. He didn't bother turning on the radio to drown her out. He could do that on his own. She finally shut up when he turned into the drive leading to the house. He wouldn't have even noticed except it felt a little easier to breathe, as if her words had eaten up oxygen, making the air in the car thin.

Once out of the car he left her to struggle with the crutches and immediately went upstairs and into Meghan's room, grabbing Ada's suitcase and throwing anything that looked like it might be hers into it. He could hear her fight with the screen door, and by the time he got back downstairs with her suitcase she had collapsed into a kitchen chair, her forehead on her arms.

"You need to call your parents," he said, the words more of an effort than climbing the stairs had been.

She lifted her face to him, horror stamped upon it, more expression than he'd seen from her since he'd grabbed the EpiPen. "What? I can't call my parents."

"Well, you're going to have to. You can't be here when they get back."

"Then take me back to school," she pleaded.

"I'm not going back to school!" he yelled. He'd found his voice. "You have to leave."

"If you won't take me then how am I supposed to go?"

"I don't care. Just go."

"You can't just . . . cast me out, Marshall. You agreed with this, you're the one who didn't have enough faith, you're the one who couldn't tough it out." Her voice began to rise, ringing off the old metal kitchen cabinets. "You were weak. She's screwed up because of you, not me. My faith is strong, it's unshakable, I am the way and the truth and the life—"

"You are nothing!" he shouted at her. "You are full of crap, and if she dies it's going to be your fault. What will your God think of that? What will he think of a little girl dying because she trusted you, because I trusted you? How will it feel when you're in hell?"

Ada drew herself up straight, closed her eyes, and began to pray out loud, rapidly and loudly. He dropped her suitcase and went for her, but she stood her ground and did not flinch when he slammed his hands down on the table in front of her.

"You're a fake!"

Her prayer only got louder, as did his accusations, and soon the kitchen reverberated with their voices, one word indistinguishable from the other, until he finally did what he'd wanted to do in the car, and fell on his knees and grasped her leg over the bandage and squeezed.

He got the response he'd been looking for. She screamed, a sound full of the pain he felt. Her body stiffened in the straight-backed chair and it tipped over, spilling her onto the floor, where she lay on her side, gasping.

"I noticed your faith didn't stop you from getting stitches in your leg," he said, crouching down beside her. "What happened? Why didn't God stop the blood? Maybe, Ada, maybe it was *your* faith that wasn't strong enough." He stood and dug the keys to his car out of his pocket, throwing them on the kitchen table. "Leave the keys with my roommate. I don't care where you go after that."

He left her on the floor and went upstairs, shutting and locking his door. He drew the blinds, and took the charms and necklaces from his drawer, pulling them off the cross and clutching them against his chest as he crawled into bed and wept his way into sleep.

When he woke, Ada, despite his locked door, was lying on her side at the far edge of the bed, turned away from him. "How did you—" he began, but when she turned over and he saw the tears shining on her face, the knot inside his chest seemed to burst. He was filled with relief, and if he were to admit it to himself, helplessness. He pulled her into him and they clung to each other, he, mindful of her knees, she, mindful of his arousal, careful of each other's individual, exposed pain.

For the first time, they stayed together all night, and after they made love—and there was no mistake that that was exactly what it was, and that, too, was a first, though they'd not known the difference before—they did not pray or ask for forgiveness, from each other or from God.

He took care of her. He carried her to the tub and gently changed her bandages, and gave her the painkillers she'd refused earlier, and then carried her back to bed. He could not heal his sister and had been cast from her presence, but he could take care of Ada, and they finally slept, entwined with each other, breathing each other's air and forming their own faith.

They did not move until morning, when the police arrived to arrest them.

Seven

No change and no change and no change. Almost forty-eight hours and there was no change in Meghan, and no change in what the doctors told us and no change in how Cal and I hovered in her room except for an occasional change of position. Neither of us ate, and neither of us talked about Marshall or Ada.

A nurse brought us a plate of breakfast but it sat on the rolling tray between us, merely a symbol of the fact that it wasn't being rolled over to Meghan's bed for her to eat. Cal took his eyes off of Meghan long enough to glance at me.

"You should go home," he said. I barked out a laugh.

"What are you talking about?" I asked. Go home? Why would I go home until I could bring Meghan with me?

He cleared his throat. "One of us should. One of us should make sure everything is...all right there. And you should shower, and change. Bring us back some food."

"Then you go," I said.

He sighed. "I will. But if I'm the one who goes home, I don't know what I'll do when I get there."

His voice was low and resigned, and I suddenly realized what he was trying to say. He didn't know what he would do to Marshall, maybe Ada. I had no idea where either of them were.

I thought it over, calculated the time it would take me to go home, get back. It was too much time. I stood and grabbed my purse.

"I'll call first," I said. Cal didn't answer, and I left the room, hesitating at the line of the doorway, superstitious of allowing the door to close behind me. But it was unthinkable to prop the door open, to allow anyone walking by on their way to visit their own damaged loved one to see my child, to see Cal, broken and ancient in the reclining chair. I let the door close softly and shuddered when it clicked.

I raced down the hall, looking for an area where I could use my cell phone. The waiting room had four people in it, their faces drawn with fear or slack with exhaustion. It was four people too many, and I continued on my way, finally boarding the elevator to take me downstairs to the lobby.

When I got off the elevator, the sunlight coming in through the automatic doors of the lobby seemed an affront, and I glanced around to find another outlet. My eyes finally settled on the sign with the hospital map on it. There was a chapel, a gift shop, and a cafeteria in the opposite direction of that obscene sunshine, and I headed that way, turning my cell phone on as I searched.

The gift shop was tiny and glass-fronted, and the cafeteria was nearly full, but the chapel not only had heavy solid doors and no signs saying "No Cell Phones," but was also blessedly empty and quiet. I sat in a pew barely large enough for three people and dialed home. The phone rang long enough for the answering machine to pick up.

"Marshall, it's Mom. We're still here. There's no change. I need you to call me back. I need to know...what's going on. I'll try your cell phone."

I hung up and called his cell. There was no answer, and I left the same message there, then simply sat, phone on my lap, and stared up at the fake stained-glass window hanging on the front wall. I felt no qualms about prayer. I did it when I wanted to, directed it at no specific deity, and expected no response.

I wondered what deeply religious people thought about this little chapel. Did they find it without reverence? If their symbols weren't there—the crosses or the robes or glass-encased Torah or Qu'ran—did it steal a piece of their faith, distract them from their purposeful prayer? In this hospital, that tried to keep sick people of any faith alive, did the faithful feel forgotten in this empty chapel?

It felt peaceful enough to me, and I closed my eyes and prayed. For my daughter, for my son, for my husband and myself. That Meghan would come out of this as whole as she had been. That Cal could one day look at Marshall without hating him. That our marriage, already in some state of flux I hadn't yet been ready to examine too closely, could remain flash-frozen until it was all over. That when we did get home, Ada would be gone and we would never have to hear her name or see her Winona Ryder face, or the dangerous glint of her eyebrow ring ever again.

I gave it ten minutes. And when my phone did not ring, I turned it off, and returned to Meghan's room, where I simply shook my head at Cal's inquiring glance and settled in for the day.

THE doctors continued their wait-and-see diagnosis. They discussed scheduling of more MRI and CAT scans, talked about Rancho and Glasgow scales, fumbled with the intricacies of the brain that they really knew nothing about, gave us tentative time limits, and threw terms like *minimally conscious* and *persistent vegetative state* around as if we were capable of processing any of it.

I made notes that Cal and I referred to, but I was unwilling to discuss anything except her swift awakening and recovery. It left little to talk about, and our silences were long and filled with nothingness. Late that afternoon, the need for real food finally overrode Cal's refusal to leave Meghan. I could go for weeks longer, months if need be. My body could sustain itself on the water the nurses brought and the dry crackers and flavorless soup from the food tray.

Cal cleared his throat. "I'm going to pick up some food."

"Okay."

"You want anything?"

"I'll take whatever you get."

"All right."

We fell silent again, and Cal did not move or appear as if he were planning to anytime soon. Our marriage had, in many ways, evolved, perhaps devolved, into daily, silent competitions. Who did more housework, who brought in a larger paycheck, who was better at money management, who got a more desirable result from our children. And now we were down to this: Who was more devoted to our comatose daughter?

The only card we had to play here was time. Who stayed awake longest, who stayed in the room longest. It was about Meghan, but on another level it was also about us. Ada and Marshall had not just placed Meghan in danger, they had forced our marital hand.

So right now my body was holding out longer than Cal's. But my mind was degenerating. Time spent in a hospital room is a void, a time warp, a suspension, and a weight at once. Time moves in great chunks at points, and slows alarmingly at others. During the slow hours there is time to see every age and shape of your child evolve under the sheets of the hospital bed. There is time to see recent memories—Meghan turning on the radio in the kitchen, twisting around on the stairs to get a glimpse of Ada, lying on the roof of the car with her beloved brother and her new friend—framed by the tubes and wires and electronic rhythm of artificial life.

The fast times were the times I saw her on the boat, the times I saw blood—blood I knew now was not my child's but from someone else's child, the child responsible for this—the times I felt the sway of the ambulance. Those times flew, and I was grateful for that.

When Cal finally pulled himself from the chair, I was in slow time, and I was relieved that he was leaving.

"So, do you want anything from home?"

"You're going home too?"

He nodded, looking at Meghan, not me. "One of us has to. Might as well do it while I'm out. I need to cancel my trips. I'll drop my book off with Kevin, have him take over what he can, call the others. Boat needs to be taken care of. You want some clothes?"

"Why don't you just pack us both a bag?"

"All right."

"What about Marshall?" I asked.

"What about him?"

"Will you bring him back with you?"

"You want him here you'd better go get him yourself. I don't want him anywhere near my daughter, or me right now, and I can't believe you would."

We were staring directly at each other now.

"This was a horrible mistake, Cal."

"No. No, it wasn't. And don't you forget it, or next time he brings home some fruitcake they're going to kill her. Or us. For all we know they were making her some kind of sacrifice or something. Still think this is some kind of fun hobby, Chloe, a *growing stage?* We did this. You did this, and I allowed it because I didn't want to fight with you. And I'll be damned if I'm going to let it happen again."

"You're the one who convinced me that this was the first normal thing he'd done since he was ten. Remember that, Cal? Marshall is our son, and he made a horrible, horrible mistake, but he loves Meghan, and he must be going through hell right now."

Cal's face darkened. "If he's not now, he's going to."

"Do we have to do this...now?" I asked, inclining my head toward Meghan.

I knew it was a risk. But it worked. His face softened and his shoulders slumped. "No. Of course not. I'm sorry."

"Me too," I said. And I was, I really was. I made an effort to soften it and said: "Thank you for going."

He nodded, took one last look at Meghan, and turned toward the door, but hesitated with his hand on the long, silver handle before turning around and approaching me. He bent to kiss the top of my head, but his lips did not land, they merely stirred the air slightly and a shiver ran across the back of my scalp, tingling to a fine point when the door clicked shut behind him. I should have felt bereft, but I did not.

There was already a divided time line, already the old, painful joke of Before and After, and in this After I was just as pleased to have time alone with my daughter as I had been Before. I got up and stretched, then started to bustle around, talking to Meghan as if we were both about to start our day at home.

"So, I was thinking about pulling your bunk beds apart," I said, adjusting the blinds, allowing more light in, but not too much, not so much that I could see every detail. I didn't want to see the grime, from who knows what, in the seams of the putty-colored, plastic baseboard, the dust in the ceiling vent. I didn't want to see how Meghan's skin wrinkled under the transparent tape holding tubes in their correct alignment. I opened them just enough to offer the illusion of allowing sunlight in.

"If we moved your desk under the window, we could put both beds against that wall with your nightstand in between them. Or maybe it's time to just get a new bed? Maybe a double? Or a queen? I think there's room to get a queen in there. We could repaint too," I said, stuffing empty water bottles, an unread newspaper, notes written and crossed out on the pad supplied by the hospital into the trash.

There was, of course, no answer. I stopped the busywork and turned around to look at my daughter from the foot of her bed, as if seeing her in it for the first time. This was coma. Life moving around you, conversations had for weeks, months, years, without your input, all the business of everyone else progressing in this one space, while you remained utterly still, the pre-Copernican, unwitting center of a one-hundred-and-fifty-square-foot universe.

Suddenly I wanted Cal back here, with me, more than I wanted anything else, and I sank into the chair he'd been in for almost forty-eight hours and sobbed in great, ugly gasps. I wasn't used to crying. I did not do it much after my parents disappeared. I had thought I'd been all cried out. Even when Meghan was in the hospital after that first episode I didn't cry, except briefly in relief when it turned out she was okay.

And when it became clear that there was a course of action we could take to keep her safe, I never shed another tear over it all. I wasn't tough, I was simply too busy. But there was no course of action to take here. Nothing. I wrapped my arms around myself and stared at the side of Meghan's face until my eyes finally closed and I slept. In that way at least, Meghan and I were together.

When Cal spoke to me I struggled against waking.

"Chloe, come on, honey," he insisted.

I wanted just another moment, just one more moment of oblivion, one more minute in which I could believe that I was about to wake up in our bedroom, and could start over, could fix whatever had come loose: in our marriage, in Marshall's life, in my baby's immune system. Somehow I had not paid enough attention. I thought I had, but I was clearly so very wrong. And I would change that.

But I was not to have that, neither the chance, nor the dream of the chance, because Cal whispered in my ear: "Come on, Chloe. It's Marshall. Marshall's been arrested."

MARSHALL

He used to watch *COPS* on television, excited by the chases, the way the police tried to trip up a person on their own lies, how at times they seemed incredibly caring and passionate about their job and at others just seemed like arrogant jerks.

He and Ira used to talk about becoming cops themselves, how they would be tough, but would make sure things were okay with the people they arrested: the druggies would get to rehab, the abused would get safe, the children would get homes.

But Ira always sided with the cops, while Marshall sometimes felt sorry for the bad guys. He often hoped they would get away when they ran. He hated it when the cops pulled up a turned-over kiddie pool to find the suspect curled under it or when the fleeing perp—a word he and Ira used with glee—tripped and went down painfully hard, cowering under a K-9.

"They shouldn't run," Ira would say solemnly. "They never get away, and it just makes it worse."

Marshall would agree, but secretly he felt their desperation, felt the leap of adrenaline in his chest and the irresistible need for escape, the urge to struggle. He always thought that if he were ever in trouble, cops-chasing-him trouble, he would run as if his life depended on it.

But he hadn't known they were coming for him.

He opened the door before the squad cars came to a full stop, he said hello, as if welcoming them to his home. He confirmed his identity. He stood next to Ada as she did the same. And then when they told him he was being arrested for aggravated child abuse he'd felt none of the adrenaline he'd expected.

He couldn't have run then if prodded with a nightstick. He was too stunned. And as one officer read him his rights and another officer informed Ada that she was being arrested too, he simply stared at them. And he simply stared at first while Ada, with her damaged knees, struggled with the female officer, and then the front hall turned into a real scene from *COPS* when he began struggling, too, when he began screaming at them to leave her alone, to take their hands off of her. But he was dragged away, out the door, across the porch, and down the steps, eventually wrestled to his knees in the sand, brittle shells cutting into his legs.

They put him in the back of a squad car, putting a hand on his head just like he'd seen them do a thousand times before on television. It was all the same visually, his hands bound behind him so he had to find some way to keep from sitting on them, or against them, the dirty back windows, the split in the seat, the black grille separating the front and back.

But on television you can't smell anything, or feel anything, and the odor of urine was an assault on his senses, the feel of the ripped seat against the back of his calf was too real for it to be a dream, and when he banged his forehead against the grille in frustration, it hurt more than he would have imagined.

The cops dragged Ada down the steps and across the yard. He couldn't help but admire the fact that she was still struggling, still making it difficult to restrain her, all hundred and two pounds of her against three cops.

They should have run. That was all he could think now. Last night, they should have just gone. Anywhere.

When they started the car and took off, they didn't turn the sirens or lights on, but they drove fast, faster than he'd ever driven down their road, stirring up such a cloud of dust and sand that when he twisted around to look out the back window, the car Ada was in was completely obscured.

He'd never been to jail, never even had a speeding ticket, though he'd received a parking ticket when he'd stayed at the beach without feeding the meter. He'd paid it without ever telling his parents. He was shaking with fear when they took him from the car, took his things, got him fingerprinted and photographed, shuffled him through doors and doors and doors, and finally got him in a large holding cell with about twenty other men, where he wasn't answered when he asked about his proverbial phone call.

Some of the men laughed, two men said something to him in Spanish, but he merely looked at them helplessly and they turned away from him in disgust. A thin, balding man in overalls, actual denim overalls like some bad *Hee Haw* joke, held a cigarette out to him, and he shook his head and turned away quickly.

Throughout all of it he never saw Ada. He didn't know if there was a separate entrance for women; he knew she certainly wouldn't be in here. He didn't think *he* belonged here. He fervently wished he were under eighteen and was being held somewhere without these men. No matter how tough juveniles were, he would have felt as though he could have faked his way in, he could talk to them, about music, or movies, or something teenagers had in common.

But it was clear he had nothing in common with these men. They all seemed broken with their years, as if they breathed different air and walked in a different world, beyond a line he hadn't crossed yet.

Within thirty minutes another guard arrived to take him to the phone. Another set of doors, and then a small table in a cramped hallway and a phone. He stared at it, its filthy receiver, the numbers worn off the pad. Who did he call? His mother was the obvious choice. But he couldn't bear to hear her voice, her bewildered, terrified voice. And where would she be? In Meghan's room, of course.

That only left his dad. Maybe his dad would leave him here. He hadn't even been able to look at him, and Marshall had gotten the distinct impression that his father had wanted to do him violence, had barely been able to restrain himself. He stared at the phone and the phone book next to it.

"You either do it or you don't," the guard said.

"I don't know who to call," he admitted. He so badly wanted to call his mother.

"You got a lawyer? That's what I'd do. Girlfriend ain't gonna want to hear from you in jail."

A lawyer. Why would he have a lawyer? Only criminals and millionaires had lawyers, and he was neither. Or perhaps he was now. Was this really it? Was this where he had been heading all his life? He wished again that he were younger. His finger itched to dial his mother's cell phone.

"Do I really only get one phone call?" he asked. "What if there's no answer?"

"I'd suggest you call someone you know's gonna be there."

He stared at the phone and finally pulled the phone book toward him hastily when the guard made an impatient weight shift coupled with a practiced sigh.

Lawyers, lawyers, lawyers. Laser vision correction, law schools, lawn service. No lawyers.

The guard cleared his throat. "Attorneys," he said, clearly bored with his charge.

Marshall flipped to *attorneys*. The pages were well-thumbed. Why didn't they just put a bookmark in it, or leave it open to the attorney page? He knew enough that he needed a criminal lawyer, and passed by the personal injury and malpractice full-page ads.

There it was. "Most Legal Matters," "Felonies and Misdemeanors," "Aggressive Representation!" "Available 24 Hours." That was his man. He made the call. True to his ad, Charles Mingus was there: He answered the phone himself, and told him to keep his mouth shut and he'd be down as soon as he could.

And now Marshall was one of those people who had a lawyer.

This time the guard, without explanation, led him to a different area of the jail, into an actual cellblock. As he walked past the cells, he was prepared to flinch, for when they threw things at him, jeered at him, told him of the terrifying ways they were going to humiliate him in the shower. But most of them didn't pay any attention to him. The ones who looked at him at all did so balefully and without much interest.

A small black man said, "Hey, little man," softly to him as they passed, but it was without threat. When they walked by the cell in which a man was crying, the guard said, "Shut it, *pendejo*," and the man, without ceasing his cries, replied, "Screw you, man."

Before the guard shut the cell door Marshall asked about Ada. The guard shrugged. "Not my department. Maybe *your lawyer* can find out."

He was alone, for now, in his cell, but the men in the other cells made their presence known. It stank of men, and sounded of men, farting, snoring, and, of course, there was still the crying. He listened to the guard's heavy steps recede down the hall.

As he passed the crying man again, he said, "Shut it, *pendejo*."

"Screw you, man."

Eight

I DIDN'T want to leave the room and Cal didn't want to tell me while I was in it. We argued in harsh whispers and when two nurses arrived to do their usual vital checks, he left, standing out in the hall stubbornly while I stood just inside the door, anxious to get back to her bedside, to entreat her, once more, to open her eyes.

"Nothing is going to happen if you step outside the door, Chloe. Now get out here so we can talk about this, unless, of course, you'd like to leave him in jail. That'd work for me. I debated even telling you."

That did it. With one last look I stepped into the hall and let the door shut softly behind me. It was the first time Meghan had been without either of us, and I felt nearly sick at the realization that eventually there would probably be more firsts. The first time I left to go home, the first time that maybe I didn't stay all night. There could be years of firsts, just like a second childhood.

Cal stood on the opposite side of the hallway, freshly showered, his hair in place, newly shaven. How long had he known, how long did he wait to tell me?

"What are you talking about?" I was still whispering.

"They've arrested Marshall and Ada for child abuse. Marshall's lawyer called and left a message on my cell phone. He said he left a message on yours, too, and one at home."

I grasped the cold metal rail that ran along the wall to steady myself. Marshall's *lawyer*?

"When? Where is he?"

"He's in jail, Chloe. That's why his lawyer called. There will be an appearance before a judge, and he says bail will be set then. We have to post bail if we want him out."

"Well then, we post bail. Child abuse?"

"Aggravated child abuse, with extenuating circumstances," he clarified, which actually wasn't a clarification at all, but only served to further muddle my thoughts.

"What does that mean?"

"I didn't think to ask."

"My God, how did this happen? Did you tell them to do this?"

"No, but I wish I had." Cal's jaw was set, his mouth a thin line.

"Because it's not bad enough, right?" I asked bitterly, the desperation for my husband's comfort forgotten at the reminder of his unforgiving nature, turned now, not against his harsh parents, but against his own child. "It all has to go to hell at once? What have you done, Cal, what have you done?"

He grabbed my shoulders and shook me. Not gently, not as a man might shake his wife to make her see reason or to startle a crying jag out of her, but a jaw-rattling, whiplash shake.

"I told you," he said, the words forced from behind his clenched teeth, "I didn't do anything. But I wish I had, yes, I do. I'd have liked to have been there for it. Don't you know she's going to die, Chloe? Our son killed our daughter."

I wrenched myself free, feeling the welts raise immediately, and hit him, across his chest and shoulders, while he stood there like a tree, immovable, intractable, and beyond my comprehension. When my fist clipped his jaw, he caught my wrists and pulled me up against himself, and for the first time in my life I felt vastly, *globally* enraged that men were stronger, that most could, whenever they wanted, overpower women, and there was nothing we could do about it.

"Stop," he said in my ear as I struggled. "Stop, stop now. Everyone's looking, Chloe, stop. It's not going to help anything."

I shouldn't have cared that anyone saw. But I did. I couldn't bear the thought that doctors and nurses and visitors would see us as a divided family. We were supposed to come together, lean upon each other, and think of nothing but our daughter, speed her healing with our combined emotional strength.

But none of that was happening. I was thinking about more than Meghan; I was thinking about my marriage and the chasms and bridges within it, and whether it might be too hard to build another bridge across this particular chasm and whether I even wanted to.

And worse, how could you speed healing when half of the team was sure there wasn't any healing to speed?

I caught my breath and stopped struggling, aware that I could lean into him, that he would put his arms around me, and that even though we were so utterly divided over our children's fates, I would gain some comfort from it for a moment, and wouldn't that feel exquisite?

But I didn't have the luxury of that moment, and I pulled my wrists from his grasp and wiped my eyes viciously with the backs of my hands.

"Okay, so, what do we have to do?" I asked.

He shrugged and raised his eyebrows. "I don't know, Chloe. The lawyer wants to talk to both of us. Marshall asked him to. But one of us needs to be here. What do you want to do?"

"Great choices," I said. Leave my daughter, or leave Marshall to Cal, who seemed to be just fine with him sitting in jail.

"Those are the only choices we've got," he said.

"What would you say to the lawyer?" I asked. What I wanted to hear was that he would tell him to do whatever he needed to, and that he would be there for Marshall.

What I heard was: "I don't know."

"Then I guess I'd better go," I said. He said we had choices, but *we* didn't. *He* did. I pushed past him and entered Meghan's room. I wouldn't be rushed on this. I pulled the chair I'd been sitting in over and got as close as I could to the side of the bed, cheap wood frame against cold metal rails, and stroked her forehead the way I did when she couldn't sleep.

"I won't be long, baby. I'm just going to get some things from home, and then I'll be right back. Daddy will be here, Daddy will take care of you. I love you, and I'll be right back."

"I brought you a bag in case you wanted to stay here," Cal said, motioning to a blue duffel bag on the floor. "But the lawyer said he would go to the house, so if you're going…"

He trailed off at my look. I stood, leaned over the railing, and kissed Meghan just above her right eyebrow before picking up the bag and walking out the door without another word to Cal. As soon as I was in the car, I turned on my cell phone with a shaking hand and listened to the message from the lawyer.

He had a soft Hispanic accent and said his name was—could that possibly be right?—Charles Mingus. He was succinct and repeated his phone number twice at the end of the call. I repeated it under my breath as I turned out of the hospital parking lot and dialed with one hand, wheeling into traffic in a way I would have berated Cal for.

"This is Charles Mingus," the voice answered quickly.

"Mr. Mingus, this is Chloe Tobias, Marshall's moth—"

"Mrs. Tobias, thanks for getting back to me. When can we meet?"

"Wait a minute," I said. "I still don't know what's going on."

"I thought Mr. Tobi—"

"My husband is with our daughter right now. I'm on my way home, and I don't want to be away from her any longer than necessary. I decided to call you directly rather than listen to it secondhand."

"I certainly understand your desire to get back to your daughter. Here's what's happening right now: Marshall is in the county jail. He and his friend, Ada, have been arrested and charged with aggravated child abuse with extenuating circumstances. Basically, what that means is that the DA feels that Marshall and Ada had clear knowledge of Meghan's food allergies and proceeded to give her food they had a reasonable certainty would cause a reaction."

A reaction. I so desperately believed that this was a horrible accident. I did, I really did. But a *reaction*? That was like calling Hurricane Katrina a thunderstorm.

"Mr. Mingus, how much do you know about food allergies?"

"Obviously I am not as intimately acquainted with this medical condition as you are, however I am trying to gain a working knowledge of it as quickly as I can in order to help your son."

I almost laughed. Help my *son*? Who would have ever thought that someone would be researching food allergies to help my son? In the privacy of my own car, listening to someone so squarely on my son's side made me realize that my own defense of him wasn't nearly as stout as I thought when forced to protect him from Cal.

"How did this happen?" I asked, still suspicious that Cal had somehow arranged for it to happen.

"From what I could find out, one of the admitting physicians found out what happened and notified the DA's office, who decided to bring charges based upon statements from her as well as a paramedic at the scene. From there arrest warrants were issued and they picked them up at your home this morning. They've also both been charged with resisting arrest."

Picked them up this morning. So Ada had still been there. My uncertainty over how I felt about Marshall grew heavier at my core. And what did resisting arrest mean? I pictured them holed up in Marshall's room like desperadoes, knocking out a pane of glass to shoot at the police surrounding our home.

"What happened?" I asked.

"With the resist charge? From what Marshall tells me, he began to struggle when they arrested Miss Sparks. I feel confident we'll be able to get that charge dismissed."

"And what about...Ada?"

"Apparently she began to struggle fairly vigorously with the female officer who was attempting to handcuff her. She has not retained me as her lawyer, but from what I understand, she has not contacted anyone, and so she will remain incarcerated for the foreseeable future."

At least she wouldn't be around my family. And like that, with a threat clearly identified and contained, my family was whole in my heart again. We were all in this together, and we would get through it together.

If I could get them to cooperate.

"So what now?" I asked, pulling into our drive, noting the ruts and spin marks in the sand and shells.

"He'll make his initial appearance in just about an hour. He'll get bail, but he says he's not sure if you'll pay it. He's given me permission to talk to you about the case, so now I need to know how willing you are to support your son."

"I will always support my son, Mr. Mingus. If we need to pay bail, then that's what we'll do. How much are we talking about?"

"Won't know that until the judge tells us. Will you be able to get to the courthouse by three?"

"I'll be there. Mr. Mingus? How are you being paid?"

"Mr. Tobias assures me that he has enough money to pay my fees."

"My husband said he was paying?" I asked in surprise.

"No. Marshall Tobias."

"You are aware that he's a college student?" I asked.

"I am."

"You're either very cheap or very new, Mr. Mingus." I was beginning to appreciate the formality of our discussion, the Mrs. Tobias and Mr. Tobias and Mr. Mingus of it all. It made it seem somehow civilized, as if it might, one day, make some sort of sense.

"I've been practicing criminal law for over fifteen years in Immokalee. I've just recently moved to this area, so I'm not very busy yet. Which is certainly in your son's favor. Shall we meet on the front steps at three?"

"I'll be there."

I hung up and turned off the engine, sitting in it just long enough to grow uncomfortable in the heat. I grasped the duffel bag and hauled myself out of the car, looking at my house as if I'd been gone for months.

It certainly felt as though I had. The gardenia was in full bloom, and the sunflowers had all been bitten to the ground by rabbits. It would not have surprised me to have walked in the house to find that the walls had been painted a new color, the floors retiled, new furniture arranged in foreign ways.

But it was all the same. The screen door caught my heel, the kitchen showed no change, nor the living room or stairs. Reaching the second landing, I glanced down the hall to the master bedroom, hesitated, then dropped the duffel bag and entered Meghan's room.

It was a wreck, as though someone had gone through it tossing things in a frenzy. I had no idea what might have happened. I backed out, then went down the hall to Marshall's room. I didn't enter, but just stood in the doorway, looking at the bed, clearly slept in, the suitcase, the bare walls, and the necklaces scattered on the floor.

It was as if little bombs had gone off in both my children's rooms, and I had no way of knowing how, or why, or how to fix it. The clock on Marshall's nightstand caught my eye, and I hurried back down the hall to my own, undisturbed bedroom, in a hurry now.

I was running late to get my son out of jail.

MARSHALL

They took him back to the same cell after he'd seen his lawyer. Charlie, he wanted him to call him, but it didn't feel right yet. Or maybe just having a lawyer didn't feel right yet. It was a tentative, uncertain thing, the way his first encounters with Ada had been.

Only the promise of Ada was one of transcendence, understanding, and yes, he'd admit it, sexual nirvana. The promise of Charlie was one of freedom, which he'd just discovered was every bit as heady a promise when it was taken from you as the others.

He had to see Ada. Charlie couldn't tell him much of anything about her except she hadn't called anyone, which meant she was just sitting there, in jail, with a bunch of prostitutes and thieves. He hoped her knees were being taken care of.

He had to get out of there.

Charlie didn't know anything about Meghan either. But his parents were still at the hospital. He couldn't think about that part of things for too long. He could still feel the water, hard under the boat, could see Meghan...

He didn't want to lie down on the bunk, didn't want his head to touch the thin pillow, the sheets. He leaned back, until his shoulder blades touched the cold concrete wall, and closed his eyes, conjuring an image of Ada in his bedroom, remembering her hips, reimagining her legs without the bandages, while doors slammed, men swore, and the *pendejo* cried.

Less than an hour later, he got a roommate. This was a bad thing. The man was easily in his fifties, but he was big, and it was clearly not his first time in jail. Marshall imagined there was some sort of protocol to follow when greeting your new cellmate, but he had not been given the handbook, and so he stood, nervously wiping his hands down his pants before he held one out.

The guard shut the door and the man looked at Marshall's hand and grunted before ignoring it and dropping heavily onto the bottom bunk. Marshall looked out the bars into the hall, then gingerly stepped over the man's feet and hoisted himself up to the top bunk. He sat there, cross-legged, and leaned against the wall again, while the man beneath him passed gas and grunted, sometimes separately, sometimes all at once. Occasionally, the man shifted violently, making the beds shake and Marshall quake in readiness for...something.

Finally, the afternoon passed, and when the guard came to collect him for his initial appearance, he jumped to the floor in relief. On his way out the door the man grunted, "Luck."

"Oh, thanks," Marshall said, strangely comforted. It didn't last long. As he made his way through the jail with the guard his stomach roiled at the thought that he would have to see one of his parents. He didn't know which one it would be, or which one would be worse.

Nine

CHARLES Mingus looked nothing like his namesake, nor did he look like I'd pictured him from his voice and manner on the phone. I'd envisioned something like a Hispanic Perry Mason, but Mr. Mingus was short, slim, and seemed like one of those men who were never meant to wear a suit and yet had managed to choose a livelihood nearly dependent upon one.

His handshake was firm, predisposing me to like him. I detested men, and women for that matter, who grasped the ends of my fingers and wiggled. But then I am notoriously unreliable when it comes to first impressions. They're rarely right; I am not that woman who can read people, or who "just has a feeling" that someone is good, or kind, or evil.

It has never stopped me from acting upon my first impressions—after all, what else do we have to go on?—and I fell into step beside Mingus, my head bent toward him, listening intently, as if we'd made this trek a hundred times. I got a brief crash course in the Florida justice system—what this initial appearance was all about and how we would go about arranging for bail and how long that would take.

He asked about Meghan, and I stumbled in my response, unsure of what I was supposed to say, unsure if there was a side, and if so, which one I was supposed to be on at this moment. Had Cal been there— But he wasn't, was he?

So I told Mingus all about Meghan, and I accepted a crumpled tissue when he offered it, and then felt foolish when he looked at his watch and I realized he didn't know how to tell me that right now, this wasn't about Meghan, it was about Marshall, and we were going to be late if I didn't pull myself together and get on with it.

I'm not sure what I expected, but what happened didn't come close. I thought I would be able to talk to Marshall, but I never saw him in person. Instead I, and at least fifty other people, sat in a courtroom with the judge and lawyers and watched a video of prisoners, one by one, some in powder blue jumpsuits, some in street clothes as Marshall was, listening attentively to the proceedings.

I thought Charles Mingus would object to the things the prosecutor said about Marshall. But he didn't say a word until he finished. I thought he would object to bail being set at all. But he quickly buzzed through a few reasons for bail to be low, pointing out that Marshall had no prior criminal history or warrants, and that he had family in the community.

I thought we would be there for an hour, hashing it out, but it lasted approximately three minutes, the majority of which was taken up with a lot of paperwork changing hands. I was shocked when the judge commented about how serious the charges were and that he was setting bail at sixty thousand dollars and it was done and over and I was left reeling.

"Why didn't you say something?" I railed at Mingus when we

were again in the long courthouse hallway. "I thought you were his defense attorney. You didn't defend anything."

He turned to me, resigned, as if he dealt with mothers ignorant of the system all the time. "This isn't the time for that," he said. "That wasn't a trial, that was simply to set bail, which we did."

"Sixty thousand dollars," I said in disbelief. "We don't have sixty thousand dollars. I know people put their houses up—"

"You'll need six thousand dollars," Mingus said. "I have several bail bondsmen I can refer you to."

I stared at him. "But why is it so high? Doesn't that seem high?"

"Aggravated child abuse is considered a violent crime," he said. "I've seen it higher."

"Well, can I see him?"

He shook his head. "He'll be transferred back to the jail. Do you have the six thousand dollars to bail him out and if so, do you want to do that?"

I thought about Cal, and about our bank account. Unlike many married couples we knew, Cal and I actually took care of the bills together. I knew what we had, where it was, and what we owed. We might have been competitive about who brought in what, but we usually seemed to agree on what we would do with it.

I wasn't used to making any major financial decisions without Cal, and though there was no chance of me not bailing Marshall out, it still felt foreign, as though I were making some sort of statement, to not confer with him. But Cal had forced me to take care of this myself, and his cell phone wouldn't be turned on while he was in Meghan's room, and so it was my decision to make without his input or approval.

"Of course," I said. "What do I do?"

*   *   *

Two hours later my son was released from jail. I held him while Mingus stood off to the side, glancing at his watch again. I pushed Marshall's hair out of his face, checking him for wholeness, for signs of despair. If I was hoping to see an unchanged boy, I was to be disappointed.

Any parent might think that after seeing their child in jail they would note the first signs of age on their formerly juvenile face, even if it were simply a new recognition of them as an adult, but I saw no such thing. If anything, he looked even younger to me, astonishingly so. But there was something else there, too, a wariness of me that I'd never seen before, and I cannot pretend that it didn't hurt.

I was the one here, I was the one helping. He remained still and stiff in my arms, and finally stepped away and turned toward Charles Mingus, turning to him to see what to do next. Mingus looked at the bag Marshall's things had been returned to him in and said, "Got everything?"

Marshall nodded.

"We can go then," Mingus said.

The three of us walked out of the justice building and stood, uncomfortably, on the steps. Marshall and I spoke at the same time.

"What now?" I asked Mingus.

"Can I talk to you?" Marshall asked him, without looking at me. Mingus nodded.

"I have to pick up my children," he replied. "Can we talk on the way to my car?"

Marshall glanced at me. "Mom, I think I need to talk to him alone."

I was taken aback. "Why?"

"Mrs. Tobias," Mingus said, "Marshall has the right to attorney-client privilege."

I glared at them both, and then walked toward my car, trying to not look back and yell at them both that I was his *mother*, and I had just *bailed him out*, and I deserved to know what was going on, and I had left my daughter for almost five hours for *this*—to be treated like nothing more than a necessary wallet.

They moved in another direction, and I seethed in my car for another twenty minutes before Marshall appeared at the passenger window. I flipped the lock switch and he slid into the seat, not looking at me.

I turned the radio off and started the car, turning toward home. He rustled through the bag for a minute and pulled his shoelaces out, then bent over and began to thread them into his shoes. I couldn't stand it.

"Are you *okay*?" I asked forcefully, nearly attacking him with concern.

He didn't startle, or look at me, just continued threading his shoes.

"Yeah, I'm all right. It was okay. Nobody hurt me or anything."

I wanted to weep at that. At the unspoken horror, the thing we all think: Had my son been beaten and raped in jail? It didn't matter if it was city jail, county, prison, federal penitentiary, there are no lines drawn between these institutions for most people. What most of us think we know about incarceration is that child molesters are on the bottom of the hierarchy; gangs, amateur tattoos, and illicit drugs are tolerated; and men are raped.

He finished tying his shoes and leaned his head on his hand, braced against the window as if exhausted.

"Are you going to ask about Meghan?" I finally asked.

He didn't say anything for a moment and then cleared his throat. "How is she?"

"She's in a coma," I replied, my voice steady. "The doctors have no idea if she'll come out of it, or what she might be like if she does."

He turned his head and stared out the window, and I could feel rage building in me. I didn't even know what to do with it. Cal and I had been at odds over Marshall for so long that however he felt about him I almost immediately countered with the opposite. And, in my defense, Cal responded in kind. But Cal wasn't here to rage, and I'd had no practice with it.

"Marshall—" I started, my voice wavering deep in my throat on the second syllable. I swallowed. "What were you thinking?"

He shook his head without turning toward me.

"Marshall!" There was no waver in my voice now. "What the hell were you thinking? You could have killed her. She could have died!"

My words were coming rapidly now, my voice rising. I wanted to beat him with them. I was his mother; he owed me an explanation. It felt like a right that would never go away, no matter how old my children got. If I wanted an answer I was going to get an answer, whether he was nine or nineteen or forty-nine.

"You talk to me! She could *die*, Marshall. Or, she could stay like this forever. You want to see her? Do you want to see what you've done to your sister?"

I slammed on the brakes, and had we not been wearing seat belts we would certainly have hit the windshield if not gone through it. Thank God there was nobody following too closely behind us, though horns began sounding immediately. I made a sharp left turn onto a side street, hauled us around, back wheels spinning, and shot back out onto the road, earning more angry horns.

Marshall clutched his seat, looking at me in terror, but finally looking at me. It was the first time I'd felt some measure of control in days, and I was determined to hold on to that feeling. His face was streaked with tears, a surprise and a relief. But they did nothing to diminish the determined rage I felt to force him to see what he'd done, see what he'd allowed to happen.

The closer to the hospital we got, the more hysterical he became, and by the time I turned into the parking lot, Marshall was pressed back into his seat and hyperventilating in great, heaving gasps. I pulled into an open space and put the car in park, then leaned forward and hugged the steering wheel, pressing my forehead into the top of its curve. It was perfectly comfortable, and after a moment my own breathing evened out. I thought that perhaps I could just sit here until it got dark, and then close my eyes and sleep through the night, right here on the steering wheel.

Marshall began to quiet, and soon we were both just sitting there, breathing together. I couldn't pull my forehead off the steering wheel, my neck simply could not muster the strength to support my head, and so I talked through the hole above the air bag.

"I think you should be able to see her. I think you should have to see her. I don't understand, Marshall. You're nineteen. You're not a child. Your father thinks it's my fault, or, really, our fault. He thinks I spoiled you, let you have your way with this religion thing. He thinks that maybe Ada is a devil worshipper or something, that you were trying to kill her."

At this Marshall made a strangled sound in his throat and my neck found the strength to snap my head upright and turn to him.

"Is that it? Were you *trying* to kill her?"

"No, oh God, no."

"Do *not* bring God into this, Marshall, not now, not ever again," I warned him sharply. "I didn't— Maybe this is my fault. If

you think this is God's will in some way, then I don't know what—"
I stopped and took a deep breath, letting it out slowly before con-
tinuing. "Don't blame this on God, Marshall, and don't blame it
on whatever religion Ada is. You did this."

"No, no, I didn't. I didn't mean to. Ada—"

"Tell me the truth, Marshall. Ada might have had the idea, but
you could have stopped it. And you didn't. And that makes you
just as culpable, if not more, because you're the one who knew
what could happen. Ada might not have realized the gravity of it,
but you did."

And with this accusation I realized how Cal felt. He was right.
He had warned me for years. I had been so stupid. My arrogance
stunned and shamed me. My smug certainty that I was encouraging an open mind, an array of experiences, a contemporary willingness to allow him choices. I thought about the parents I grew
exasperated with at restaurants and grocery stores, the ones
who spent an extraordinary amount of time presenting their five-
year-old with twenty different choices, despite the child's clear
bewilderment.

How was what I'd done any different?

And Cal. Cal had grown up seeing the dangers of unchecked
beliefs, of extremism. And now, of course, he felt as culpable for
this as I, and with this realization came another: We would not get
through this. Not as a family, and not as husband and wife. I stared
at Marshall, who was trying to tell me something, but all I could
do was search his face for signs of the little boy Cal and I had made
together.

He was stuttering his way through some sort of explanation, and
I watched his mouth move, trying to match the words up with it, like
a badly dubbed movie. "I didn't think, such a small bit, Ada, she

had researched exposure therapy. And we do, we really do believe in the power of prayer, and I swear, Mom, it was working, it was."

"When was it working, Marshall? After you gave her the Epi-Pen? That wasn't prayer, that was epinephrine." There was nothing he could say. I understood that now. There was simply nothing he could say that would explain it to me.

I put the car in reverse and backed out of the spot carefully. I needed to get him home and needed to turn my attention back to my daughter. There was only one person I could do anything for now, and I'd been gone for too long.

"Where are we going?" Marshall asked in a small voice.

"I'm taking you home."

"I—will Dad let me stay there?"

"I don't know," I said. "I hadn't thought about it."

Neither of us had a solution and we drove in silence.

"What's the deal with Mingus?" I finally asked.

"I have an appointment with him tomorrow to find out what the next step is. He told me to not talk about it with anyone."

"Really? He was able to talk about it with me enough to get bail for you. He says you're planning on paying him. How do you think you'll be doing that?"

"I have money."

"Oh yeah? How much money do you have? And where did you get it? Your job at the frame store suddenly a real money-maker?"

He looked out the window again, biting his lower lip. "I have money," he repeated.

"Well, great," I said. I couldn't force him to tell me, and right then I didn't really want to know. Maybe he'd gotten a raise, maybe he'd sold a kidney. How would I know?

I pulled beside the house and didn't bother putting the car in park, but shifted back to reverse and waited for him to get out. He put his hand on the door and turned toward me.

"Mom, I'm—I'm so sorry."

"Oh, Marshall, I can't, I just can't right now," I said, my voice beginning to waver again. "We'll talk later. I don't know when we'll be home. Call the hospital if you need me. I can't have my cell phone on."

"Tell Meghan, will you? Tell her that I'm sorry?"

I shook my head, my teeth clenching. He still didn't get it. I replied softly: "She can't hear me, Marshall. She may never know that."

He got out of the car and I drove away without looking in the rearview mirror, my thoughts only on Meghan now. Things would work out with Marshall, one way or another. The lawyer would get the charges dropped, someone, they, Marshall, would pay him. Marshall would find another girlfriend, would graduate from college. Marshall would move on with his life.

I didn't know what Meghan would move on with.

MARSHALL

He did have money. He had an entire bank account fat with the student loan check he hadn't done anything with yet, not to mention his paychecks and various gift money. He hadn't yet paid his rent, or next semester's tuition. He was going to do it when he got back, because he had an e-mail in to his student advisor asking if he could drop a class and he hadn't wanted to pay anything yet.

It wasn't like he'd be going back to college anyway. Not after this, not now. Everything had changed. God was leading him down a different path, and he needed to listen. He'd spent so long searching, when if he'd just listened he could have skipped all of it. It really was like they said: Let go and let God.

He watched his mother drive out of sight. He understood more than she thought he did. He understood that a line had been crossed for her. In fact, he thought that perhaps he understood more than she did. Because he knew that he'd been slowly crossing a line with his father for most of his life. The line with his father was miles thick, and it was possible that he'd never step all the way over to the other side but would remain in a sort of limbo.

But the line with his mother had appeared suddenly, and it was hard, straight, and thin, and there was no going back. He'd always thought she was the flexible one, the open-minded one. But when it came down to it, she was just as narrow as the rest of the world.

As soon as the taillights disappeared, Marshall raced inside. He had his car. He had money. And he had a little time. He wasn't going to waste it, and he wouldn't make the same mistake twice. God was leading him now; he saw it all mapped out ahead of him.

He found the phone book and called the jail, then made a series of calls to bondsmen, figuring out the process as he went, and finally found one who was willing to do the work for him. He threw everything he could think of into his suitcase, stuffed bags and backpacks. He grabbed Ada's suitcase and rummaged through his mother's things in search of anything else she might need.

He packed everything in the trunk, then grabbed a wheeled cooler from his father's workroom and filled it with food. He walked through the house, glancing around, looking for anything they might need, grabbed some magazines, the blankets off his bed, a fishing rod from the workroom.

The car was stuffed, and he stood staring at it for a moment before mixing a little mud from the dirt beneath his mother's gardenia and splattering it across the license plate. He didn't know what else to do.

The bank in the mall was open until eight and it was his last stop, before the bail bond place, and then, at last, the jail. When they finally released Ada, limping heavily on her crutches, her face pale and frightened, he knew he'd made the right decision. He shook his head at her while the paperwork was completed so she wouldn't talk, and it wasn't until they were outside and had concluded their business with the bail bondsman that he allowed her one brief embrace.

"We have to get out of here," he whispered in her ear. She hesitated for a moment, but then pulled back and looked into his eyes. When she nodded he felt anointed, when she pressed her lips to his he felt as if a minister had just declared them man and wife, and when she placed her hand in his he became responsible for them both.

As they drove out of town, she asked, hesitantly, if they should pray. He reached across the front seat and grasped her hand, and they prayed. It cleared the frantic silence, and though he didn't slow their speed, it did seem as if things were back on an even keel between them.

Ada put her window down, and as the stars came out she turned the radio on low, and finally they were able to speak.

"Do you know where we're going?" she asked.

He nodded. "My grandmother's place is about five hours away. I figured we could stay there for a few days, figure out what we're going to do, maybe she'd give us some more money, and then we'll leave the state."

"Won't they think to look there?"

"No way. That's exactly why we're going. They don't even know I know about her, and any hotel these days is going to want a credit card. They'd be able to track us that way."

"Well, how do you know about her?"

"She writes to me sometimes. I found out about her when I was, like, sixteen. My dad threw out a letter from her, and she sounded, I don't know, sort of cool. I kept the envelope so I had her address, and wrote to her when I got to college. We've been writing back and forth, I don't know, maybe every few months, ever since. My parents don't know. My grandfather was a minister, you know?"

She shook her head, wide-eyed. He'd been afraid to tell her before, afraid of what she'd think about their backwoods ways, afraid she would think him more of a dilettante than she already did. But everything about their relationship had changed, and now he was the one in control, and she watched him, waiting for him to continue.

"It was real old-fashioned stuff, I think they even used to handle snakes, stuff like that. But he died a long time ago, before I was born. My dad never got into any of it, and I guess there was some kind of fight. She writes to them, but they never write back that I know of. Anyway, we never go to see her. She told me I could come anytime."

"You've never met her?"

"I guess we went there when I was a baby. I don't remember it."

"Does she know we're coming?"

"No."

"Marshall, what are we doing?"

"I—I'm not sure. But, I felt like we had to leave. Did you?"

She nodded solemnly, her eyes wide, and again he felt that wide open space in his chest, the feeling he recognized now, and though he'd already felt it on the steps of the jail he thought he should make it formal.

"Ada, I love you. Maybe this happened for a reason. Maybe

we're meant to do something with our lives that this is leading us to. Whatever it is, I feel like we're supposed to be together. Do you?"

She nodded again, rapidly, clutching his hand.

"Marshall, we could go to Nebraska. We could go back to my family."

He shook his head. "We can't go there. They'll definitely look for us there."

"They won't let them find us," she said matter-of-factly.

"What do you mean?"

"They've done it before. They'd take care of us."

"They've done what before? What are you saying?"

"A couple of years ago there was...a problem. One of the families in North Carolina, this girl, she led one of the ministers on, and then she said he raped her. She just said it because she got pregnant and had to say something. Then she got her friend to say he raped her too. It was totally bogus, like *The Crucible* or something, but they arrested him, so they sent him to us and we got him out of the country. He's doing God's work in Brazil, helping build houses."

His wide-open feeling plummeted for a moment. A test, it was a test. Girls were raped all the time, but sometimes they did lie. He recalled the cases he'd read about in the paper. It did happen. And what about the people's lives they ruined? Even though they were innocent. It would taint them forever. He took a deep breath. If Ada believed, then he believed.

The thought of having not just family, but an entire community support them, believe in them, and help them on their journey, compared with his own family's response, was the most beautifully hopeful feeling. His father was ready to do him physical harm, or at least anxious to cut him out. His mother didn't know what she thought except she wanted him taken care of, shut away for a while so she didn't have to think about anything but Meghan.

Here was another crossroads; they were coming at him fast. He glanced at Ada, then stared straight out the windshield at the winding black length of Route 29 stretching before them.

"Let's do it," he said and hit the gas.

Ten

CAL was pulled up next to Meghan's bed when I returned, curled as close to her as he could get, the bed rail pressed into his side. It looked like it hurt, and it should have touched me. He was talking to her, as I had been, entreating her to open her eyes, stroking her hair away from her forehead as if its weight might be keeping her lids from finally lifting. I should have been filled with enough compassion to want to stand there quietly for a moment and take in this sight of pure, fatherly love and pain.

But instead I quickly walked over and placed my hand on his shoulder and said: "Be careful, you're pulling on the sheet."

He pulled himself sharply away from me, and I could have eased it then, I could have softened my hold, slid my hand down to rub his back, leaned down to kiss him softly, somewhere, his forehead, his cheek, his lips. But I could not bring myself to do it.

"What happened?" he said.

I wanted that chair back. But there was no way to lay claim to it without coming off as completely irrational. He wasn't sitting in the chair to bother me, I knew that. But I had been there earlier, and had gotten used to the view, used to that particular angle on Meghan's face, used to being close enough to reach out and touch her when I wanted.

I put my purse down on the floor next to the chair and remained standing.

"Well, I met the lawyer, we went to the initial appearance, and then I bailed him out. He's at home now, he's got an appointment with the lawyer tomorrow."

"How much?"

"What?"

"How much was the bail? How much is the lawyer going to be?"

"Bail was six thousand dollars. Marshall says he can pay for the lawyer."

"Oh, really? With what?"

I shrugged.

"What happens next?" he asked

"I told you. He has an appointment with the lawyer tomorrow."

"What is going on here, Chloe? Why do I have to drag this out of you? Would you just tell me what's going on?"

"I don't know. And maybe if you wanted to find out, you should have been there. I was not privy to their conversation because of *attorney-client privilege.*"

"So we're just supposed to sit back and wait for him to tell us what's happening?"

I shrugged. "I don't know what else we're supposed to do, Cal. I asked; he wouldn't tell me anything except that he had an appointment."

"Did he at least ask about Meghan?"

I wanted to be able to say yes. "I told him what was happening," I said carefully.

"What about Ada? Her parents arrive to bail her out? They'd better not show up here, I'll tell you that."

I wondered what scenario he had worked out in his imagination. I'd worked out a spectacular few myself. I'd seen myself confronting Ada, confronting her parents, interrogating them about what kind of parenting had produced a child who could do this, who could so cavalierly take another child's life. And about what kind of faith had so little respect for others.

But it wasn't just their child, was it? It had been mine too. And what would I say when asked about what kind of parenting could produce a child like Marshall? Would I counter that Ada was a Jezebel, a siren that Marshall couldn't refuse? What would I say when asked about Marshall's faith? That he had none, or that he'd had them all and it had still come to this?

"I didn't see Ada," I responded, and finally admitted defeat and sank down into the other chair. "Mingus told me—"

"Mingus?" Cal asked.

"Charles Mingus is Marshall's lawyer."

"You mean like the musician?"

"Yep." I pulled the lawyer's card out of my back pocket and handed it to him. He read it and rolled his eyes before tucking it in his wallet and flashing me a grin. I couldn't help but smile back, but the moment was quickly past.

"So, he told you what?"

"He said that she hadn't called anyone. That's it. Frankly, I don't care. I don't want to know. Let her parents deal with her."

"We'll have to deal with it sooner or later if they go to trial."

"You think this will get that far?"

"They don't press charges unless they're serious, Chloe. What do you think will happen? You know we'll have to testify, don't you?"

I stared at him. No. I hadn't thought about that. And who would we be testifying for? Against? Weren't there laws against having to testify against family members?

"And if—if…things don't go well," he said, gesturing toward Meghan, "the charges could be upgraded."

"How do you know that?" I asked, unwilling to allow my mind to even approach the possibility of what he was intimating. "What is going on? Are you just making this stuff up or do you actually know something you're not telling me?"

"If I tell you—"

"If you tell me? *If* you tell— How dare you *not* tell me anything! How, exactly, do you think not telling me something you know about this situation is an option?"

"I talked to the doctor."

It rang no warning bells in me. The doctor. Which doctor? We'd talked to doctor after doctor. The neurologist had been in several times a day, the specialists, the interns, the therapists. One doctor we'd never seen before had come in the previous day, ordered blood tests, disappeared, and nobody had any idea who he was.

"And?" I asked impatiently.

"The doctor from the emergency room."

I still wasn't getting it, and then, just as I was about to lay into him, I realized who he meant. *The* doctor. The one who called the police to report a crime. The one responsible for our son going to jail. The unnamed emergency room doctor who'd doubled our family emergency with one call, as if he hadn't even considered what the combination would do to us, as if he didn't care. First do no harm, right? I sank back down into the chair.

"When?"

"When you were gone."

Of course he had come when I was gone. I had to wonder if

he'd watched, waited until I left before coming to see what he'd wrought, unable to face the hysterical mother.

"Who is he? What did he say?"

"*She* said she was sorry she missed you."

It shouldn't have mattered. But somehow it did. The mental image of a hard-eyed man in scrubs was replaced by one of the woman, in white, hair pulled back, no makeup, single, no children. Straight-ahead career, no place for family, no consideration of others' families.

"Why did you let her in here?"

"I didn't know it was her. She just came in and started checking Meghan out. She asked if you'd be back soon. I think she wanted to talk to you rather—"

"Well, what did she have to say? Did you tell her I was off bailing our son out?"

He nodded. "She said she was sorry. She wanted—"

"She's *sorry*? Really?"

"If you'll stop interrupting me—"

It wasn't me that time. Two nurses entered and stood at the door, looking back and forth between us. I wondered how long they'd been outside the door and what they'd heard. They must have thought we were horrible. Talking about this in front of Meghan. It was a common enough theory that patients in a coma might be able to hear what's going on around them, but we'd been reminded, with varying degrees of certainty, of that by almost every nurse and most of the doctors. Which meant that it was possible that Meghan had heard our entire conversation.

"Dr. Vaughn found a room on the fourth floor that he'd like Meghan moved to," Delia said, the nurse who'd written her name on the dry-erase board next to Meghan's bed. This was the third day in a row she'd been with us through the day shift. It was astonishing how quickly I'd grown attached to her. There was something nearly primal about my need for the nurses to like me. They had so much power here.

If they liked me, if I treated them well, was patient, then they would make sure Meghan was receiving the care she needed, they would check on her more frequently, would give me tidbits of information the doctors wouldn't share, would see that our needs were attended to first.

And it was useless, I knew that. But I couldn't help ingratiating myself with them. Anything could make a difference. And so I was ashamed of them catching us having words in front of Meghan, as if my stock might go down.

"Why is he moving her?" Cal asked.

"She's stable enough to leave ICU, and it's a much more private room, away from the elevators. It's better set up for...a longer-term visit."

The only noise in the room was from the machines keeping Meghan alive. It sounded like progress until she said "longer-term visit."

"Will she be okay?" I asked. "You know, on the move?"

The other nurse, one I didn't recognize, nodded. "She'll be fine. Everything is on a battery backup. If y'all could gather up any personal items and maybe give us a little room, you can meet us up in room four eighteen in about twenty minutes?"

It took me a second to realize that they wanted us to leave. "Oh, okay," I said, and awkwardly gathered up my purse and Cal's duffel bag while he grabbed his newspaper and magazines. Delia held the door open for us and patted my arm when I hesitated.

"She'll be okay," she said. "Promise."

Cal and I straggled down the hallway feet away from each other and stood waiting for the elevator, not looking at each other.

"Where do you want to go?" he asked.

"There's a little chapel downstairs," I suggested. "It was empty last time I looked."

He looked at me askance. I shrugged, and we got on the elevator. He followed me into the chapel, which was, again, empty, and I sat in the pew in front of the one he chose, piling the empty space beside me with my bags.

I turned in the pew and eyed him in this new, softer light. He still looked exhausted, the circles under his eyes even more pronounced. I didn't imagine my own countenance had improved any either.

"So," I said. "The doctor."

"She wants to talk to you," he said, digging in his wallet and pulling out a business card. I examined it. Dr. Camille Kimball.

"Wasn't Camille a hurricane?" I murmured.

"Sixty-nine," Cal replied.

"Why does she want to talk to me?" I asked.

"I guess she wants to explain why she did it."

"Oh, she has some specific reason?" I asked. "Besides trying to hurt us more than we already were?"

"Her son died after eating peanut butter her mother-in-law gave him. He was three years old."

And all the air disappeared from the room. I could feel my head shaking. My grandmother, my mother's mother, had had Parkinson's disease. She died when I was nine, and I didn't remember much about her, except she had a wonderful laugh and her head shook on the top of her neck as though it were a gyroscope, but with no pattern, and no illusion of control. This was how my head felt.

I couldn't cry for my own child, not now, not yet, but cry for another's I could, and I did. I cried for that three-year-old little boy, and for his mother, and even for the mother-in-law. Cal, to his credit, did not seem to be going through the same detached examination of our marriage as I was, or if he was, he put it on hold long enough to lean over the pew and hold as much of me as he could.

But he remained dry-eyed, and I had to wonder at it a little. Just the sight of tears in his eyes had been enough to make me cry in the past. How did he hold me, sobbing, and remain steadfast? How did he tell me that our daughter was going to die and our son should be in jail with such belief, his own version of faith, and not explode with the enormity of it?

I pulled away from him and took some deep breaths, before inspecting Dr. Kimball's card again, its heavy stock dry as dust against my fingers, and felt a resentment well up in me.

"So, because her son died we're supposed to be . . . what? *Grateful* she pressed charges against our son?"

"Chloe, just talk to her, okay? She's the one who saved Meghan's life. I think she at least deserves a conversation."

I couldn't speak for a moment. I froze in place, certain that I could not have just heard what I just heard. "She deserves a conversation? Since when are you concerned with what someone deserves, Cal? What about what our son deserves? Don't you think that perhaps your *son* deserves a conversation? Doesn't your son deserve some benefit of the doubt? Some support from you? You don't seem too concerned about what he deserves. But this doctor you've never met before, this woman deserves your consideration?"

Cal's face darkened and his eyes narrowed. I knew what that meant. What woman, married for more than six months, doesn't know every expression, every warning eye narrow, every irritated mouth tightening, every drawn down eyebrow?

It went both ways, of course. In our daily life, I expected him to take note of my head tilt, my raised eyebrow, my crossed arms. I always responded more quickly than he did to these unspoken cues, and I rarely ignored them. But this time I did not acquiesce.

"No, you don't get to look at me like that. I'm the one who had to do it all alone today. You didn't see him there, you didn't get to learn about bail, and you didn't have to drive home with him. So don't act like I've somehow gotten off easy on this one."

"You spoiled him—"

"Spoiled him? What the hell are you talking about? The kid never asked for anything. It was your idea to buy him a car, and as soon as he could he got a job."

"Not materially. You spoiled him by letting him think he was adult enough to make decisions on his own. You think that if he were afraid of what we, you, thought that he'd have let this happen? If she dies—"

"Stop that," I said, surprised at my own vehemence. "You stop saying that right now. She's not going to die. Do you *want* her to die? It seems to me like you've just decided she's going to. How can you do that? What is wrong with you?"

He looked anguished, and I wanted to hit him and wrap my arms around him at the same time, but my overwhelming feeling was exhaustion, and when he finally spoke I listened with my eyes closed.

"I can't do this the way you do, Chloe. I can't just—take it all at the same time. I feel like if I prepare myself, you know, if I let myself touch on the worst, then maybe if it happens I won't just die. Because I have to tell you something, you should know, right now, that if she does, if she does die, I won't survive. And if I don't die on the spot, then I will blame Marshall and that fucking nutcase he brought home and I will hate them both. And if I hate my son, well, that's going to kill me anyway."

"No," I murmured, shaking my head, unwilling to open my eyes and see his haggard face. When he spoke again, his voice was hoarse and pained.

"And I will be sorry to leave you with all of it, but I will have to. I won't make it, Chloe, I just won't make it. And I'm convinced that all of this is going to happen because I should have known. I did know, maybe not this, but I knew that something would happen if you kept letting him just think whatever he wanted, but I didn't do anything about it. And for that, I hate myself."

"Cal—"

"No. I hate myself, and...I hate you a little too."

Had he punched me in the face I couldn't have been more shocked and filled with pain. Marshall and Meghan had both told me that they hated me when they didn't get their way over some petty thing or another. Childish, whiny little stones thrown to hurt me. And it had stung a little, but just a little, because I had understood that they were children, and they didn't hate me, and they didn't yet understand the power of such words.

But I had always been so sure that Cal would never use that power, not like this, not at a time like now. I turned forward again, and stared at the stained glass set high in the otherwise unadorned wall. A dove on a blue background, wings spread, paused forever in mid-flight, olive branch streaming from its beak. I suppose it was meant to represent peace, God's promise to mankind.

But I felt as frozen as it was, and there was no peace in me. Cal touched my shoulder, and I did not move. It was a stranger's hand, and it meant nothing. I stood and grabbed my purse, leaving Cal's bag on the pew, and left. I heard him come after me, and we rode up in the elevator in silence.

Meghan's move was successful, and she looked exactly the same as she had two floors down. The room was larger, and the nurse showed us how the recliner could turn into a bed, filled the water pitcher for us, and left, and neither of us said a word. I took the chair next to the bed, Cal took the recliner, and that was how Dr. Kimball found us almost an hour later.

She looked nothing like I had imagined, and yet I knew immediately who she was. She was older, much older, than I had imagined, and her gaze was direct and calm. I had expected her to be nervous, but she trained her bright blue eyes on me and walked over to my chair without hesitation.

She nodded to Cal once. "Mr. Tobias," she said.

"Hello, Doctor," he replied, maneuvering the recliner upright and straightening his clothing.

"Mrs. Tobias, I'm Dr. Camille Kimball," she said, holding her hand out. I would like to be able to say that I simply stared coldly at her and ignored the hand, but I have never been able to do that. If someone holds out a hand to me, I grasp it before I can stop myself. It is the same with friendship, and reconciliations, and when I was younger, with romance. I did not often make the first move, but once one was made I responded eagerly, and then often did the heavy lifting of the thing.

But I reminded myself, even as my hand slid into her cool, powdery grasp, that this was the woman responsible for my son going to jail, and I cut the handshake off before I would have in any other circumstance.

"I would very much like to speak with you," she said, shooting a glance at Meghan, "if you have the time. Perhaps I could buy you a cup of coffee?"

"I'm fine here," I said, proud of myself for the flat tone of my voice.

She nodded. "Yes, I was just thinking of Meghan," she said softly. "I think this is an adult conversation."

And I was again ashamed at the fact that I still considered Meghan nothing more than asleep. All of her hives were gone, all the swelling had receded, and aside from the tubes and wires, she looked like Meghan...asleep. The difference had been explained to us, the MRI and CAT scans and nerve tests had all been done, explained. There was nothing unusual about Meghan's coma as comas of this nature went, and nothing unusual about her treatment.

And so, to me, we were merely watching over her while she slept, while she rested from her ordeal, while her body and mind reknit themselves from the temporary unraveling. Cal might have been on a deathwatch, I was just waiting for her to wake up, to open her eyes and see me sitting there, just as I always had been when she was sick at home and woke from fevered dreams.

I immediately rose and shot Cal a look. He shrugged and said, "I'll stay here."

I allowed Kimball to take the lead and followed her down the hall. We didn't speak in the elevator, which she seemed perfectly comfortable with, sliding her hands into the pockets of her immaculate white coat, her shoulders relaxed, hip resting against the stainless rail, calmly watching the digital floor countdown.

I watched her. Her age was a surprise; I pegged her as approaching her mid-sixties, but I could see the hard, younger woman I'd originally imagined under the slackening skin. She wore her gray hair clipped short in back and longer in front so it swung forward, partially obscuring the side of her face.

We headed for the cafeteria and got our coffees in silence. She took hers black, I liberally dosed mine with milk and sugar, then followed her to a small table in the back corner. Those in scrubs and white coats ignored us as we walked by, but the others, the ones like me who were here looking for a miracle, followed her hungrily with their eyes, looking for something in every medical professional they saw, some extra piece of information, some sparkling shard of hope.

She sighed as she sat down and then clasped her hands around the foam cup as if they were cold. Having so recently grasped one, I knew they weren't. I took a sip and waited for her to start.

"I've already spoken to your husband," she said.

I nodded. "Yes, he told me."

"I feel that I should explain why I did what I did. I understand that it must have placed you under a great deal of additional stress."

"I can't imagine that you would understand."

"I understand more than you realize."

"I'm sure you think you do. And I am sorry for your loss, but that doesn't give you any right to send my son to jail."

"I didn't send your son to jail. I merely—"

"You didn't *merely* do anything. You decided you knew what the situation was—"

"Which was what, Mrs. Tobias? Do I have the story wrong? Did two young adults, well old enough to know better, not purposely feed your daughter something that had the potential, no, was nearly *guaranteed*, to kill her? You're damn lucky she isn't dead right now. And if she had died, I'd be pushing for murder charges," she said, nearly hissing, jamming her index finger so hard into the laminate tabletop that I winced. She took a deep breath and leaned back in her seat, folding her hands around her coffee again as if in prayer. "And if she does, I will."

"Is this what you wanted to say to me?" I asked, leaning forward, keeping my voice as low as hers had been. "That you wish it had been worse so you could punish them more?"

"No," she said. "No, I wanted to tell you about Bobby. I wanted to . . . I just wanted to tell you. But I get caught up, still." She cleared her throat and took a sip of coffee. I hadn't touched mine.

"So say what you have to say," I said. "Because I'd like to get back upstairs, and I don't want you to feel any need to come see me, or my daughter, again. So I suggest you get it all out now."

She nodded. "Fair enough. Bobby was a Down syndrome child. I was forty-three when we had him. Our families were horrified," she said, smiling slightly. "Jim, my husband...his mother was angry. She thought we were selfish to have a baby at our ages. And when he was born, well, I think she felt vindicated. She wasn't a bad woman, she was just from another time."

She stopped as if waiting for me to respond, to empathize, or sympathize, or otherwise encourage her to continue. But I remained silent. She'd have to push forward without help from me. Which she did once the pause grew too long for her.

"I had a hard time being around her, but of course it wasn't fair to Jim or to Bobby to cut her out of our lives, and she often babysat when both Jim and I were working. She was pretty good about it all, once she got the hang of his needs. But he was a picky eater, and it drove her crazy. It bothered her that he was heavier than other kids, and she felt it was up to her to make sure he was eating nutritiously. It was even sweet, in a way, like this was how she chose to bond, to show that she cared about him.

"Anyway, he had a thing, with his food, he didn't like certain textures. And she was always trying to fix things a different way to get him to eat them. We tried him on peanut butter once, when he was two. He hated it, and he had an allergic reaction, but it was mild. It was just part of his medical needs to us. We were both doctors, okay, he has a peanut allergy, in addition to everything else."

She stopped talking for a moment, her eyes locked on her coffee, before she raised her gaze to me and continued softly: "She wasn't trying to hurt him. She always followed our instructions. And we trusted her, we both did. But she also thought we were too protective. She thought some of his medical issues were due to our strict regimens, she thought we were doctors instead of parents. She thought...that she knew better.

"Peanut butter on saltines. Just a little. His stomach was upset, and she didn't know what to do. She gave him peanut butter on saltines and ginger ale. He only had a little bit. He was gone before she knew what was happening. He didn't even have a chance."

Her eyes didn't fill with tears and her voice didn't shake, and I found myself staring at her in fascinated horror. How did any mother tell the story of her child's death and not fall apart? Cal worried that he wouldn't survive Meghan's death.

I was terrified that I would.

Because I would have to say it for the rest of my life. And I would not be calm like this woman, this doctor, who had, perhaps, seen too much death.

"She never got over it. *We* never got over it."

"You seem all right."

She smiled. "I am not. It has been seventeen years and I still blame myself. And I blame her, and I blame my husband. And my husband blamed himself, and her, and me. My mother-in-law moved to Arizona. She died about five years ago, but we hadn't spoken for a long time before that.

"Jim and I tried to stay together. We found something in common: alcohol. He lost his medical license, and I almost lost mine. We were divorced within two years. I don't know where he is now."

"That is a horrible, horrible story," I agreed. "Is this what you wanted? To make me thankful? That she's alive, that Cal and I aren't alcoholics yet, that the object of blame is gone? I'm sorry, but you're greatly misguided. Now I have to get back upstairs. I like to be there for shift change."

She reached across the table and grasped my forearm, holding me to the table, her grip strong. I struggled against it and pulled away, furious at her presumption in touching me. I didn't want to be touched, especially by her.

"When your daughter came in I wasn't in Emergency. I haven't practiced emergency medicine in fifteen years. I heard about it and went down because I felt compelled. I had to save her, and Mrs. Tobias, I did. I did save your daughter. And when I heard what happened, how it happened, I knew what you would go through. You will all be able to get on with your lives much faster because of what I did."

"Your logic escapes me, Dr. Kimball."

"You need to focus. You and your husband need to, together, focus on your daughter's care. Knowing that the people responsible for this situation are being held accountable for it will allow you to do so, even though it's your son, especially since it's your son. Now *you* won't feel the need to punish him, or each other, for the rest of your lives."

I stood, making sure to avoid her grasping hands, leaving my untouched coffee on the table. "Thank you for saving my daughter's life. I will always be grateful for that," I said carefully. "But you know nothing about me, or my family, and what you did will not now, nor ever, make anything easier. Please don't approach me again, and please stay away from Meghan's room."

She looked up at me sadly. "It's the law too, you know. At the very least it's aggravated child abuse, and I am obligated by law to report that. If asked to testify, I will."

"Stay away from me," I whispered and finally escaped. I was shaking as I hurried down the hall. I wondered if the woman was still drinking, or if the power of her position had overcome her sense, or perhaps she was just insane.

I couldn't imagine riding up the elevator and having to walk in and see Cal right then. I couldn't possibly relate this exchange without becoming furious with him for allowing her near me. I ducked into the chapel, which was still empty. I was sure that one day I would walk in, see someone sitting there, and feel usurped, but for now I sank down into my usual pew and gazed at the white dove and tried to regulate my breathing.

I finally pulled my cell phone from my purse, waited for a signal, and called home. I wasn't sure exactly what I was going to say, but I felt the need to hear Marshall's voice, to tell him that no matter what happened, I did love him, and things were going to be okay. He didn't answer, and I tried his cell phone. It went immediately to voice mail, which meant he must have turned it off.

I envisioned him curled up in bed, perhaps crying himself to sleep, or praying, or whatever it was that Marshall did when he was devastated and scared. I left a short message on his cell, letting him know that I would call him the next afternoon to find out what had happened at the lawyer's, and then I turned the phone off and returned to Meghan's room.

Where nothing had changed.

MARSHALL

They reached his grandmother's town on the edge of Okeechobee by three in the morning, and then spent over an hour wandering back roads, lost. Massive oaks canopied over the roads, blocking out the sky for miles at a time, and raccoons and armadillos scurried in front of the car on a regular basis, making Ada gasp and Marshall slam on the brakes.

When they finally found the lane leading to her house, Marshall turned off the headlights and coasted into a dirt courtyard. He cut the engine and they sat in the dark, staring at the little brick house his father had grown up in. An old blue and white Chevy pickup truck was parked in the carport, and something skittered out from underneath it and raced past Marshall's window too quickly for him to decipher what it was.

The surrounding woods and scrub encroached on the sides of the house, as if it might swallow it and just keep on growing. Palm fronds rustled dryly in the breeze, and in the break in the trees over the courtyard the sky spangled with stars. They both craned over the dashboard, looking up into that vast blackness, and smiled softly at each other.

"Let's try to get some sleep," Marshall said, then leaned over the center console to kiss Ada, a certain kiss. She nodded and they maneuvered their seat backs as far down as they would go, then prayed, and fell asleep holding hands.

IT wasn't quite full light yet when Marshall woke, his eyes gritty and head pounding. His right arm was asleep and he untangled his fingers from Ada's and rubbed some tingling feeling back into it as he cranked his seat up. Ada sniffed and turned over toward the door. He stared at her back, so slender that he thought his hand could span it.

The house looked dingier in the soft pink and gold of sunrise. The visible blooms of rust on the Chevy spread as the rays of the sun did, and he could see where the beams of a front porch had been torn from the house. The only part left of it was a wide concrete slab with rotting remnants of board screwed into its perimeter.

He touched Ada gently on her shoulder and she groaned as she turned back over. She opened her eyes at him and smiled, and then, as she started to stretch, she shrieked in pain and clutched at her knee.

"Oh shit," she moaned. "Remind me not to do that again."

"Are you okay?" he asked. He hadn't given her knees much thought beyond the fact that they would need to keep an eye on the stitches and would likely have to remove them themselves.

She puffed a breath out to get her bangs out of her eyes and smiled ruefully at him. "Yeah, I'm okay. Just need to get centered." She looked out the windshield at the house, then back at him with troubled eyes, her brows drawn together. "So what do you think?"

He looked at the front door of flat, unpainted wood, and for the first time since he'd put this plan into action, felt a flutter of uncertainty.

"I really have to pee," Ada said, eyeing the woods around them.

"I— Hey, did you see that?" He pointed to the house. "I just saw someone at that window."

Ada straightened up and ran her fingers through her hair. "Oh, God, Marshall, what are we going to say? Are you sure she won't already know? How do I look?"

He looked over at her, her cheeks in high color, biting her lip in her nervousness, and murmured, "You look beautiful," just as the front door swung open and a woman, tall and rangy, wearing a blue quilted housecoat that zipped up the front, strode onto the porch.

She shielded her eyes from the sun and yelled at them. "What do you want? I don't need any of what you're sellin', and if you're them Jehovah's Witnesses again you can just go on and ease on down the road. I been saved already, don't need your help with it."

Ada inhaled and then laughed as she looked at Marshall in a mixture of fear, despair, and amusement. "Oh shit."

"We'd better go before she pulls out a shotgun," he said. "Come on." He opened the door and stood from behind the safety of it and let his grandmother get a good look at him. He knew he looked like his father. Everyone commented on it, and he could see it himself whenever he caught a surprise glance in a mirror. "It's Marshall, it's me," he called, and slowly stepped out from behind the door.

She looked closer, making her way across the concrete slab, and then he saw recognition dawn. "Well, my Lord," she said. "Get up here, boy, let me get ahold of you."

He moved toward her slowly, taking in the ways his father looked like her, the ways he didn't, the stains on the housecoat, how hard she looked, like she'd been plowing fields for most of her life. He stepped up on the porch and she did, indeed, grab ahold of him. She was nearly as tall as he was and she was strong, but her crushing embrace was mercifully quick. She let him go and stepped back to take a good, long look at him.

"My Lord, you look like your daddy. Nearly took my breath away seeing you get out of that car."

He heard the passenger door open and turned around to motion Ada up to the porch.

"Oooh, and you brought someone. Well, come on, girl, bring it on up here. This girl's too old for Meghan?" she asked, glancing quickly at Marshall. He nodded and helped steady Ada as she used her crutches to step up onto the porch.

"This is Ada, Grandmother Tobias."

"Little thing, aren't you?" she asked, clearly not expecting an answer, but pulling her to her for another brief, hard hug.

"Well, I imagine there's a reason you're both here. Let's get off the porch before the dogs get a whiff of you." At this she turned without further explanation and preceded them into the gloom of the house.

Marshall took a quick look around for dogs and then pulled

Ada with him and entered his grandmother's house, following the lights she turned on for them. He was relieved to see the inside of the house. Though it was aged and worn, it was spotless and smelled fresh. They followed her down a long hallway, and, just like in his own house, the walls were lined with faded family photos. He was dying to stop at each one and examine it; he could pick out his father in them, and the other boy was obviously his uncle, Randy, and of course there was his grandfather, the minister, a gaunt man in black trousers and a white shirt in most of them.

But his grandmother didn't slow down, and they caught up to her in a surprisingly large main room, a combination of living room and dining room, with a cool terrazzo floor, corduroy-covered recliners, and a long dining table with enough chairs for ten people. Windows lined the wall behind the dining table and looked out onto the yard behind the carport.

Unlike the courtyard, the backyard was a lush garden, where tomato plants hung heavy with fruit on tall wire forms, orange trees bordered the yard on one side, and masses of giant sunflowers seemed to hold back the wilderness on the other. Ada immediately gravitated to the windows while Grandmother Tobias banged some pans onto a stovetop in the kitchen.

A coffeepot was already filling, and she grabbed mugs from open shelves and brought them to the table, quickly followed by cream and sugar. Instead of sitting down, she started pulling things out of the old refrigerator, got the pans filled with something, and timed it all exactly so that she was done when the coffeepot was finished.

"Okay," she said, as she settled herself into the chair closest to the kitchen, and poured coffee for all of them as Marshall and Ada sat in chairs on either side of her. "I don't imagine you children showed up here before daylight because you just wanted to visit. So let's have it. What kind of trouble are you in?"

"No trouble—"

"You pregnant?" she asked, turning to Ada with a frown.

Ada shook her head vehemently. "No, oh no."

"This have anything to do with those legs?"

"No, Grandmother Tobias, no, she just fell on the boat," Marshall protested. "We just...wanted to get away for a little while and thought we'd come for a visit. Mom and Dad—"

"Your daddy doesn't know you're here," she said flatly, a statement, not a question.

"No," he said.

"Well, I hope you don't think you can come here and shack up," she said. "I want you here, but the two of you can't stay together."

"Of course not," Ada said quickly. "We never thought that."

"What about school?" she asked. "You didn't leave school?"

He shook his head. "It's spring break." The words felt absurd on his lips. It had been four days, and in that time he had gone from a college student bringing his girlfriend home for a carefree spring break boating the Ten Thousand Islands and backwaters of the Everglades, to a fugitive, holing up at his grandmother's and making plans to flee the state. He looked at Ada and saw her staring back at him, the same uncertainty in her eyes.

"What about you?" she asked Ada. "Your parents know you're here?"

"They know I'm in Florida with Marshall's family for break," Ada replied steadily.

"Where are your people from?"

"I was born in Canada, but we live in Nebraska."

Marshall looked at her in surprise. He'd never known she'd lived anywhere but Nebraska.

"I knew I couldn't place your accent," Grandmother Tobias said, as if it had affirmed something. "And how long do you plan to stay?"

"A couple of days," Marshall said. "We have to get back to school next week."

"You need to let your parents know where you are, that you're safe. You too," she said to Ada. "I'm happy to have you both here, but I won't have your folks worried sick about you."

Marshall nodded and lied. "We'll call as soon as it's a decent hour," he said. "I'd like to talk to my mom before I talk to Dad," he added, and she nodded understandingly, swallowing it whole. He looked down at the scarred table, feeling sick to his stomach, thankful that she didn't know him well enough to pick up on any subtle clues that he was lying.

"Mrs. Tobias?" Ada asked. "Could I please use the restroom?"

"Of course, girl. Head on down that hall, it'll be on the right. Take your time, breakfast'll be ready soon. I don't imagine the two of you had much of a dinner last night sleeping in that car in my yard," she said, startling them both with a hearty laugh. "Oh Lord, reminds me of some of the stunts Randy and your daddy used to pull."

She scraped her chair back as Ada headed down the hall. Marshall tucked his head down and took a long sip from his coffee and gratefully inhaled the scent of sausage and biscuits wafting from the kitchen. He couldn't bring himself to tell her that Ada wouldn't eat most of it.

He wasn't sure what was going to happen. But right now, he was safe for a few hours, with a hot breakfast on the way and the woman he loved by his side. He closed his eyes and thanked God for his good fortune.

Eleven

IT is astounding what you can sleep through. It was our fourth night in Meghan's room and the nurses came in every hour to take her vital signs. They weren't always quiet, and they often turned the lights on suddenly, but I had slept through most of it last night.

Cal talked the nurses into moving another recliner bed into the room, and it was surprisingly comfortable. With the exception of a couple of nights in the hospital when Meghan was born, Cal and I hadn't slept apart since our third date. Of course, for me "slept" was a rather strong term for what I actually did.

In our first years together I slept little. I've always needed dark and quiet to fully sleep, but Cal breathed heavily, and occasionally snored, and turned over often, and he liked a nightlight on in the bathroom in case he needed it in the middle of the night.

I appreciated his concern for aim, but everything was exaggerated when I couldn't sleep, and no matter which way I turned, that little glow from the cracked door managed to seem like a klieg light by two in the morning. And his heavy breathing was like a rushing river, which made the snoring like a freight train and the tossing as if someone were leaping about the bed.

But my need to be with my husband at night superseded my need for eight straight hours, and so, over the years, I had gotten used to it all, the light, the breathing, the shaking bed. My father had snored loudly enough for me to hear in my bedroom upstairs, and I suppose that perhaps I viewed my sleep deprivation as a wifely rite of passage, and even a way to feel closer to my mother.

But Cal's snoring had been imperceptible with Meghan's respirator running and his distance from me, and of course I could not feel his restless tossing at three in the morning from across the room. I may well have slept more in that recliner in a busy hospital room than I had in all the days of my marriage, and for the first time since Cal and I began sharing our sleeping space, I wondered what it would be like to sleep alone in a bed.

He brought a couple of coffees up for us, and that was nice too. We'd always woken at staggered times, Cal up first for fishing, me later to get the kids off to school and then into my studio to get some restoration done. He usually left coffee in the pot for me, but on the whole my mornings were spent alone, and I always thought I liked it that way.

All of this, of course, was temporary, and as such took on the luster of fantasy, of a different life. The alternate roads in life are not just a poetic conceit; they are so real and heartbreaking in the details that are occasionally revealed to us, the glimpses of how things could be, if we were braver, if we had listened to our parents, if we had, or hadn't, had children.

I had always been the woman who smiled smugly and said that I was happy with who I was and that everything that had happened to me made me this person and blah blah blah, and I could cheerfully smack that smug smile off my face now. I wish someone had done it every time I'd said it, and I imagine that quite a few had wanted to.

Yes, all of my choices, mistakes or not, had made me this person that I was today. This wife who was so vaguely unhappy in a thousand roundabout ways that she couldn't even face it head-on until she was confined with her husband in a hospital room. This mother who had so utterly failed her son that he was facing a jail sentence—nutty, bereaved Dr. Kimball aside—and this mother who, unable to protect her own daughter, instead watched over her comatose, tiny body and lamented her own marriage.

My self-pity had not blossomed overnight, but I felt a right to it now and claimed it like a bride's thrown bouquet. It was the only emotion I could identify, and so I clung to it, inhaling its sweet, slightly rotting aroma and growing heady with it.

Cal and I took turns showering, and I embraced the opportunity to have a good cry, perfectly at home sobbing in the shower, its noise covering my own, its water mingling with mine. I could not say that I was refreshed when I dried off, but cleaner, yes, at least I was a little cleaner and the stink of self-pity had lessened a bit.

When I got out of the bathroom the nurse was just leaving, and Cal was pulling a small card out of a large plant arrangement. I couldn't imagine who even knew what was happening, though of course Cal had gotten Kevin to cover his trips for him, so perhaps it was from the marina or Kevin's wife.

He held it out to me after reading it, and I was surprised to see Sandy's signature at the bottom of a short message saying little more than the standard Get Well Soon. I had liked Sandy so much, but I could not get the image of those cookies at her register out of my mind, and the ghost of a scent of peanut butter haunted me whenever I thought of it. She was forever associated with it, adjacent to blame, close enough for me.

"That was nice of her," Cal said, alternating peering at the digital numbers on Meghan's respirator and searching her face.

"You know they got it there," I said. "That's where they got the cookie. Sandy made it, just the night before, she told me. Nice and fresh."

"So, it's her fault now?"

I didn't bother answering him. I had spied something sticking out of the pothos and ferns in the arrangement and pulled out a long, gray envelope. I sank down in Cal's chair and drew out a single-page letter.

> *Dearest Calvin, Chloe, and Marshall:*
>
> *Words cannot express the deep sorrow I felt upon learning about Meghan. I am, of course, aware that it must have been the cookie bought at my own store, and hope you know how very sorry I am for that. I couldn't have known, but it still feels as though a piece of my heart has broken, and I feel the need to seek your forgiveness.*
>
> *Kevin and Stacey Greaver are members of our congregation, and Stacey called me as soon as she heard the news from Kevin. We have been in touch with the hospital, and while they are protective of how much information they're giving out, they have let us know that Meghan is in a coma and that her family is there constantly, which must be a great comfort to her.*
>
> *We have started a prayer circle for Meghan and your entire family, and our service this Sunday will be in honor of you all,*

*with special prayers being made at every service until Meghan
is well and home again.*

*Please consider me at your disposal, and if there is any-
thing that needs to be done at the house or in any capacity, I
urge you to call, day or night.*

Most sincerely,

Sandra Wells

Her number and the number of the church were at the bottom
and I stared at them, feeling an urge to go down to the quiet little chapel and call. Instead, I silently handed the letter to Cal and
walked down to the vending machine for a tiny package of potato
chips and a sugar-filled soda. When I returned to the hallway I
found myself walking behind two men in sport coats. To my surprise, they stopped at Meghan's door and spoke quietly before one
of them raised a fist and rapped lightly on the door.

I turned into an empty room and peeked out around the corner.
Meghan's door opened and they stood in the hallway while they
talked to Cal. As soon as I heard them introduce themselves as
detectives, I hurried down the hall. If they were detectives, then it
meant that it was about Marshall, and I wasn't going to stand by
and let Cal indict our son.

"—think it's appropriate to talk in my daughter's room," Cal
was saying when I neared.

"I'm Meghan's mother," I said loudly, making them both turn
in surprise. "How can I help you?"

"Chloe, they're here to take statements from us."

"Statements about what?"

"Mrs. Tobias, I'm Detective Hernandez and this is my partner,
Detective Rhoades. We've been assigned to the case against Marshall

Tobias and Ada Sparks, and we'd like to speak to you and Mr. Tobias at your convenience."

"Well, this isn't convenient. As you can see, my husband and I are busy with our daughter."

"Yes, ma'am. And we're sorry for your troubles here," Detective Rhoades said. "Could we set up a time that would be better for you?"

"I know my wife doesn't want our daughter to be alone," Cal said. "So now that she's here I'll be happy to go downstairs and talk for a few minutes. But they both need me back here as soon as possible."

Both of the detectives nodded, pleased looks on their faces, but I was seething.

"I would like to speak with my husband about our daughter in private for a moment," I said, shooting him a meaningful look. "He can meet you down there."

The two men looked at each other, but Detective Hernandez nodded. "We'll be in the cafeteria," he said to Cal. "Thank you both for your time."

"I'll be down in a bit," Cal said easily. We both waited for them to get on the elevator before we entered Meghan's room. Sandy's plant arrangement looked obscenely alive and green on the windowsill.

I went straight to Meghan and stroked her forehead before turning to Cal.

"What are you planning to say to them?"

"I'm going to tell the truth," he said simply. "I'm going to tell them what Marshall told us. What else am I supposed to say, Chloe? Everyone has heard the exact same story. I'm not the one who's talked to him since he told us. I imagine you'll have more to say to them than I will. So, what are *you* going to say?"

I didn't know. Fact was, Cal was right. We hadn't given a thought to the possible ramifications of repeating what Marshall had told us. We had been too shocked, too worried about Meghan. They   the doctors, the nurses—had asked how it had happened. We had told them what Marshall told us.

And Marshall hadn't said anything to me after I had picked him up that deviated from or added to his original story. It was all incredibly, stupidly simple.

"Give me back that lawyer's card," I said suddenly, holding out my hand. Why had I not thought of this before?

Cal's hand moved to his back pocket cautiously. "Why?"

"Don't you think we should talk to one?" I asked. "If we're being questioned by the police—"

"They're not charging us with anything, Chloe. The case is against Marshall and Ada."

"They're still questioning us. And I think we should have someone who knows about the law on our side. What if they put words in our mouths? Make it seem like we said something we didn't?"

"I think you've been watching too many cop shows. If we don't have anything to hide—and we don't—then we don't have anything to worry about."

"I think you're being naïve," I said in exasperation.

"And I think you're being evasive and combative, and you're going to wind up causing more problems than we already have," he replied hotly.

I dropped my head in my hands and pressed my fingers against my eyelids, the chill from my fingertips easing my swollen eyes. I pressed harder, feeling the give, feeling the pressure move through the bridge of my nose.

"If we can't get together on this—this thing with Marshall, Cal—then we already have more problems."

"What's that supposed to mean?"

I took a deep breath. "It means that I need to get your support on this. I need for you to at least act as though your son's future matters to you. We have been on opposite sides of this for, well, for most of Marshall's life, and the thing is, you're just wrong. You just are. You have this blind spot—"

"I have the blind spot? No, Chloe," he said, and his voice was shockingly gentle, "my eyes have finally been opened. I care deeply about Marshall's future. And if he doesn't take responsibility for this, and he *is* responsible, then I see nothing in Marshall's future but misery. I *was* wrong, I'm not anymore."

"Then we are in deep trouble."

He nodded. "I guess we are."

Oh, how close were we to saying what? I had never been good at ultimatums. I was always too aware of both sides, too afraid that perhaps I would have to follow through on whatever threat I was making. Especially with Cal. I almost always caved first. Except when it had come to our children.

Cal had often accused me—sometimes jokingly, sometimes seriously—of being unable to make a decision. Where we went to dinner, what movie to watch, when to buy something. But he never appreciated all the decisions I made on an hour-to-hour basis for our children.

Choices in groceries, clothing, school supplies, homework expectations, cultural education, hairstyles, dental care, a million decisions made without his input. Because that's what mothers did. Mothers were the ones who knew what was best for their children: It was a biological right.

Right?

"Cal, if we're not together on this..."

"Yes?" His challenge was clear.

"Then we're not together." It had been said, and there was no going back.

"Be very careful about what you're saying here, Chloe," he said.

"Okay. I won't speak with the police without a lawyer present. I don't want you to, either. I won't say anything that might implicate our son or further their case. I don't want you to, either. I assume, every day, that our daughter will open her eyes. I want you to, also, vocally and with feeling." Now that I had stepped over that line, I was calm. "If you don't support our children, then you don't support us, or me. And that's not a marriage."

His face drained of color, leaving his tan a sickly color, and he somehow seemed more fragile than he had a moment ago. "I can't believe that you don't see that I am supporting our children," he said. "I am supporting Marshall's need to take responsibility for his actions, and I'm supporting our daughter's right for..."

"Vengeance?" I filled in for him. "Isn't that what this is about for you? Don't make it about Meghan. Do you think that if she opened her eyes and talked that she would want Marshall in jail? Do you think Meghan would be happy about what you're doing?"

"I am not encouraging anyone to send him to jail. I am saying that he should be held accountable!" He finally couldn't hold it any longer, and as his voice rose at me, his color flooded back until he was red in the face. "I'm going downstairs now, to talk to the detectives. I'm going to do what I have to do."

"Then I will too," I said, turning away from him and sinking down into my chair as he stormed out. The soft click of the door seemed an incongruous period rather than an exclamation point on the end of his anger, and there was some sort of satisfaction in that.

He didn't come back for almost two hours, and I didn't speak to him when he entered. The nurses were making their usual checks and the neurologist had been in while he was gone, but nothing had changed and there was nothing to say to Cal.

"I told them you didn't want to talk to them," he finally said after inspecting Meghan's respirator number and settling into his chair. His constant attention to the numbers on the respirator grated on my nerves. He wasn't a doctor, or a nurse, he had no training. He just had to look like he was doing something, some outward appearance of control, some useless male trait.

I simply nodded at his statement. I imagined he wanted me to thank him, but I would have been happy to tell them that myself. I didn't need a buffer.

"I'll be back in a while," I said, feeling generous in giving him that much information, and went downstairs to the chapel. As I knew would happen eventually, there was a couple in there, clinging to each other, their heads nestled in each other's necks. They turned grief-ravaged faces toward me as I stepped inside, hope burning brightly in the woman's eyes before she saw I wasn't anyone of importance in her life.

"Sorry," I mumbled, backing out and turning toward the cafeteria. The doors were propped open and I scanned the tables carefully, looking for Dr. Kimball and the detectives before I entered. It was long past the lunch hour and there were only a few people sitting at tables, grouped loosely around the coffee machines.

I wove my way through the tables and got myself a bottled water from the cooler, then found a table behind a low wall topped with anemic-looking pothos, and scrolled through the missed calls on my phone. One from an art dealer I'd done some work for a few months ago, and two from Charles Mingus. I hit the call button, and as before he picked up himself.

"Charles Mingus."

"Hello, Mr. Mingus, this is Chloe Tobias."

"Oh, I tried you earlier. Thanks for calling me back," he said, but his voice was guarded.

"I've had my cell phone off. Why were you calling me?" I asked. I should have called Marshall when I saw that Mingus had called, should have found out about their appointment before I talked to him. I steeled myself for the inevitable conversation about who would be taking care of the bills.

"Have you heard from Marshall?"

"No," I said cautiously. "I've been at the hospital. Should I have? Did your appointment go all right?"

"He didn't show up," he said. "Calls to your home and his cell phone have gone unanswered—"

"I'll call you right back," I said and hung up on him while he was still speaking and hit the speed dial for home. No answer. I left a message, then dialed Marshall's cell. Straight to voice mail. I left a message for him there too, and then sat at the table with the phone clutched in my hand, wondering where the hell my son was.

I called Mingus back. He answered the phone coolly. Who could blame him? I didn't like being hung up on either.

"I didn't get him either," I said by way of greeting.

"Do you have any idea why he would miss our appointment?" he asked.

"The only thing I can imagine is that he's scared," I said.

"I've been a criminal lawyer for a long time. Clients missing appointments comes with the territory, but Marshall doesn't strike me as the type to just blow it off. Do you think your son would flee?"

"Flee? Of course not. Where would he go?" I asked. It was true. My family was gone, his father's family might as well be. He had friends at school, but I couldn't imagine he would hop in the car and go back to college, or, if I were honest with myself, that he would leave Ada while she was still in town. I wondered if her parents had arrived yet, or if she were still too afraid, or stubborn, to call them.

"Mrs. Tobias," Mingus started hesitantly, "I am in a bit of a quandary on what to do here."

"Well, as I said, I imagine he's scared. He probably took the boat out to fish, clear his head. I'm sure he'll call one of us soon," I said, but I felt no real certainty of that. More likely I would go home to find him staring at the television, ignoring the phones ringing around him, trying to forget how much trouble he was in, as if it might go away. Which only underscored Cal's misgivings about Marshall's maturity level.

"Besides," I said, "he wouldn't leave while Ada's still here."

"And that's what concerns me. Ada Sparks was bailed out by Marshall last night."

"What? That's impossible. I dropped him off last night. He was at home," I protested, but even as I did a cold pit grew in my stomach. Of course he did. He said he had money in his account, and I left him alone, with his car, with time. Of course he did. I groaned, and Mingus was silent.

"I don't have a great feeling about this, Mrs. Tobias. There's nothing to panic about yet; Marshall isn't due in court for almost two weeks, and there's no reason for me to tell anyone anything at this time. But, I suggest you do what you can to find him and get him back here, or we're looking at some pretty serious charges compounding already serious charges."

"I'm sure he's just hiding out at home. He's probably got her there and they're just trying to figure out what to do about her parents," I said, seeing it as I was saying it. Of course that's what they were doing. He thought he loved her, he rescued her, and now they were comforting each other. "I'll go home, get this figured out, and will have him call you as soon as I can."

"Great. Now, was there a reason that you called me earlier?"

"Oh, yes, I—my husband has spoken to a couple of detectives here at the hospital. I don't want to talk to anyone without a lawyer with me."

"I can certainly recommend someone."

"Yes, I would appreciate that."

"Hang on a sec..."

I could hear the sound of computer keys being rapidly pecked. "Ready?"

I quickly pulled a napkin from the silver dispenser and fumbled a pen out of my purse. "Go ahead."

He gave me the office and cell number for Tessa Barker, a lawyer, he said, who would be particularly sympathetic to my concerns as a mother.

"I don't need someone motherly," I said. "I need someone tough."

"I don't think that's going to be an issue," he said. "Let me know if she doesn't work out and I'll give you another number, but I think you'll like her."

From the tone of his voice, I thought that perhaps it was Mingus who liked Tessa Barker, but I promised to call her, and to have Marshall call as soon as I found him.

A woman with two teenagers in tow sat down in the booth behind me and started explaining, in a cracking voice, what a stroke was. I didn't hear whether it was the children's father or an older relative, and didn't stick around to find out. I was discovering that if I stayed in any one place for too long in the hospital, misery was sure to find me, and I had enough of my own to deal with.

I tucked the phone number into my jeans and left the cafeteria, cracking the door of the chapel and peeking in. The couple was gone and the pews were again empty. I sighed as I flopped down into one and stared at the dove. He offered no answers, what with his mouth being full of olive branch, and I finally dialed Tessa Barker.

Unlike Charles Mingus, she had a secretary, who informed me that Ms. Barker was in court, but that she was happy to take a message. I left my name and cell and Mingus's name, and hung up feeling empty.

There was only one thing left to do. Find Marshall. Like Mingus, I didn't have a good feeling about it.

MARSHALL

Luckily, Grandmother Tobias didn't feel the need to hover while he made his fake phone call. He and Ada walked out to the backyard while his grandmother cleaned the breakfast dishes. He could see her peering at them through the window over the sink and he made a great show of opening his cell phone.

He turned it on and it immediately began to beep with messages. He picked them up, and, as expected, they were from his mother and Mingus, escalating in concern levels. In Mingus's last one he told him in no uncertain terms how he felt about wasting his time, and Marshall felt guilt course through him. He deleted it and pretended to dial a number.

He mimed speaking into the phone for his grandmother, even giving a few sullen head shakes before faking a laugh and then mouthing *I love you too* for her benefit. Ada leaned on her crutches and grinned at his superb acting skills. She held her hand out and went through the same routine, though she skipped the head shaking and made the call much shorter.

When she handed it back to him, her fingers brushed his and he ached to touch her. She looked like hell: a tragic day on the boat, a night in a hospital, almost three days in jail, and then another night sleeping in a car would drain anyone's good looks, but he still desired her more strongly than anything he'd ever felt before.

He shut the phone off before it could start ringing and slipped it in his pocket while Ada thumped around the garden, fondling tomatoes and caressing the sunflowers. He watched her, with the sunlight filtering through the sharp-leaved oaks to scatter across her hair and face. It didn't matter that she looked like hell, she still sparkled, glowed.

A cloud passed across the sun, and when she turned to him she was in shadow, no warm halo around her, and he saw how tired she looked. He took one of her crutches, wrapping his arm around her waist, and helped her inside.

His grandmother was sitting at the dining table, watching them through the windows, a leather-bound Bible open in front of her and a glass of orange juice in her hand. She appraised them as he helped Ada in the door.

"Get ahold of your folks?" she asked.

"I talked to Mom," Marshall said. "She wants us to come home tomorrow."

"That all she said?"

"She said to give you her best," Marshall said hesitantly. He wasn't sure what his mother would have said. But his grandmother nodded and turned her attention to Ada.

"And you?"

"My parents trust Marshall and his family. They're happy I'm meeting you," Ada said. Marshall nearly believed her.

"Well," Grandmother Tobias said. "I guess we're all right then. Why don't you two get cleaned up and we'll get to know each other."

"Do you have any bandages?" Marshall asked. "I'd like to help Ada with her knees."

She looked at Ada's dirty, bloodied bandages and narrowed her eyes. "There's some things under the cabinet. But you need to remember whose house you're in now. I don't know what all your daddy's taught you, but you'll behave yourselves in my home."

Marshall was speechless, his mouth gaped open and he took a quick glance at Ada. Her face was bright red and she stared at the floor, all the light gone out of her.

"I was just going to help—" Marshall protested.

"No. I'm fine," Ada said, raising her head and looking straight at him. "I'm fine. She's right. I can do it myself. You shouldn't be...touching me that closely." She turned to Grandmother Tobias. "I respect your home."

"No room for whores and fornicators in my house."

Marshall gasped, but Ada reached out and put a hand on his arm. "She's right. We're in her home, and we'll respect that. She's right, Marshall, we're here for a reason. Listen to your grandmother."

"I—" He didn't know what to say.

"Do you know Jesus, girl?" Grandmother Tobias asked, looking pleased.

"Yes, ma'am," Ada said softly.

"Well, but you don't have to talk to her like that," Marshall said. But his words went unheard by the two women. They gazed levelly at each other until Ada gently removed her second crutch from his grasp and made her way down the hall to the bathroom.

"Why don't you have a seat, son," Grandmother Tobias said, closing her Bible. He looked down the hall where Ada had disappeared and then out at the garden before sitting down. "Now why don't you tell me why you're really here?"

"I just—I wanted to meet you," he said desperately. "I mean, it's crazy. It's crazy that I have this family that I don't even know about."

She fixed him with that look again, and he could almost feel himself wither. He'd not encountered this particular brand of faith before. He'd always found it easy to ask questions before, questions about their God, their rituals, their history. But there was something too forbidding in this big woman.

Almost every religious person he'd encountered had been so ready to talk to him, eager to explain their side, nearly frantic to prove their openness to his inquiries. He had the feeling that if he began questioning his grandmother she would, instead, want him to prove his worthiness to her.

"So you came here to get to know me," she repeated. She looked down the hallway and seemed to make up her mind about something. "Well, that's nice. I wish your folks would come sometime. I'd like to meet that sister of yours. How is she doing? She a smart girl? Good in school like your mama was?"

Marshall's mouth dried up. Meghan was smart. She was smart enough to skip a grade, but his parents hadn't wanted her to have an even harder time than she already had. He thought about her on the boat. Before the...thing. She hadn't been all giggly like he'd thought. She'd been so serious. She'd been asking Ada questions, about her diet and about school.

And for the first time, she'd asked him about the things they were passing in the boat, letting him show off for Ada, letting him be a big brother. They hadn't spent much time alone together. She was always so spoiled by his parents. He'd thought that maybe she'd been too protected. They'd both been so intent on her. And he'd never seen anything that made him think she was as sick as they'd said.

They had felt like a family out there on the water.

"Yeah, she's smart," he said. "She's, uh, she's real smart." He finished in a whisper.

She narrowed her eyes at him again, then slapped her hand on the table, making him jump. "Your daddy was a helluva fisherman. Did he at least teach you that?"

"Yeah, I can fish."

"Why don't you get little Squaw Broken Knees out of the bathroom, and I'll take you up to the river, see what you got."

"I don't know—"

"Sure you do," she said, rising. "You want to get to know me? You want to know about your daddy? Then we got to do some fishin'."

Twelve

I CHECKED on Meghan and told Cal I was going home for some clothes and other things. He asked me to pick up a few items for him, and I said that I would. We were polite now.

He would wait for Meghan to die and would walk Marshall to jail. I would wait for Meghan to open her eyes and would fight to keep our son from having his life ruined by a horrible mistake. Our sides had been chosen and declared out loud, and there was nothing left to fight about.

I drove home as quickly as I could, and was almost sorry for it when I pulled into the drive. Marshall's car was gone. I didn't know what to think. I was almost relieved, because I did not want to see Ada. I had been almost successful at putting her out of my mind throughout this.

Enough of my heart and mind were occupied with my own two children that I could barely remember what the girl looked like. And I didn't want to remember. I didn't want to see her, and, perhaps the way Cal felt about Marshall, I wouldn't know what I would do if I did.

The house was quiet. I walked through the kitchen as silently as I could, as if sneaking through my own home. A cabinet door was hanging open and I closed it, then made my way through the downstairs. As expected, nothing.

Upstairs was a different matter. Not for what I found, but for what I didn't find. The suitcase that Marshall had so cavalierly dropped on the floor was gone. Ada's, in Meghan's room, was gone. My closet had been riffled through. A tracksuit was gone, a couple of pairs of shoes.

I knew the house was empty, but I checked my studio and office on the third floor, and then went downstairs and out to Cal's workshop, where I found nothing.

They were gone.

I walked back inside and stared at the two photos on our old, noisy refrigerator. Meghan's school photo, and one of Marshall, taken right before his high school graduation. He was in a purple gown and cap, and he was grinning as if his life had just started.

"Who are you?" I whispered to it.

I waited for an answer, searching his face, but the glossy surface showed me nothing but a happy young man. I jerked my head up at a sound and strained to isolate where it was coming from. It was a car, and it was coming down our road.

"Oh, God, please," I said out loud, my hand on my heart. I stepped out the kitchen door and waited for it to turn into our drive, but it wasn't Marshall's car. It was an unmarked police car, the darkly tinted windows obscuring the occupants. Marshall and Ada could be in there.

I didn't know whether to hope for that or not. From what Mingus had said, neither of them were in trouble unless they didn't show for a court appearance. And I didn't imagine they'd just drop them off at our home if they had been picked up.

But when the car came to a halt, the same detectives from the hospital stepped out. I backed up into my kitchen and pulled the screen door closed, slipping the hook into the eye to hold it, the silvered crosshatch of the screening like a confessional.

But I had nothing to confess. They couldn't force me to talk to them. And they couldn't come in without a warrant. I felt rather like some superstitious medieval, certain that unless I invited the vampire across my threshold, it could not hurt me. The screen door that had once represented all my unhappy thoughts about my marriage had turned into my safety.

Hernandez and Rhoades—that was how I thought of them, like a country music duo, and I'd never been a fan—squinted up the height of the house, then said things too low for me to hear before walking toward the door.

"How are you, Mrs. Tobias?" Rhoades asked. "I'm sorry we weren't able to talk at the hospital."

Keeping the screen door closed I said, "Are you following me? I haven't done anything, and I consider that harassment."

"No, we weren't following you. We figured you were still at the hospital with Meghan," he said.

I didn't like his use of her name. After all the legal formality— with their and Mingus's use of Mrs. and Mr.—it felt entirely too familiar, aggressive.

"Where I am is of no concern to you," I snapped. "Now what do you want?"

They glanced at each other, and Hernandez gave some sort of deferential nod to Rhoades.

"Marshall here, Mrs. Tobias?" he asked, taking a step up onto the porch. I stood my ground behind the screen. I shook my head.

"No."

"Is Ada Sparks here?"

"No."

"Do you know where they are?"

I wanted to lie and say that I did, and it would have been easy. But Mingus said they hadn't done anything illegal, and I wanted to let them know that I knew that, that I was informed and they couldn't intimidate me.

But I was intimidated. I was nearly sick to my stomach with it. Yes, at forty years old, never having done a single illegal thing in my life, I was afraid of cops. So I lied.

"They're visiting family," I said.

They glanced at each other again and I clenched my teeth. I didn't care how long they'd been together as partners, they weren't psychic, and their little looks and raised eyebrows and carefully practiced wry smiles couldn't communicate anything to each other that I didn't recognize myself. They were cats with a mouse, so full of power that they didn't even have to make an effort at it, just a little swat here and there would keep me running in circles.

"Mrs. Tobias, we would really like to speak with Miss Sparks. Could you possibly let us know how we could get in touch with her?"

I was nonplussed. They'd already had Ada. And why were they specifically asking for her and not Marshall?

"They'll be back soon," I said cautiously. "Why do you need to speak with her? Have you gotten ahold of her parents?"

"In a way," Hernandez said.

"How much do you know about Ada Sparks?" Rhoades asked, overriding his partner's comment.

"I— What do you mean?"

"Did you know that both of her parents have been in the system?"

In the system? What the hell did that mean? Okay, I'd seen my share of cop shows, how could you miss them these days? TV was filled with murder and mayhem and corpses, limbs and autopsies, detectives and crime scene investigators, and all manner of violence and substitute porn. I could guess what "in the system" meant, but it irritated me that they took it for granted that I would.

I wasn't a cop. I wasn't a criminal. This wasn't my world, and I wasn't going to pretend that it was.

"I don't know what that means," I said. "I've never met them."

If Rhoades had been being careful of our tenuous communication so far, my professed naïveté obviously irritated him as much as their self-assurance irritated me, and he was silent for a moment before speaking in a flat, no-nonsense clip.

"Ada's mother was arrested eight years ago on suspicion of manslaughter. Her father has been incarcerated in several of our finest state pens on various fraud and theft charges and is currently wanted in New York State for grand larceny."

My knees didn't weaken, go soft like you read about. It was my whole body that went limp, my fingertips slid down the old wood of the screen door frame, my eyes closed involuntarily, even the arches of my feet felt as though they'd lost their support. *Oh, Marshall*, I thought. *Who did you fall in love with?*

Rhoades stepped up to the screen door and said softly, "Want to know more?"

Hernandez appeared behind him, and though I knew it was the wrong thing to do, yes, I did want to know more, and so I unlatched the door with my rubber fingers and it swung slightly toward them. I backed up into the kitchen and pulled a chair out from the table and dropped into it as they came into the house, the screen door catching Hernandez on his battered loafers. I waited while their eyes adjusted after the brilliant sun in our side yard.

I pushed a chair out with my foot and they both sat down at the table. Nobody spoke, and I stared at them in turn while they pulled out small notebooks and pens. Rhoades needed a haircut. Hernandez needed dental work. They both needed new shirts. I would have said something, asked something, but I was unable to form words, and was exhausted with the fact that I was, again, speechless.

I just closed my eyes and prepared to listen, as if I were waiting on a bedtime story. Rhoades flipped through his notebook and began to speak.

"Adaleide Marie Sparks was born to Oriole and Daniel Sparks in Alberta, Canada, in 1988—"

"Eighty-eight? She's twenty?" I asked, truly shocked. I'd thought she was eighteen, at the most nineteen. It was only a year or two older than I had assumed she was, but somehow the absence of the "teen" suffix changed her, made her more menacing, as if had I known that then perhaps I could have avoided all of this. Maybe I wouldn't have allowed her frail appearance to soften me, I wouldn't have chalked her tattoo and piercing up to an immature frontal lobe.

He nodded and continued. Hernandez watched me closely, and I shut my eyes again, shutting him out.

"Daniel is an American citizen and Ada has dual citizenship. They moved to the States when she was nine and moved around a lot. Daniel was in and out of prison and, from what we can tell, Oriole found places for them to live by joining communes, fringe churches, a few of them have been investigated as cults."

I must have made some noise. I know I didn't scream because my mouth never moved, so that was only happening in my head, but I did something because Rhoades stopped speaking and reached his hand across the table as though to pat me.

"You okay?" he asked.

Hernandez cleared his throat. "Mrs. Tobias, we're not here to upset you. We know you haven't done anything but raise two pretty good kids. But, ah, there's more you should hear."

I nodded. "Did you tell my husband this?"

They both shook their heads. "No, ma'am," Rhoades said. "We didn't know a lot of this ourselves when we spoke to him. When we found out, we came straight here to see if she was here. We didn't expect to see you."

I took a deep breath. "Okay. What else?"

"While Daniel Sparks was serving time in North Carolina for forgery, Oriole evidently met someone else, and they took Ada and her sister, Zyphyr—"

"Zyphyr?" I repeated.

He looked at me solemnly. "Yes, ma'am. They took Ada and Zyphyr and moved to Nebraska to join the man's community, which is sort of a weird mix of everything, from what we know. They've not quite achieved cult status, but they have been investigated several times.

"It looks like the whole thing's just a hodgepodge of whatever individual beliefs people bring to the group. They don't believe in Western medicine, no immunizations or vaccines, no medical intervention, healing by laying on of hands and rebirthing, speaking in tongues, polygamy, we're pretty sure they're involved in illegal sexual practices involving minors, and there's some sort of end-time component, which would seem to be at odds with their environmental concerns."

Rhoades shook his head and shrugged. "There's no one guiding principle apparently, and not one single guru-type person heading it up that they've been able to discern, though these types of groups sometimes go to great lengths to protect that person from being discovered. There is some kind of council that the authorities can't figure out yet. It seems to mostly be a group of loosely related fringe religious beliefs and environmental practices.

"Of course, most of these things aren't illegal and are protected under the laws of our country, but then some of it is illegal and so they're definitely a group on Nebraska's radar."

I huddled over the table, my stomach heaving just slightly, the way it had when I was pregnant with Meghan, not enough to get sick, just enough to be miserable. "She said they sent her to school on a scholarship. I thought, you know, maybe they were just— Marshall has always had an interest in religions. He likes to explore them. Everyone he's ever brought home has been...interesting." I looked up at them and could tell there was more.

"They have been paying for her college. Nothing as organized as a scholarship, just paying her tuition and books. They're sending another member to college to get a medical degree."

"She never mentioned that."

"They think they're doing it so they have their own doctors and lawyers to protect them. Keep the kids out of regulated medicine, defend their right to their practices, keep the state out of their business," Hernandez said. "It's kind of, well, it's kind of brilliant if you think about it."

Rhoades glared at him and he shut up. I got the impression that Hernandez was the observer, detached, while Rhoades got more involved. Against my own judgment, I was starting to like, or perhaps respect, him a little. At least he was giving me information, which was more than I could say for anyone else.

"Thing is," Rhoades said, "some of their religious practices aren't exactly benign. So, Zyphyr was born with several medical conditions—she was autistic, and deaf, with multiple learning difficulties. Rebirthing is some psychological thing where they put the person in something supposed to represent the womb, like a sleeping bag, or a sheet. Then they, I don't know, they lean on the person, sort of squeeze them, trying to re-create the birthing process, like contractions, and the person is supposed to fight their way out of it, be rebirthed, and their emotional issues are supposed to be gone, I guess. So these people decide that they're going to adopt that, only they're going to make it a religious thing, heal physical ailments instead of emotional ones."

"Oh no," I said weakly, almost a protest at what I knew was coming.

"Yeah, they decided to do it to Zyphyr. Only it didn't turn out so well. She died. Cause of death was suffocation, but she also had multiple broken ribs and one of her lungs had been punctured. Good, God-fearing people they are." Rhoades sounded disgusted, even angry. His notebook flapped like a bird with a broken wing on the table as he jittered his hand up and down.

"They tried to cover it up, buried her without reporting it, gave her a service, a headstone, everything. Said it was God's will, that she was healed when she went home to him, so it had actually worked, just not quite how they had intended."

"Her mother, Oriole...?" I didn't even know what I wanted to ask, didn't know what I wanted to know.

"She was arrested, along with several other members. They all told the same story and said that Oriole hadn't participated physically, but she had allowed it, and encouraged her other daughter, Ada, to participate."

I gasped. Hernandez nodded. "They wound up dropping the charges."

"But how—how come you didn't know this?" I asked. "Why didn't it show up?"

Hernandez shrugged. "She was a minor, the charges were dropped, and her record was expunged. We only found out about it because one of our colleagues thought she recognized the name and found a news story on it. We got the mother's records, followed her info, found Ada."

"Where's her mother now?"

"Nobody knows," Rhoades said. "Her charges were reduced, she got out with time served, spent a couple of years with the group, got Ada married, and then disappeared."

"Married?" I asked faintly. "Ada's married."

"Well, no, not legally she's not. There was some sort of community-sanctioned ceremony. Probably danced around a drunk duck or something, who knows? They lived together for a time, then when she left for college they had some sort of annulment," Hernandez said.

"Lucky they didn't rebirth her," Rhoades muttered.

"So, Mrs. Tobias, can you tell us where Ada and Marshall are?" Hernandez asked, clicking his pen and preparing to write in his notebook.

"No," I finally said. "I can't."

Rhoades sighed. "I can tell you that this sort of information could be pretty important to any defense Marshall is planning to mount. It would likely make him look more sympathetic to a jury if it goes to trial."

"What are you saying?" I asked. "You're willing to offer some sort of plea bargain?"

He held his hands up. "Whoa, now we can't do anything like that. That's all big-time DA stuff. We're just saying that if we could get a handle on exactly what happened, how Ada was involved, if she was the instigator. We just want to talk to her. This could put a different spin on things, that's all."

Hernandez leaned forward. "We don't want Marshall. We want Ada," he said.

"We just want to talk to her," Rhoades said.

They both got silent all of a sudden, and the quiet descended like smog—unpleasant, dirty. They shot each other another look, and Rhoades said, "We think she might have information on a pretty bad guy, Mrs. Tobias. A pedophile out of North Carolina. We figure she might give up some information in exchange for a reduced charge. Federal marshals will be here soon."

"Oh, God," I groaned, cupping my forehead in my palms. They remained silent. "Look," I finally said, not raising my head. "I don't know where they are. I don't even know if they're together. I assume they are, and I assume they'll be back, but I can't get ahold of him and he hasn't gotten in touch with me. So. I just don't know. That's the truth."

"Do you have any family he'd go to?" Rhoades asked. "Friends who'd take them in?"

I shook my head. "My family is gone; he doesn't even know Cal's family. And Marshall's friends are at college, and I wouldn't know the first place to start there."

"I guess that's where we'll begin then," Hernandez said. He recited all of Marshall's personal information from college, his address at the dorm, his home and cell phones, his job at the frame shop. I nodded along. They already had the information; there was no sense in denying any of it. And at this point I wasn't so sure I should be viewing them as the enemy anymore, though I wasn't so naïve as to believe that they were telling me everything they had or everything they were considering.

They both stood and reached inside their blazer pockets for their cards. Hernandez slid his across the table toward me, Rhoades handed his directly to me and waited for me to take it.

The ease at which I fell into the good cop/bad cop cliché was surprising to me, but then clichés are born of reality. Put any two people together and one will stand out as the more difficult, one will be warmer, one will seem more intelligent, one more dour. Any marriage, any friendship, any business partner.

The way married people made friends, or didn't, with other couples, had always made me uncomfortable: evaluating how the women related to each other, the men, and then the cross-relationship. There had to be a certain amount of attraction, enough for friendship, but not too much for the partner's comfort.

I'd imagined that I was the warmer partner when I had been in college and Cal and I had met, the more intelligent, the more desirable friend. But when we'd moved here, it had been made clear that Cal was the preferred half of the couple, including, no, *especially* with the women. I was not to be trusted, and it took a long time for me to realize that I was the one seen as cold, distant, self-absorbed.

My intelligence, the way I had defined it, did not matter. My talents with reversing microscopic damage to a canvas and matching medium and color were considered ephemeral and stumbled upon, not essential and time-honored, at least not here.

This tenuous foursome—Rhoades and Hernandez, Cal and I—was reminiscent of those early overtures. Cal was the cooperative, forthcoming one, I the recalcitrant bit of yolk in the meringue. But my loyalty was to my child. I took the cards and remained seated while they let themselves out the door.

MARSHALL

By the time they were paddling up Fisheating Creek, the sun had warmed central Florida's wilderness to a steamy mid-nineties and the only one who looked perfectly comfortable was Grandmother

Tobias. She wore an old baseball hat with a Lykes logo on it and her gray hair foamed out the sides in frizz.

Ada had emerged from her shower looking like someone else. She hadn't reapplied any makeup and had drawn her hair back into two low, spiky pigtails. She'd removed her eyebrow ring, and she looked about twelve years old, as innocent and clean as Meghan. She'd only rebandaged one knee, the worst one, and the other one glowed with bruises, but was no longer swollen.

Grandmother Tobias's eyes had roamed over her and she seemed to approve of something. Marshall took a shower while she and Ada loaded up the old truck with rods and a cooler, and by the time they were jouncing down dirt roads to the edge of the creek, he could tell they had spoken enough that they were comfortable in each other's presence. He was the one who felt like an outsider.

But now that they were in the canoe, he took over the ways he knew how, steering upriver over the tea-colored water according to Grandmother Tobias's directions while she showed Ada how to work a fishing rod. He was surprised to see that Ada did not flinch at threading a worm onto the hook. Apparently her vegetarian reluctance to hurt any living thing didn't extend to invertebrates, and he was torn between an uncertainty about who she really was and pride.

"Arms holdin' up okay?" Grandmother called to him, glancing up the waterway. She pointed to a small inlet overhung by lacy cypress limbs, with an alligator sunning itself on a short bank. "See there? That's where we're headed. We'll get some bluegills maybe. I've gotten bass there too. Your daddy caught a twelve-pounder there when he was just eleven."

"No way," he said, peering over the edge as they glided into the inlet.

"Don't ever underestimate your daddy's fishing skills, boy," she said, adjusting Ada's fingers on the reel and pulling her arm back, showing her how to cast lightly into the water. "He was like magic on the water."

"Still is," he said. "I do okay too, you know."

"Lotta talk on the Creek," she said. "Got to prove yourself. Now, Ada, you feel a nibble, don't go jerkin' it out of the water like you got a marlin on, you just let him take it before you set, and just reel, don't jerk. I don't feel like gettin' hooked when it comes flyin' out of the water. This is easy fishin', not deep-sea fishin'."

While his grandmother was teaching Ada, Marshall chose a rod and got busy tying a weight and sorting through the small tacklebox, settling on a four-pound spinner rather than hooking a real worm. His grandmother watched him out the corner of her eye as she got Ada used to the motion of casting, and she smiled at his choice.

They fished for over two hours, quietly, only conversing when one of them caught a fish. Marshall was proud of Ada. She was excited when she caught a fish, but she didn't squeal or act grossed out. Instead, she allowed him to show her how to remove the hook and hold the fish in the water for a moment before letting it go, catching on more quickly than he had when he was a novice.

Grandmother Tobias was the only one who kept her catch, and she twisted her lips whenever she watched them let one go that she thought might be good eating, but she didn't say anything. Ada stopped after the first hour and just watched, and finally Marshall saw what he'd hoped to see the last time they went boating.

She did soften. She practically melted in the heat, and eventually her eyes drifted shut and she began to hum, a fine sheen of perspiration making her glow. Marshall didn't recognize the tune she was humming, but within a moment Grandmother Tobias began to sing softly

"—and we shall go a'down, and go a'down to the river, and he calls to us where they laid him down, and we go a'down, and go a'down to the river, and we raise our voice—"

Ada began to sing too, and he closed his eyes and thought that he might never have an opportunity to feel so perfect again, here on this water, with fish biting, swallowtail kites sailing overhead in the palest blue sky, the sun's edges sharp, without the blur of even the wisp of a cloud, and women singing a hymn he'd never heard before yet felt his soul recognized.

But perfection eluded him, because he could not forget.

He could not forget about Meghan and his parents, about the jail cell, the *pendejo*, about anything. He tried to think of nothing but the pull at the tip of the pole and the heat on the top of his head, filtering down through his body and making him one with the creek, but it all stayed with him.

When Grandmother Tobias decided they had enough fish for dinner, she picked up a paddle and she and Marshall slowly wended their way back. The water level had dropped a bit, and they had to get out and wade twice, pulling the canoe along the mucky bottom of the creek, before they were able to pull the canoe up the bank they'd pushed off from.

Marshall shoved the canoe back into the brush alongside several others.

"Are all of these yours?" he asked.

"Nope, just a bunch of us keep 'em here. Most folks don't know about this spot 'less they live here. Don't even know about these trails we took to get here. Only the old Glade people know this land like this."

Ada looked up from stowing the rods in the back of the truck. "I thought we were far away from the Everglades," she said, shooting Marshall a look.

"Well, you're not too far," Grandmother Tobias replied. "But I'm talkin' 'bout Belle Glade, honey, not the Everglades. Two different places, different fish, different folk. I imagine Calvin'll be back before long. You don't get this place out of your soul for long, just like you don't ignore Jesus in your heart for too long, neither. Sooner or later, no matter how they lose their way, everybody comes back. You're here and you didn't even know it, if that doesn't just show you. Some things are in the blood."

She pulled the door of the Chevy open and climbed behind the wheel as Marshall and Ada scrambled to get in the cab, and they bounced back to her house under the blaze of the midday sun, their windows down, the heavy air blowing through.

As they pulled into the clearing and came to a dusty stop beside the house, the brush surrounding the carport began to shake, and Ada clutched his leg when a pack of dogs burst out of the dry scrub and surrounded the truck, baying and barking ferociously.

Grandmother Tobias inched the truck up and yelled at the dogs out the window. "Get on back, get back or I'll get one of you, go on! Damn dogs!"

Marshall jumped when one leapt against the door just before she pulled into the carport, and Grandmother Tobias laughed. "They won't hurt you," she said. "They just want some fish. You think we're gonna be able to eat all this? I'll get them going while you get this one in the house," she said, patting Ada's arm. "I don't want them jumping on her legs."

She got out and whistled, pulling the dogs to her like a magnet, and Marshall twisted around to watch her pull the cooler to the end of the truck bed and start throwing fish over her shoulder. The dogs tumbled after the fish, snapping at each other, and Marshall and Ada got into the house without incident.

Inside the gloom of the front hall, Ada peered at him and said, "Oh, my God. That's crazy."

"*She's* crazy," Marshall agreed.

Ada turned serious. "No, no she's not, Marshall, and don't ever talk like that about her. She's...touched. Not nutty touched, but she's holy, she knows God."

Marshall looked out the front window at the pack of dogs scrambling for the rest of the fish and shook his head. "You think?"

"She told me..." Ada trailed off, biting her lip.

"What? She told you what?"

"She said she knew we were coming. She knew we were in trouble, and God told her we were coming."

He wanted to believe that, but the big-woman in the carport with the crazy gray hair throwing raw fish at wild dogs, well, she just didn't strike him as a visionary. Which was his fault, he knew. His own lack of faith, his own lack of courage.

"What else did she say?" he asked, taking her hand. She looked at him tenderly, tilting her head. If she'd looked twelve years old earlier, now she looked as though she contained the wisdom of age. She gently removed her hand from his.

"She said we weren't to continue on our road together."

"What? What are you talking about?"

She shrugged. "I'm just telling you what she said. She said you weren't ready."

"What the hell? Ready for what? Listen, Ada, our plan stands, doesn't it? We needed a place to hole up for a couple days, get some rest, well, we got some. We'll get out of here tomorrow, we'll head to your people. Once we're on the road, you can get in touch with them, make sure it's safe. You said—"

"Shhh," she cautioned him, holding her finger to her lips. "We'll talk about it later."

Grandmother Tobias huffed in from the porch, wiping sweat from her forehead and dragging the cooler in behind her. Marshall hurried to take it from her, noting that the color had drained from his grandmother's face.

"Whew," she said, sitting down at the table to catch her breath. "Those dogs'll be the death of me yet. I don't get 'em fed, they're like to eat me up one day." She laughed and Ada joined her, but Marshall couldn't muster a smile. He pulled the cooler into the kitchen and began stacking fish in the sink while Ada got a glass of water for his grandmother.

"We'll fry those up later," Grandmother Tobias said, watching Marshall. "Know how to clean 'em? Got newspapers in the utility room there."

Marshall nodded. He knew how to clean fish. He remembered his father teaching him how to do it, how to hold the knife, hold the fish so he didn't slice a piece of himself off, how to slip the guts out with a minimum gross factor.

He got newspapers and started on the fish while Grandmother and Ada moved to the sofa and Grandmother began pulling out old, fabric-covered photo albums. They leaned their heads together over the albums, and he slowly worked himself into a snit, fairly vibrating with jealousy and self-pity.

He didn't come here to clean fish. He came here to...what? The fish scales fell like glitter off the edge of the knife, and he remembered teaching Meghan to scale a fish the way his father had taught him, the way she'd been fascinated at the colors as light played against them. Tears—a surprise, he hadn't even felt them come, they just sprang into his eyes the way his mouth watered when he smelled his mother's barbeque sauce—blurred his vision. He stopped scraping; he'd be sure to cut a finger off if he couldn't stop crying.

He used the back of his hand to wipe his eyes and started back on his task, half-listening to Grandmother Tobias talk about his father and his uncle Randy and the trouble they got up to as boys. He'd never been much trouble himself, not the way she was talking about, anyway. He'd never taken the car at thirteen the way she was telling Ada his father had, never been arrested...Well, that was no longer the case, was it?

He had come here to escape, to get Ada somewhere safe. But it didn't seem so safe to him here now. Grandmother seemed more interested in Ada than in him. She looked at him as if he were missing something vital.

He looked over his shoulder at the two women on the sofa, their heads bent close, their voices low. Ada was nodding, her dark hair blurring through his still-watering vision. He wiped again with the back of his wrist, the knife slipping past his nose.

Before he knew it, Ada was beside him, looking down at the fish guts distastefully. He sniffed, trying to hide it by clattering the knife in the sink, but she turned to him and looked up into his eyes.

"You have such a rich, interesting history," she said, reaching up to wipe a scale away from beneath his eye. "You really should learn more about it."

"Yeah, well, I'm in here cleaning fish, aren't I?" he muttered, picking up the knife again. "She doesn't seem to want to tell me."

Ada glanced over at Grandmother Tobias, who was still flipping through photo albums. "She just doesn't think you're ready to hear."

"What the hell is that supposed to mean? I'm not ready? I'm tired of..."

She searched his face. "What?"

He shook his head and hefted a fish in his hand, the weight of it satisfying, the size of it perfect in his hand. "I don't know," he finally said.

Thirteen

I JUMPED when the phone rang in the still kitchen. The caller ID showed Tessa Barker's name, the lawyer Mingus had referred me to. I cast a quick glance out the window before I picked it up to make sure Rhoades and Hernandez's car was out of sight.

Her voice was tight, devoid of any accent, and I couldn't tell how old she was. I could hear heels tapping, and she sounded almost out of breath as she identified herself.

"Charles Mingus suggested I give you a call," I started, hoping that perhaps he'd already filled her in. But all she said was "Uh huh," the heels still tapping quickly.

"I — My son is in trouble, and he's representing him. But my husband and I are being questioned by the police, and I wanted to speak with a lawyer about what I should do."

"What kind of trouble?"

"He and his girlfriend are both charged with several things, including aggravated child abuse with extenuating circumstances and resisting arrest."

"Where's the victim?"

The victim? I thought that perhaps Tessa Barker and Hernandez would get along just fine. "The victim is my daughter. It was an accident. And she's in the hospital, in a coma."

"And you need me why?"

The heel tapping stopped and I heard a thump, followed by the jangle of car keys. "Because the police continue to question me and my husband, and I don't know what's best for us, or for Marshall, and I thought I should talk to someone."

"I'm really not sure what I can do for you," she said, and a car door slammed, a motor turned over. "Why did Charlie send you my way?"

"I don't know," I said in exasperation. "You're obviously too busy to talk to me."

"Look, I just got out of a trial I worked my ass off on for the last five months. And my client ruined everything. So forgive me for my impatience, but I'd like to go pick up my kid and go home and pour a massive scotch, and as you've not been charged with a crime, I don't see how I can help you."

I sat back down in my chair and sighed. "I just wanted a consultation, some advice," I said. "That's all."

"Did they beat her? Your daughter?"

"What? No, I told you, it was an accident. Well, not quite an accident. They gave her a cookie with some peanut butter in it. She's allergic."

"Oh." There was a silence. "Oh. Okay. When can I see you?"

"What?"

"I'll meet you? When is good for you?"

"Why the sudden change?" I asked, mystified.

"I imagine Charlie sent you to me because of my son, Owen. He's allergic."

"Oh," I said. "To what?"

"Everything," she said flatly.

We made plans for her to visit the hospital the next day, and I hung up the phone, drained. I checked the clock. I had been gone for too long, and I remembered my awareness days ago that there would continue to be firsts. This was the first time I'd been gone for this long, but I needed a few minutes to pull myself together.

I checked the refrigerator and found a bottle of wine we'd kept in there for last-minute guests. It had to be at least a year old. I pulled it out, opened it, poured a glass, and took an exploratory sniff. It seemed fine. Taking a sip worked out well, and I walked upstairs to Meghan's room and sat down on her lower bunk, on her pretty, peony sheets.

She'd called them "pee-ony" sheets when she'd first spotted them in the store and fallen in love with the bold reds and oranges of the overblown petals. They didn't smell like her yet, and despite their journey through the washer and dryer, they still smelled new. I huddled against the back post and sipped my wine while I tried to pretend that she was here, that Marshall was just away at college, and that my biggest concern was finding some common ground in my marriage again.

I had looked forward to Marshall graduating and Meghan going off to college. I had thought that Cal and I would have time to fall in love again, as though it had just been put on hold for a little while, but was still there, waiting for us to pick it back up and nourish it back to health. I had counted on it, taken it for granted.

I thought we had time.

I took a deep breath, gulped the rest of the wine, and climbed out of my daughter's bed. It was time to get back to the hospital. To my daughter's new bed, and my new marriage. I had been right all along. New was dangerous. And very, very sad. And I would never let it sneak up on me again.

I tried to decide what I should tell Cal as I drove back to the hospital, and came up with two choices: tell him everything, or tell him nothing at all, and there were valid arguments for both sides. By the time I arrived, I still hadn't decided.

The nurse was showing Cal how to work the controls on the side of Meghan's bed. It took me a moment to figure out what was different. Her respirator. Meghan was off the respirator and it was sitting in the corner, its tubes and cords hanging limply, its digital display dead. Meghan's throat was wrapped in brilliant white gauze.

My hand flew to my chest and everything, *everything*, evaporated: my concern over Marshall, the crazy doctor who put it all in motion, the problems within my marriage, all gone, and I could not help the cry that escaped me.

Cal and the nurse turned in surprise and he caught me as I rushed to the side of her bed, the smile on his face as unguarded as my own feelings had been.

I ran my hand along her forehead and the side of her face, but she was nonresponsive. I stroked her again, whispered, "Baby?"

"No, Chloe, no, they just, the doctor said she could come off the respirator, they're confident she's strong enough. There's no...there's no other change."

I wanted to wail out loud. It was my fault, the hope that had expanded so quickly inside of me, it was my fault. The doctor had told us about the respirator, that it would be coming out, that there was a chance of infection if they left it in and that as soon as she healed enough they would take her off of it.

He had told us, but who thinks rationally about those things, who considers each step until it happens? The people who think rationally about it are the people who have been living with it for long enough that the fog has cleared, the people who have had enough firsts under their belts to think long-term, the people who finally accept that they might live with this situation for years.

I was not ready to be that person.

I would never be ready to be that person.

The nurse bustled around, pulling the sheets taut, keeping her eyes down. I realized I'd had another first, hard on the heels of the last one; they were coming faster now. For the first time, I did not care what the nurse thought of me. What, after all, did they have to judge me against? Other parents? How many marriages did they watch crumble? How many mothers and fathers did they see slowly lose their grip on their sanity?

And so another first; I cried in front of the nurse.

She left the room and I slid out from under Cal's hand.

"It doesn't mean anything," he said, as if he meant to comfort me. At the look I gave him he tried to elaborate. "It doesn't change her prognosis."

"And what is her prognosis, Cal?" I asked. "Nobody can tell us that. Why do you think you know? All I get is a bunch of 'we don't knows' and 'we're still learning' and 'when she's ready.' So are you hearing something I'm not? Are you privy to information I don't have?"

He looked at me blankly. I knew the look. I wasn't going to affect him. I wouldn't get anything out of him, no reaction, positive or negative. He'd gone neutral, which always succeeded in making whatever reaction I had, no matter how measured and reasonable, seem like a nuclear incident.

I needed to tell him about Rhoades and Hernandez, about Marshall and Ada, about the lawyer who would be coming to the hospital tomorrow, but he beat me out with his own news.

"Kevin called," he said. "He can't take my charter tomorrow."

"So did he cancel it?"

He shook his head. "I'm going to go out."

I stared at him. He was going to leave. It hadn't been a week yet, and here it was, the slow shift back to daily life. He was going back to work, to spend his days on the water fishing.

"Don't look at me like that," he said. "What do you want me to do? We still have bills to pay, Chloe, and we're going to have a ton more before any of this resolves itself. We can't do...this, forever."

Ah, but I could. I'd ship every Highwayman painting in mid-restoration back to its owner, would not take another commission from the fine art galleries in Naples, would figure out what to do about the bills.

But I also knew, did not want to admit, but knew, that I could afford to do that. Because, really, Cal did bring in more money, more regularly. What did the mothers do who didn't have a husband to help support them, or who were the main breadwinner for their family? How did they make that shift?

I didn't have to answer that. Because this was my situation, my family, my husband. And I was torn between punishing him for his realism and falling on my knees in gratitude for it. Because it would allow me to stay here, with Meghan, as long as I needed to.

"No sense going all the way home," he said, studiously not looking at me. "I'll just stay on the *Trill*."

"What do you mean you'll stay on the *Trill*?" I repeated.

"It's closer to the hospital than home," he said.

"So, you're not going to stay here overnight?" I asked, ignoring the larger question looming in the back of my mind.

"I have to get up at four in the morning," he said. "I need a decent night's sleep. I think you should get one too."

"I'll be staying here," I said, enunciating each word, pointing to the floor.

"You can't be a martyr forever."

"I'm not being a martyr. I'm being a mother."

"You're being stubborn."

"And you're shutting down so you don't have to hurt over any of this."

"We can't keep doing this."

"What? You want to go down to the chapel and bitch at me there?"

He sighed. "No, I don't mean where. I mean—" He waved his hands between us, as if he were guiding a plane in. "—*this*. We can't keep doing this."

"You know, Cal, people go through hard times. Sometimes they fight through it, but they get through it."

"Believe it or not, Chloe, I've been through tough times before. And we've been going through tough times for a lot longer than just this particular tough time."

My heart was beating so hard in my chest that I could feel it bumping against my ribs, and my breathing was shallow and becoming more so with every moment that I continued to stare at him. "What are you trying to say, Cal? Just say it."

"I'm not trying to say anything. I'm just— Chlo, I'm just going to stay on the *Trill* for a little while, okay? What do you care? I thought you said we didn't have a marriage, and you're not at home anyway."

I didn't say anything. He was right. "Do you want to know about Marshall?" I finally asked, looking away from him, my arms crossed tightly over my chest.

"He home?"

"No. Wait, is that it? You don't want to go home because Marshall is there?"

He hesitated, and I could tell he was weighing something, but I could not tell what it might be, and I ached for that, for the fact that I couldn't read him when he was closed off like this. "No, that's not it."

"Well, I don't know where he is."

"What do you mean?"

I took a deep breath. "He bailed Ada out last night after I dropped him off at home. Nobody's seen him since."

His jaw tightened and he leaned in toward me. "What are you telling me here? He jumped bail?"

I almost laughed. Cal had never been one for cop shows or detective mysteries. I'd never heard him say anything like "jumped bail" in my life. We had grown apart. There was no denying that. Somehow, we had grown apart and not made an effort to change it. Not a real effort. We made token efforts, and I wasn't willing to take all the blame for that, we had *both* only made token efforts. We'd gotten lazy, it was that simple. We'd gotten lazy with our affection.

But I could not help but remember how cute he was when he said something out of the blue, something that surprised me, that arranged his lips in unfamiliar shapes, that reminded me of how much I had wanted to kiss him that first time we'd been aware of each other in the airboat. Attraction was still there, and if that was still there then did that mean there was still hope? Did you really still want to kiss someone if it was over?

I wouldn't know. Cal had certainly not been my first kiss, or even my first lover, but he had certainly been my first love. And yes, absurd as it sounded, him saying "jumped bail" made me want to kiss him.

I didn't.

He was, after all, talking about our son, about whom I was even more conflicted than I was about Cal.

"No," I said. "He didn't *jump bail*. He's not due in court for almost two weeks. For all we know, he's just holed up in some hotel because he's afraid to bring Ada to our house."

"Yeah, he'd better be," Cal said darkly, and all thought of kissing him fled. I had never been, and never would be, attracted to anger against one of my children, no matter how deeply under the surface it simmered. It made things easier. Cal would find out about Marshall and Ada sooner or later. But it wouldn't be from me.

If we were separate but for our physical presence in Meghan's room, then I supposed we would just have to discover what else was happening in our once shared lives on our own. I had Rhoades and Hernandez, I had Mingus and this new lawyer, Barker, and I knew that when Marshall realized he was out of his depth, I would be the one he came to.

Cal was—consciously or subconsciously, I didn't know yet—removing himself from the life of this family. And I wasn't sure I was terribly sorry about it.

"So, you're moving onto the boat."

"For now, Chloe, just to make things easier . . . on all of us."

I nodded. "Fine."

It did not feel monumental. It simply felt sad, and I looked at Meghan, wondering what she heard. We had never hidden our relationship from our children. I had never known if my parents had problems with each other. If they did, they were well hidden from me. Cal and I did not have the kinds of disagreements that needed to be hidden.

I had often thought that in order for our children to realize that something might be wrong with our marriage, they would have had to develop more finely tuned sensibilities. They had not yet appeared to realize that their parents existed outside of their lives.

But if Meghan had heard what was happening in her room over the past five days, she could not help but know that her parents were in trouble. Even a girl in a coma could tell that we were falling apart. I motioned to Cal.

"Can we talk in the chapel?" I asked.

He looked at Meghan. "Could you give me a minute?"

"I'll meet you down there," I said, and walked out the door. Almost ten minutes later Cal eased himself into the pew beside me.

"We have to come to some sort of understanding," I said quietly.

"About what, Chloe?" He sounded exhausted. But so was I.

"About how we're going to handle this. We can't talk in front of Meghan as if she can't hear."

"Do you really think she can?" he asked. I almost snapped at him, but when I saw his face I realized that he was asking the question earnestly, as if he truly wanted to know my ideas on it.

"Everybody tells us she can. I think we just have to stop thinking about her as asleep. She's not asleep. She's in there."

He shook his head. "I don't get it."

"I don't either, but when she does wake up, do you want her to remember that while she was lying there we did nothing but fight?"

He turned toward me, the rough seam of his old jeans rubbing my knee through my thin cotton skirt, and then leaned in, closing us off from the empty room, from the glass gaze of the dove.

"Do you really, really believe she'll wake up, Chloe?" His voice was pleading.

"Yes," I whispered. "Yes, I do. I'm so sorry you don't."

His shoulders slumped and his leg moved away from mine. "Me too," he said. He left, taking his bag with him. Before he did, he leaned over the back of the pew and kissed the top of my head. His mouth connected this time, and as he pressed his lips against my hair, I breathed in deeply of him.

MARSHALL

Ada placed her hand on his wrist and he dropped the knife. He wasn't exactly sure what they had just agreed to, but he was as terrified as he'd been in that boat. Ada looked into the living room.

"Why don't you go sit down with your grandmother? I'll finish this."

"It's not as easy as it looks," he said. "Besides, do you really want to touch fish guts?"

"I had a life before I became a vegetarian, Marshall," Ada said with a grin. "Believe it or not, I've done this before."

He remembered her ease hooking the worm, how quickly she'd picked up casting, how she managed to unhook a fish and release it without flinching. He wondered what else he didn't know about her. He thought they knew everything about each other.

But he hadn't been completely honest either, had he? This was the first she'd heard about his grandfather, the first time she'd heard about this family at all really. He hadn't told her about his grandparents, and she hadn't asked. The first time he'd told her about Ira had been on the drive down.

So she hadn't told him about being born in Canada. There was no crime in being Canadian. And she hadn't told him about what her life was like in the other states she'd lived in. Still no crime. But there was no question that he was starting to wonder about what else he didn't know.

She took the knife from him, gently moving against him until she was standing in front of the sink. He breathed her in, and then joined his grandmother on the sofa.

"Hey," he said.

"Well hey yourself, son," she said. "That girl of yours is a real firecracker, isn't she?"

He laughed. "Yeah, she is. She likes you."

"Hmmm, well, she don't know me yet, really. I know I'm a tough one to get on with sometimes."

"I don't know," he said. "You seem all right to me."

"What's your daddy told you about me?"

"Nothing much," he admitted. "I got the feeling there was some kind of fight—"

"Wasn't no fight."

"Well, I don't really know then."

She nodded. "It's hard to hear about where we come from sometimes. Sometimes people think they have to get away from their people. Your girl there, she seems like she wants to get back to her people."

"She does," he said with a nod. "She comes from solid people, people of faith."

"Mmm hmm, she mentioned that. She knows her Bible, that's for certain."

"She's helping me to know it better."

"You know, you want to know your Bible better, you can come to me."

"I didn't—"

"Why don't you tell me what kind of trouble you're in, son? What are you two runnin' from?"

"We're not running."

"I raised two boys. I know when one's in trouble. And, your Ada, she's got a spark, I can see that. But she's not in the same kind of trouble."

"I don't know what you're saying, I don't know what you mean," he said desperately.

"You got some kind of trouble of the conscience. That one's got trouble in her soul. You got trouble can be taken care of. Hers, I'm not so sure."

He stared into the kitchen. He could just see a bit of Ada's hair, her shoulder, a slender leg cocked to the side as she worked over the fish.

"I'm in love with her," he said.

She nodded. "Oh sure, I can see that much."

"She loves me."

"Your folks like her?"

"Yeah," he said, his face flushing. He could feel Grandmother Tobias's steady gaze on him. He couldn't look at her.

"Calvin ever tell you about your granddaddy?"

"Just that he was a minister," he said, relieved that she'd dropped the subject of Ada. He wouldn't leave them alone again.

"You ever seen any pictures?"

"Just the ones in your hallway. My dad looks just like him, doesn't he?"

"He does. Randy takes after my side more. Now here," she said, opening up a heavy, blue, cloth-covered photo album across his knees, and pointing to the first photo, a black-and-white group shot taken in front of a tiny house with a single window. "These are your granddaddy's people. He's right here." She touched a shaky finger to the brittle, yellow plastic protecting the photo, pointing to a lanky teenager with a nearly shaved head, wearing a short-sleeved dress shirt and squinting somewhere beyond the camera.

He looked strong, as though his lankiness, his casual stance was hiding long, lean muscles ready to burst into action. He looked...tested, proven somehow. He was clearly younger than Marshall was, but he seemed more of a man than Marshall had ever felt.

It made him ashamed of his soft life, of his freedom to choose how he spent his days. It made him ache to run a plow behind a horse, to fish for dinner because he had to, not for sport, to have dirt creased into his calloused hands. He felt spoiled by the heaviness of the cell phone in his pocket, his electronics-filled dorm room, the classes he took.

The classes he used to take.

He felt a sudden cramp in his middle, and he hunched over as his grandmother turned the page in the photo album, touching the hard faces of his ancestors, pointing out everything he wasn't.

Ada brought them both tall glasses of lemonade, and then took her own out to the backyard, where Marshall saw her stretch out in the grass, apparently unconcerned about the dogs. He couldn't tell if she was gazing up at the sky or closing her eyes, but he knew that what she was really doing was giving him time with Grandmother Tobias, and they stayed on the sofa looking through album after album for almost two hours.

She told short anecdotes about the people, occasionally telling the same one over again whenever she came upon the same face. But the one he sought out in all of the pictures was his grandfather. He watched him change from the hard teen into a hard man, with his parents and siblings, fishing, driving, preaching in front of small groups of men as hard as he.

Finally he had his own wife by his side, Grandmother Tobias, looking much like she did now, he saw in amazement. Yes, she'd gotten older, much older, but everything was recognizable, the shape of her face and eyes, the gaze direct and knowing, the body sturdy and capable as a man's. And then the children, two boys who grew tall, their eyes less hard when they were young, both of them looking uncertain and wary.

Until the pictures progressed to their early teens, the photos turning from black-and-white to color, that was when they finally changed, when they grew shuttered. Even in the photos that showed them at play, in a canoe or with long shotguns cradled in their arms, posing over gutted deer or fowl, their faces were inscrutable.

The album ended abruptly, blank pages for the last half of it, and Grandmother Tobias pulled out a final, slim one, covered in vinyl, and slid it onto his lap. To his surprise, it was filled with pictures of his own family. Mostly of him at first, baby pictures, photos of him tearing open Christmas presents, school photos. There was an occasional one of him with his father, and after staring at photos of the males of his father's family, he was struck by how alike they all looked.

He could even, for the first time, see his grandfather, his uncle, and his father in his own face, his own eyes. And like his father and uncle, his photos changed at some point. He flipped the pages back and forth, looking for the exact moment it happened, and, at last, he thought he found it. He remembered the day at school that it had been taken, remembered the shirt that drove him crazy because of the high collar, it had made him feel as if he'd had a noose around his neck, as if it were keeping the air from filling his lungs completely.

But Shelly Williams, an eighth-grader with long blonde hair and the astonishing beginnings of a chest, had once told him that his arms looked good in it, and he wanted to make sure he was immortalized wearing it.

It was *before* Ira died.

If he had ever been asked to point to a defining moment in his life, he would have pointed to Ira and the train. Would have talked about seeing him hit, how he saw Ira place the penny on the tracks, saw it tip off the edge, catching the sun and blinking bright and gold and copper for a half second as Ira darted away. And saw the thing that everyone asked about later. Saw Ira turn back, even as the train bore down, saw him *turn back* to right the penny, saw him fall over his own clumsy feet, in the brand-new, too-big Nikes he got just the day before, an early bar mitzvah present.

He didn't remember reaching for him, but he must have, because when the train hit Ira—hit him as though he were soft as a pillow, as though he had never had bones—the rush of wind from the train knocked him off his own feet. When he fell, blinded by the swirl of grit and dust kicked up by the hungry metal wheels, he ripped his shirt, a jagged tear that exposed the right side of his chest. He didn't remember how it happened. Later, all he remembered was the wink of the penny.

And he had been profoundly changed. Everyone around him looked at him differently, and in the mirror he looked different to himself.

But this photo had been taken before that day. Bewildered, he flipped the pages again, but yes, he remembered that photo very well, because of Shelly Williams, because of the irritating neckline, and because it had been that shirt, the same shirt that he'd torn the day that Ira died.

And he'd already changed.

Grandmother Tobias had been talking during Marshall's frantic page-flipping, but he'd barely heard what she said, something about his mother sending the photos, but rarely any proper letters, and how her own letters went unanswered and how her son had forsaken her. Long, rambling, righteous talk that reminded him of when she'd sat at the table and told them that she'd not have whores and fornicators in her house.

He turned the page again. Meghan had started showing up. Baby pictures, pink blankets, tiny hair bows that he remembered his mother struggling to fasten with Velcro in Meghan's fine hair. School pictures, Meghan's eyes already sad, long before she had anything remotely like Ira happen to her.

She'd never had anything like that happen to her.

But then, nothing like that had really happened to *him*, had it? After all, he was not the one hit by the train. In fact, nothing had ever really happened *to* him. And Meghan had. She'd almost died when she was little more than a baby.

He hadn't been home when the babysitter gave her the peanut butter. He'd been at school. All he'd been told was that she'd gotten sick, and then his parents were busy with her. He hadn't been jealous; in fact, he'd felt heady with independence. He spent a lot of time with Ira and his parents, sure, but he'd also taken care of himself. He'd felt grown-up.

Photos started appearing that he didn't recognize, photos without him in them, photos with his father and Meghan, rarely ones of his mother, but of course she'd been the one behind the camera. Meghan grew up within a few pages, and the last one in the book was her current school photo, her eyes wide, as if someone had surprised her just as the camera went off.

It wasn't a great picture. And he knew Meghan hated it. She was so sensitive. A splotch appeared on the plastic over her face, and he hastily wiped it away, hanging his head and turning away from his grandmother so she wouldn't see him crying. He closed the photo album as she noted that Meghan looked like her mother, but that she'd gotten her father's nose.

He nodded, agreeing with the genetics lottery, letting her talk, and stared out the window at Ada, her better knee bent up into the sun, her bandaged one hidden in the thick grass.

"You told Ada that we weren't going on the same road together," he said, interrupting her.

She stopped talking and was silent for a moment before nodding, slowly. "That's true. That's what I believe."

"Why?"

"Because that's what God told me."

"God told you that?"

"That's right."

"What else did God tell you?"

She looked at him steadily for a second, her eyes full of certainty and what felt to him like a solid judgment, heavy, pushing against him, knowing that he was questioning her.

"You're in trouble, son. I know that. Don't know exactly what it is, but I imagine I'll be finding out soon enough. That one there," she said, nodding out the window, "she's something different from you. She's got trouble, too, but she's...alone with herself. She's alone, Marshall, and that means she's not with you."

He wanted to protest. Not against Ada being alone, but at the assumption that he wasn't. The only times he hadn't felt alone were the times he'd been with Ada, the times he'd held her, the times they had prayed together.

He'd always been alone.

"What did God tell you about me, besides me being in trouble?" he asked, hating the quiver in his voice.

"Well, that's something between me and God, I guess," she said. She patted his back and hauled herself off the sofa. Marshall winced as her joints cracked and studied her as she limped into the kitchen with their empty glasses. "She did a right good job on these fish," she called to him, and again, he considered what he didn't know about Ada.

He opened the photo album to the last page to look at Meghan and her sad eyes, and wondered how alone she felt.

Fourteen

AGAIN, after Cal left I tried to resume some sort of normal relationship with Meghan. It was easier now, without the respirator, though everything else was still hooked up, the catheter, the GI tube, and the transducer. Still, things seemed different without the respirator. The nurse brought me a shower cap, an ingenious little thing that she heated in the microwave and had a no-rinse shampoo built into it. I washed Meghan's hair, trying to believe that somehow she felt and enjoyed the pressure of my fingertips against her skull, knew that it was me and felt safe.

Years ago, after they called off the search for my parents' boat, effectively declaring them dead, I spent days curled up in bed. Cal never entreated me to get up, and he never appeared surprised or irritated when he came home and found that I hadn't moved all day. Instead, he came home from work on the fourth day, still smelling of the Gulf and sunscreen, and kissed me gently on the forehead before he went to the bathroom and ran hot water in the tub.

He lifted me from the bed and stood me in the tub, drawing

the T-shirt of my father's that I had been sleeping in over my head, and then silently lowered me into the water. It was so hot that it stung, driving the breath from my lungs as I sank down, but I never flinched. And when my chest slid under the water, finally extinguishing every bit of oxygen from my body, it was as though I were born again, taking in a great gulp of air, as if it were my first on this Earth without my parents in it.

He'd let me soak, changing the sheets on the bed, laying out a new T-shirt, one of his, on the bed, before coming back in and cupping the back of my head to support it while he dipped it beneath the water, then raised me up and lathered my hair with strawberry-scented shampoo. His fingers on my scalp made things start to make sense again.

I hoped that would happen for Meghan. For the first time in my life I did not bemoan my bitten-short nails. I knew I wasn't hurting her, pressing my fingertips through the plastic of the bathing cap. I wasn't afraid to use some pressure, and I watched her forehead move with my ministrations, pulling her eyebrows, tugging her eyelids up. She looked alternately hopeful and surprised, and I fully expected her lids to fly open at any moment.

It did not happen.

And that was okay. That was okay for the moment. Because I had this project, this cleaning up to take care of, the way I hadn't been allowed since she'd turned eight. I pulled off the cap and towel-dried her hair, letting it fall in wavy wisps around her face.

One of the nurses helped me bathe her, using the same sort of no-rinse bathing cloths, and she showed me how I could do this myself next time—how to hold her up, how to use my own body as a prop for hers. It was easier than I would have thought. She was still so small, so light.

We dressed her in a new gown, and then the nurse left and I did

Meghan's nails. Meghan had just recently started getting interested in the feminine side of life. She'd spent so long trying to catch up to Marshall, chasing after her daddy, and she had been rightly called a tomboy. But along with developing her flirtatious glances, she'd also begun pilfering nail polish and lipstick from my jumbled drawer of rarely used beauty products.

And so I painted her feminine. I glided the shiniest shell pink I could find across her nails, reacquainting myself with these little bits of her, remembering how I'd held her feet in my hands and kissed her toes until she screamed with delighted laughter when she was a toddler, how amazed Cal had been with the sharpness of her tiny fingernails when she was an infant. We'd had such fun with her when she was a baby, so thrilled when she came along so many years after Marshall, an accident we joked at first.

I hadn't even known I'd wanted another baby until I was already pregnant. It was heavenly to enjoy those nine months the way I hadn't when I was pregnant with Marshall. I'd been so convinced that something was going to go wrong with him, and I exhausted the library books about all the rare ailments and desperate situations of childbirth.

After Cal paged through a couple of them, he'd looked at me in horror and then refused to allow me to read any more. I had resorted to sneaking them up to my studio and reading them on the sly. I thought that if I were prepared, if I knew what the tiniest symptom might mean, then I would have time to save my baby.

I blew on Meghan's nails, as if she might move and smudge her polish, and knew that no matter how many books I'd read about food allergies I could never have predicted this. I couldn't possibly have known that Ada was a symptom, a glaring one.

"If you opened your eyes, you could see what a fabulous mani and pedi I just gave you," I said to Meghan. "Heck, this is probably a perfect opportunity to pluck your eyebrows, isn't it? That'll make you open your eyes." I grinned, looking at her thick eyebrows, carbon copies of my own at that age. I'd finally plucked them myself, badly, at thirteen, mortifying my mother and sending my father into paroxysms of laughter.

I ran my finger across Meghan's, and then suddenly leaned forward and whispered fiercely into her ear, "Dammit, Meghan, open your eyes. Come on! Open your eyes, baby, please. Do it!"

Nothing.

I sniffed, not even aware that I had begun to cry. "You look so pretty, sweetie," I said. "When you're through all this, we'll get your hair cut. And—"

A soft knock at the door startled me, and before I could say anything it opened a crack, then slowly eased forward just enough that I recognized Sandy. I jumped from the chair and met her at the door, as reluctant to allow her in Meghan's room as I'd been to allow Hernandez and Rhoades into my home.

"Chloe," she whispered. She looked into my eyes, not trying to look past me to Meghan. "I—is this a bad time?"

What was I supposed to say to that? Was it a bad time? Could there be a worse time? Her shoulders rounded and her chest caved in as she sighed.

"Such a stupid question," she said.

I nodded. Yes, it was a stupid question. And I had thought that I would never want to see Sandy again, but there was suddenly nothing in the world, besides seeing Meghan open her eyes, that I wanted more than to have a friend, and Sandy was the closest thing to a friend I'd had in years. If she'd held her arms out, I would have fallen into them.

"Come on," I said and opened the door. It felt as though a sweet breeze came with her.

She stepped across the threshold without hesitation, as though she were a nurse, a doctor, someone well acquainted with hospitals and broken people. And when I closed the door and turned to her, she did open her arms, and I did fall into them.

But it was brisker than I imagined. I did not cry, and she did not rock me as a mother might a child. Instead she squeezed tightly enough that I felt compressed, and then lighter when she released me, as if I'd just cracked my back after a long day bent over a painting.

She held my shoulders in her hands and scrunched down to peer into my face, searching for I didn't know what. I felt embarrassed, as if she were about to kiss me, and my gaze slid to the side, toward Meghan.

"You look okay," she finally stated, releasing me. "Tired, but okay."

"Well, I've been sleeping in that," I said ruefully, pointing to the recliner. She didn't bother looking at it.

"Cal?"

I was torn. A part of me ached to be petulant, to explain how he had left me here, left me alone with our daughter, left me alone to take care of Marshall's situation. But even as the wailing sentences formed in my mind I knew I couldn't do it. I could paint him a monster in my head because I knew I could change my mind, and because I needed that target, but I could not paint him a monster for someone else, no matter how pathetic I felt.

"He's on the boat," I said. "I told him to go."

She nodded. "Kevin told me he was taking a tour for him tomorrow. I imagine all this is going to be pretty expensive."

I didn't know what to say to that. Yes. Of course it was. And what do you do about that? Tell them to stop?

"We've been taking up collections," Sandy said, reaching into her purse.

"Oh, no," I said. One hand covered my mouth and the other reached out to stop her from going any further. I did not want to see an envelope stuffed with the creased bills of fishermen and housewives, of the neighbors we barely knew and the parents of my children's classmates. No, this was not a step I was willing to take.

She looked up at me in surprise. "We thought—"

"I know, I know." I slumped into the chair Cal had been using and covered my face with my hands. "I—thank you, Sandy. That's such an amazing thing to do, and I don't mean to seem ungrateful. I just— I don't think we need it yet. I mean, there are so many people who do. We always try to give to St. Matthew's or the Guadalupe Center in Immokalee. Maybe you should give it to them."

She tilted her head, much like a puzzled puppy that can't understand why you wouldn't want your shoe vigorously chewed upon. But she didn't argue and pulled her hand from her purse before sitting in the recliner next to Meghan and finally looking at her.

"I think I've gone about this the wrong way," she murmured. "And I'm sorry. Again. Chloe? What do you need? Tell me how I can help. Please?"

I considered that. People say those things a lot in a crisis. And you answer in nothings. You say things like *Pray*, or *I don't think there's anything*, or *We're just glad you're here*. But the truth is that we want people to intuit what we need and then just do it. We want people to see our needs as easily as they would hear us if we cried them out loud. Don't you *see* what I need?

How often are solid answers given to these inquiries?

I sighed. "I need Meghan to open her eyes. I need to find my son. I need to read my husband's mind. I need to go home and climb in bed and pretend that none of this is happening," I said softly. "I need for this to be over."

Sandy pulled her lower lip into her mouth and held it there. It was as good as biting her tongue, I imagined.

"I can't do any of that," she finally said, as though we had agreed on something. "What else?" she asked.

I gestured at Meghan. "Ask me about my daughter."

She looked at her and considered. She took in every detail, and I felt some sort of satisfaction for that. *Yes,* I thought, *bear witness, maybe this is what I need. See her.*

"How is Meghan?" she asked.

"I have no idea," I admitted. "Nobody does. Her body seems to be recovering. But we have no idea if she'll wake up. And if she does, there are no guarantees that she'll even be...Meghan. If she'll have lost motor control, language, everything, or nothing. All of this," I said, waving my arm around the room, "seems temporary. But it might not be. I might just sit here for the rest of my life. Well, that's not completely true. They won't let us stay here forever. At some point they'll want us to move somewhere else. A nursing facility or something."

She nodded. "What do they think the chances are that she'll wake up?"

I shrugged. "They give us statistics, but everyone seems very careful to make sure that we know that they can't tell us. A neuropsychologist from Miami has been in once to evaluate her and talk to us. But he says it's too early to know anything. I keep asking her to open her eyes."

"I wonder if that helps," Sandy said. "May I?"

"Go ahead," I said, and watched as she leaned in toward Meghan and talked to her.

"Meghan, it's Sandy. Now, come on. Open up your eyes. Your mom misses you. Everybody misses you. Now open your eyes and look at me."

I stood and walked over to Meghan's other side, and we talked to her together, imploring, and cajoling, and making vague threats about missing school and good meals and fishing trips.

And nothing happened. But at least there was someone else there for nothing to happen to. At least there was someone who simply shared this part of it with me, this part that seemed so pointless when I did it alone. And in a way, it was like praying, and I started to understand why people gathered together to pray, why two voices were better than one, and suddenly I was filled with hope that an entire congregation, small though it was, was praying for Meghan every Sunday.

"Sandy," I said, "I think I know how you can help."

"Just tell me," she said.

"When y'all say a prayer for us, for Meghan, could you be specific? Ask for her to open her eyes? Just...open her eyes."

I called Cal twice that night. We said little, but I heard anguish in his voice, and I don't imagine I was able to keep it out of mine either. I continued to try Marshall, both at home and on his cell phone, leaving brief messages, and finally I slept, just Meghan and I and the endless stream of nurses in and out.

Waking early was no longer a problem for me, and I was showered and dressed when Tessa Barker arrived. She was too young to look as tired as she did. She was slight enough that I wondered if she had an eating disorder, but her grip on my hand when she shook proved there was no weakness there, no frailty. She might not have much meat on her bones, but the bones themselves were like steel.

Unlike Sandy, she went right to Meghan's bedside and stood looking down at her with an indecipherable expression. "So this is Meghan. How long has it been?"

I wasn't sure what she meant by "it," but I assumed she meant the coma. "A week now," I said. "Not that long, according to the doctors." Sandy's visit the previous day had brought me back to the idea of time, and despite the fact that it seemed as though Meghan's eyes had been closed for years, it had been, indeed, only a week.

"A week," she repeated, then raised her voice and said, "Meghan, I'm Tessa Barker, and I'm here to talk to your mom. You go ahead and listen in, and if you have something to add, if we're getting something wrong, I want you to open up your eyes and let us know. My son's name is Owen and he has allergies, like you. I don't want this to happen to him, Meghan, and I know you don't either, so I want you to come on back to us as soon as you can and give us a hand, okay?"

For a moment, I was shocked. She'd not asked, as Sandy had, to speak to her. She'd not gotten the lowdown on treatment or expectations from me yet. Maybe I didn't want her yelling at my daughter. But following quickly on the heels of my shock was a vast relief. Good. Yes, let Meghan hear as many people around her as possible demanding that she return.

A good child, who followed directions, that was Meghan. I'd always told her that following directions might save her life one day. But maybe I had been wrong about how that would come about. Maybe I needed to stop asking, and start telling her how to do it. Maybe I needed to give her directions to follow.

Tessa Barker turned to me next. "Tell me."

And so I did. I told her more than I should have. I told her about my fears while pregnant with Marshall, I told her about Ira, and about Cal's family, and even about my family. And she just sat there and listened. She never took her eyes off me, and she never interrupted. When I paused, she simply waited, when I choked telling her about seeing Meghan on the boat she just gazed at me, when

I told her about Rhoades and Hernandez she made notes without looking at her notebook, and when I finished she was silent until she was sure I was done.

"I talked to Charlie this morning," she said. "He says he thinks Marshall skipped town."

"I don't know," I said. "I hoped he was just at a hotel or something. He hasn't called me back, but I imagine he's scared. I don't know where to look, and I can't take much time away from being here."

"Okay. What do you think I can help you with?"

I shrugged helplessly. "I don't really know. I just felt as though I was being railroaded into indicting my son, making him take the blame for this, and I wanted to know how I should talk to these detectives."

She leaned forward in the chair, her sharp elbows on her hard little knees. I wondered if all that bone meeting bone hurt. "Why *don't* you blame, Marshall, Chloe? What if someone you didn't know did this? What if some guy, who you barely knew, purposefully gave Meghan a peanut butter cookie?"

I am not an idiot. Perhaps these people thought I was, to defend my son, to defend the person who was, I admit, partially responsible for this. But the fact was, he wasn't some guy I barely knew. He was my son, as surely as Meghan was my daughter, and how did I choose which one to protect? Were they not both worthy of my protection? Was that not my most important job as a mother? To protect my children?

"But he's not," I said. "He is my son, and I can't understand this sudden objectivity everyone seems to have about that. As if that's changed. How many children do you have, Ms. Barker?"

"Owen is my only child," she replied.

"And how old is he?"

"He'll be five this summer."

"And do you love him?"

She looked at me with distaste. "Do I love him? What kind of question is that? He is my world."

"Of course he is," I said. "And I think that for parents of an only child it might be hard to imagine that you could possibly love another child as much, with that same intensity. But you do, it just happens, you can't help it. They both need my help right now, and I couldn't possibly choose between them. And I don't see why I should have to."

She nodded. "I can see that, but aren't you angry with him? I don't know if my love could overcome my anger at seeing my child like this."

"Of course I'm angry. I am so furious with him it scares me. But no, it doesn't change my love for him. What would change your love for Owen?"

She looked at Meghan and didn't answer.

"What is he allergic to?"

She rattled off a list long enough to daze me, and when she finished I felt like crying. I knew what she was facing, trying to let this child live in the world at large, trying to get him through the school system, trying to make his friends—if he could develop any—and their families understand, the fear whenever he was out of her sight.

"What are you going to do about school?" I asked her. She shook her head.

"I've gone to three kindergartens so far. I'm considering homeschooling."

"Do you worry about his social life if you homeschool?" I was always curious about this. I had wanted Meghan to be as fully integrated with society as she could be, and, in truth, I had not trusted myself or Cal to be social enough to give her the interaction she needed to become a happy adult. Though she was an outsider at school already. Perhaps what I had given her instead was a massive inferiority complex.

"Of course," she said. "But what can I do? When I explain the extent, the number of things he can't come in any contact with, they just look at me in horror. I can practically see their brains working out how they can possibly get all of their teachers and students and employees to change their lives around one little boy."

I was nodding along with her as she spoke. We'd gone through it all, and Meghan wasn't allergic to half the things this little boy was.

"And things are bound to start getting litigious over this stuff. Look at what's happening right here," she said. "It's not going to be much of a leap from a criminal case to a civil case, and once schools and individuals start getting sued, nobody's going to want to deal with it."

It was my turn to not know what to say. I couldn't think of anything that would make it easier on her. All I could think about was trying to make things easier on my own family, and me, and I hadn't been able to come up with a single idea to accomplish that.

"Is Owen's father in the picture?" I asked, simply to make conversation, cover the awkwardness. And how funny was that? In most situations, asking about an apparently absent father would create an awkward conversation. With us, it served as a pressure valve.

She shook her head. "No, not really." She left it at that and I didn't push it.

"And how do you know Mingus?"

She smiled. "His son is in the same day care as mine. It's just five kids, so all the parents know each other."

There was no question that there was interest there, and even in the middle of everything happening, in and out of this hospital room, it brought a smile to my lips. Nothing changed, not really. There is always romance, there is always sex, there is, and always will be, attraction. And in the beginning, it is so lovely, even when it's not you that the loveliness is happening to, even when what is happening to you is the very opposite of loveliness.

"So, tell me again," she finally said, "what can I do for you?"

"Well, I'm nervous about talking to these people by myself."

"So you just want someone beside you whenever you talk to anyone about Marshall and Meghan?"

"Yes," I said firmly.

"Marshall's lawyer could do that," she said.

"I want someone objective. I want someone who has my entire family's best interests at heart, not just Marshall's."

She looked at me searchingly and took a long look at Meghan again.

"Yeah, okay, I'll do it. Do you have contact information for—" She consulted her notes. "—Hernandez and Rhoades?"

I riffled through my purse and handed her their business cards. She copied the information down and gave them back to me. "I'll contact them and let them know that if they want to talk to you they'll need to make an appointment with me. Now, I'd like to ask you to do something for me."

I nodded. "Of course. What is it?" I asked, expecting her to lay down some rules, some instructions that would protect my family and me.

She looked at Meghan. "I don't know anyone else with a child with food allergies. I belong to an online forum and have gotten some great information there, but to talk, really talk to someone who's been through it, it's different. Could you keep me posted on what's happening here? And, could I call you once in a while? If I had a question, or something."

Does it make me a bad person that I wanted to say no and then curl up in a ball and go to sleep? I couldn't, of course. But I wanted to. After all, I was asking for her support, but it was her job and I was paying her. What she was asking was, would I be her friend?

And a friend was a responsibility. One I wasn't sure I wanted to take on right now. Sandy was different. She was a friend I could lean on, while Tessa was asking to lean on me. I couldn't imagine that I was going to be able to support that particular weight now, or anytime in the near future.

But at least she was asking outright. At least it wasn't taken for granted that I would, the way the added peripheral responsibilities of wifedom and motherhood eventually turned into silent assumptions.

It was nice to be asked. And so I said yes. She gave me several business cards, and before she left she held Meghan's hand for a moment and told her that it had been nice to meet her, and that the next time she saw her she was looking forward to seeing what color her eyes were.

After she left I went down to the chapel and tried Marshall again, unsuccessfully, then called Charles Mingus and left a message on his machine that I'd spoken with Tessa, and he was right, I did like her. I sat gazing at the dove for a moment, acknowledging the fact that I was able to leave Meghan's room without pause now, acknowledging the grief that came with that...and that was then so quickly gone.

I sat in the cafeteria to eat my lunch and made notes about Meghan and her treatment while I ate a bean sprouts and turkey sandwich. I would have liked to complain to someone about the food, the way you complained about airline food, as common a conversation as any. But, in fact, the cafeteria food was delicious. Different every day, fresh, a surprising variety, and incredibly reasonable.

If I worked close by, I thought I would probably come to the hospital cafeteria by choice for lunch, but then a man who had to be in his seventies shuffled by me on a walker and fell heavily into a chair just a table away. He pulled out a cell phone and fumbled with it, sighing in frustration, before finally making his call and telling the person on the other end that things didn't look good.

A reasonable lunch was not worth the contagious misery and grief. I was not here for a pleasurable lunch break. I finished my sandwich, tasteless now, and gathered my notes.

Meghan had been shifted when I returned. I checked my notes and remembered my idea to give her directions, and began my self-devised treatment in the same no-nonsense voice I had used when we taught her how to use her EpiPen. First I shut off the lights and closed the blinds, making the room nearly as dark as it was at night.

I pulled the chair as close to her bedside as I could get it and took a deep breath, silently said a short prayer, and *believed*. I had broken down the steps the same way I broke down colors to their individual components in order to make a perfect match in a fifty-year-old painting. What is the base, what is the tone, the tint?

And we began.

"Okay, Meghan, I want you to think about waking up. I know it feels good to sleep, it feels good to keep your eyes closed, you think it might hurt to open them. But things are nice and dark and cool in here. It's not going to hurt to open your eyes. It's already mid-afternoon and you've slept too long, but there's lots of time to just laze around in bed. Wouldn't it feel good to stretch, and to get something good to eat? I'm going to make pancakes, and you'll get lots of butter and maple syrup.

"There's a television right at the end of your bed, and all we're going to do is sit here together and watch some TV. So, do you feel your eyelids twitch? Right there. Feel that?"

I reached out and gently pushed up the outside corners of her eyes with my index fingers, fluttering them.

"See, it's not too bright in here, it's not too bright." I brushed my fingertips across her eyelashes, tickling her eyelids, in truth, trying to irritate them open. If she couldn't open her eyes, then maybe she'd lift a hand, a finger to brush me away. I lightly tickled across her cheeks, the end of her nose, hoping that she'd feel me as if I were a swarm of no-see-ums flying about her face.

"Raise your eyebrows," I commanded her. "Come on, raise your eyebrows and your eyelids will follow. You can open your eyes. I need you to open your eyes now, Meghan."

Nothing made any sort of difference. No muscle twitch, no wrinkle of her nose, no crease in her forehead. Nothing. I kept trying and didn't bother stopping when the nurses came in. They indicated a sort of silent approval, slight dips of their heads, and then quickly left me to it when their jobs were done. One even said, "Good," before she left.

When Cal arrived, I was taking a break, as tired as if I'd been working on a painting all day. He came in with a large bag from an electronics store in town, and after greeting me quietly he began to unpack it, making little comments as he pulled each item out.

First was a small CD/DVD player, followed by Meghan's stack of Winona Ryder movies, then brand-new CDs in their maddeningly secure shrink wrap.

"I thought that maybe, I don't know," he said as he unboxed the DVD player, "if she's listening, maybe she'd like to listen to something besides doctors and nurses and her parents talking about her."

I was ashamed that I'd not thought of anything like that myself. The only items that could be called personal in the room were my purse and books and the quickly wilting arrangement Sandy had sent.

I immediately made a mental list of other things I could bring in, but realized that none might be able to reach my daughter the way the things Cal had brought could. As he got it all set up, fitting headphones on his head first to adjust the volume and then gently finding the right spot for them on Meghan, I realized that perhaps this meant that Cal had rethought his conviction that our daughter would not wake.

As if sensing my thoughts, Cal got *Beetlejuice* set up in the machine and then sat down and spoke softly. "Good trip today. These guys knew what they were doing already, didn't need much from me but a boat, so I got to fish, got to think."

He stopped and looked down in his lap, rubbing his hands together as if applying lotion. I could hear his rough skin rasping, remembered its feel on my own smooth skin and wondered if I would ever feel it again.

"You know, I kind of thought: Does it matter?"

"Does it matter?" I repeated. "I don't know what you mean." I did not want to assume anything, because what I was already assuming was not only not flattering, but was raising my all-too-familiar flags of anger at Cal. *Does it matter?*

"Don't get me wrong, yeah, it matters a lot that she's here, that this happened at all. But, even if I'm sort of having a hard time with…whatever, hope, I suppose, should what I'm willing to do be any different than if I wasn't?"

I had to take apart what he was saying. Cal could be willfully obscure at times, but the times that he spoke of the important things in our lives, he was obscure without malice, his words caught in his feelings like a bird in fishing line, and I had to slowly, carefully unravel things if I wanted to get to his meaning and intent.

I had often felt like a detective in our marriage. And that was not a complaint. I enjoyed the slowing down of our altercations, the time it forced me to take to understand each word, the time it gave me to formulate my own responses. In our home, fights were quick and then quickly over, whether they were resolved or not.

But the discussions, the real ones, they were often slow enough to last until the early morning hours. And in most cases, by the end of them we, or at least I, felt as though we had reached some new level of understanding of ourselves and each other and how a marriage, our marriage anyway, worked. We hadn't had one of those discussions in a very long time, and I did not know why, but I had a sneaking suspicion that it might have been at least fifty percent my fault.

It was another example of the loss of "try" in our relationship. And I realized, as I untangled, and sorted, and considered, that he was acknowledging that too, only with Meghan. Perhaps he did not believe, but he was willing, perhaps even needed, to act as though he did.

I nodded. "Okay. Good. I started really working on her to open her eyes today," I said. "Maybe between us we can get something."

He nodded, and we had sealed something new. Our differences over Marshall were still on the table, as was our marriage, but on Meghan, we seemed to finally agree in some basic way.

"So tell me about the trip," I said, leaning back and closing my eyes. I hadn't asked for a fishing story in a long time. I used to ask him to tell me about his day every night when we climbed in bed, falling asleep to his deep voice vibrating through my pillow the way my father's bedtime stories of Euclid and Aristotle used to.

And I did fall asleep in my recliner, the lights on bright overhead, with images of Cal, shirtless, fishing rod in hand. He was doing the thing that he was meant to do in this life, coming to epiphanies, decisions, resolutions, surrounded by the things he loved most, birds and fish and gators, mangroves and cypress and water.

He didn't spend that night on the boat, but stayed with me after I woke, and we watched Winona Ryder movies with our daughter, hoping for a movie ending, and holding hands across her still body, ignoring everything outside her room.

MARSHALL

Dinner had been quiet, all of them exhausted with sun and fishing, and Marshall was embarrassed when he fell asleep on the sofa and woke to hear Ada and Grandmother Tobias talking softly at the dining room table. He wasn't sure he wanted them talking so much.

He felt his pocket, grasping the edges of his cell phone. It felt like a time bomb. He knew that when he turned it on this time the calls from his mother, and perhaps some from his lawyer—or his former lawyer—would no longer be mildly concerned. They would be angry and demanding, and what would he do then?

His grandmother patted the Bible that lay on the table in front of her, and Ada glanced over at Marshall. He smiled faintly at her. She didn't return the smile. In fact, the ends of her mouth turned down, and she murmured something to Grandmother Tobias.

"I guess it's time for all of us to turn in," his grandmother said, turning toward him. "Time to wash up, Marshall."

He still felt groggy, and her tone suddenly irritated him. He wasn't a child, and she certainly hadn't known him long enough to speak to him as if he were. He'd had Ada all to himself at school. At home, he'd had to share her with Meghan, here he was sharing her with his grandmother. They should never have gone home for spring break. If they had stayed at school, none of this would have happened.

And now they were probably never going back to school, never going back home.

He got to his feet and walked over to Ada, placing his hand on her shoulder. "I'm not quite ready for bed," he said, trying to keep his tone light and confident. "I thought Ada and I would go for a walk."

His grandmother's face darkened, and Ada looked between them quickly. "I don't think I'm really up for a walk," she said, looking down at her knees. He immediately felt like an idiot.

"No, of course not," he said, trying to salvage his pride. "I just meant out to the backyard, to see the stars. Come on, I'll help you."

"No, really, it'll be buggy, and I'm tired," she protested. "We should just get to bed."

She rose and gave him a pointed look he chose to ignore. "Well, I'm going to go, but you go ahead," he said, returning her look as best he could. It didn't affect her at all, and when his grandmother pushed back from the table and Ada walked down the hall to the guest room, he felt an irrational anger well up in him.

Grandmother Tobias said, "Maybe we'll get some more fishing in tomorrow."

He shrugged. "Maybe," he said, watching Ada's retreat, desperate to pull her back to him somehow. It already felt too late. She had attached her loyalty to his grandmother, accepting without question her assertion that they were to proceed apart.

Because God had told her so.

Told her. Talked to her. Put a voice in her head and formed words and proclaimed.

She turned away from him and he watched her walk down the

same hall Ada had just disappeared down. He stood in the living room in the dark until he saw the light under Ada's door wink out, and then he opened the back door and wandered out to the middle of the yard, the grass still warm under his feet.

He stretched out in the same spot Ada had been in that afternoon and watched the night sky, ignoring the pinpricks of the mosquitoes and the rustle of the night creatures in the oppressive woods beside the house, but listening for the telltale barking of the pack of dogs.

His cell phone rebuked him from his pocket. It felt like a living thing now, a constant reminder of his failures. He didn't know why he kept it, and since he hadn't bothered charging it in days, it would be dead soon enough anyway.

He stared at the stars, at the banks of dark clouds that were rolling over them from the west, illuminated from within when lightning sparked in them, bringing a promise of thunderstorms and rain, and asked God to speak to him as He had spoken to Grandmother Tobias. It stood to reason that if God spoke to both his grandmother and grandfather, then perhaps He would speak to him.

Though if faith was passed down through the genes like eye color, why didn't his father believe in anything but the gods of fish and water? His mother he could understand: Being the daughter of academics, her genes had contained loads of curiosity, yet little concrete faith, not just theologically, but in anything, including her own opinions.

When he'd asked his parents about their beliefs—and he had asked, nearly relentlessly—he'd been met with silence from his father and an open lecture series from his mother. Neither had answered his questions. Neither had told him, in any sort of specific way, what *their* beliefs were.

The clouds moved across the sliver of the moon and he felt a raindrop on his left cheek. When Meghan was little, she used to crawl into bed beside him when there was a thunderstorm at night. She would shiver for a few moments, and then fall deeply asleep, as though simply being with him was enough to keep her safe. She drove him crazy on those nights. She thrashed and rolled and kicked, all while asleep. He'd finally told her that she could no longer come in if she couldn't stay still.

The next time she came in, she lay gingerly at his side on her back, her arms straight at her sides, legs stretched out, taking up as little room as she could. She finally fell asleep, and to his amazement she managed to maintain this perfect form throughout most of the night.

Ironically, her very stillness left him sleepless, and he kept checking to make sure she was breathing. When she'd made her presence known, felt in every kick and roll, he'd wanted nothing more than to get rid of her. But the fact that she was strong enough to change her sleeping habits, was strong enough to maintain it while not even awake, simply to stay with him, fascinated him.

She'd stopped being afraid of thunder by the time she was ten, just in time for him to go to college. Now he wondered if she had weaned herself off of his protection in anticipation of his departure. It seemed reasonable that someone who could change their behavior even in sleep could do that.

He heard the back door open and close softly, and when Ada lowered herself to the grass beside him, he rolled over toward her, burying his face in her neck, breathing her in. She stroked his hair, but when he ran his hand down her thigh, she stopped him. He tried again and again and she stopped him.

Within moments, they were grappling with each other on the lawn, and he finally, to his horror, burst into tears when it was clear that she was not simply playing hard to get, wasn't mock wrestling with him, but was determined to keep him from the solace of her body.

"What?" he demanded, savagely wiping the damning tears away.

She sat up, breathing heavily, and brushing the sides of her legs free of grass. "Marshall, we have to move beyond that."

"But we've already—"

"I know," she silenced him. "And that was wrong."

"No, it wasn't," he protested. "It was beautiful. Ada, I love you."

"No," she said harshly. "You used me."

He gasped. Perhaps he could have expected her to rethink their sexual relationship, but he hadn't expected her to blame him completely for it, or to think so unkindly of him.

"I did not," he said.

"You did," she insisted. "But I don't blame you. I let it happen. I wasn't strong enough. I got distracted. If we're going to do this, if we're ever going to work, then we have to start over. We have to atone, be made clean. Especially if we're going back to my family. I can't go back there . . . like that."

"I thought we weren't traveling *on the same road*," he said bitterly.

She gave him a long, considering look that felt heavy on his cheek, as if she'd placed a hand there to try to read his thoughts.

"We have to leave," she said softly and watched him. "We shouldn't have come here. We have to leave soon. The sooner the better. Your grandmother's asleep. We could leave tonight."

He looked away from her. "Ada? How come you never told me that you were born in Canada?"

"It didn't seem important. How come you never told me about your grandparents?"

"How did you get into my room?"

"What do you mean?" Ada asked, slanting a cagey glance at him.

"That night at the house, when you came into my room, I had locked the door. How did you get in?"

"It's not like it was a deadbolt or anything, Marshall," she said. "Those little locks are pretty easy to get open."

They were silent. Something being pursued, or perhaps the pursuer, in the wildness of the thick brush screamed, and Marshall felt a chill rise along his backbone, spread beneath his thighs.

"I—can't go with you. I have to go back," he said, his voice quivering with the anguished truth of it. The fresh silence in the backyard made him feel more alone than ever before.

"I know," she finally said. "But I can't."

This time it was his turn. He looked in her eyes. "I know."

"I'm sorry," she said softly. "I'm so sorry."

He did the only thing he could for her. He gave her the keys to the car and as much cash as he could. They moved quietly about the house, getting her ready, and he held her tightly before she got in the car. "I love you," he whispered fiercely in her ear.

"I know," she whispered back. "Take care of yourself, Marshall. Have faith."

He couldn't even watch her drive away. As soon as she started the engine, the dogs came out of the brush, yipping and howling as they converged on the car. He backed into the house, gently shutting out the sounds of their hunger and desperation as the car faded away.

Fifteen

OUR détente didn't last long. Cal strode into Meghan's room later that week and came right to my chair, holding his cell phone up as if it would explain things.

"Why didn't you tell me about Ada?"

I was going to tell him. But then he had come in full of hope for Meghan, and all I wanted was to keep things peaceful between us for as long as I could.

"I was going to tell you," I said.

He paced the hospital room, anger radiating from his set shoulders, his tight mouth. I stayed silent. There was nothing I could say right now that would be heard the way I meant it. But then this was the direction things seemed to be moving in, the inexorable slide—started at some point in the past that I'd never been able to pinpoint—into the pool of separateness.

Cal could stand separation. He'd been alone when I met him. But I had still had my parents, I'd had a boyfriend, I'd had a large circle of friends, a larger circle of acquaintances, and larger still, the very world open to me.

Everything had gotten smaller. I had broken up with the boyfriend to be with Cal, lost my parents, slowly lost touch with all of my friends, and with the birth of my children, the very thing that I thought would open up worlds to me, I had given up my vast possibilities in this one.

And it continued to shrink. Marshall left for school and was now so clearly beyond the son I thought I knew; Cal had moved away from me and I didn't know what his world was like anymore; and my daughter, the one I'd thought I had so much more time with, the one I thought I would always have, had gone somewhere I could not follow. My world had shrunk, constricted around me, to this hospital room.

When I was pregnant with Meghan, I hadn't had a baby shower. Gifts had always embarrassed me; I hadn't even wanted a baby shower when I was pregnant with Marshall. I hadn't wanted a bridal shower when we got married, and I hadn't had a birthday party since I was seven and ran from the room, sobbing, when confronted with a great mountain of brightly wrapped presents and the expectant faces of my classmates.

But I had always been touched by the little gifts Cal occasionally surprised me with. When we brought Meghan home from the hospital, this exact same hospital, he had scattered small bits of love throughout the house, for me to discover in time, without fanfare.

The first time I reached for a onesie, my hand fell upon a small ceramic plaque, the sort of hokey little tchotchke that I usually couldn't stand. It had a fat silk rope to hang it on a wall, and in brilliant pink calligraphy it said, *A son is a son till he takes a wife, but a daughter's a daughter for the rest of her life.* Little garlands of white flowers surrounded the words, and this new part of me, the mother of a daughter part of me, did not laugh out loud at the sentiment of it.

Instead I found a hook, and hung it on the wall above her changing table, and then kissed Cal when he came home that day and whispered "thank you" softly in his ear. We had become a family when Marshall was born, but we were complete when Meghan came along, and I'd never even realized that there was an absence to begin with.

Now I knew more about the absences in our lives than I did about what we had. And we had a new one: the absence of easy apologies. They had never been hard before. Once, *sorry* had rolled off our tongues as easily as Cal caught fish. I should have said I was sorry that I didn't tell him what the detectives had told me. But it simply felt like more effort than I could muster.

He finally dropped into the recliner and dug in his duffel bag. "I wasn't going to show you this, but I guess you better know in case anyone tries to get in here," he said, pulling out a newspaper folded in half.

"I went by their office—those detectives you said you wouldn't talk to—this morning to see if there was anything we could do about it," he said, handing it to me. "I looked like a real ass when they mentioned the long conversation they'd had with my wife."

I scanned the section he'd given me quickly, unsure of what I was looking for, then gasped when I saw it, the headline I hadn't even considered could be about us.

"Girl near death, brother disappears," I whispered, reading the accompanying article quickly, then going back to read it word for word. Cal talked in the background but I barely heard him.

"Kevin told me a reporter had been by the marina to talk to me, and I imagine they went by the house too. All I can figure is that someone from the hospital called them, that doctor, I guess. The detectives said a journalist called and asked about Marshall, but they didn't give out any information except to ask if the journalist had talked to Marshall. I guess that's how they figured out he's gone."

The article was brief, but damning, and seeing it in black type, with our names attached to this outlandish story, made me ill. I rushed to the bathroom and fell on my knees in front of the toilet, but all I could do was try to catch my breath. The nausea stayed, hovering somewhere just under my lungs, making every breath a risk.

Dr. Kimball hadn't been mentioned by name in the article, but who else would have been so callous about a family's personal crisis, our family's personal crisis in particular?

I sat back on the tiles and leaned against the wall, cool against my shoulder blades, and stared dully at the toilet, the white ceramic sculpture, and thought of the oddest things. I wondered if I would have to teach Meghan to use one again someday, or if we would ever even get to that point. I remembered how easy she had been to potty train, especially after the difficulty I'd gone through with Marshall.

I remembered how Cal had delighted in allowing him to pee off the side of the boat, how the first time he did it, a fish jumped and startled Marshall so that he fell in the water. How Cal roared with laughter as he hauled him out and how Marshall had trembled on the edge of sobbing and laughing, finally coming down on the side of hysterical laughter with his father.

Such a simple thing, a toilet. So bitterly stupid to sit there and make it a poignant symbol of a possible future. But it did represent a line between infancy and independence, between the drudgery of diapers and freedom. I turned my cheek to the cool wall, my ear pressed tightly to it, and could hear Cal moving things about, muffled thumps and mutterings.

I took a deep breath and slid up the wall, not bothering to wash my face clean of tears. I used to be careful of the ravages of crying, stress, illness, and daily indifference. Even if my use of makeup had declined over the years, probably just when it ought to have increased, I was still conscious of how I looked to my husband.

I still brushed my teeth first thing in the morning, I still washed my face, showered, and used deodorant daily, still paid attention to how shabby I would let my clothes get. I still shaved my legs, under my arms, carefully tamed anything that got unruly in a bathing suit. I had not, at any point, let myself go to hell.

But frankly, I simply did not care anymore. I paused to remember if I had showered that day. I hadn't. God only knew how long it had been since I shaved my legs. I wouldn't even consider raising an arm for a look there, much less a whiff, and the thought of applying a razor anywhere else was nearly laughable. I felt a vague satisfaction at the knowledge that I had, indeed, brushed my teeth that morning, as if that proved my descent had its limits. For now.

Cal looked tired, but other than that it seemed that men, in addition to their unfair aging advantage, weathered stress better. Perhaps it was simply a matter of the amount of upkeep necessary to keep women presentable. Men looked good with stubble, a little scruffy around the edges. A little scruffy around the edges for women meant disaster.

I jerked at the soft knock on the door.

"Chloe? You okay?" Cal called.

"Fine," I called back, and turned on the faucet as if to prove that, clearly, if I was able to work a sink, I must be all right. Perversely, I did not allow my hands to touch the water, and refused to ruminate about what this might signify.

When I returned to the room, I saw with surprise that Cal had rearranged the chairs. He had dragged them over to the windows and opened the blinds. That light wasn't going to do much to improve my countenance. It splashed through the room, as loud and harsh as heavy metal, and I immediately went to Meghan's bedside, to shield her from this intrusion.

"What are you doing?" I asked. I couldn't keep my voice from rising accusingly. I had always tried to keep that shrillness I so often heard in other women's voices from invading mine. I hated hearing women speak to their husbands as if they were dull children they barely tolerated.

But right now, Cal *was* very much like a dull child I could barely tolerate.

But the mirror-bright bars of light that fell across Meghan didn't extend up to her face, and there was little I could say to support my irritation. I adjusted her sheets, straightened a couple of wires across her pillow, smoothed her hair back from her forehead. High-pitched beeps made me whirl around to check the digital displays on the machines that were keeping track of her vital signs, her "very promising" brain activity. The beeps weren't coming from any of the machines, and I finally turned Cal's way.

He was working both of our cell phones, his flipped open on the little table between the chairs, mine in his large hand, pushing the tiny buttons as dexterously as any fifteen-year-old. One of Meghan's spiral notebooks was open on the table, and he was making notes from whatever he was finding on my phone.

"What are you doing?" I asked again, my voice just as shrill as before. I pulled the phone from his hand and he just as quickly grabbed it back, catching my wrist in his other hand, hurting me, though I knew he couldn't have meant to. I had nothing to hide from him, but he had never been one of those husbands who felt a right to go through my things whenever he felt like it. We'd always been polite. All of the common courtesy levees that made our relationship work were being breached.

"Sit down," he commanded, pointing my phone toward the chair across from him.

I sat.

He leaned forward and flipped my phone closed before he looked at me intently. He just looked for a moment, and I wanted to say "What are you doing" again, but I wasn't going to give him the satisfaction of it. Instead, I remained silent and gazed back at him, hopeful that I appeared calm and unperturbed on the outside. Inside, my heart was beating hard, and I still felt nauseous. I felt as if I were sitting across from my father, a feeling that infuriated me. I'd found that the only way to combat it was to act as much like an adult as I could muster.

"Where is he?" Cal said.

I looked down at my phone and at his scribbled notes, buying a little time to figure out exactly what he wanted. I assumed he meant Marshall, but I wanted us on even footing in this conversation, and I wouldn't be rushed into making a misstep. But Cal wasn't waiting for me to catch up.

"Where the hell is Marshall, Chloe? You can't protect him like this. You're going to make it much worse than it already is."

"I don't know where he is," I said. His expression didn't change. He didn't believe me.

"Dammit, Chloe, I can't believe you can be so stupid—"

"Whoa, you can stop right there," I interrupted him. "Don't you dare ever say that I'm stupid. I don't know where he is. I have no idea. He didn't tell me, he hasn't called, and he's had his phone turned off for days. All I know is that he bailed Ada out and they took off. That's all I know. I'm not covering for him, I'm not aiding and abetting, and I'm not about to let you make me feel guilty about something I didn't do."

He pinched the bridge of his nose, right where he'd developed tiny indentations from the sunglasses he had to wear constantly. His face looked vulnerable without them, the way faces do when people first get laser eye surgery and forget they don't have to squint to focus. Cal squinted whenever he was without his sunglasses, even when it was dark out, and it had emphasized the lines radiating from the corners of his eyes.

Now he looked at me through his fingers, squinting as though I were a mile away, across sunlit water, trying to decipher who I was, what I was, and whether it was worth getting closer for a more intimate look.

"I don't know where he is," I stated, slowly, carefully forming each word for him so there was no mistake.

"You really don't?" he asked, softly now.

"I really don't."

He sighed heavily and leaned back in his chair, his hand now covering his eyes. "All right. Well, I think we need to do everything we can to find him. Call his friends...does he still have friends?"

I shook my head and shrugged. "I don't know."

"Well, do what you can. I've been onto the cell phone website. He hasn't made any calls in the last week. I thought—" He waved my cell phone in the air before leaning forward and dropping it onto the table. "—maybe you were calling him."

"I am calling him," I said. "I'm not getting any answer, but I've been leaving messages for days now. I've told you that."

"I think," he said, pushing the newspaper with his toe, "that we need to make a concentrated effort to find him before this girl manages to really screw up his entire life."

I loved him right then. I loved him so much for the relief that coursed through me, and I felt like crying, loose-limbed and light-headed with the release of it. Suddenly, I was not alone, we were a team again, and I wanted to curl up in his lap and wrap my arms around his neck and let him tell me how he was going to fix this.

"So what's your plan?"

"First we have to manage this somehow," he said, tilting his head toward the newspaper. "There was a message at home from a reporter. I don't think we should talk to them at all. What do you think?"

I shook my head. "No. No, I don't want any part of it. What are they going to want to do? Come in here and take pictures of her? Splash the grieving parents all over the front page? No."

He nodded. "Okay, then I think we'd better talk to someone here about their policy on who they let in."

"Sandy just walked right up to the door the other day."

"Exactly. So, we'll do that, we'll keep trying to find Marshall..." He trailed off and sighed, leaning his head back and staring at the ceiling for a moment, and I finally moved. I crossed the small space between us that had seemed like such a distance before, and climbed into his lap.

He folded his arms around me so quickly that tears welled in my eyes when I realized that he needed to be touched too. Perhaps it didn't fix anything permanent, but it would be nice, just for a moment, to be us again.

Our breathing synchronized, and I rested my forehead in the curve of his neck, coming together the way we'd perfected over the years. It amazed me that it hadn't changed. Shouldn't—after agreeing that we had come to an impasse in our marriage—our curves and angles have shifted slightly? Shouldn't the chemicals that made the smell of him mean safety and love and happiness have altered now that I wasn't so sure he meant any of those things anymore?

But nothing about our bodies had changed, and I breathed him in just as deeply as I had when he embraced me on our first night together. I felt him do the same; felt his hands seek out and settle in the places he loved the most on me, my hip bone, the span between my shoulder blades. It had always felt as though he were holding me together, as if were my bones to suddenly disjoint themselves I would not collapse, accordionlike, to the floor.

It was a lovely moment, suspended there.

MARSHALL

He couldn't sleep. He regretted letting her go, or regretted staying behind, he wasn't sure which, as soon as the door closed and the sounds of the dogs faded away. He walked down the hallway and slipped into the room Ada had been in, slid into the bed she'd lain on and tried to smell some bit of her. But she hadn't been there long enough, and all he could smell was fresh sheets atop an old mattress.

He returned to the sofa and stared into the dark, his eyelids jumpy with exhaustion. He was what his mother used to call "mad at sleep," and the longer he cursed not being able to find it, the further away the possibility sailed.

He finally eased himself off the sofa and roamed the house, stopping at each window to stare out into the night, listening, waiting for something to happen. He developed a track and made the loop more times than he could count before he finally returned to the sofa and fell upon his knees in front of it, clasping his hands together and resting his elbows on the sagging, sheet covered-cushions, like a child, to pray.

He had nothing to say. He did not know what to ask for, whom to praise, how to make the words work anymore. But he stayed there, determined that something would eventually come to him, determined that he could escape into it and quiet the anger, the pain, the uncertainty.

He tried the rote prayers, recited the chants, even whispered a song under his breath, swaying from side to side, and none of it worked, none of it moved him, and he had never known the power of the word *forsaken* before but he knew it now, and that became his prayer.

You have been forsaken, you have been forsaken.

He heard a noise behind him and his heart skipped wildly as he turned to see what had appeared, what manifestation his disbelief had conjured up. He would not have been surprised to see the things he only imagined at three in the morning: a demon, Satan himself, Iblis, Mara, Angra Mainyu.

It was Grandmother Tobias, but seeing her there rather than the demon of his midnight imagination did not ease his fear, or his anger. He rose quickly, feeling it in his head, and sat on the sofa as she crossed the room.

"What are you doing?" she asked, leaning down and taking his cheeks between her thumbs and fingers, as if she were a doting aunt, but squeezing, so he had to look up at her. He was shocked at how much it hurt. "I know what you were thinking," she hissed at him.

He was bewildered. *He* hadn't known what he was thinking, how could she? He gaped up at her, and she gave his face a little shake before releasing his cheeks. His hands flew to them, rubbed them back into shape.

"I wasn't doing anything," he protested.

"You were going to try to sneak in there, in my house, under my roof. I gave you shelter and you were going to go in there—"

"No," he protested. "No, I wasn't. I couldn't sleep, I was walking around, and I was—I was praying. I was praying."

She became still and glanced down the hall, uncertainty stamped on her face, better than the strange rage that had been there a moment before.

"Praying?" she asked.

"Yes," he said. "I was, you saw me, I was kneeling."

"Don't have to kneel to pray, son," she said, sitting on the sofa beside him, lowering her voice, trying to not wake a girl who wasn't there anymore.

"I know, I just, I thought it would be easier."

"Ain't hard to pray either," she said, chastising softly.

How he wanted to argue. It was. It was hard to pray, when you didn't know what to pray to, when you didn't know what to pray for, when you didn't have faith that anyone, anything, was listening.

"Marshall," she said, "you can be his vessel."

"What?"

"You can be his vessel."

"I— What the hell does that mean?" He wanted to shout this, but he was aware, still, that Ada was supposed to be in the room down the hall. He wanted to buy her time, time enough to get out of the state, to get as far as she could. And so he put as much of the idea of yelling as he could into his half-whisper. "What does that *mean*?" he demanded again, satisfied when she shrunk from him.

But Grandmother Tobias was clearly not a woman accustomed to shrinking from much and she came back at him as quickly as she had retreated. "Don't you push me, child, don't you question me. You open yourself, and you let him fill you, and you *will* find the way, you *will* find the path. You refuse His love and you will be lost, you accept His love and you will be released."

"From what?" he asked.

"From your doubts."

"I don't think I can be," he whispered. "How do you do it?"

She tilted her head at him, uncomprehending, as if he'd asked her how to speak Japanese. "You just do," she said simply.

He shook his head. "No."

"Yes," she corrected him. "Your girl there, she knows. She just knows, she doesn't question, she knows. Now, I'm not altogether clear on just what she thinks about it. Seems to me she's mighty confused on that part of it. But she knows. She'll get there. You'll get there too, but you have to stop fighting it."

He slumped back on the sofa, all the anger gone out of him, everything gone out of him, and closed his eyes. "I'm not fighting anything," he said.

She patted his knee, as if the conversation had somehow made sense, somehow been satisfying to them both, and was now over. "Go to sleep," she said, and left him there.

He watched her move slowly down the hall through half-open eyes and had a moment of fear when she stopped at Ada's door, listening. Whatever she hoped to hear she obviously convinced herself she had, and she turned away and entered her own room, quietly shutting her door.

He threw himself back on the sofa and stared at the windows. There were no prayers in his mind, there was nothing in his mind but Ada, and everything he had just lost, had just willingly allowed, *encouraged*, to drive out of his life and into some unknown future without him. He pictured her speeding to the coast and then turning north onto the freedom trail of I-75, windows down, one graceful arm cocked out the window, wings of dark hair fluttering about her face.

Sometime in the predawn hours, Ada's hair turned to water, her limbs turned to fish, and he slept and dreamt. When the windows became hazy with the pink of sunrise, he opened his eyes as though he'd never closed them, rose, and quietly made coffee.

He poured two cups, looking over his shoulder, dumped one in the sink, and then sat at the table until Grandmother Tobias emerged from her room, shuffling in like an old woman, devoid of any of the stealthy visitor of the night before.

"Good morning," he said. "We were up early so I made coffee. Can I pour you a cup?"

She lowered herself into a chair with held breath, dropping the last couple of inches, and he suddenly wondered exactly how old she was. At times, when she turned on that faith, that passion, she became ageless, but now, without that fire and in the dawning humidity of a merciless Florida morning, she could easily have been well into her eighties or beyond.

"Nice to have it ready," she said, her voice matching her aged appearance. She accepted the cup gratefully and looked at him closely as she took a sip. "Your girl gone back to bed?"

"No," he said, taking his seat and keeping his eyes on his coffee. "Actually, she's got family a little farther up the east coast, so I let her have the car for a couple of days so she could visit. She waited, but we weren't sure when you'd be up, and I wanted her to get on the road before the weekend traffic got too bad."

He had lied so much already. He would start making things right soon, but for now he was going to continue to do what he had to do. He'd deal with the consequences later, and he knew, knew already, that the consequences might be dire indeed. He pulled his cell phone from his pocket and held it up for her to see, as if it were a calling card of credibility.

"Talked to Dad before he got on the water to let him know I wanted to stay the week to get to know you a little better. I hope that's okay?"

Her face changed as quickly as the sky at sunset, from suspicion, to acceptance, to a flattered hopefulness that twisted in his gut like fish twisted in his hand to get free.

"This will be nice," she said, hesitantly, as though she weren't quite used to looking forward to something, or letting on that she was. He resigned himself to the fact that, apparently, there was no bottom to how badly he could feel. There was still another depth to reach.

The deep pool he kept looking for within himself was never full of faith. If he had a deep pool of anything, the catfish, the bottom-feeders, would be feasting on regret, guilt, maybe some well-earned self-hatred. He felt as old as Grandmother Tobias. How did anyone get to an advanced age without becoming stooped and angry with guilt?

There were only two answers he could come up with: There were either very few people who did bad things, made horrible decisions, or there were millions who had no conscience, or who at least had incredibly selective memories.

Perhaps memory loss was not a curse of old age, but a gift. He was ready to be eighty, eighty-five, ninety. He wanted to already have his life behind him. Wouldn't it be easier?

Life was messy and long, with countless opportunities to make the wrong decision, to hurt other people. Exhausting.

Grandmother Tobias made breakfast, and he ate it, but tasted little. He didn't bother feeling badly about eating the sausage.

Over the next week they fished, paddled Fisheating Creek and Lake Okeechobee, ate, and looked through more pictures. His grandmother brought out shoeboxes filled with more photos, and seemed to know and, more surprisingly, respect that he did not want to talk about Ada or his family. At least the family he'd grown up with.

The rest of his family, her family, he heard all about. She produced a wealth of ephemera: sermons scribbled on tissue-thin paper, birth, marriage, and death certificates, Christmas cards, and report cards. It was all too overwhelming to complete a picture in his mind of exactly what genetic material had distilled down to form who he was, but it was certainly more than he'd ever had to work with before.

Perhaps his grandmother thought it would help him. But all it did was confuse him more, make him retreat further from understanding any sort of clear truth. As she became chattier, he became more quiet, and he drew out the days with fishing as much as he could, eventually taking the truck back out in the afternoons to fish the creek himself, getting back as late as he could to toss more fish to the wild dogs than they could possibly eat.

Eventually, two days after he was supposed to appear in court, after Grandmother Tobias asked him over breakfast if he was certain that Ada was coming back and he had to tell her that no, she wasn't, he finally turned on his cell phone.

He didn't listen to any of the messages, and there were many. Instead, he made a call to the hospital. They wouldn't tell him anything. He looked at the phone, its technology as foreign to him now as his own face in his grandmother's tiny bathroom mirror. He finally dialed.

"Dad? It's Marshall."

Sixteen

THANK God for lawyers. Lawyers on my side anyway. Tessa met with Cal and me and swung into action with remarkable efficiency. It felt, a little, as if all of us—Cal and me, Tessa and Mingus, even the detectives and, to a lesser extent, the two FBI agents who spoke with us—were working together.

None of us agreed on why we needed to find Marshall, but we all agreed, with varying degrees of desperation, that finding him was the goal. The FBI agents filled us in on the information they had on Ada, but overall they seemed rather bored with the whole thing. It seemed to simply be a lead for them, not a break in their case. They were both young, and I had the feeling that their idea of what being an FBI agent would be like and what it was turning into were wildly different.

I had no sympathy for them. What in life turns out the way we thought it would? Our jobs, our marriages, our children, ourselves. When they sat across from me with bored sighs, barely taking any notes, I wanted to say, "Welcome to the world, welcome to your lives. Sucks to be on the other side of your dreams, doesn't it?"

I didn't, of course. I answered their questions, but when they left I knew we wouldn't hear anything from them. They would go back to Miami and hope to get assigned to a case that was more exciting than trying to find a couple of kids who might, just might, have some idea about where an alleged pedophile could be, but most likely did not.

I had never met anyone who worked for the FBI before. I thought they would be different, more…streamlined. A piercing, intelligent gaze, edgy, clever dialogue, sharply parted hair. What they looked like the most, to me, was someone Marshall might have grown into.

Except now Marshall's future was going to be limited in a way I'd never even considered before. Working for the FBI was quite likely out of the question, as were many things now. Even had this happened before Marshall was eighteen, they'd found Ada's sealed juvenile records. This would follow Marshall for the rest of his life. It would follow them all for the rest of their lives, though, so why should he be spared?

We retreated from these meetings to Meghan's room, now moved to the end of a hallway after our meeting with hospital administrators about the media interest in the case. Tessa came with us for everything. I was sometimes surprised to find myself in the bathroom without her. Hernandez and Rhoades kept their distance, as did Mingus, and once Marshall missed his court appearance he had little to say, but shook his head often. He had not, of course, been paid, and Cal wasn't yet about to offer to take on more of Marshall's mistakes.

Our tenuous connection lasted only in Meghan's room. We

came together over our daughter. He continued to bring in movies, and I continued to demand that she open her eyes. We each supported the other's methods, and the doctors did too. The neuropsychologist came over from Miami again, and continued to say the same things the neurologist in the hospital said: *Good brain activity, there is hope here, hang on, keep doing what you're doing.*

But they also continued to say the same things the nurses and other doctors said: *We don't know, so much we don't know, don't know, don't know, don't know.*

Cal continued to track Marshall's phone usage, but no outgoing calls were made. I continued to try him, but his message box had filled quickly with the messages from me and Mingus and Cal, and all we got was a recording that the mailbox was full.

Cal also had the idea to track Marshall's credit cards, the two we'd given him for emergencies and necessities at school, but he'd not used either of them. I got the feeling that Cal at least had a grudging respect for the fact that Marshall wasn't so stupid as to have used anything that could lead anyone to his whereabouts, combined with absolute fury that he was one of the people who couldn't find him.

He continued to go back to the *Trill* each night. That had not changed. Perhaps more significantly, the day after Marshall missed his court appearance, I went home.

Sandy met me there. She had a basket of vegetables and fresh bread dangling over her arm as she got out of her car and followed me up the steps. I had been home, of course, to retrieve clothes, personal items, more of Meghan's things to decorate her room. But this was different. I was going to sleep in my bed.

Everyone had an opinion on it. Everyone agreed it was time. One nurse had even suggested that Meghan was waiting for me to leave to open her eyes, that she was waiting for a quiet time, to come to terms with what she would find by herself.

Of course, I knew that was a load of crap. But I knew what people were trying to do. Cal made me step on the digital scale by the nurses' station one day, and I was shocked to find that I'd lost almost twenty pounds. I'd noticed my clothes were loose, but it simply didn't register as important.

As Sandy followed me into the kitchen I said, "Oh, watch the—" But it was too late. She yelped as the screen door caught her heel, and for a moment I closed my eyes and wanted to cry. It felt like a bad omen, but then she laughed and I opened my eyes in surprise. She plopped her basket on the kitchen table, obscuring my view of the blue ceramic bowl I'd placed back on the table after contemplating giving it to Ada, and she never noticed my momentary lapse.

"Don't worry about it," she said, reaching into her basket and pulling out beautiful tomatoes still on their vine and arranging them in the bowl as if she'd been here a hundred times before. "I love those old wood screen doors. I hate the new ones, all plastic and metal. Snagging my heel is just part of the character. Mine does it all the time too."

I looked at it skeptically. "You don't think we should replace it? It doesn't hold tight, it lets bugs in, which I'm pretty sure is exactly what a screen door shouldn't do."

Sandy looked up at me in surprise at my serious tone. I wasn't sure why it was important, but that damn screen door had played too large a part in my family, if only in my own mind, over the last couple of years for me to allow her comment to pass.

She must have seen something on my face because she took me seriously and placed the two jars of preserves she'd pulled from the basket on the table. She turned and gazed at the screen door, walked over and pulled it shut by its center bar, and secured it with the hook and eye, pulled once or twice on it, inspected where the edges met the doorframe.

"Well," she said, "it's your door, of course, and if you want a new one you should get a new one. It's a little warped, but overall it seems sound, and it mostly does what it's supposed to do. And I guess I feel like sometimes people get rid of things too easily now, even when they're perfectly good, even when they're better, because they're just tired of them and have stopped seeing the beauty in them, or seeing them at all. And maybe when they catch your heel, hurt you a little, hurt the ones you love, you just want to get rid of the whole thing, rather than fix the little thing."

She turned around and looked at me with a troubled and questioning twist to her mouth. "Just my opinion," she said quietly.

I nodded, took a deep breath, and smiled at her. "Peach?" I asked, touching the preserve jars. "They're beautiful."

"These were my mother's jars," she said, holding them up to the light, the preserves within glowing like topaz and amber.

"I'll get them back to you," I assured her, but she looked at me quizzically.

"That's okay," she said. "So, why don't I put a little something together to eat while you go have a nice, hot shower? Take your time, I'll find my way around. You know, Stacey's home alone tonight while Kevin and the kids are up at his folks. Want me to call her?"

I didn't, not really. But then I didn't think I had wanted Sandy here, and yet I was almost desperately relieved that she was. I tried to sound casual as I said, "Sure," but my voice broke when I said it, and Sandy smiled at me encouragingly.

"Okay, go on then. You're going to feel so much better."

I didn't know how that would happen, but I trailed my way through the house, taking in the dust and the stale air. I didn't lapse into a morose study of our family pictures the way I had the last time I was here. I didn't go smell Meghan's peony sheets, I didn't try to decipher clues in Marshall's room, I didn't agonize about Cal when I walked into our master bedroom.

Instead, I looked at our bed and almost swooned. Yes, I wanted to get clean in my own old, subway-tiled shower. I wanted to take the time to condition my hair and shave my legs (my God, my legs hadn't felt like this since I was eleven, and maybe not even then). And I wanted to slide open my dresser drawer and pull out and pull on my softest jammies. But what I wanted, most of all at that second, was a *bed*.

I pulled the comforter off, ripped off the sheets and pillowcases, and jammed them in the washing machine in the hall closet with an overloaded cup of detergent and four glugs of bleach. I would run it on an extra rinse cycle, dry them with extra dryer sheets, and sink into them later with the fitted sheet taut beneath me and the comforter pulled up to my ears.

The shower was better than I expected, even with the loss of water pressure and shortened hot water cycle from the washing machine running. By the time I managed to fight my way through the thickets on my legs, the water was running cold, but I was happy for that, too, because it energized me enough to not just crawl onto the bare mattress right out of the shower.

By the time I got downstairs, Stacey had arrived with a bottle of wine and some grocery bags that were piled on the floor of the kitchen. She smiled shyly at me as I came through the swinging door, my wet hair wound up into a clip, dressed in pajama pants and a tank top, and my face shiny with moisturizer.

I didn't know Stacey very well. Kevin and Cal were friends, but friends the way men were often friends, at work, talking fish, gas prices…fish. Of course Stacey and I knew of each other, the way wives are aware of other wives, curious about each other, but enough time had gone by without making a concerted effort that we had grown content to let the opportunity fade.

Now that contentment was a bit embarrassing. Her husband had worked overtime to take care of my husband's business when we needed it, and yet she'd never been to our home, and we'd never exchanged more than polite greetings.

"I'm so glad you're here," I said, trying to sound warm, certain I simply sounded tired.

"I'm s-s-sorry I d-d—" She stopped and took a deep breath, and Sandy laid a hand on her arm.

"Just take your time, honey," Sandy said cheerfully. "Chloe's a friend."

Stacey nodded. "I-I know. I'm sorry, I didn't, come, to the hospital."

I am sure that I loaded my karmic scale so heavily at that moment that I am doomed to come back forever more as some dirt-scuffling, vermin-eating, low life-expectancy cur on the outskirts of Hell. Forgive me: I laughed.

I did. I laughed. But I suddenly realized that everything wasn't about me. For the first time in weeks, maybe years, yes, very possibly years, I didn't need to take on all the blame for something. Maybe I didn't know Stacey well because *Stacey* had been too uncomfortable to meet strangers without a compelling reason. Shame on me for not knowing, but...it wasn't me.

Stacey and her stutter suddenly and swiftly decapitated my inner martyr, and, oh, how I enjoyed seeing her die, even if she was a Hydra and would come back with a vengeance tomorrow, for right this second I felt freed.

They both looked at me, stunned for a moment as my laughter went on, but Stacey's arms rose around me as I threw myself at her and held her tight. What had it taken for her to get in the car and come over here? To support a woman she'd met once and said a few well-rehearsed words to?

"I'm so glad you're here," I said in between my gasps for breath. "Oh, I'm *so* glad you're here. Thank you."

"Okay," she said. "Th-thank you."

"All righty, I think we could all use a glass of wine," Sandy said, pulling a chair out for me and raising her eyebrows at Stacey as I sat and caught my breath.

"Please, let me," I said, pulling the wine toward me and grabbing the corkscrew—not mine, I noted—lying on the table. I stuck the sharp tip right through the foil and threw my newfound energy into getting the cork out.

Sandy and Stacey bustled around, and as I poured the third glass of wine they had plates of fresh bread, fruit, preserves, and cheese on the table and were making small talk about the condition of the church steps. They finally sat down in the chairs to each side of me and wrapped their fingers around their wineglass stems, and we immediately all got shy.

"Really," I said, "thank you so much for being here. I'm not sure I could come back here alone."

"You n-n-needed a . . . break," Stacey said, not looking at me.

I took a sip of the cool chardonnay and folded my hands around the bowl of the glass. I know that wine enthusiasts would shudder, but I preferred my wine, both red and white, warmer than the recommended temperatures. I rarely drank to excess, mostly because I drank slowly, and if white wine was cold I seemed to mistake it for water and downed it as if I'd just gone for a run.

I had no interest in getting drunk. I'd not forgotten Meghan and had no plans to, and I needed to remain alert in case the hospital, Cal, Marshall, anyone called. So I warmed my wine and formulated an apology.

"Stacey, I wasn't laughing at you—"

"It's okay," she said quickly.

"You must think I'm losing it," I said ruefully. "I am sorry, Stacey. I don't know what came over me. I was just feeling badly for not having had you over before, and then you came out with your stutter, and I guess I realized that maybe you were just shy. It felt...good, I know that sounds awful, but it felt good *remembering* that other people had problems, and I felt like an ass for forgetting that. And it felt good just to feel something different for a minute."

Stacey nodded, but Sandy shook her head. I sighed. "I had been thinking that Stacey thought I was a jerk and didn't like me for being distant. But I don't know her at all. And maybe I'm not the only distant one."

"I am," Stacey said.

"But—" Sandy started.

"It's t-true," she insisted. "You're not. You take...over."

I grinned at Sandy, who looked slightly affronted. "In a good way," I added, and Stacey and I smiled at each other in understanding. I slathered a piece of bread with preserves and moaned as I took a bite. I couldn't remember ever tasting anything so good in my life.

Sandy drank faster than Stacey and I and kept pushing me to eat more, and by the time the buzzer on the dryer sounded for my sheets, we were talking like friends. Maybe not old friends, but there was something to be said for the conversation of new friends, with the subtle probing questions, the quick retreats from noticeably sensitive subjects, and the gentle competition to be clever.

They followed me up the stairs, and grew quiet as they passed the pictures along the wall. I gave them a very short tour: "That's Marshall's room, Meghan's is there, and here we have the laundry." I pulled out the warm, sweet-smelling sheets and headed toward the master, Stacey trailing behind me with a dropped pillowcase and Sandy behind her, peering up the stairs to the third floor.

"That's just my studio and office," I called over my shoulder, dumping the sheets on the bed. Stacey and I got right to work as if we'd been making up beds together for years, and within a couple of minutes we were done. Sandy stood in the doorway looking on approvingly.

"You should sleep well tonight," she said.

I nodded in agreement, but despite my earlier anticipation I knew that I would likely not sleep well. It was getting late, Meghan had been at the hospital alone for longer than she ever had, and I considered saying good-bye to Stacey and Sandy and heading back. I'd had a break, I'd had some fattening food, and, surprisingly, had enjoyed some company.

I felt refreshed, but lonely.

"I'd love t-t-to see where you work," Stacey said.

"Sure." I led them down the hall and up the stairs, feeling them glance into the kids' rooms again, and when I opened the door at the top of the stairs, the smell of paint hit me and I felt tears in my eyes for the first time in days.

It hadn't even crossed my mind that I might miss my work, but there it was. I went straight to the fire sky painting I'd been working on the day it happened. I turned on the two lights I always used and forgot completely about Sandy and Stacey wandering around behind me as I noticed things I'd never seen before in the painting, minuscule bits of paint loss, the small section in the lower left that had been touched up by someone else, someone good, but not as good as I.

I leaned down, looked at it from different angles, made mental notes about which colors I would have to mix, which areas to start on first, where I'd need a lighter hand, which spots I'd have to build up. My hands hovered over my brushes, and I picked up a palette knife and felt its slight heft in my fingers, made a mental note to black-light the painting again.

I had started this business quite by accident when Marshall was a baby. My OB/GYN was on the outskirts of Naples, north of us, and I would often make a day of my appointments in order to wander the art galleries in town. Because it was a wealthy area, most of the galleries carried high-quality, upper-end art, and though I could no more afford to buy such art than I could afford to buy a Bentley, I loved just being around it.

In one gallery I'd become friendly with the manager, and in my sixth month, feeling fat and sluggish, I collapsed on her sofa to gaze at the new paintings she was still positioning on the wall. We'd previously discussed my background, my artistic aspirations and utter lack of real talent, and that day she asked me if I'd been painting lately. I'd had to confess that no, I hadn't.

"I have something sort of interesting to show you," she said, and retrieved a beat-up painting in a rickety frame from the back room. It couldn't have been more different from the gold-leafed traditional oils on the walls.

She carefully propped it on a small, wooden easel and maneuvered it in front of me so I could inspect it without moving from the sofa. I was so horrified at the condition of it that I barely noticed the painting itself, and it looked as though the frame might have actually been put together with some sort of household baseboard or door trim.

But once I got past the dirt and the homemade surrounding, I was taken by the Florida landscape. This was an unschooled hand, yes, but there was something there that niggled at my memory, and it wasn't just the backcountry scene, a small, serene inlet surrounded by palms and moss-hung oaks, with a lone crane fishing in the water, crossed palms against a beautifully clouded sky.

"Who is this?" I finally asked, searching for the signature. I found it at the same time that she said the artist's name, but it rang no bells.

"This was painted by a man named Harold Newton, one of his earlier pieces. Crazy, isn't it?"

"It reminds me of someone, though. I can't put my finger on it, but there's definitely an influence there."

"You're right. Good eye. Newton studied with Beanie Backus. Look, you can see it here, and here, see the clouds, this light?"

We pored over the painting and she told me the story of the Highwaymen while I listened, completely rapt. "So how'd you get this?" I asked. "Doesn't seem like your usual thing."

She laughed. "No," she said ruefully. "It's definitely not for this gallery. But I saw it stuck in the corner of a garage when I went to look at a painting a client wanted to sell. The painting wasn't anything, I didn't wind up taking it, but he was showing off his wife's new Mercedes in the garage and this just caught my eye. He said it had been his grandmother's and had been in the garage for years. I gave him a couple hundred bucks for it and started doing some research."

"Wow, it's really neat," I said, embarrassed at my less-than-worldly expression.

"You want to play with it?" she asked.

I looked up at her in surprise. "What?"

"Well, it needs a lot of work, obviously. You've just said you're not painting, you've talked about your interest in restoration, and you need something to do."

I bit my lip and inspected the painting again.

"Am I wrong?" she prodded me.

"No, I guess not. But, Leigh, I'm not a restorer. I mean, I'd be experimenting on this. You must have a great restorer."

"I do," she said. "And I give him plenty of work. This is a personal thing. You want it or not?"

I stared at the painting again, and realized that yes, I did, I wanted it. "Okay," I said.

That was twenty years ago. I'd developed a good enough reputation that I turned down work on a regular basis. Fifteen years ago, Leigh died of breast cancer, and she left the Harold Newton to me. It hung on the far wall of my studio, and reminded me of how far I had come, and how sometimes your life's work can sneak up on you. Now my hands were nearly itching with the desire to get in there on the fire sky and make things whole again, fix the wrongs with all the skill I'd developed over these twenty years.

These I knew how to fix. But there were too many other things broken in my life now, more important things, and they were not going to allow me the time for this, not for a long time.

Sandy and Stacey were going through my portfolio of before and after photos and exclaiming over the differences, and I smiled as I turned off my work lights. It felt good to remember that I had once been good at something. I made a mental note to call the fire sky client and let him know I'd be shipping the painting back to him.

I knew what was happening. I knew that with this night at home, with my decision about my work, that I was *settling in*. I was accepting that it was possible that Meghan was going to be like this for a long time and it was time to find a new normal.

It was the first time since I'd watched Ada and Marshall walk down the road to the bay that I'd considered *new*. I had been right about the dangers of that after all.

"Chloe?" Stacey called to me from across the studio. "Are you getting tired?"

I imagined that she'd seen my shoulders slump, that if the view of my back looked tired, my face must be a craggy map of exhaustion. I nodded and headed for the door, not trusting myself to turn around and see their kind, concerned faces.

We trooped back downstairs, and once in the kitchen Sandy and Stacey started the bustling that women do when they realize they've left too much of a mess to take their leave as quickly as they'd like to, or have been made to feel they should.

They were right. I was ready for them to leave, but wasn't sure I wanted to be alone, either. As if reading my mind, Sandy said, "Are you sure you're going to be all right here alone tonight?"

Stacey turned from where she was washing wineglasses at the sink. "Oh, will Cal stay at the hospital all night?"

The innocence of her question was genuine. Sandy flashed me a look and shrugged slightly, and I felt a surge of appreciation for the fact that she had obviously not been gossiping about me. And obviously Kevin hadn't mentioned anything to his wife about Cal staying on *Trillium's Edge*. Though I supposed it was possible that Cal had not said anything to Kevin.

But things apparently weren't going to change anytime soon, and there was no reason to not start getting used to saying it.

"Cal has been staying on *Trill*," I said. "I think we're separated."

Stacey whirled around with a gasp. "Oh no," she cried. And then, for the first time since they'd arrived, she said something that made me remember how she and Sandy knew each other to begin with. It was also the first sentence I'd heard her speak in which she did not stutter over at least one word. "Oh Lord, bless your heart, how can he do this to you right now?"

"He's not doing it to me. We just—it's been okay. I'm okay."

She looked confused, and when she spoke, her stutter was more pronounced this time. "But this is when the t-two of you should be su-su-supporting each other the most. Th-that's wh-wh-what m-marriage is."

"Stacey," Sandy cautioned.

"It's okay," I said to her. "I think it's been coming for a long time. And, believe it or not, I think it might even be easier this way. We can each deal with things the way we want to, without fighting with each other over what should be done, or who's to blame. Though we've done plenty of that anyway."

"Oh," she said, but she clearly wasn't convinced. Perhaps her parents had never had problems, maybe she and Kevin were still madly in love with each other. Or perhaps she had religious objections to our separation.

Whatever it was, I wasn't quite ready to discuss the particulars, with anyone.

"I am so tired," I said, shooing them out. "Y'all should go on. There's hardly anything left to do."

They both protested politely, but we finally exchanged hugs and promises to call and keep each other updated, and I stood at the screen door and watched them drive away, raising my hand at their taillights. The night had lost some of the humidity of the day, and I breathed in the scent of gardenias wafting from my wildly untamed little tree and the tangle of night-blooming jasmine beside the house.

I started when the phone rang and turned to answer without closing the door, allowing the scent to fill the kitchen.

"Hey, Chlo," Cal said, and I immediately thought of Meghan.

"What's wrong?" I asked, so afraid to ask the question, unable not to.

"Nothing's wrong, everything is fine," he answered. Of course that was patently untrue, but at least there was no new emergency. "I'm just calling to check on you, make sure you're okay there."

I listened to the creak of the house in the breeze, smelled the flowers. Cal never liked leaving the doors open—a breach in safety—and there were too many airborne irritants for Meghan to do it very often, but tonight I thought that I might even sleep with my window open.

"I'll be okay," I said cautiously. Was he offering to come over? Looking for an invitation?

"Good. Everything is all right at the hospital. I left around eight, and I just got off the phone with the nursing station and they said Meghan is fine, nothing has changed."

Well, Meghan wasn't fine then, was she? I bit my tongue. "Anything new on Marshall today?" I asked. Cal had bought a laptop in order to keep tabs on Marshall's cell phone use and to try to track him down through his friends. Neither his online efforts nor my phone calls had come to anything.

"No," he said. "I got a lot of information about comas today though. I printed a bunch of stuff out and left it in a file in her room for you, along with a couple of other things I picked up."

"Okay," I said. We fell silent for a moment.

"Well, sleep well," he finally said.

"You too." We hung up without saying, "I love you."

I returned to the screen door and looked out at the yard. The house might have survived my absence with little more than dust to show for it, but the landscape had quickly deteriorated. The taming of southwest Florida was a constant battle, and while you might be able to get away with an occasional week of disregard, two weeks was pushing it, and three weeks made a real statement. Let it go longer than that and you might as well raze the place and start over.

I pushed open the door and walked over to the gardenia, wincing as the crushed shells dug into the soles of my bare feet. The kids ran, used to run, across the driveway all year long without shoes on, making the soles of their feet as tough as the soles of shoes. I never knew how they did it.

The transition to the weed-choked grass made me sigh with relief, and I knelt down and began to gather up the spent, rotting gardenia blooms that had fallen to the ground. There must have been two hundred and they made a fragrant little pile on top of the old, barely-there-anymore, cypress mulch.

Not a single sunflower had survived the rabbits, but I'd rarely had a good year with them, and whenever I sowed the seeds I knew they had little chance of maturing. I got a certain sense of satisfaction that I was making little bunnies happy, giving them a treat. But year after year did get old. I couldn't see myself doing it again.

I pulled suckers off the base of the jasmine and added them to the pile, pulled tiny mahogany saplings with their attached seed pods from the ground, and, despite the fact that I actually sort of liked it, pulled the Florida pussley flowering at the edge of the grass.

The more I put to rights, the more I saw that was falling apart, and soon I was sweating, with dirt smeared across my forearms and staining the knees of my old cotton pajamas. I wound up at the end of my planting bed, with piles of weeds and broken-off overgrowth at regular intervals. I'd need to get some bags to put all the detritus into; I needed to pull out the mower and the edger too.

Gold light fell out of the open kitchen door, unrestrained by the screen, glowing upon the steps as if beckoning me back inside with the promise of a home-cooked meal, a pleasant evening, a happy family. I realized I was breathing heavily enough that I was rasping deep in my throat. I dropped the handful of dead purple queen stalks I'd been clutching and took a deep breath.

It was almost eleven o'clock at night. I was not going to mow the lawn, or edge the drive, but I wasn't quite ready to walk through that golden light into that lie of a house. I walked over to my car and studied it for a moment before carefully stepping up on the bumper, crawling across the hood—hearing it buckle beneath me slightly—and up onto the roof where I lay, gazing at the stars for long enough to catch my breath.

Then I slid down the windshield and off the edge. I stared at the rectangle of light and then walked into the house, where I pulled the tomatoes out of the blue bowl, and threw it into the garbage, where it lay there, upside down, rebuking me.

I fished it out. I couldn't throw it away. It had been my mother's, now it was mine, and one day it would be my daughter's. Maybe I thought of Ada when I looked at it now, but maybe one day I wouldn't think of Ada for any reason.

I dragged a chair over to the refrigerator and climbed up to open the cabinet above it. All of the little items we never used but I couldn't bear to toss were stored in there. I slid some old wine-glasses over and pushed the bowl to the back of the cabinet. It would be there for Meghan when she was ready for it.

I closed the cabinet doors softly and returned the chair to its place, the kitchen almost in perfect order but for the full garbage, something that had always been Cal's job. I tied the red plastic handles tightly together and hauled it out to the big, green garbage can beside the outbuilding. The garbage would be picked up in the morning, so I tilted it onto its big, black rubber wheels and pulled it to the curb, dropping it with a *thunk* next to the mailbox.

It had been years since I'd taken the garbage out. What a simple, satisfying chore. Why had wives encouraged this division instead of, say, cleaning toilets? I checked the mailbox, knowing it was unnecessary, Cal had been picking up the mail to take care of the bills, but it seemed a waste to not check since I was all the way out there.

I slammed the door on the empty box, marched back up the shell drive without flinching, through the door with its promise of family, and up the stairs, where I stripped out of my dirty pajamas and put on jeans and a T-shirt. And then I drove back to the hospital.

MARSHALL

He'd almost expected Grandmother Tobias to get all flustered and start hustling around getting things ready; cooking, cleaning, maybe nervously talking about how she wished she'd had time to get her hair done. But in the time he'd been there he should have realized that his grandmother never had been, and was not now, a typical woman. Instead, she got a gleam in her eyes and immediately pushed him into the truck to go fishing.

She didn't want to greet her son with cakes and a nice manicure, she wanted fresh fried fish and homemade ice cream and, based on the way she thumbed through her Bible and moved worn Post-its around, a few appropriate verses. He wondered what kinds of things she'd found that she wanted to make sure she remembered enough to bring her Bible along in the canoe, but he didn't ask and she didn't offer.

What he did do, though, was try to record everything in his mind that he could about fishing this creek. The light was different from the coast, and even from the bay. This central Florida light was softer and more golden than the bright, white heat on the Gulf of Mexico; heavier, closer than the air on the bay.

He filed the color of the water away, absent the deep blues and greens he was used to, and though the browns and yellows of it initially seemed somehow intrinsically wrong to him, he'd come to appreciate its layers, the clear iced-tea sparkle on the top, the deceptive depths where the big fish hovered.

He could not see, despite what his grandmother said about people who belonged always coming back, that he would ever return. If there had been something to glean from his family about faith, he had already gotten it with the early morning visit from his grandmother.

If someone who claimed to hear God's voice could not satisfy him, he did not know what could, and so he tried to remember the light and the color and the flash of the fish and the air on his skin.

His grandmother had already moved beyond his presence. In the same way that he had been hurt when she seemed to be more interested in Ada than in him, he felt that same sullen irritation now. He'd been interesting after Ada left, and now that his father was coming, it was as if she'd forgotten him, and forgotten the fact that the only reason his father was coming was because of *him*.

They arrived back at the house about three hours before his father was due to arrive, and his stomach began to lurch around the three-hour mark. It got worse with every half hour that passed and by the time his dad was due to turn into the drive he'd had three bouts of diarrhea. There was only one bathroom in the house, and it was pretty difficult to hide the fact that he was afflicted with nerves in this humiliating way.

Grandmother Tobias didn't say a word, but she looked at him knowingly over her glasses whenever he reappeared in the living room. He finally took to avoiding her, lying down on the guestroom bed, sweating in the heat and the still air before rising again for another trip across the hall.

When his grandmother called to him to ask for help cleaning the fish and he stood swaying over the sink, he actually thought that he might have to add fainting to his list of embarrassing symptoms.

But not only did he live, and somehow manage to stay on his feet, it appeared that his hearing improved, because the old, wood-rimmed clock that hung in the living room ticked incessantly throughout his remaining time.

Seventeen

THE nurses smiled wearily at me as I passed the station. Neither of them commented on the fact that I was supposed to be spending the night at home, and I imagined that they saw a lot of well-intentioned promises to family and friends broken.

I dropped my purse into my chair and leaned over the rail to kiss Meghan, slipping my hand across her cheek and back into her hair, tucking it behind her ear, the way that used to make me crazy when she did it herself. It fell forward, and I tucked it more firmly this time.

And her hand moved.

On purpose, not one of the twitches we'd gotten used to. It raised up, as if to brush my hand away from her ear.

Her right hand definitely moved. Her manicure had never chipped or worn, because of course she hadn't used her hands in weeks, but had just grown out so that she had little semi-circles of bare nail in front of each cuticle. When her hand moved, *raised*, it led from the thumb, and the bit of pink iridescent polish flashed in the low light.

I quickly, frantically, took inventory of my movements and how they might have caused the movement, but I hadn't tugged on the sheet, hadn't jostled the mattress, and it had moved *up*. Nothing could have done that. I held my breath for a moment and then whispered, "Meghan?"

Then quickly on the heels of the whisper I nearly yelled, "Meghan! Meghan, move your hand again!" while I jabbed at the nurse button on the railing. Reva, the nurse on duty for the past two nights, hurried into the room.

"We okay?" she asked.

"She moved her hand," I cried, "she moved her hand!"

Reva immediately began to work. She pulled a small flashlight from the pack she wore about her waist and checked Meghan's eyes, then grabbed her chart and began to take all her vitals.

"Tell me what happened," she said, as I hovered around her.

"I kissed her cheek, I touched her face, and then I tucked her hair behind her ear, and I saw her hand move, like she wanted me to stop. What's happening? Is anything different?"

"Not yet," she said, her eyes intent on the numbers on Meghan's transducer. "Which hand moved and how did it move?"

"Her right hand," I said, holding up my hand and showing her the motion, demonstrating over and over again. "Like this, like this."

"How many times?"

"I—once. I only saw the once," I said, desperately wanting to lie, to tell her it was four times, seven times, just to make sure she took it seriously.

"Okay, do what you did again," she said, making notes on the chart and stepping back, motioning me forward. "Do it again exactly the way you did it the first time."

I took a deep breath and tried to still my shaking hands, clenching and releasing them several times while I tried to remember exactly what I did, in what order, with what pressure and speed.

As I gathered my courage to start, the other nurse, Jessica, slipped into the room.

Reva glanced at her and quietly said, "Her hand moved." I heard Jessica's little gasp, and had I not been steeling myself to lean over the railing at the perfect degree I would have hugged them both to me. Reva had not said, "She *thought* her hand moved," and Jessica's gasp had been a hopeful, optimistic sound. Neither of them thought I was deluded, and I was suddenly very glad that I had not lied.

I did it. I leaned over, I kissed her, ran my hand over her cheek, then back into her hair, tucked once lightly, tucked a second time, harder. I kept an eye on her hand. It didn't move. "Meghan," I said, "move your hand again. Do it, honey, move your hand, please."

"Do it again," Reva said quietly.

Lean, kiss, hand on cheek, into hair, tuck once, tuck twice. Nothing. I started trembling, and realizing that I'd been holding my breath, I let it out in a rush and then inhaled again quickly, feeling light-headed.

"Again," Reva encouraged.

Lean, kiss, hand, cheek, hair, hair. *Nothing*. Oh, God. I groaned in frustration and began to do it again, did it three more times before Jessica silently backed out the door and Reva finally put her hand on my arm and handed me a tissue from the box on the side table. I hadn't even realized I had tears on my face.

I fell back into my chair and dropped my head into my hands as Reva rubbed my back. "Okay," she said. "It's okay, I know it's hard."

My usual anger at anyone telling me that they "knew" anything about this, about me, didn't flare at all, in fact, all I felt was relief and a desperate longing to turn into her arms and let her tell me it would be okay for a few hours. Instead, I took a quivering breath and said, "Thanks. Should I keep doing it?"

"I certainly don't think it could hurt," she said. "I'm going to call Dr. Tyska and let him know what's happening. Buzz me if anything happens again, okay?"

I nodded, a little surprised and excited that she didn't just believe me, didn't think it was the desperate imaginings of a broken-hearted mother, but that she believed me enough and felt it significant enough to call the neurologist at a rather ungodly time. I thought about calling Cal, but he'd be rising just after four for a full day on the water, making our only paycheck.

If it had happened again, if it had turned into anything, if the nurse had said anything particularly hopeful, then I would have called him. As it was, I thought it kinder to let him sleep. There could be a hundred little instances like this, a hundred little hand motions that meant nothing. Would we call every time?

I kept my eyes on Meghan while I pulled my purse out from behind my back, where it was lodged uncomfortably. As I did I felt something come with it and stood to clear out what I thought was a newspaper Cal had left behind.

But it was a manila envelope filled with paper, and I remembered Cal telling me he'd printed out some information for me. The bag he'd told me he'd left was beside the chair, unnoticed by me in the excitement of Meghan's hand, and I pulled it onto my lap as I started reading, stopping just long enough to peer into it and see two pieces of wood, a small flashlight, and more music CDs.

I lowered the bag to the floor and settled back to read Cal's research, regularly looking up to check on Meghan, and occasionally rising to repeat the whole lean, kiss, cheek, tuck, tuck process, with no luck. An hour later, I was rubbing my eyes, but fascinated by the things Cal had found.

In many ways I felt good about the fact that I had spent so much time at the hospital. I was doing the only thing I thought I could for Meghan, the only thing I thought I could for me. But seeing the amount of information Cal had managed to put together made me feel short-sighted.

I could have spent some time at home, researching on our computer. I knew I didn't use our computer the way other people did, and I couldn't blame it on age. I was only forty, certainly young enough to have been fiddling around expertly on the Internet for years now. But, as evidenced by our dial-up connection, I took a certain amount of pride in my Luddite status.

I didn't need to get online to know how to manage a particular shade of green, and Cal certainly didn't need it to find new types of fish. Our professions did not rely on, or even benefit from, computer use. The kids used the computers at school until we got a laptop for Marshall when he was a senior, and Meghan had no use for high-speed access yet.

But had I known how much was out there, I could have been learning more than I had been from the library books Sandy brought me. This was real information, things I could be doing, and he'd even printed out pages of parents' conversations, actual back and forth between mothers and fathers whose children were in the same or similar situations.

I was determined that I would ask Cal to show me how to use the new laptop and leave it with me so I could put any downtime to better use than I currently was with alternately feeling sorry for myself and angry at everyone else.

I had read through all the pages twice by the time Reva returned. She squatted down next to my chair to talk to me. "Dr. Tyska is going to come in by seven, but he's asked me to call if we see anything else."

"It really happened," I said. "I really did see it."

She nodded. "I believe that you did. It's just, it doesn't always mean anything—" She held up her hands as I tried to talk over her. "Sometimes it does though. People have opened their eyes, spoken, and then gone back into the coma. Other people have been in a coma for years, wake up, and have almost all their memory, start talking as soon as they open their eyes. The thing is, we just don't always know, and, well, we're a pretty small hospital here, Mrs. Tobias."

"You think we should take her somewhere else?" I asked. "What about the other guy? Who comes over from Miami? He's supposed to be a specialist."

"He's great," she agreed. "But he's only here every six weeks. I'm just saying that if this goes on for much longer, you might want to think about transferring her somewhere that's better equipped to handle things for her, give her the most up-to-date treatments. We've got great trauma people, but there are better places for longer-term care."

"I've just—" I started, holding up the sheaf of papers, "I mean, my husband has just started doing some research online. Maybe we should start looking around."

She nodded. "If you talked to Dr. Tyska, I'm sure he'd help. I know we all want her to get as well as she can."

"I know," I said, but I wasn't so sure I did. Why weren't they doing some of the simple things Cal had printed out? Why weren't there people in here strobing lights in her eyes every forty minutes? We had physical therapists, neurologists, everything we thought we needed, but there was still more that could be done, and it was clearly up to us to find out what those things were and to do them.

"Would you mind shutting off the lights when you leave?" I asked Reva, and she patted my shoulder before she left, flipping off all the lights but the ones that illuminated the machines beside Meghan's bed.

I fell asleep rereading Cal's papers and didn't wake until the next morning, when Tessa and Mingus arrived.

THE nurses, as instructed, would not allow Mingus to pass, only Tessa, Sandy, Cal, and myself were allowed beyond the nurses' station. Reva had been the first one challenged by a journalist the previous week. He'd been escorted out by security, and there had been at least one a day since then. Security accompanied me out whenever I left the hospital, and only one person had dared to approach Cal.

Another article had appeared, but there had been little new information in it, only a brief interview with the prosecutor, in which he mostly declined to comment. Tessa had brought the paper that day with a grim look on her face, and when she woke me that morning she had the same fixed scowl.

I steeled myself and looked for a newspaper in her hands, but I was completely unprepared for what Tessa said.

"Chloe, Cal's gone to get Marshall."

I bolted upright, gasping at the pain that shot through my lower back as I did so. "What?"

"Charlie's at the nurses' station. Could you let them know it's okay for him to come down and he can tell you."

I didn't even bother answering, I just scrambled out of my chair and ran for the door. Mingus pointed me out to the nurse as I hustled up the hallway, and when she turned I waved for him to come on and she gave him a nod. He met me halfway and took me by the elbow as we hurried back to Meghan's room.

As soon as we got through the door I turned to him. "What's going on? She said Cal's gone to get Marshall? What happened? How come nobody called me?"

"Hang on, let's sit down, we need to talk about some things," he said, looking around the room, at everything but Meghan, whom Tessa was talking to, her hand gripping Meghan's tightly. Mingus dragged the chairs over to the little table and Tessa joined us, leaning against the windowsill.

"Let me just say this quickly," she said, holding a hand up to Mingus to keep him from speaking immediately. "I am here as Chloe and Cal's attorney, their friend, too, but Chloe, you don't have to say anything, okay?"

I nodded. I didn't care, I just wanted to hear about Marshall. "Is he okay?" I asked, reaching my hands across the table, not even sure what I was reaching for.

Mingus nodded. "Yeah, he's okay. Hang on a sec." He looked at Tessa. "You all set now? What do you think I'm going to do, Tess?"

"Just making sure, Charles."

"Can I tell her what her husband said now?"

"Yes."

"Thank you." Their eyes held for a moment longer than necessary, and I wanted to scream that they could take their *Boston Legal* banter elsewhere after this and screw each other's brains out, but right now I wanted to hear about my son. Luckily, he started to speak, to me this time.

"Cal called me early this morning. Evidently Marshall called him from his grandmother's—"

"What?"

"Cal's mother? In central Florida, I think he said, about five hours away."

"How the hell did he get there? How did he know where to go?"

"I don't know," Mingus said patiently. "He said he wasn't staying. He was going to go, pick him up, grab something to eat, and come home."

"What then?" I asked, glancing between them, suddenly nervous.

"I advised your husband that Marshall was a fugitive and that the only thing I could advise him to do is to drive him to the police station immediately on their return and have Marshall turn himself in. He said he would call from the road so that I can arrange things, and I'll be there when they arrive."

"He's not going to get out, is he?" I asked, my hands gone cold.

"No. He will be considered a flight risk and new charges will be filed against him. No, he won't get bail this time. I'm sorry."

I sighed. "What are we going to do?"

"Mrs. Tobias?" Mingus asked. "Forgive me, but, you don't have to do anything."

"What do you mean?"

"Well, Marshall is an adult in the eyes of the law. He'll be charged as an adult, incarcerated as an adult, and tried as an adult. There's not a whole lot you can do, except decide how cooperative you want to be with the prosecution and defense. You're not responsible for anything else."

"Wait, why is Cal picking him up?" I inhaled sharply and put my hand to my chest. "Where's Ada?"

Mingus nodded as if wondering when I would get there. "Ada's gone. She took Marshall's car and left over a week ago."

"You can't be serious?"

He nodded. "I'm afraid so."

Tessa leaned in. "When did he call?"

"About two hours ago," Mingus said.

"Had he already left?" she asked.

"Just. So he won't even get there for another three hours or so."

She looked at me and clearly decided I was too shell-shocked to ask any more coherent questions. "Is there anything else you can tell us?"

Mingus shook his head. "That was about it. Like I said, he told me he'd call when he had him and was on the way back."

"Why the hell didn't Cal call me?" I asked, just now realizing this fact.

"He said he did, but you didn't answer at home. He left a message there and on your cell phone. He asked me to come talk to you in person so you weren't alone."

My anger at Cal melted slightly at that. Of course, he thought I was at home.

"I thought Tessa would want to be here, so I stopped by and picked her up."

"And you knew she wouldn't talk to you without me here," Tessa said smugly.

I was glad that Tessa was so confident. It helped me to be confident, gave me an example, a pose to emulate. But she was so very wrong. If Mingus had told me he had news about Marshall, I wouldn't have waited a heartbeat to ask him in.

They all—the lawyers, the doctors—amazed me. They worked hard to know their uncooperative client, their comatose patient, but the ones they often had to deal with the most, the parents, the caregivers, the decision makers, they seemed to forget that they weren't simply an extension of themselves. I had my own ideas, my own concerns, and yes, even my own agenda, and it seemed as though few of the professionals I'd dealt with so far even considered that.

I didn't bother correcting her. I sat back in my chair and tried to digest Marshall fleeing to Cal's mother. How the hell had that happened? How had he even known where she was? And why hadn't the woman called them? I thought about her staring at Marshall when he was just a toddler, the way her face had transformed, narrowing and hardening before my eyes. This was the person he ran to?

And speaking of unlikely saviors, it suddenly hit me that Marshall had called *Cal*. He'd called his father, the one who'd never understood, never *tried* to understand him. The one who was perfectly willing, no, adamant, that he go through a trial, possibly go to jail. I suppose I could understand Cal wanting to be the one to get Marshall, but I couldn't understand Marshall choosing to call his father.

Except... Cal hadn't been able to reach me. I was supposed to be at home last night. And my cell phone was on the kitchen counter, hooked into its charger. I'd left so quickly I hadn't even given it a second thought. Oh, Marshall, I mourned. He must have called me. And I hadn't been there.

He must have been so afraid to call, and then to not have me available, it must have just killed him. I'd always tried to be there for him, even when I was angry with him, uncertain of his intentions.

How bad had the conditions at Cal's mother's house been for him to call his father? I shuddered just thinking about him stuck in that place. The only thing the woman might have gotten accomplished was to drive Ada off. Or, I supposed Ada drove herself off, in Marshall's car.

"What do we do about Ada?" I asked.

"Well, obviously they're going to be pretty interested in questioning Marshall about her whereabouts," Mingus said.

"She stole his car," I said. "Can he press charges for that?"

"We don't know that she stole his car," Mingus said. "Maybe he gave it to her. I think that right now we should concentrate on Marshall."

I looked over his shoulder at my daughter. She had splints on her legs, keeping her toes from pointing and shortening her calf muscles. Her toes formed tents at the end of the bed, and I remembered how she'd always hated her sheets pulled tight at the end of the bed because she didn't like the way the bedclothes felt on her toes, she said she liked her feet to be free.

Instead of tucking her into bed at night, I was always pulling the peaks up off her toes. Instead of arguing with her over what movies were appropriate, I was playing *Heathers* at top volume on a laptop computer resting on her stomach, a stomach that I hadn't made a meal for in almost a month.

I had worried about Marshall when he was gone. I had berated my husband for his lack of support of our son, I had beat my own chest wondering how I could have done something different. And, as Mingus said, I certainly had concentrated on Marshall during this whole time.

But as I looked at Meghan's little toes pushing against the sheets just over Mingus's right shoulder, I couldn't stop concentrating on Ada.

If Marshall was coming back here to face the consequences, then I wanted her back here too. If I was going to have to see Marshall in a courtroom, then I wanted her in a courtroom too. If Marshall was in handcuffs, then I wanted to see them restraining her too. I thought I had never wanted to see her again, but I was wrong.

I very much wanted to see her again.

If Marshall had to pay, then she had to pay.

"I think I'm going to go home for a bit," I said, rising slowly. "I want to check my messages." I also wanted to get some things together. As soon as Marshall was back I was going to call the FBI agents who had been there. I'd give them all the information I had on Marshall's car, as well as Cal's mother's address. Now that Marshall wasn't with her, I wanted Ada found.

Mingus stood, obviously surprised, and Tessa looked at me questioningly. "You okay?" she asked. "I thought you'd be pleased."

"Oh, I am," I said. "Thank God he's safe. At least I know where both of my children are. Thank you for coming to tell me." I was waxing formal again. Something in Charles Mingus brought it out in me and I clung to it now, nodding calmly at both of them, a beatific smile curving my lips as if I were the mother of the bride thanking guests for coming.

As I drove home, I drummed my fingers on the steering wheel, imagining what I would find. Would Marshall be obviously upset, perhaps even crying, in his messages? Or would he be defensive, demanding that I come get him? I let up on the gas when I noticed I was going almost fifteen miles an hour over the speed limit. Then I looked in the rearview mirror, didn't see a car in sight, and floored it.

I didn't care what he said or what tone he said it in. I wanted to hear my child's voice. I hadn't heard either of my children in over three weeks, and I craved it the way I'd craved Cal's voice in the early days of our relationship. I careened into the drive, creating ruts as deep as the cop cars had in the crushed shells, and ran up the steps.

As I hurried to get into the kitchen, the screen door didn't just nip my heel, it caught it at the top, just where my Achilles tendon was its most tender. I fell into the kitchen, the pain in my heel in screaming competition with the pain that exploded from my right wrist when I tried to break my fall on the unforgiving tile.

I cried out, trying to roll on my side and curl into a ball around my wrist, but the screen door held my foot and I kicked out in rage against it, succeeding in freeing my trapped foot, but at the expense of most of the flesh on my ankle. I pulled into myself and moaned as the pain bloomed, and finally screamed at the screen door, "God *dammit!*" and lashed out to kick it again and then again.

I finally stopped and lay there gasping for breath, eventually sitting up, cradling my hand and wrist against my chest as I tried to determine the damage. It looked as though my ankle was the real concern, the skin raw and starting to ooze blood, but as I used the hand I was supporting my wrist with to reach out and touch it, fresh pain shot through the side of my wrist and up my arm and I clutched it again, completely forgetting about my ankle.

Once supported it felt better, and I held it tight while I gently rotated my foot to see if it, too, would be shockingly painful. But aside from the tattered skin it seemed intact, and I struggled to my feet while trying to keep my arms from moving. It was not nearly as easy a maneuver as I would have thought, but I finally managed and hobbled over to the table, scooting a chair out with my undamaged foot so I could sit down and gingerly lay my arm on the table for further inspection.

It was already swelling, and I grimaced when I saw that there was definitely something off in the shape of my wrist, a hump of sorts, like the top of my wrist had suddenly turned into an old hunch-backed crone. I closed my eyes for a moment and tried to breathe steadily. This simply couldn't be good.

I carefully picked my hand up, trying to keep it as motionless as possible, and limped upstairs to my bathroom, where I pulled the cupboard open with the side of my good foot and toed out the plastic basket I used for various medical supplies. I sat on the floor and pulled a tightly rolled ACE bandage out and managed to wrap my wrist, with slightly more skill than I had hoped for.

Getting the top off the Tylenol bottle was a little more tricky, and I scattered the pills across the floor when I finally ripped it off with my teeth, but luckily several landed near me and I swallowed them dry and tucked a few more in my pocket.

I had intended to go through my records in the office to find the information on Marshall's car, as well as gather some other things I thought might be helpful to Meghan based on Cal's printouts, but I simply did not have the energy anymore. I managed to make it down the stairs and checked the messages at home, hoping the sound of Marshall's voice would make me feel good enough that I could forget about my wrist for a few moments.

But there was only one message, and it was Cal's voice that came out of the speaker, not Marshall's. It was brief enough, but not unkind. He told me Marshall had called, he was at his mother's, and he was heading out to pick him up, to call him on his cell when I got the message.

I stared at the machine in disbelief when it told me that was the last message. I played it again and then deleted it, and checked again for messages. Nothing. That was it. If Marshall had called, he hadn't called home. I turned on my cell phone and it rewarded me with the horrible piercing notes that meant I had a message.

Same thing. It was Cal, and Cal only.

I scrolled through the missed calls feature. Nothing. Marshall had not called me at all. His father had been his first choice, the one parent who was least likely to support him. I dropped it back on the counter, wondering if there would ever again be a time that I thought I knew my son.

I checked the clock and then called Cal.

"Chloe?" he answered, AC/DC loud in the background. "Hang on." The music stopped and then he was back. "Hey, did you get my messages? Did Mingus get you? Where have you been?"

"Yeah, I just got the messages. I couldn't sleep so I went back to the hospital last night. I forgot my cell phone on the counter. Where are you? What did he say?"

"I'm about an hour away. It was a hell of a surpr—"

"Is he okay?"

"He sounds okay, but—"

"What did he say about Ada?"

"Chloe! It was a *short* conversation. If you'll be quiet for one second, I'll repeat it to you word for word."

I was silent.

"Okay, I was already on the boat but the party hadn't showed up yet. He, obviously, called my cell, and I nearly dropped it in the water when I saw it was him. I swear, I thought..."

He stopped, and I heard him put the phone down.

"Cal? Cal, what's going on? Are you okay?" I had a sudden vision of him being upset and running the truck off the side of the road, into some canal God knew where, or having a heart attack because of all the stress. And it almost felt right. Yes, sure, why not? *Why not?* Why shouldn't it all go ahead and finish exploding?

Just as I started to really panic, he picked up the phone.

"Chlo?"

"Oh my God, what happened?" I cried.

"I'm sorry, I'm sorry, I got upset, I had to put the phone down for a second."

I had to think to recall what he had been saying before he stopped talking, and then remembered. "You'd thought what, Cal?"

He sighed. "I thought he'd been hurt or something, in an accident, I don't know. I saw his name on the caller ID, but I didn't think when I answered the phone that it was going to be his voice."

So I wasn't the only one imagining the next level of devastation. Nothing is ever *the worst*. There is always something more out there, to make things just a little more horrible, and I had no idea when it would stop. Perhaps you are only allotted so much joy in life, so much luck, and I had used it up on my childhood with my worry-free days playing with friends, my evenings of interesting discussions with my parents, and my nights of falling asleep within seconds, safe in my double bed with its white eyelet coverlet.

In fact, I had fallen so easily into this mode that I had to believe that it was a natural state for humans. I knew people who never seemed to acknowledge that anything could be a good thing, there was no reason for optimism, ever, and they used to exhaust me. I searched for a reason why I had not become that person, and, astoundingly, I found it.

"Cal!" I said. "I almost forgot to tell you. I think something happened with Meghan."

"What do you mean? What happened?"

"She moved her hand. I was talking to her, and she moved her hand. It was just a second, just a little twitch, but it moved."

"When? Why the hell didn't you tell me?"

"I didn't want to wake you—"

"What the hell?"

I knew he would be irritated at first, but I hadn't imagined this anger in his voice. "Hang on, I know how hard you're working, Cal. And I—I appreciate it. I know you're the one making it possible for us to pay our bills right now. I was going to watch the clock and call you as soon as I knew you were up, but I fell asleep, and Tessa is the one who woke me up to tell me about Marshall." I took a deep breath, and for the first time in a long time, made the first move. "I'm sorry, Cal. It was such a small thing the doctor didn't even come in, but it's a good sign."

I could hear him breathing erratically and knew he was trying to process, trying to balance his anger at me not telling him immediately with the fact that it was good news and my apology.

"Tell me about it?" he asked softly.

I tried to do the story justice. I did not embellish, I didn't want him to think it was more than it had been, but I tried my best to give him every nuance of the feeling of seeing life in your child for the first time in weeks. He'd gotten Marshall's voice, yes, but I'd gotten Meghan's hand, and perhaps we simply both needed to be thankful that either of those things existed at all.

"That's amazing," he said when I finished, and then it was my turn. He told me about Marshall's call, and I could tell he tried to wring as much life from it for me as I had for him. But the fact was, the conversation had been as brief as he said.

He'd called, said hi, I'm okay, I'm at Grandmother Tobias's, I don't have my car, could you please come get me. And Cal had been in the truck within minutes.

"So," I asked, "he didn't say anything about how he decided to go *there*? How did he know where to go?"

"I have no idea. I was going to ask you if you'd told him about her, maybe thinking you were doing the right thing?"

"No, Cal, I would never have done that without talking to you first," I protested. But that wasn't necessarily true, and we both knew it. It is quite likely that had I believed it was in Marshall's best interest, I might have put them in touch. Luckily, I didn't believe it was in his best interest, but the fact remained that I had felt no qualms about those things falling under my domain.

And suddenly, I realized that Cal was going to see his mother for the first time in over fifteen years. "Are you going to be okay?" I asked.

"I'll be fine," he said, and I could picture him shrugging. "I made my peace with this stuff a long time ago. I'm going to pick up Marshall, not have a family reunion."

"I'm sorry, Cal," I said. And I was, terribly. Something about our separation had allowed me to see him at a distance. And what I saw was not a man who had slowly come to ignore my needs and passively let me assume the leadership role of our family, but a man who had to come to terms with the fact that he had no family left from childhood, and had quietly, without fanfare, taken care of the family he'd created in the less obvious and yet just as important ways.

We were a "traditional" family, no matter our politics. I made some money, yes, but if I were honest, if we put it down on paper, I knew that the bills were paid by Cal. Why it hurt for me to admit that, just to myself, especially to myself, I didn't know. He allowed me to do the work I loved—but that would never pay our mortgage—without ever making me feel as though I were handling less of the load.

And in that same traditional sense, I did the majority of the housework and the child rearing, yes, but I didn't do it quietly. It was all front and center and well-known, as if my contributions were more important. And perhaps I needed to feel that way because I didn't feel that I had anything tangible, cash, to point to. Dust-free floors didn't pay the bills, and a part of me resented that, and so I had made sure everyone knew that the dust-free floors were work, dammit.

And while I didn't think I was wrong for that, somehow the work that Cal did got pushed to the back burner of the appreciation stove. It frustrated me that nobody ever said thank you for the clean toilets, but, except for just a moment ago, I couldn't remember the last time I'd said thank you to Cal for getting up at four o'clock most mornings and working a twelve-hour day to pay our bills.

Cal never demanded appreciation, while it had become my currency. And I realized that this must have been at least partly why Marshall had called his father rather than me to pick him up.

I wondered if Cal saw me differently now, but no longer felt I had the right to ask.

"Thank you," I finally said, the only thing I could think to say.

"Thank you for being there with Meghan," he replied, and for a calm, quiet moment in our lives, we were on the same page.

"What's your plan?" I asked, my wrist beginning a slow, warm throb.

"I'll get there, probably have something to eat, thank her for taking care of him, try to not get in a fight, and then turn around and drive home. Did Mingus tell you what we have to do?"

"Yes. I understand what has to happen. I'd like to ask you a favor though."

"Okay."

"I'd like to see him before you take him in."

He sighed. "Chloe, I want you to see him. But I don't want him at the hospital."

"Call and leave me a message when you're on your way back. I'll meet you at home, and . . . we'll take him in together."

"Are you sure? You don't have to do this, Chloe."

"I'm sure."

MARSHALL

Fry oil and expectation hung heavy in the house in the afternoon, coating his nose and mouth and skin, and he finally burst out of the back door and into the backyard to gasp fresh, if humid, air. He'd not been out there for more than twenty minutes—inspecting the grass where he and Ada had tussled, looking for evidence that she had once been there, that a girl, a woman, had once been a part, a sexual part, of his life—before he heard the steady, well-maintained thrum of his father's truck.

His heart hammered in his throat, and if his bowels had been loose before, now his entire body was clenched tight. He wanted to walk through the tiny walkway into the carport and out to the courtyard, but his legs refused to move and he remained still, barely breathing as he heard the truck gear into park and then the engine fall silent.

Nothing in the world moved. He didn't hear the truck door open, he didn't hear his grandmother open the front door, and he certainly wasn't moving enough to make a sound. He envisioned them all frozen—he in the backyard, Grandmother Tobias in the kitchen, his father in the truck looking through the windshield at his childhood home—and knew he was going to have to be the one.

He closed his eyes for a moment, the disk of the sun black on his lids, and just as he took his first step he heard Grandmother Tobias move inside and the latch of the truck door engage. The three of them formed a sorry triumvirate of wary, weary, and worried when they stepped into the yard from their respective hiding places, but Marshall saw that his father only had eyes for him.

His own eyes immediately filled with tears, and what he wanted to do more than anything, more than see Ada again, more than forget that any of this had ever happened, was to fling himself across the yard and into his father's strong arms, sobbing "Dad!" as he ran, and be enfolded, lifted up, and held tightly to his chest the way he'd been as a child.

And after a second of locking eyes with him, to his mortification and relief, he did just that. He somehow managed to keep the "Dad!" from flying out of his mouth, but when he reached him his knees went so soft that his father did nearly have to lift him just to keep him upright.

"Okay," Cal said. "Okay, it's going to be okay."

And for a few astonishing, pristine seconds, Marshall let himself believe that. This was all that faith was, all that God was, every religion in the world searched for this, this little bubble of time in his father's arms in which he was assured that everything was going to be okay.

It had to end, of course, and as soon as he felt his dad test his stability he stiffened his knees. The support was drawn away by degrees, until they were standing a foot away from each other,

Marshall looking at the ground, his father looking over his head to study his mother on the front porch.

"Don't make me come down those steps with my knees, Calvin," Grandmother Tobias called, and Marshall saw the resignation on his father's face. Marshall had gotten used to his grandmother's rough voice, her accent, her aggressive style, but he heard it now as if for the first time, grating on him, making him wonder how he, how his father, could have come from this.

He didn't just want to go home, he wanted to leave here, and for a moment he entertained the fantasy that he would leap into the truck and he and his father would strike out across Florida, leaving everything behind them on a cross-country father/son road trip.

He didn't know what his dad was thinking, but in the part moan, part sigh that he made he thought it must have been something a little similar. Marshall stayed by the car and watched him walk across the yard and up the steps, saw his father's head swivel as he took in the rotting boards along the edge of the rough concrete, the chipped edges of the steps, the slab of the front door.

He looked away when his father bent to give his mother a one-armed hug and a brief kiss on the cheek, and then glanced away again when he saw his grandmother clutch at him, just as desperately as he himself had just a minute ago. He felt the weight of all that desperation like a solid force touch on him, and wondered how his father remained upright throughout his life with so many people depending on him.

Maybe he didn't want a family after all. Maybe it was better to just do what his uncle had done, take off, not with a girl, not for love, but alone, to make his own life without the constant tugging on a conscience. He knew he was going home now, knew he was going to have to face some unknown consequence, but it wouldn't last forever.

And when it was over, well, maybe he would say his good-byes and start over somewhere he'd never been before, someplace it got cold in the winter, maybe with snow, Colorado, the Dakotas. He filed this plan away, next to the childhood plans he and Ira had made to be cops, the high school plans he'd made with his parents to graduate from college, the pseudo-adult plans he and Ada had made to live their lives together seeking redemption and light.

"Let's go, Marshall," his dad called to him from the porch, and he made his way across the dirt yard and up the steps to face the waning afternoon trying to reconcile his father to this place and feed his nerves for the ride home.

"...about this trouble," he heard his grandmother say from the kitchen, pouring his father a glass of tea she'd brewed on the back patio with thick slices of lemon and a tooth-aching amount of sugar.

"It's family business," Cal said as Marshall silently approached.

She thunked the glass down on the counter in front of his father, a scowl Marshall had not yet seen fixed upon her face, making her look old to him for the first time. "And I'm no longer family, is that what you're saying?"

Marshall pulled the wood stool out and sat next to his father. Grandmother Tobias glared at him and then poured him a sweet tea and set it in front of him. His father took a long draw of the tea and sighed; Marshall couldn't tell if it was in pleasure at the tea or in frustration at the situation.

He took a sip of the tea and almost felt it splash into his nervous, empty stomach. He cleared his throat but neither of them looked at him.

"I, uh, I told her about Meghan," he said softly. But his father didn't turn on him angrily as he might have expected. Instead, he continued to look steadily at Grandmother Tobias.

"We don't know what's going to happen," he said. "But the most important thing now is to get Marshall home. The last thing Chloe needs is to have to worry about him too. She's already lost too much weight and too much sleep being at the hospital all the time."

He knew his father didn't mean it to hurt him, but it felt like a punch in his already queasy stomach. He loved Meghan, he did, but her condition was too...foreign to imagine, too exotic and intense to think about without collapsing in self-hatred and sorrow. But thinking about his mother grown thin and exhausted with worry over Meghan and, even worse, him, was only too easy to comprehend, and it made him ill enough to consider another rapid trip down the hall to the bathroom.

Grandmother Tobias's face softened. "It's no good having a sick child," she said. "Takes it out of you, and she's a slight enough thing as it is."

"Meghan's not sick, Ma. She's in a coma. There's a big difference."

Marshall flinched at the word *coma*. He could tell his father felt it, but he still didn't look at him.

"And what's going to happen with this one?" she asked, nodding her head at Marshall.

"I don't know," his father answered. "We have a lawyer who seems to still be willing to talk to him, so we'll see."

His grandmother snorted and gave Marshall a twisted smile that he didn't know how to respond to. " 'And if the blind lead the blind, both shall fall into the ditch,' " she said ominously.

"And if you start with this, I'm taking my son and leaving right now," his father said mildly, almost pleasantly.

"How far you've fallen, Calvin," she said.

His father's attention finally descended upon him. "Go get your things," he said, "and get them in the car."

"Shouldn't we—"

And now his father's attention was so fully upon him that he got spooked and rose so quickly that he nearly knocked the stool over. He retreated to the bedroom he'd taken over after Ada left and began to throw his things into the duffel bags he'd retrieved from the car before she took off.

As he worked, he heard snatches of conversation from the kitchen.

"...gonna leave just like you did...don't take no genius to see that boy's got...a real little hellcat you ask me..."

And answering Grandmother Tobias, his father, in a voice Marshall had never heard before: "...leave it...it doesn't matter...happens or it won't..."

He stopped several times in order to eavesdrop, but their voices fluctuated in volume, giving him just the hint of their conversation. He tried to make it not matter, tried to remember that in all likelihood, this visit, this *thing*—he wasn't sure he could call it a bond—with his grandmother was nothing more than a temporary situation. The time he'd spent here was a blip in comparison to the drive home with his father. That car ride was going to be as intense as a sweat lodge.

He made a sudden dash across the hall to the bathroom and collapsed on the toilet, huddled over in misery as the decades-old argument continued in the same rooms it had been born in, his father and his grandmother at such opposite ends of the spectrum that it felt as though they tugged his insides back and forth between them.

He finally emerged, shaky and weakened, to silence. He peered down the hall toward the kitchen and saw no one, listened hard and heard nothing. He moved cautiously into the living room, nearly expecting to find that one had the other by the throat, or perhaps they had managed to kill each other, but found nothing.

He heard a noise from outside and whirled around to the windows. His father was lighting an old propane grill with a match held at the tips of his fingers, while his grandmother was setting a plate of sliced tomatoes on the patio table. Neither of them were moving their mouths, and they both looked grim enough to be in mourning, but at least they weren't sniping at each other.

He backed away from the windows before they could catch sight of him and completed his packing, loading his bags in the back of the truck, before sitting down with his father and grandmother to a mostly silent dinner of fried fish and grilled vegetables.

Nobody said grace.

Eighteen

BY the time I got back to the hospital I'd eaten two more Tylenol, but my wrist was only increasing its insistent throb. When I got up to Meghan's room, I actually felt a bit faint, my forehead slicked with sweat. The nurse at the station, Kendell, lit up when I stepped out of the elevator.

"Dr. Tyska is in with Meghan," she said. "Reva told us about Meghan's hand. We've been watching closely, but nothing else, yet."

I loved her for the "yet," and nearly forgot about my wrist for a moment, but then it sent a throb through me designed to make sure I remembered. She must have seen a grimace because she cocked her head and inspected my face more closely.

"Are you okay?" she asked.

I nodded. "I'll be fine," I said. "I just had a little fall. Thanks. I'd better go talk to him." I smiled at her and hurried down the hall.

Meghan's door was slightly open, and I could hear two voices in her room. I stopped just outside and listened, not at all ashamed to eavesdrop in the hope that I might find out some tidbit they hadn't told me yet. Hearing Dr. Tyska's deep voice soothed me, and nothing he was saying was of concern to me. In fact, I felt a little spectral pat on the head when I heard him say, "The mother's been here constantly. She said she saw her right hand twitch last night—"

A woman's voice interrupted, indistinct, as though she were farther away from the door than Dr. Tyska, and I assumed it was a nurse. There was a low laugh from both of them, and then quick footsteps.

"I'll keep you posted," Dr. Tyska said, still in the room, and the door opened the rest of the way, allowing Dr. Kimball out, her head with its gray pageboy turned back into the room.

"Thanks, Matt," she said. "I hope things progress."

"I told you to stay away from my daughter," I said, my fury completely taking my mind off my wrist, the smell of the hospital antiseptic strong in my nose, making my head clear for the first time in hours.

She maintained her composure and stood up straight, sliding her hands into her pockets as if to show she wasn't concerned about having to defend herself against me, and tossing her hair out of her face. "Mrs. Tobias," she said, nodding professionally at me, causing her hair to swing forward again. "I heard Meghan made some movement. I simply wanted to check in for a moment. I assure you I've crossed no boundaries here."

"You being here at all is crossing a boundary. Get out of my sight—"

"Is there a problem here?" Dr. Tyska asked as he stepped into the hallway, looking concerned.

"Don't you ever allow this woman in my daughter's room again," I said, turning on him, forgetting my wrist and pointing the index finger of my bad hand at Dr. Kimball, causing me to gasp and clutch it to my chest again. Dr. Kimball immediately stepped forward, her hands reaching for me.

"What's wrong? What did you do?" she asked.

I jerked away from her, protecting my wrist the way I'd not been able to protect my children, turning away from her grasp. "Get away from me," I said, raising my voice, causing the nurse to peer down the hall. I edged around her as Dr. Tyska shot her an uncomprehending look and followed me. She raised her hands and mouthed, "Sorry," to him before she turned and strode down the hall, stopping briefly at the nurses' station.

I hurried to Meghan's bedside, taking in her changed position, her right arm stretched to the edge of the bed, palm up. I glanced at the machines, their readings, their charts and cords, as if I expected to see them pulled from the wall. Kimball might have saved Meghan's life, but I was certain she was a danger to it.

Dr. Tyska followed me in and stood on the other side of Meghan's bed. "Are you all right?" he asked. "What happened out there?"

"I've been very clear that she is not allowed near my daughter," I said, my voice shaking with adrenaline now that she was gone. I wanted to fall into my chair, but wanted to look as strong as my words while Dr. Tyska remained in the room. I could fall apart when I was alone.

"But—why?" he asked. "She was the admitting physician—"

"Because she's the one who caused my son to get arrested. I think we've got quite enough on our plate right now without having to see her, don't you?"

He shook his head. "I didn't really know about that. I mean, of course I know about Marshall, right? But I didn't know there was friction there. For what it's worth, she's not been here before as far as I know. I'll certainly respect your wishes in the future. And, she really was just checking on her. When we have a patient like

Meghan, a child especially, who looks like they might be making a change, word tends to get around."

The words drove everything else away. "You think she's making a change?" I asked, reaching out and grasping Meghan's hand.

"I don't know," he said. "I heard it from Reva, but why don't you show me what happened."

I went through the story again, showing him all the steps I'd been repeating with her. He watched so intently that I fully expected Meghan to do it again. But she didn't. Like Reva, he asked me to do it several times, checking her eyes with his light, watching the readings. He pursed his lips.

"I think we're going to want to schedule another MRI. Dr. Makarushka will be over on Thursday, so let's get it done Wednesday and we can see where we're at."

"Did you see something?" I asked excitedly. This is what you wanted from doctors, ability that nobody else has, finer eyes, keener hearing, faster synapses. Did he feel a vibration through her skin when he touched her, observe the slightest quiver of an eyelash? But he shook his head.

"I didn't," he said. "But we rely on the family a lot. You're here more often, you're more attuned to what's normal, what's not. It's almost always the family who sees the first signs."

I was counting on the doctors to be supernaturally observant, only to learn they were depending upon me. I nodded, disappointed. "Okay, MRI on Wednesday."

"Now," he said, "let's see what's going on with you." He motioned me over to the table and held his hands out on it. I hesitated, but the throb was too insistent, so I laid my wrist down on the table and allowed him to carefully unwrap the bandage.

"What happened?" he murmured, stopping for a moment when a pain shot through me and I sucked air in through my teeth.

I cleared my throat, trying to stave off tears. "I tripped, well, really I was viciously attacked by my screen door. I guess I tried to break my fall, but it didn't do much good. I think I must have sprained my wrist pretty badly."

The last loop of the elastic bandage sprung off my wrist and I gasped. My wrist had doubled in size, and yes, it definitely looked... wrong. Dr. Tyska traced his fingers over the top of my wrist and nodded.

"We'll get you to X-ray and I'll send the orthopedist in to take a look, but definitely looks like a Colles' fracture."

"What's that?"

"That's what you get when a screen door viciously attacks you and you try to break your fall," he said, raising his eyebrows, trying to make me laugh. I could only manage a weak smile. "It's a break in the radius, right here," he said, tracing the top of my wrist again. "You'll need a cast."

"Great," I said faintly. "Shall we check for cancer while we're at it? I'm sure that's right around the corner."

"Hey," he said softly, "listen, you're going to get through this. This? This is just a little broken bone. This is easy stuff. Easy to diagnose, easy to treat, easy to recover from. Save your energy for Meghan. You're doing great, okay?"

I sniffed and bit my lip before nodding. A broken wrist was painful, and it couldn't come at a worse time, but for a little while, during the x-rays, the orthopedist's exam, and the application of the cast, I was being taken care of, and it felt like lying back in a cloud.

I checked my cell phone when they finished with me, hoping for a call from Cal telling me that he and Marshall were on their way, but there was only a message from Sandy, asking if there was anything she could get me, and telling me how nice the previous night had been.

I grabbed a sandwich from the cafeteria and ate it in Meghan's room, feeling the painkillers slowly, beautifully kick in. The afternoon took on a drowsy, dreamy quality as clouds slid over the sun, making it even darker in the room. I leaned my head back in the chair, and finally gave in and put my feet up, thinking about Marshall, feeling the frustration over him calling Cal instead of me well up again.

I slept, I don't know for how long. When I woke, in that foggy way you do when you've been drugged, not sure if you're going to wake all the way or just go back under, my frustration was gone. I thought for a moment I was dreaming, the drugs acting as a genie in a bottle, granting me my wishes. I blinked once, twice, and then slowly began to smile.

Because looking back at me from her bed, was my daughter.

Meghan had opened her eyes.

MARSHALL

His dad hadn't said anything for almost an hour. He'd cranked up the music, the old classic stuff he liked. Marshall could never understand his father's complaints about his music, which was a hell of a lot lighter on the bass than some of this stuff from the seventies he wouldn't stop listening to.

Marshall looked over at him at one point during the second playing of "Black Dog" and his father seemed less to be enjoying the music than internalizing it, his eyes locked on the road, silently mouthing the words when his mouth wasn't clenched, bobbing his head.

It seemed to wind him up and relax him at the same time, and a half hour later he finally reached some balance and turned down Neil Young wailing away just when Marshall thought his head would explode if he heard about anyone else dying in O-HI-O one more time.

"Marshall?" His father's voice was measured, and very, very calm. Marshall had spent the day in fear, but it had receded to some manageable level over lunch, what little of it he'd eaten. Now, hearing that voice made Marshall glad he hadn't had much fried fish or he'd have to make his father pull over and make a dash for the bushes.

"I'm going to say this, and I don't want any pretending that you don't know what I'm talking about, I don't want anything left out, and I don't want any lies. I want it all. You hear me?"

He took his eyes off the road long enough to look at him, and Marshall swallowed. "Yeah."

"Okay. Now, I want you to tell me what happened. You can start with how you met her, or if there's something important before you met her, then start there. Do not make me ask questions."

"Her" was perfectly clear. His father thought it had all started with Ada. It hadn't, of course, but no, he wasn't going to be coy. He'd start where his father wanted him to. At the beginning. With him.

"You never told me about your father," he started.

"God dammit, Marshall. That's not what I want and you know it. You can blame me for all your problems, but you're gonna have to be a man one day. I suggest you make it today."

Marshall had to think. *Make it today.* He shook his head, his lip trembling, determined to not cry. "But you want to know where it started. Ira—"

He jumped when his father hit the dashboard hard enough to rock the car.

"No!" he bellowed. "Don't you blame this on that poor kid!"

"He died right in front of me," Marshall screamed back at him. "And you never even asked me about it. You never even..." And damn if he didn't start crying anyway. Huge, horrible, humiliating gasps of sobs. His father punched the button for the glove box and pulled out a stack of fast-food restaurant napkins, throwing them in Marshall's lap.

Oh, shit, what a mistake this was, Marshall thought. He should have left with Ada, he should have stuck to the plan. He grabbed a wad of the napkins and tried to pull himself together, tried to match his father's stoicism, tried to work up some manly rage to counteract the childish fear, but they both seemed like the same thing to him, and the tears took longer to get under control than he would have thought.

"Fuck," he finally said, kicking the front of the footwell in frustration and savagely wiping his face. His father stayed silent and Marshall put the window down and took great gulps of wind. His father was grim-faced and just reached out and turned the music up, Jim Morrison, screaming himself hoarse at the end of "Moonlight Drive." Perfectly fitting.

He finally caught his breath and slid the window up, wishing for a crank to turn instead of a button to delicately press, wishing for hard mechanical things to put his hands on, vinyl to press his sweaty head against instead of soft, fragrant leather.

His father turned down the music again and they rode in near silence, but it didn't last for long. "Got that out of your system, you little shit?"

"Whatever," Marshall answered, exhausted.

"Okay," his father said, suddenly swerving the truck off-road. Marshall gripped the seat and the door, something more than fear blooming in him as he realized that there were no cars around, these were still the little-traveled roads of backwater Florida, and this was his father's country, not the open waters of the Gulf he was more familiar with.

The truck, nice as the interior was, was still a real truck, and it ate up the dry grasses beside the road in great jouncing strides as his father headed toward the heavier brush. The ride got notice-ably rougher within seconds, and Marshall would have screamed again when a canal suddenly loomed in front of them, but terror had seized up his throat, and he clutched the door when his father made a hard left and took them along the canal and into a stand of melaleuca trees before slamming on the brakes and throwing open his door.

As soon as his father hit the ground and slammed his door shut, Marshall punched the automatic locks and watched in terror as his father rounded the back of the truck and came for his door. Sadly, his dad had the keys and he quickly hit the unlock button and jerked the door open at the same time, while Marshall franti-cally poked at the button.

"Dammit, Marshall," his father yelled. "I'm not going to hurt you. Now get down here. When have I ever touched a hair on your head? Hell, I probably should have, I probably should have beat the crap out of you the way my father did me and Randy. But I didn't, did I? And I'm not gonna start now. So get down here."

His father stepped away from the truck and folded his arms across his chest, as if to prove he wasn't going to wrap his hands around Marshall's throat. Marshall wasn't convinced, but he slid down from the seat and sidled against the truck, watching his father carefully, his heart racing. His father didn't move.

"Shut the door," he said, and Marshall leaned over without tak-ing his eyes off his father and slammed the door shut. He jumped at the sound of the doors locking, and then his father turned around and set off through the melaleuca, calling over his shoulder, "Come on. I want to show you something."

He stood by the truck for a minute. It felt a lot like a mob movie, and even though his father was telling the truth—he hadn't ever laid a hand on him—he felt a lot safer near the truck. But his father just kept going and Marshall finally followed him, his back suddenly feeling vulnerable.

The melaleucas had nearly ruined the Everglades, but Marshall loved them, their mellow, camphor smell, the way the trunks shed their silvery, paperlike bark in velvety sheets. He used to peel it off and tell Meghan that the Indians used to pound it flat and make paper from it. Complete crap, of course. But she swallowed it, like she swallowed everything he ever fed her.

Had he shelled a peanut right in front of her and held it out she would have opened her mouth and stuck out her tongue like a novice taking communion. Jesus, she was so stupid and naïve and trusting. He tramped behind his father, breathing in the scent of his childhood, his feet trudging through softer and softer ground.

His father finally broke out of the stand and stood waiting on the banks of a wide canal, the remains of an old, wood bridge crossing to the other side, where palm trees curved out over black water. His dad was looking hard at the bridge, and Marshall followed his gaze, taking in the rotting planks, the sagging supports.

"We actually used to drive across that," he father said, shaking his head, a small smile on his lips. "Randy had a Scout, that thing could do about anything. He used to pull people out of the canals with it all the time. We'd come out here on the weekends." He turned, looking over the overgrown banks, the palms. He pointed to a palm dripping with dead fronds like a giant's hula skirt. "Used to jump off that into the water. Randy could do a flip off it. I'd like to break my back when I tried it. Come on."

His father made his way to the edge of the bridge, and Marshall watched in disbelief as he slid his foot forward and tested his weight on it. The plank held and he looked back at Marshall. "I'm going over."

He left it open, but the challenge was clear. Marshall watched him, almost crying out when his foot broke through, but his dad gained his balance and grinned over at him. "It's just water, you know."

Marshall looked down at the water. It looked safe enough, but the "just water" could have anything at all in it. Water moccasins, gators, amoebae that could crawl up his nose or his urethra and grow in his brain, his gut. But his dad was making it, even seemed to be enjoying it.

Marshall picked his way down to the end of the bridge and gingerly edged his foot forward, feeling for a solid base. He closed his eyes as he transferred his weight. It held. He toed his way across like that, only glancing at his father once. Cal was standing on the bank, watching him intently. To Marshall, he looked like an outfielder with a killer at bat, tense, waiting for the ball to come straight at him. He knew, without a doubt, that if he fell, it was likely that his father's body would hit the water before his did.

He felt more confident with that, and covered the second half of the bridge more quickly, jumping the last five feet of nothingness to land, crouched low, on the bank beside his father. He grinned up at him. "Holy shit," he said, forgetting for a moment that this was anything other than a testosterone packed day out with his father, proving his manhood by daredevilry and swearing.

His smile faltered when he recalled that his father had asked him to prove his manhood in another way not fifteen minutes ago in the truck and he hadn't been able to. He considered Ira and the ritual of a bar mitzvah. How much easier it would be if he'd had some cultural, public agreement that yes, he was a man, instead of these constant, fluctuating, daily tests in life that he was never certain he'd passed, but nearly always knew, undeniably, when he failed.

"Come on," his father said, walking along the bank, swishing the hard, broken stem of a dead palm frond through the grass in front of him. Marshall followed his father's path, remembering the king snake he'd found as a child and brought to his father, planting his mother's gardenia near the house. His father had gone white, and with his perma-tan that had been an astonishing sight indeed.

"Throw it," he'd said quietly to him, pointing toward the side of the garage. Marshall hadn't known why but he'd known that tone of voice was not to be contested, and so he'd thrown it. The instant he did his father had taken two giant steps in between him and the snake and used the shovel to cut the head off the snake.

Marshall had wailed in protest, and his father had picked up the body of the snake, still squirming, and shown him the markings, so similar to a king snake, but actually that of the poisonous coral snake, just a simple inversion of band colors, and taught him the rhyme he still repeated whenever he was in snake terrain. *Red to black, you're OK, Jack; red to yellow, you're one dead fellow.* He muttered it under his breath now as a black racer darted in front of him, and he heard his father laugh softly.

His dad stopped at the base of one of the palms curving over the water and looked up it, shaking his head. "Jeez, I can't believe we ever got all the way up that thing," he said, with the wonder of a middle-aged man remembering his ill-spent youth. He turned to Marshall and said, "Want to give it a try?"

Marshall squinted up the length of the tree and then out over the water. "No thanks," he said.

"Yeah, probably kill yourself," his father agreed.

That would solve a lot of things for a lot of people, Marshall thought.

There was a large, cleared area in a rough semi-circle behind the palms, with a rickety, silvered picnic table under the overhang of a feathery poinciana, its spent orange blooms scattered across the top like spilled gems. An unofficial, unpaved road led away through the brush, its deep ruts testament to how long it had been there.

His father brushed some of the flowers off one of the benches and sat down. Marshall slowly sat across from him, the air nearly ten degrees cooler under the massive old poinciana tree.

"We skipped a lot of school to come here," his dad said. "Brought as many girls as we could, hoping for some skinny-dipping. Never happened, but we never stopped hoping. Randy drove that Scout like he was trying to kill us all. Threw me right out of the back one time." His father pulled the hair behind his ear back and traced a thin white line. "Should have gotten stitches for that one, but we were having too good a time, I guess. Bled like a bastard."

His father looked around the clearing and Marshall stayed silent, hoping for the next tidbit. He'd never noticed the scar before. He himself had no scars, except four round ones on the top of his foot from fire ant bites when he was seven. Hardly the stuff of adventure, hardly the stuff of family lore.

"I'm not gonna sit here and tell you my life story," his father said, pushing his sunglasses up on his head, squinting across the table at him. "I'm gonna tell you a couple things because you seem to think I owe it to you, and if it helps you get past whatever the hell it is that's got you so screwed up, well, all right."

"Could I—"

"No," his dad said. "You just get to sit and listen. I don't know what my mother told you, maybe nothing, but I figure she told you some bull about how great my father was and how misunderstood Randy was and how she was such a loving mother and how loving Jesus can make it all better. Am I right?"

Marshall looked down at the table and shrugged. If he had to wrap up everything his grandmother had told him in a few sentences, yes, that was probably how it would come out.

"Yeah, well, your grandmother was so busy loving Jesus she didn't have time to love anybody else. You remember that."

His dad let out a guttural, frustrated moan and raked his fingertips against the sides and back of his head, hard enough that Marshall winced.

"I left all this, Marshall," he said.

"I'm sorry," Marshall whispered.

"Yeah. Okay, so, my father was a minister, a preacher, really. We were raised on the Bible. I didn't know there were any other books until I went to school. I could probably still recite the thing from memory. Bet I could whip you on it." He looked at Marshall as if about to challenge him right then and there.

Marshall remained silent. He was pretty sure that there wasn't a thing in the world his father couldn't whip him at. He'd given up the challenge for good by now.

"You already know that your grandmother is one tough woman, but my dad was a hell of a lot tougher, so how you figure me and Randy wound up? I grew out of it all pretty quick, though. I always knew I wanted to get out, but I don't think Randy thought he could. He got heavy into drinking, drugs. She tell you he's a criminal?"

Marshall nodded. "She didn't say what he did, just that he couldn't come back because he'd be arrested."

"Yeah, well, I imagine he would. He got started young, burned down a deserted church when he was ten. Nobody found out about that one, I was the only one who knew. But, he kept doing it, burning down churches. Got caught when he was fifteen and wound up in juvenile hall 'til he was seventeen. He came back and lived at home for a year or so, then my dad's church got torched."

"Oh no," Marshall said. His father nodded once and tightened his lips before answering.

"Yep. Dad came home, grabbed his gun, and him and Randy

went at it in the carport, but he was just too old and Randy was too strong and all pumped up from the fire. I tried to stop it, Ma tried. There wasn't anyone stopping what was happening though. Randy got the gun away, and I don't think he meant to do it, I really don't, but Dad got shot. Last time I saw Randy, he was taking off down the road in the Scout with my mother shootin' after him. My dad died three days later. Ma dug the bullet out of him, sewed him up, and everybody prayed. Didn't help him, either, Marshall. He died on our couch."

"Why didn't you ever tell me before?" Marshall whispered, suddenly afraid of the woman he'd been staying with.

His father just looked at him for a moment as though he was even stupider than he'd thought. "That's not something you tell your kids, Marshall. I was *ashamed* of it. I am ashamed of my family, of what I come from, bunch of hellfire-and-brimstone nuts. Christ, all I ever wanted was to get away from it, make my own family, have a decent life. Your mother doesn't even know. I'm gonna have to tell her now, and I want you to know that I am pissed off about that. I'm pissed off at a lot, I admit that, but that part…having to hurt her like that…" His dad trailed off, shaking his head.

His father's meaning was clear. Marshall had dragged them all down. "So, you asking me all those questions about God and faith and everything, I was just trying to keep you steered away from all that, but you just kept goin' after it and goin' after it. I thought if I let your mom handle it, she'd, you know, do it in a *scholarly* way. She had me convinced it was you just learning, like history."

Marshall shook his head. "No," he said softly.

"Yeah, well, I get that now. So, okay, ask me what you want to ask me now, and then we're done with this. If you still have to experiment, you're gonna have to keep it to yourself. I won't have any more of it. Got it?"

Marshall nodded, his mouth dry. He looked around the clearing and wished desperately for a cold Coke. "Then you don't believe in God?" he finally asked.

"I never said that. I don't believe in my parents' god. I don't believe some old man with a beard is up there punishing us, giving AIDS to gay people, making terrorists blow up innocent people to teach us a lesson, sending us to Hell if we're not white, right, and baptized in a river. I'll never believe that."

"Then what?"

His father sighed and looked over at the palm tree again. "God? I don't think about it much, Marshall. I figure when the time comes, I'm going to know one way or the other anyway. I don't think you have to think about it all the time, wear it like a badge. I think you have to do the right things in life. You see a turtle in the road, you pull over and stick it in the canal. Your neighbor's in trouble, you take over a casserole. Kids need clothes, you send what money you can. Feed your family, love your wife, teach your kids how to tie their shoes, balance their checkbooks, tell right from wrong."

He looked in wonder at Marshall. "I thought I did that. I really did."

Marshall looked down at the table. "You did," he croaked out.

"Then, what the hell, Marshall? Maybe I didn't understand you, maybe I didn't tell you I loved you enough, all that crap, but I gave you everything I could think of. I never beat you, I never asked for more than I thought you were capable of. You want me to talk about faith?

"I've had faith, Marshall. I had faith in you, in our family, in how we were living our lives. *That's* what faith is, knowing you've done what you needed to so the people you love can do the things they need to. Religion just gives you a language, things to say for people too ignorant to figure that out."

"I just don't believe that," Marshall protested.

His father slammed his open palm down on the table. "And nobody's asking you to! That's what I believe, and you asked, dammit. I'm not some idiot who doesn't believe somebody else can believe something else. Faith is nothing but opinion to me, Marshall, and you got a right to one, but dammit, when your opinion threatens my family, all bets are off, period. That's *my* religion, buddy, and you ever cross it again, you'll wish there was a Hell you could go to."

His father was red in the face and breathing heavily. He spread his hands, with the scars Marshall knew better, the ones from fishing line and hooks, fish and motors, open flat on the table as if he were going to rise, but he continued to sit there. Marshall was afraid—he'd be a fool not to be—but he was also fascinated that they were having this conversation at all. He remembered what his father said to him in the car. *You're gonna have to be a man one day. I suggest you make it today.*

He took a deep breath and started, this time where he knew his father wanted him to. With Ada. With her skin, and her hands, and her calm, knowing center. And the sex. And the way it had gotten all mixed up with the praying. He didn't know why he'd become so obsessed, but he guessed his father was right; it didn't really matter. All that mattered was that he'd allowed something to happen to Meghan. It was just that simple.

And he didn't have a good answer for how, or why, except he'd gotten caught up. Maybe the way Randy had gotten caught up in the fire. He could understand that. But he'd never tell his father that. And he had really believed, he had.

For a few moments on that boat, when Meghan breathed again and Ada turned to him with her eyes wide and her cheeks just starting to burn, he had felt what he'd always wanted to feel.

He got through finding Grandmother Tobias's letter and getting in touch with her, through making the decision to take Ada there, their plan to go to Nebraska and then let her "community" help them go underground, and then his father interrupted him and told him all they'd learned from the detectives and the FBI agents.

Marshall was smart enough to be scared all over again.

"And then she stole your car and left you in the middle of the night?" his father asked, almost—*almost*—sympathetically.

"No," he answered in surprise. "No, I gave her the car."

"What? What the hell did you do that for?"

So much for sympathy, Marshall thought. "I'd made my decision, but I couldn't make hers," he said with a shrug. "I felt like, in a way, I'd gotten her into this. So I gave her some money and told her to go."

His father looked confused. "So, wait, you gave her the car because you decided, you *chose* to come back?"

"Well, yeah. Of course, I mean, yeah, I knew I had to come back. I couldn't just leave. I…couldn't."

"You know how much trouble you're in, Marshall?"

He nodded. "Yeah. I don't imagine I'm going back to school any time soon."

His father shook his head. "No, that's true. It's going to be rough. Marshall, we're going to do everything we can to help you, but I don't think there's any way we're going to be able to get you bail now. You're going to have to spend time in jail. Jail, Marshall. At least until your trial; after that, well, I guess it depends on what happens."

"I know," Marshall said. "I'm not stupid, Dad." He flushed. "I did some stupid things, but I'm not stupid."

"And you chose to come back anyway," he pressed, staring intently at Marshall.

He had to think about what his father was going on about for a second. Then he got it, and even though he knew it was dangerous, he smiled a little. "Yeah. I did."

"Okay." His father looked at him appraisingly. He didn't think his father approved of him, that was not going to happen for a long time, but there was something else there that hadn't been present before. "Okay then. You all right?"

"Yeah," Marshall said. "I guess."

"Yeah? You guess? Okay, well, unless you're gonna jump off that palm tree, I *guess* we should get home."

Marshall looked up the palm tree. It wasn't a dare, it wasn't really even a metaphor for anything. It was just a tree. It hadn't made Randy a man. It hadn't made his father a man, either.

He'd done that himself. He'd fed his family, loved his wife, and taught his kids right from wrong.

"Let's go home," Marshall said.

Now

MARSHALL never got to trial. The prosecutors listened to the FBI, who listened to Mingus, who listened, very carefully, to Cal and Marshall. The Brazil link turned out to be true, and they traced the pedophile there, though he was gone by the time they managed to send someone out to check into it.

Ada was gone too. The community in Nebraska, recently disbanded after fifteen members were arrested for running meth labs in three of the houses right next to the apple orchard, swore that she never came back. Marshall's car was found in Texas, driven by a man who claimed he bought it for eight hundred dollars in cash from a woman and her daughter in Oklahoma.

In exchange for his help, and based on the depositions of everyone involved, with the conspicuous exception of Meghan, Marshall agreed to a plea bargain. He had to serve time for jumping bail, as well as for resisting arrest. Those were not happy days for Cal and me.

We spent our time in rehab with Meghan, visiting Marshall,

and alternately avoiding talking about our problems and beating each other about the head with them. The worry over what Marshall was enduring in prison wore us down to nothing but exposed nerve endings.

Not that Marshall ever had anything to say about his experience except that things were "okay." It was the things we imagined that drained us. All I could hope was that my imagination was worse than the reality. He did some good while he was there. He volunteered to teach other inmates to read, he helped develop a program for those entering the system with food allergies, and he wrote a lot of letters to Meghan.

I read them out loud to her. She understands most of them now. She didn't at first. That day at the hospital, when she opened her eyes? It was both a celebration and a sober, stunning realization that our troubles were certainly not over. The neuropsychologist came over from Miami immediately, but it was still a long time before we understood that Meghan was not just going to snap out of it.

She was forever changed, and, like Marshall's letters, there were a lot of things she didn't understand. But now, over a year later, at least she is home. The rehab center was necessary, and we still go twice a week for physical therapy, but it wasn't home. When we reached the point that she could be released from the hospital, I insisted on bringing her here.

Everyone tried to talk me out of it; Cal even flat-out refused to allow it at first, but I was adamant. I had schedules worked out, contingency plans, the living room turned into a makeshift bedroom so we didn't have to deal with the stairs. Therapists would come out three times a week, and I had help in the form of Cal, Sandy, Stacey, Tessa, and her now-official boyfriend, Mingus—Charlie to us finally. Stacey and Kevin's kids, Tessa's son, and

Charlie's children all felt at home with us, and I've actually come to enjoy the sounds of a full house.

Dr. Kimball even calls occasionally to check on us, and while we had had some doozies of conversations in the beginning—after I stopped hanging up on her—I have come to almost appreciate her tenacity. In many ways, we are the family she lost, and some compassionate part of me kicks in now when she calls. She always keeps the conversation brief, and always asks if there is anything she can do, then follows it with a comment about likely having done enough. I never know if it is self-congratulation for having saved Meghan's life, or some sort of apology for Marshall, and I never ask for a clarification.

I thought I was the best person to care for Meghan. I knew what to do, and though she was much like a three-year-old, well, I was the one who had taken care of her when she *was* a three-year-old, so I felt confident that I could do it again.

I was wrong.

It took almost two months and a grim three-hour intervention by Tessa (fully supported by Cal, who took Meghan to the beach while it was happening), involving a full-length mirror, threats to end our friendship, a bottle of wine, and an entire box of tissues for me to admit defeat. Leaving Meghan the first time was even harder than finding out she was in a coma to begin with.

But she advanced so much more quickly at the center than she had at home. Leaps were made in just the first few weeks at the center, and after my resentment over this indication of my failure waned, I was excited and hopeful about her future. And when we talked about bringing her home the next time, everyone agreed it was the right decision.

Many things, basic things, have changed. She has no interest in Winona Ryder. The first time Cal and I tried to watch *Beetlejuice* with her she knocked the computer off her lap. After the third flight of the laptop, we agreed that poor motor skills weren't to blame and stopped trying. We pulled the posters down, repainted her room, and got her a new bed.

She's interested in cooking now. Jamie Oliver is of specific interest, and we have cable and TV in her room so that she can watch his reruns on the BBC whenever she wants. Oh yes, she can watch TV anytime. And my determination to upgrade our computer and connection has been an amazing experience for both of us.

Not only do we both belong to online support groups for coma patients, families, and caregivers, but we've also joined food allergy groups, and I've even become something of a mentor for several mothers dealing with their children's allergies for the first time. Tessa is on with me, and we discovered enough parents in Southwest Florida that we started our own support group that meets in person once a month.

I will never go so far as to say that this was all a blessing in disguise. It was certainly not a blessing, but there is no question that our lives are fuller now than they were, especially Meghan's. She has not gone back to school yet, but she has more friends now than she ever had, kids like her, from the rehab center, children of the people in the support group, friends she chats with online.

As I said, a lot of things changed, and that includes the old rules. Cal and I agreed that rules were a more flexible thing than we thought. And it was nice to agree with him. Oddly, it seems that he is more present now that we're separated than he was when he was living here. Of course, I had to have a lot of help with Meghan at first.

Sandy and Stacey were rocks in those early days. They still are, but at that time I was never alone with Meghan. If Cal wasn't there, Stacey or Sandy were. They were there for the first time Meghan maneuvered the stairs by herself, the first time she bathed herself, the first time I collapsed, convinced I could never do everything that needed to be done.

They are still there, but things have progressed so that when they come over, it is for dinner or b-b-ques, usually prepared partially by Meghan. She badgers Sandy for fresh, organic ingredients, and Sandy delights in showing up with unusual offerings, like loquats or pawpaws.

The most unusual thing, to me, is that Meghan has retained so much of her music, though it didn't seem to surprise her piano teacher. She is not technically a better player, but the way she approaches it has changed dramatically. While we struggled with getting her shoes tied, she went at the keys with a passion. When we worked for so long on the motor skills necessary to floss her teeth that we both wound up in tears, she calmed herself down by voluntarily practicing scales.

At first, every day was a discovery of something else she couldn't remember how to do. Now every day is a discovery of something else she can do, or a favorite children's book remembered, or a face in a photo she attaches a name to.

Even our personalities have changed. Her patience got frighteningly short and mine got long, with everything and everyone, even myself. I'd spent so much time getting her and Marshall through their childhood stages, as if they were to be navigated as quickly as possible, that sometimes I realize I am appreciating her more fully as her own person than I ever did when we were going through those stages the first time.

And thank God for that, because Marshall is proving less knowable and appreciable all the time. According to the terms of his plea bargain, he went straight from prison to a mental health facility in north Florida. Cal and I alternate weekend visits. When we compare notes, it feels as though we are talking about two different people.

He is shy and withdrawn with me, while Cal says he'd never talked so much to him in his entire childhood. The therapist assures us that he is not deeply depressed or suicidal the way he was for a time in prison. He takes antidepressants and has taken up smoking, which infuriates me. I try to not show it.

His main topic of conversation with me is Meghan. He wants every detail of her slow recovery. He researches coma recovery online and tells me things I already know. He makes copies of pages from books in the library and always has a sheaf of these things for me when I visit. He never asks if she talks about him.

She doesn't. Though she does remember him, pointing him out in photos and saying his name. She's often quiet afterward, and her counselor—oh, yes, *everyone* is in counseling at this point—tells us to let it be and allow her to work things out, and in time she'll want to talk about him. Everything doesn't have to happen at once, he says.

I think Cal has taken this advice more to heart than I have. Perhaps it is because he is a fishing guide. Sometimes a favorite spot isn't happening, so you move on to another one. You go back the next day, or the day after, or maybe a week, and suddenly things are biting again. I want more immediate results, and when I feel the need for this most strongly I climb the stairs to my studio.

I did send back the paintings I was working on last year. But about a month ago I contacted my usual galleries and clients, and the work has been coming in steadily since then. I turn on my lights, the problem areas reveal themselves to me eagerly, wantonly, and I know what to do to fix them and make them whole and perfect again.

Meghan often plays piano while I work, and I leave my door open and listen to the music my daughter makes until I have fixed enough of the damage to feel able to return to my new life. We give each other space during these times.

She has not asked about why her father does not stay the night. She accepted our changed circumstances as though it has always been this way. And she loves visiting Cal on the boat. Cal sold *McKale's Ferry* to a man who was planning to give it to his son farther up the west coast, and continues to live on *Trillium's Edge*. We never discussed him coming back, but we've also never discussed making our separation more legally binding.

When he comes over he mows the lawn, and he uses his workroom just as he always has, to fix a motor, maintain his records. I visit him out there if I'm at home and bring him lunch or dinner, depending upon the time of day. Meghan often makes him simple dishes to take back to the boat.

I miss him—now that there is slightly more time in my life, now that he has been gone long enough to stop thinking that he's just in the next room. I thought that I would get used to it, and then it would be a better life for me, one free of the extraneous emotional entanglement. But now I am used to it and have discovered that Cal was never extraneous.

I told Sandy that I liked being alone, but didn't like being without *Cal*, and she seemed to understand that. We circle each other now, tension of a different kind thick between us. I see him watching me, the way he did on that airboat in the Everglades. Last week, while Tessa and Charlie were at the house with their kids, he took me for a walk around the bay.

We watched the spaces around the trees turn scarlet with the sunset, as though the woods were on fire, and we held hands on the way back. My wrist still pains me at times, and he was careful of my hand, making sure it wasn't bent in the wrong way as it tucked into his.

My sex drive has returned with a vengeance, though I've not let this little nugget loose, and the way his palm rubbed against mine nearly had me pulling him down to the pine needles right then and there.

When Stacey picked us up for church last Sunday, she told me that Cal told Kevin he thought I looked more beautiful than he'd ever seen me.

Yes, church.

I started going when Meghan was in the center, and even helped paint it this year. The chapel in the hospital had given me a quiet place to think, and despite the fact that the tiny white church was filled with people, it is that place for me now.

There is less talk of God and more talk of peace than I had expected, and that is all I am looking for now. Meghan enjoys the music, and the people there care for us in a less pressing way than I feared. We usually sit with Sandy in the back, while Stacey and Kevin sit with their kids in the first pew, and then we meet back at my house for lunch, where Tessa and Charlie and their combined kids join us.

Nobody has been maimed by the screen door on these Sundays. I unscrewed it from the door frame as soon as my cast came off and, after blasting it with the hose, painted it slate blue and hung it on the wall next to my inherited Harold Newton painting.

I am not sure of what it teaches me yet, but when I look at it I take a deep breath and nod, and that seems to be something.

MARSHALL

He had three months left. Sometimes the time passed with agonizing slowness, other times his release date frightened him with its proximity. Progress, they'd made a lot of progress, that was what Dr. Reif said. There were plenty of guys in there who talked about ways to fake "progress." But he didn't want to fake anything, and he was suspicious and nervous as hell of Dr. Reif's optimism.

He still thought about Ada, especially late at night, when he heard some of the others move around, knew they were seeking comfort in the dark, with each other. They'd never talk about it when they got out, and maybe it helped while they were here.

It wasn't for him, though he'd considered it, at least twice seriously enough that he got close to one particular man in prison. But he had backed out, and had been allowed to. He'd known others, heard others, who had not been so lucky.

It was Ada who kept him clear. He understood more now about her purity angle, and he was repentant about having pressured her. Oh, she'd folded quickly enough, he knew that. And she'd used her sexuality to manipulate him, he knew that too. But the things she'd *said* about purity resonated now. There were different types of purity, and in prison he achieved one, in here perhaps he would achieve another.

But he didn't count on it.

All he wanted after he got out of here was to go home, work on his dad's boat, somehow make things up to his family, and live a decent life. He no longer had any thoughts about escaping to another state. His parents wouldn't be around forever, and Meghan was eventually going to need him.

And he was going to be there.

He was allowed some personal possessions now. He'd asked for his iPod and his jewelry. He was only allowed one necklace, so his dad brought him the leather cord and slid all the charms off the others and brought them jumbled together in a small plastic baggie. Marshall had strung them all on the cord and wore it constantly.

He'd taken to lightly touching the jagged bulge under his thin

T-shirt, just a brush of his fingertips. It was enough, most days. Most days, nobody noticed.

"Are you comforted by wearing the charms, Marshall?" Dr. Reif asked him after taking note of the gesture. He'd shrugged.

"I guess," he'd answered. But the truth was, he didn't know what he felt when he touched them. He'd believed in them all at one time or another. But now they were merely a reminder that he no longer believed in anything at all.

Fishing. He just wanted to go fishing.

And the Screen Door

I've been abandoned today. Well, technically, I was abandoned yesterday. But I've come to enjoy my big "family" Sundays, and while yesterday I'd felt an exhilarating sense of freedom, today I miss everyone more deeply than I ever would have expected.

Tessa and Charlie took Owen and Meghan to the Flagler Museum on the East Coast because they'd both recently declared an interest in trains. Or Owen professed an interest, and Meghan had jumped on the train too, so to speak.

Kevin and Stacey took their kids to Busch Gardens and Adventure Island, the water park next door to it, for the weekend. And Sandy had left on Friday to visit her brother, whose wife had just given birth to their fourth boy, making the lone girl, aged eleven, desperate for her aunt. Sandy left the care of the produce stand in my hands, but as she had never opened on Sundays anyway, I would be at loose ends after church.

But if Meghan has taught me nothing else, she taught me that I could only live one day at a time, and if I am not in the present, then I am missing all that is important in life. So I tried to make everyone's absence into a good thing.

I considered skipping church and sleeping late, a decadence I've not indulged in for a very, very long time. I still don't get up as early as Cal, but the days of lounging in bed until nine seem forever gone.

And I tried. I lazed, propping pillows behind my head to read when I couldn't fall back asleep after seven, but it was no use. I was habituated, and my stomach was growling. I was, however, able to take my time in the shower after having an English muffin, and I stayed in long enough to drain the old hot water heater. It made me laugh out loud for some reason, and I kept the smile on my face as I dried off, using two towels, slathered on lotion, and blow-dried my hair.

But all my selfish ministrations left me late for church, and as I hurried out the door I felt a loneliness descend, and it only intensified once I was in the car. I turned the radio on but could find nothing but commercials and finally switched it off, arriving at church just as the doors were closing.

I slipped into the last pew and nodded at the family sitting beside me. It was strange to be in church alone, and my attention wandered throughout the service. I tried to concentrate, but my eyes kept returning to a man in the third pew. He had a new haircut, and the line of a tan was clear across the back of his neck, the previously protected strip above it white and vulnerable.

He, too, seemed to be distracted, looking straight ahead when others bowed to pray, remaining seated when others rose. He, too, cast his gaze left and right, as though looking for someone.

It was CAL.

Cal was in church.

Cal was in *my* church.

I must have made some noise, because the little girl next to me looked up questioningly and put her hand in my lap, as though to comfort me. Her mother reached out immediately and took her hand back, mouthing *I'm sorry* at me with a bemused smile. I smiled back at her shakily and patted the little girl's shoulder.

I slouched down in the pew and watched Cal as one would watch a secret crush at a party, holding my breath whenever it seemed as though he would turn his head enough to see me, but he never did. I finally slipped out the next time everyone rose to sing, and hurried to my car, afraid he might have seen me.

I drove home, rattled.

But now that I am here, I am still rattled, and wander from room to room, nervously jumping at every sound and car going by. I finally change into my bathing suit, grab a book and my towel, and walk down the path to the beach.

Meghan and I go to the beach more now than we did when she was a small child. Somehow, having it right there during our daily lives inured us to its call. We thought of it as a place for tourists, people who didn't work for a living, or go to school, or have to manage the countless little chores of daily life. But things are slower now, and it's a rare day that we don't get down to the beach, or across to the bay, or both.

As the sand shifts beneath me, conforming itself to my curves, and the sun warms my back and legs, I stop wondering about Cal and his appearance at church, the last place he would ever have gone when we were together. I breathe in the air of the Gulf of Mexico and its salty moisture infuses me, softening my thoughts, relaxing my body.

It is nearly as good as church, and with the Gulf lapping quietly in the background in a mesmerizing rhythm, I do something on the beach I haven't done since I was a teenager. I fall asleep.

When I wake, the sun is high in a cloudless sky, and I wince as

I stretch and turn over. I'm going to have a painful sunburn later, but it feels wonderful right now, my skin taut and alive, as if the sun were as healthy as we'd believed it was when I was a child. I sigh as I turn my face up to the heat, wishing for the scattering of freckles I'd had across my nose back then instead of the unevenness and blotches of my middle age.

The beach is almost empty but for some diehards, and I watch a couple with a young boy crouched between them in the wet sand at the water's edge from behind my sunglasses. They lean over the boy's back and kiss each other, and tears spring to my eyes, taking me completely by surprise.

It's time to go home.

I shake my towel out, wrap it around my waist and walk back to the house, slowing considerably and then stopping altogether when I see Cal's truck in the drive. The tailgate is down though the back is empty, and I run my hand along its edge as I walk around the back and approach the house.

Cal is standing on the steps, adjusting the tension on a brilliant white, aluminum screen door. Its newness assaults my eyes. It makes everything around it, the doorframe, the house, the steps, the yard, seem old and decrepit in comparison.

"Hey," I say, startling him.

"Oh, hey," he replies with a slow smile. "What do you think?"

"Wow," I answer. There are other things I want to say.

"Yeah," he says, opening it, letting go, and watching in pride as it slowly closes and latches by itself. "Works great, huh? Come on up, give it a try."

I climb the stairs and hand him my book and extra towel. He hops off the steps and stands back with his arms folded and his legs set wide apart to watch me try out the door. I open it, let it go, watch it close, and nod my head at him and smile.

"No, no," he says. "Go in like you'd go in normally. Go ahead." He looks like Marshall looked the Christmas he'd given me an insanely inappropriate nightgown and badgered me to try it on. He'd been so proud that he'd shopped for and wrapped it himself, but neither Cal nor I could keep from spluttering when I opened it. Marshall had looked so pleased with himself, and later, after dinner, I saw him curl up on the sofa with it, rubbing it against his cheek until he fell asleep.

The nature of the gift, its sheer lace inserts and clear intent—to adults—as a sexy nightie had been completely lost on him. He'd thought it was soft, and he'd wanted me to have that. I'd never worn it—it wasn't just inappropriate; it was also two sizes too small—but I'd kept it tucked in the back of my drawer, though I haven't thought about it until this other gift arrived.

It, too, seems shockingly inappropriate and out of place, but I suddenly realize that to Cal, measuring for it, shopping for it, installing it, is likely a very, very soft thing he'd wanted to do for me.

And so I start at the bottom of the steps, climb them, open the screen door, open the kitchen door, and step inside, trying not to cringe as I let the screen door go. But I am two steps safely inside the kitchen before it latches behind me.

I turn around to see Cal grinning at me through the screen. He places his fingertips lightly against the fresh black netting and says, "What do you think?"

I touch his fingertips with mine through the screen, eerily reminiscent of the way Marshall and I had "touched" through the glass on visiting day, before he'd been transferred to the minimum-security prison. "It's perfect. Thanks."

He holds up a finger and bounds back down the stairs. I'm dying of thirst, and I enjoy the waft of cool air as I pull a couple of waters out of the refrigerator. The tailgate slams shut on the truck, and I hear the jangle of Cal's keys as he pulls them from the ignition and slips them into his pocket.

I hold a water out to him as he comes in the kitchen, smiling as he takes exaggerated, slow steps and doesn't get caught by the screen.

"Have a seat, Mr. Fix-it," I say. "I'm making spaghetti bake with sausage. You staying?"

"You asking?"

"I guess I am," I say as I pull ingredients out of the pantry.

"Sounds great. Hear from Tessa yet?"

I shake my head as I cut up an onion. "No, but I didn't ask her to call. They should be back in a few hours."

"Good."

"Oh?"

"Well, I just thought, maybe we could talk a little, just you and me."

"Okay," I say, my heart racing. "Do I need wine for this talk?"

He laughs, a rich, male laugh I haven't heard in a long time. It makes me consider telling him to be quiet and take me upstairs, but I don't. Cal is ready to say something, and no matter what it is, I am ready to hear it.

"I don't think you *need* wine," he says. "But maybe we should both have some. In the pantry?" he asks, as if I've rearranged things in his absence.

I nod, and he pulls out a bottle of red wine, pours us both a glass, and splashes some into the sauce. I grin at him. "All right, hands off the food, mister." God it feels good to banter with him.

He leans against the counter and watches me cook, occasionally handing me an ingredient or utensil. "So, I've been thinking about Marshall."

"Mmmm," I answer, draining the pasta.

"He'll be out in three months, you know."

"I know," I say, shaking the colander.

"Have you talked to him about what he wants to do?"

"Not really. I thought we'd cross that bridge when we got there."

"Have you given much thought to having him back here?"

I don't answer for a bit, and Cal lets me think while I build individual dishes of spaghetti, sausage, sauce, and cheese. I feel his eyes on me, watching my hands work, and I know he wants me too, as much as I want him. I place the dishes on a tray and slide them into the oven before I look at him, feeling my face flush.

"Let's sit in here," I say, nodding at the kitchen table. "It's nice with the door open now."

He gives me a small, appreciative smile and pulls a chair out for me, and when we sit in tandem, we look at each other directly for the first time in a long time.

"I've thought about it," I finally answer. "I'm not sure how I feel. Obviously he's not going back to school any time soon. He needs someplace to live, and I feel that my—our home should always be open to him, but—"

"But you're worried about Meghan," he interrupts. I take a sip of wine.

"Yes, but not why you think."

"I don't think he'd do anything to harm her, do you?"

"No, I don't."

"You're worried about how Meghan will feel about having him here, if *she'll* feel safe."

I laugh. "Okay, I guess it is why you think then. Yes. I talked to her therapist about it a little. He doesn't think we should move so quickly, you know, force her to talk about him if she's not ready."

"So have you been thinking about anything?"

"Well, I thought that maybe we could get him a small place in town, you know those new apartments they built last year? They seem affordable enough, and of course he'll need to get a job. I guess it is time to start getting things rolling, isn't it?"

It had seemed as though Marshall would never be free again, but suddenly the three months seem like entirely too little time. My sip of wine turns into a gulp.

"Well, we've been talking about it," Cal says.

I hate the jealousy that still courses through me when I'm faced with the fact that Marshall talks to Cal more than me now.

"And?" I ask, trying to not sound irritated.

"I think he'd be a pretty good fishing guide," he says, completely taking me aback.

"Really?"

"Yeah, he seems to want to give it a try."

I raise my eyebrows as I consider, coming around it as slowly as I had Cal's truck earlier. It seems as good an option as any, I suppose. I certainly don't have a better plan. And of course everyone in town knows everything, thanks to the newspapers. He probably wouldn't be able to get any sort of decent job.

"And you want to take that on?" I ask.

He nods, and it's obvious that he's given this plenty of thought. "Yeah. I do. I think he'd be good at it, and I think I'd like to work with him. I think…I think I can help him. My way."

"I saw you in church today."

He looks startled at my sudden shift, and I feel a little jolt of pleasure knowing that I can still surprise him.

"I looked for you," he says quietly. "I didn't think you were there."

"Is that what this is about?" I ask, but I ask gently. "You going to get God and teach your son a trade and save him?"

He shakes his head. "I never lost God, Chloe. I lost religion.

Always seemed like two different things to me. I went to church because Kevin said you'd been going with them, and that you seemed...good, you know, peaceful. I wanted to see that. I want to see you peaceful. And maybe I want to be peaceful too."

I don't know what to say, so I nervously sip my wine, trying to get it past the lump in my throat.

"I thought Marshall could come back, live on the boat, and work the business with me."

"Live on the boat?" I repeat. He could still surprise me too. "What about—you?"

"Well, it's three months away," he says, as if cautioning me about something. "So, you know, maybe you could start to think about..." He clears his throat, but I don't help him, just watch helplessly as he lays his heart bare in front of me, speaking so rapidly that he is nearly tripping over his words.

"Maybe we could start thinking about us, Chloe. If it's okay with you, what you want too, maybe I could move into Marshall's room. I'd be more help with Meghan, and...I miss you, so much, Chloe. I miss everything about you. I miss our marriage, and, I don't know that I miss our life, because it got pretty screwed up there for a while, but I—"

"Cal," I interrupt him, but with a smile, feeling our lives expand in front of us, with plenty of time. "We have three months. You know what?"

He stares at me, and I can tell that he'd had more rehearsed. I didn't need to hear it. I reach over and take his hand in mine.

"It's a beautiful night," I say. "We've got the next few hours alone. Let's have dinner, and see what happens."

He looks at me questioningly, and then nods. "Yeah, okay," he agrees, his voice hoarse.

I take a deep breath of the sweet Gulf air flowing through the screen and rise to take dinner out of the oven. But I am finding it hard to be around him without touching him.

I pause behind his chair and bend to kiss the strip of soft white skin, smelling him for the first time in so long that it is new again. It makes me wonder if we will even get to dinner, or if I will pull it out of the oven and let it grow cold on the counter.

He shivers as I draw away.

"Thanks for fixing the screen door, Cal," I whisper, and he stands and turns in the same instant, turning his chair over as he reaches for me.

I am ready.

Readers Guide

Suggested Questions for Discussion

1. After meeting Ada, Cal is surprised when Chloe asks whether there's a difference between being in love and thinking you're in love, saying, "Well, yes, there's a difference. Damn, Chloe. That's pretty cynical." Do you believe there's a difference? And, if so, what distinguishes "thinking" from "being" in love?

2. "[Marshall] was pretty sure there wasn't a thing in the world his father couldn't whip him at. He'd given up the challenge for good by now." How does Marshall's defeatism inform his spiritual pursuits and his relationship with Ada?

3. When Meghan is first taken to the hospital, Chloe finds herself unconsciously competing with Cal to prove herself the better parent. "It was about Meghan, but on another level it was also about us. Ada and Marshall had not just placed Meghan in danger; they had forced our marital hand." What does Chloe mean? What do

you think would have happened to their marriage if nothing had happened to Meghan?

4. After pressing charges against Marshall and Ada, Dr. Kimball attempts to justify her actions to Chloe, telling her, "You will be able to get on with your lives much faster because of what I did." Do you agree or disagree? Should the death of Dr. Kimball's son make Chloe more sympathetic toward her?

5. Do you think homeschooling a child with severe allergies is the best way to protect him or her? Why or why not?

6. Grandmother Tobias tells Marshall that he came to her because it was inevitable, saying, "You're here and you didn't even know it, if that doesn't just show you. Some things are in the blood." Do you think he would have sought her out if he hadn't needed a place to hide out?

7. Do you think it was Chloe's leniency or Cal's uncommunicativeness that allowed Marshall to commit such a grave act? Or are Chloe and Cal responsible at all?

8. Did Cal do the right thing in hiding the full history behind his estranged family from Chloe and his own children? When would be the appropriate time to share a complicated emotional issue with a child?

9. As an art restorationist, Chloe spends her days repairing the mistakes of the past. How do you feel her work affects her response to mistakes in life that she is unable to correct?

10. After Meghan is hospitalized, Marshall is angry with Ada but forgives her soon afterward. "He could not heal his sister and had been cast from her presence, but he could take care of Ada." Is Marshall being honest with himself? Is his reconciliation with her a betrayal of Meghan?

11. Chloe does daily battle with her broken screen door, yet she doesn't replace it, even when it trips her so hard that she fractures her wrist. Why do you think she won't fix it?

12. Should Meghan ever forgive Marshall?

13. While it is Marshall's misguided beliefs that allow him to endanger his sister in the first place, it is Chloe's return to the Church that allows her to cope with Meghan's condition. What do you think Kiernan is trying to say about faith? What role do you think it should play in our lives?